The Falcon
and the
Sparrow

The Falcon
and the
Sparrow

M. L. TYNDALL

BARBOUR
PUBLISHING

Cover Design: Müllerhaus Communications Group

Published by Barbour Publishing, Inc., P.O. Box 719, Uhrichsville, OH 44683, www.barbourbooks.com

Our mission is to publish and distribute inspirational products offering exceptional value and biblical encouragement to the masses.

 Member of the
Evangelical Christian
Publishers Association

Printed in the United States of America

DEDICATION/ACKNOWLEDGMENTS

This story is dedicated to everyone who has ever felt too timid, too weak, and too insignificant to be used by God for a grand purpose.

Acknowledgments:
I offer my heartfelt thanks to Rebecca Germany and everyone at Barbour Publishing. Bless you, bless you, bless you for loving my stories and for all the hard work you do to put them in print. To my agent, Greg Johnson, for all his diligent work on my behalf. To my critique partners, Laurie Alice Eakes and Patty Hall—thanks for being so tough on me. To my wonderful editor and friend, Susan Lohrer. Thanks for making me laugh at myself! To my family who inspires me, but most of all to my Lord and King, Jesus, who through His awesome grace gives me the talent to write and the gift of each story. *Soli Deo gloria.*

CHAPTER 1

Dover, England, March 1803

Dominique Celine Dawson stepped off the teetering plank of the ship and sought the comfort of solid land beneath her feet, knowing that as she did, she instantly became a traitor to England. Thanking the purser, she released his hand with a forced smile.

He tipped his hat and handed her the small embroidered valise containing all her worldly possessions. "Looks like rain," he called back over his shoulder as he headed up the gangway.

Black clouds swirled above her, stealing all light from the midmorning sun. A gust of wind clawed at her bonnet. Passengers and sailors unloading cargo collided with her from all directions. She stepped aside, testing her wobbly legs. Although she'd just boarded the ship from Calais, France, to Dover that morning, her legs quivered nearly as much as her heart. She hated sailing. What an embarrassment she must have been to her father, an admiral in the British Royal Navy.

A man dressed in a top hat and wool cape bumped into her and nearly knocked her to the ground.

Stumbling, Dominique clamped her sweaty fingers around her valise, feeling as though it was her heart they squeezed. Did the man know? Did he know what she had been sent here to do?

He shot her an annoyed glance over his shoulder. "Beggin' your pardon, miss," he muttered before trotting off, lady on his arm and children in tow.

Blowing out a sigh, Dominique tried to still her frantic breathing. She must focus. She must remain calm. She had committed no crime—yet.

She scanned the bustling port of Dover. Waves of people flowed through the streets, reminding her of the tumultuous sea she had just crossed. Ladies in silk bonnets clung to gentlemen in long-tailed waistcoats and breeches. Beggars, merchants, and tradesmen hustled to and fro as if they didn't have a minute to lose. Dark-haired Chinamen hauled two-wheeled carts behind them, loaded with passengers or goods. Carriages and horses clomped over the cobblestone streets. The air filled with a thousand voices, shouts and screams and curses and idle chatter accompanied by the incessant tolling of bells and the rhythmic lap of the sea against the docks.

The stench of fish and human sweat stung Dominique's nose, and she coughed and took a step forward, searching for the carriage that surely must have been sent to convey her to London and to the Randal estate. But amidst the dizzying crowd, no empty convey-ance sat waiting; no pair of eyes met hers—at least none belonging to a coachman sent to retrieve her. Other eyes flung their slithering gazes her way, however, like snakes preying on a tiny ship mouse. A lady traveling alone was not a sight often seen.

Lightning split the dark sky in two, and thunder shook it with an ominous boom. For four years she had longed to return to England, the place of her birth, the place filled with many happy childhood memories, but now that she was here, she felt more lost and frightened than ever. Her fears did not completely stem from the fact that she had never traveled alone before, nor been a governess before—although both of those things would have been enough to send her heart into a frenzy. The true reason she'd returned to her homeland frightened her the most.

Rain misted over her, and she brushed aside the damp curls that framed her face, wondering what to do next. *Oh Lord, I feel so alone, so frightened. Where are You?* She looked up, hoping for an answer, but the bloated clouds exploded in a torrent of rain that pummeled her face and her hopes along with it. Dashing through the crowd, she ducked beneath the porch of a fish market, covering her nose with a handkerchief against the putrid smell.

People crowded in beside her, an old woman pushing an apple cart, a merchantman with a nose the size of a doorknob, and several seamen, one of whom glared at Dominique from beneath bushy brows and hooded lids. He leaned against a post, inserted a black wad into his mouth, and began chewing, never taking his gaze from her. Ignoring him, Dominique glanced through the sheet of rain pouring off the overhang at the muted shapes moving to and fro. Globs of mud splashed from the puddle at her feet onto her muslin gown. She had wanted to make a good impression on Admiral Randal. What was he to think of his new governess when she arrived covered in filth?

Lightning flashed. The seaman sidled up beside her, pushing the old woman out of the way. "Looking for someone, miss?"

Dominique avoided the man's eyes as thunder shook the tiny building. "No, *merci*," she said, instantly cringing at her use of French.

"Mercy?" He jumped back in disgust. "You ain't no frog, is you?" The man belched. He stared at her as if he would shoot her right there, depending on her answer.

Terror renewed the queasiness in her stomach. "Of course not."

"You sound like one." He leaned toward her, squinting his dark eyes in a foreboding challenge.

"You are mistaken, sir." Dominique held a hand against his advance. "Now if you please." She brushed past him and plunged into the rain. Better to suffer the deluge than the man's verbal assault. The French were not welcome here, not since the Revolution and the ensuing hostilities caused by Napoleon's rise to power. Granted, last year Britain had signed a peace treaty with France, but no one believed it would last.

Dominique jostled her way through those brave souls not intimidated by the rain and scanned the swarm of carriages vying for position along the cobblestone street. If she did not find a ride to London soon, her life would be in danger from the miscreants who slunk around the port. Hunger rumbled in her stomach as her nerves coiled into knots. *Lord, I need You.*

To her right, she spotted the bright red wheels of a mail coach that had ROYAL MAIL: LONDON TO DOVER painted on the back panel. Shielding her eyes from the rain, she glanced up at the coachman perched atop the vehicle, water cascading off his tall black hat. "Do you have room for a passenger to London, monsie—sir?"

He gave her a quizzical look then shook his head. "I'm full."

"I'm willing to pay." Dominique shuffled through her valise and pulled out a small purse.

The man allowed his gaze to wander freely over her sodden gown. "And what is it ya might be willing to pay?"

She squinted against the rain pooling in her lashes and swallowed. Perhaps a coach would be no safer than the port, after all. "Four guineas," she replied in a voice much fainter than she intended.

The man spat off to the side. "It'll cost you five."

Dominique fingered the coins in her purse. That would leave her only ten shillings, all that remained of what her cousin had given her for the trip, and all that remained of the grand Dawson fortune, so quickly divided among relatives after her parents' death. But what choice did she have? She counted the coins, handed them to the coachman, then waited for him to assist her into the carriage, but he merely pocketed the money and gestured behind him. Lifting her skirts, heavy with rain, she clambered around packages and parcels and took a seat beside a window, hugging her valise. Shivering, she tightened her frock around her neck and fought the urge to jump off the carriage, dart back to the ship, and sail right back to France.

She couldn't.

Several minutes later, a young couple with a baby climbed in, shaking the rain from their coats. After quick introductions, they squeezed into the seat beside Dominique.

Through the tiny window, the coachman stared at them and frowned, forming a pock on his lower chin. He muttered under his breath before turning and snapping the reins that sent the mail coach careening down the slick street.

The next four hours only added to Dominique's nightmare.

Though exhausted from traveling half the night, rest was forbidden her by the constant jostling and jerking of the carriage over every small bump and hole in the road and the interminable screaming of the infant in the arms of the poor woman next to her. She thanked God, however, that it appeared the roads had been newly paved or the trip might have taken twice as long. As it was, each hour passed at a snail's pace and only sufficed to increase both her anxiety and her fear.

Finally, they arrived at the outskirts of the great city capped in a shroud of black from a thousand coal chimneys—a soot that not even the hard rain could clear. After the driver dropped off the couple and their vociferous child on the east side of town, Dominique had to haggle further for him to take her all the way to Hart Street, to which he reluctantly agreed only after Dominique offered him another three precious shillings.

The sights and sounds of London drifted past her window like visions from a time long ago. She had spent several summers here as a child, but through the veil of fear and loneliness, she hardly recognized it. Buildings made from crumbling brick and knotted timber barely held up levels of apartments stacked on top of them. Hovels and shacks lined the dreary alleyways that squeezed between residences and shops in an endless maze. Despite the rain, dwarfs and acrobatic monkeys entertained people passing by, hoping for a coin tossed their way. As the coach rounded one corner, a lavishly dressed man with a booming voice stood in an open booth, proclaiming that his tonic cured every ache and pain known to man.

The stench of horse manure and human waste filled the streets, rising from puddles where both had been deposited for the soil men to clean up at night.

Dominique pressed a hand to her nose and glanced out the other side of the carriage, where the four pointed spires of the Tower of London thrust into the angry sky. Though kings had resided in the castlelike structure, many other people had been imprisoned and tortured within its walls. She trembled at the thought as they proceeded down Thames Street, where she soon saw the massive London Bridge spanning the breadth of the murky river.

Her thoughts veered to Marcel, her only brother—young, impetuous Marcel. Dominique had cared for him after their mother died last year of the fever, and she had never felt equal to the task. Marcel favored their father with his high ideals and visions of heroism, while Dominique was more like their mother, quiet and shy. Marcel needed strong male guidance, not the gentle counsel of an overprotective sister.

So of course Dominique had been thrilled when a distant cousin sought them out and offered to take them both under his care. Monsieur Lucien held the position of *ministère de l'intérieur* under Napoleon's rule—a highly respectable and powerful man who would be a good influence on Marcel.

Or so she had thought.

The carriage lurched to the right, away from the stench of the river. Soon the cottages and shabby tenements gave way to grand two- and three-level townhomes circled by iron fences.

Dominique hugged her valise to her chest, hoping to gain some comfort from holding on to something—anything—but her nerves stiffened even more as she neared her destination. After making several more turns, the coach stopped before a stately white building. With a scowl, the driver poked his open hand through the window, and Dominique handed him her coins, not understanding the man's foul humor. Did he treat all his patrons this way, or had she failed to conceal the bit of French in her accent?

Climbing from the carriage, she held her bag against her chest and tried to sidestep a puddle the size of a small lake. Without warning, the driver cracked the reins and the carriage jerked forward, spraying Dominique with mud.

Horrified, she watched as the driver sped down the street. *He did that on purpose.* She'd never been treated with such disrespect in her life. But then, she'd always traveled with her mother, the beautiful Marguerite Jean Denoix, daughter of Edouard, vicomte de Gimois, or her father, Stuart Dawson, a respected admiral in the Royal Navy. Without them by her side, who was she? Naught but an orphan without a penny to her name.

Rain battered her as she stared up at the massive white house, but she no longer cared. Her bonnet draped over her hair like a wet fish, her coiffure had melted into a tangle of saturated strands, and her gown, littered with mud, clung to her like a heavy shroud. She deserved it, she supposed, for what she had come to do.

She wondered if Admiral Randal was anything like his house—cold, imposing, and rigid. Four stories high, it towered above most houses on the street. Two massive white columns stood like sentinels holding up the awning while guarding the front door. The admiral sat on the Admiralty Board of His Majesty's Navy, making him a powerful man privy to valuable information such as the size, location, and plans of the British fleet. Would he be anything like her dear father?

Dominique skirted the stairs that led down to the kitchen. Her knees began to quake as she continued toward the front door. The blood rushed from her head. The world began to spin around her. Squeezing her eyes shut, she swallowed. No, she had to do this. *For you, Marcel. You're all I have left in the world.*

She opened her eyes and took another step, feeling as though she walked into a grand mausoleum where dead men's bones lay ensconced behind cold marble.

She halted. Not too late to turn around—not too late to run. But Marcel's innocent young face, contorted in fear, burned in her memory. And her cousin Lucien's lanky frame standing beside him, a stranglehold on the boy's collar. *"If you prefer your brother's head to be attached to his body, you will do as I request."*

A cold fist clamped over Dominique's heart. She could not lose her brother. She continued up the steps though every muscle, every nerve protested. *Why me, Lord? Who am I to perform such a task?*

Ducking under the cover of the imposing porch, Dominique raised her hand to knock upon the ornately carved wooden door, knowing that after she did, she could not turn back.

Once she stepped over the threshold of this house, she would no longer be Dominique Dawson, the loyal daughter of a British admiral.

She would be a French spy.

CHAPTER 2

Admiral Chase Randal sat stiffly by the fire in his drawing room, thumbing through the latest issue of the *London Gazette*. "Blast these politicians," he cursed aloud to no one in particular. "We cannot cut the fleet now, not with Napoleon threatening us from France." He tossed the paper into the fire and delighted in watching it burn—the only delight he perceived he would have that afternoon. With a sigh, he rose and began to pace across the elaborately woven Chinese rug. Another rainy afternoon in London. He itched for action, not the sedentary life of the city.

If only Sir Thomas Troubridge hadn't fallen ill, then Chase wouldn't have been called to take his place temporarily on the Admiralty Board. Chase wished the man would recover soon so he could get back to sea. Though honored to be chosen, and even more honored to know that the Lord Admiral was considering Chase for a permanent post to the board, Chase hoped that would never come to pass. He couldn't imagine being confined to land for months at a time, especially in London, where memories haunted him at every corner.

He stomped to the tall French windows, straightening his navy coat, and gazed upon the dismal scene through streaks of rain lining the glass. The blurred shape of a woman caught his attention, and he watched her circle around the steps that led down to the kitchen and instead approach the front door. Another beggar—the city was full of them. Why didn't she go down to the kitchen like the other vagrants?

The expected knock echoed through the front parlor, and Chase waited to hear Sebastian, his butler, direct the person to the kitchen, where the cook had been instructed to give handouts to anyone who came asking. But no footsteps sounded in the empty hall. The knock came again. Charging from the drawing room, Chase scanned the dark hallway and down the stairs to the entrance hall. Nobody was in sight.

"Sebastian!" His voice roared through the house, bouncing off walls and fading around corners. Where was that infernal man? If Chase were on his ship, men would be running to attention, all ears straining to hear his next command, but not here, not in his own home. Chase huffed as the silence taunted him from every direction, finally interrupted by another knock on the door.

Storming down the stairs, Chase flung open the carved oak slab. A small, drenched woman clutching a bag and huddling against the rain flashed before him. "If you want something to eat, please go down to the kitchen," he stated and shut the door. Brushing his hands together, he headed back up the stairs, shrugging off the moist chill that had seeped in from outside.

He had just resumed his seat by the fire and picked up a book when the woman knocked again. *Surely I made myself clear.* Slapping the book down, Chase jumped to his feet and stomped toward the hall when Sebastian appeared in the doorway.

"Where have you been?" Chase planted his fists on his waist. "Never mind." He shook his head as Sebastian parted his lips to reply. " 'Tis but a beggar. Send her to the kitchen door." He waved a hand in dismissal.

"Very good, sir." Sebastian bowed.

Chase heard the door open, the rain hammering on the walkway, and voices, muffled and hesitant. Finally, the door thumped shut, and he nodded in satisfaction as he picked up his book again and began to browse its pages.

"Begging your pardon, sir—a Miss Dominique Dawson to see you." Sebastian's haughty voice floated into the room like a taunt. Chase swiveled around to see a woman shivering from the cold and staring at him with vacant eyes. "Who the blazes is Miss Dawson?"

"She says she is the new governess, sir."

Was that a smirk on the butler's face? Chase's stomach roiled. *The governess.* He glared at the pathetic woman as guilt assailed him. What was the date? The tenth of March. Yes. Of course, the day she was to arrive. And he'd forgotten.

And he had not sent a carriage to retrieve her.

Gripping the book, he slammed it onto the table and crossed the room. Her gaze lowered under his perusal. He would expect a lady to be furious at him for his blatant disregard, but here she stood, cowering like a common servant.

"Are you Admiral Stuart Dawson's daughter?"

"I am," she replied with a quivering voice.

"You look nothing like him."

"So I am told, Admiral." She brushed chestnut curls from her forehead as drops of rain seeped from the long strands and splattered onto the floor.

"Humph." Could this sopping creature actually be the daughter of the great Admiral Dawson?

"Take her cloak and bag, Sebastian, and have Larena prepare the coal grate in the governess's chamber. Then return and escort Miss Dawson to her quarters."

Sebastian eased the frock from the lady's shoulders, holding the wet garment at arm's length, then hefted her dripping valise and left.

Chase gestured toward the fire. "Would you care to warm yourself while you wait, Miss Dawson?"

She offered him a flash of the most brilliant amber eyes he'd ever seen before sloshing past him into the drawing room.

The sweet scent of rain perfumed with lilacs followed in her wake. Chase noted the way her gown clung to her tiny waist and the way her chestnut hair bounced in wavy strings as she walked. A rush of warmth surged through him that surely was caused by the fire. "I'd offer you a seat, but. . ." He allowed his eyes to rove over her, but remorse abruptly dampened his perusal when he remembered again that this poor girl's sodden condition was his fault.

"I understand," she said without looking at him. Still trembling, she eased up to the fire, crossed her arms over her chest, and stared into the flames.

In the flickering light, shadows of glittering gold gave her skin the rich luster of pearls reflecting the sunlight on a warm day. She gave him a sideways glance.

Chase cleared his throat. Egad, he'd been staring at her. He clasped his hands behind his back. "Have you any experience as a governess?"

The lady bit her lip and began to speak, but Chase could not make out her words.

"Speak up, woman," he barked, causing her to jump, but he suddenly regretted his harsh tone. He was no longer on board his ship dealing with hardened seamen.

Her delicate fingers clamped onto her arms as if she were frightened—or perhaps angry. He would prefer the latter. He had no place for weaklings, either on his ship or in his house.

He raised a brow, waiting for her to contain herself and respond. If she couldn't handle a few questions, she certainly couldn't handle governing his son. The sooner he discovered the truth, the better, for he had a sudden urge to dismiss her. Her presence was having a strange effect on him.

"As you are aware, Admiral"—she surprised him with a determined look—"I am well educated in all the classics: Latin, philosophy, mathematics, history, music, and natural science. I assisted my mother in my younger brother's instruction."

Guilt showered over Chase. The woman had recently lost both of her parents, and she couldn't be more than five and twenty. "I was most grieved to hear about your mother's illness."

She turned her chin aside and hid her expression from him.

Chase shook off a surge of compassion. He was already doing enough by giving the poor girl a position that would provide for her needs. He owed that much to her father for his exemplary service in the Royal Navy. "But there'll be no need for you to instruct William in mathematics, science, or any of the more difficult subjects. I have hired a male tutor for those topics, which are no doubt beyond your feminine knowledge and ability."

The woman's creamy skin deepened to dark red, and he wondered if the warmth from the fire had suddenly penetrated the icy chill of the rain. Her jaw jutted forward, and she snapped her sharp eyes his way. "Then I fail to see why I am here, Admiral."

"You are here as a favor to your father, miss," Chase huffed then chided himself for being so blunt. "But also because my son needs a woman's touch. By all means, teach him reading, writing, music, and art, but leave the more challenging endeavors to the men."

She folded her lips together and stared into the flames, silent for a moment. "If you wish to waste your money, that is your affair," she said without looking at him. "But I assure you that you will find my *female* knowledge and ability more than adequate."

Chase leaned against the mantel and crossed his boots at his ankles, a surprising delight welling within him at her curt tone. "You have a slight French accent." The sound of the enemy tainted her lips, yet why did he find it so charming?

"*Oui*. I mean yes. I have lived in France these past four years." Though her lips trembled and she failed to meet his gaze, there was the hint of spite in her voice. Toward him or toward France?

"How was your mother able to bring you and your brother into France during the war, if I may ask?"

"My mother has—had—friends in high places who were able to transport us in through Guernsey, monsie—Admiral." She shuddered, perhaps remembering the reception she no doubt received as the daughter of a British admiral.

"Quite difficult to live among the enemy, I suppose?" Chase gauged her reaction. Surely her loyalties lay with Britain.

"My mother was French," she replied, narrowing her eyes upon him, then offered him a hesitant smile. "But my allegiance lies and always will lie with England."

"I would expect nothing less." He snorted. "But I suggest you keep your French heritage to yourself while here in London." Chase cocked his head and studied the way her chest rose and fell with each swift breath. Why was she so nervous?

She lowered her gaze again, and her long ebony lashes cast tiny shadows over her cheeks. A quiver lifted her shoulders, and she pressed a hand to her stomach.

"Are you ill, Miss Dawson?"

"No." Her hard gaze snapped to his. "Just wet and cold."

So she was angry at his blatant disregard. Good. At least she possessed some pluck. He cleared his throat. "I forgot you were to arrive today."

"Indeed." She raised a slender brow.

He frowned and waved a hand through the air. "Nevertheless, my son needs a strong hand, Miss Dawson." Chase crossed his arms over his chest and began to pace in front of the floral-patterned ottoman. "You seem somewhat frail for the task." He stopped and stared at her. "Are you able to handle a six-year-old boy?"

"Father, Father!"

Chase looked up to see William skipping into the room, blond hair flopping and eyes alight with excitement.

"What have I told you about raising your voice in this house?" Chase scolded him, and the elation on the boy's face fell to the floor. Chase tensed his jaw, rebuffing a niggling feeling of self-reproach. But he could not have his son behaving like an animal. "Out with you now, and enter the room like a gentleman."

His housekeeper, Mrs. Hensworth, entered behind William and, after directing a sour gaze toward Chase, led the boy from the room. A moment later, the boy entered again in silence, his blue eyes straight ahead and his arms by his sides. He reached his father and raised his gaze to Miss Dawson, who had turned from the fire to face him.

"Father, is she my new governess?"

"Yes, William, this is Miss Dawson."

The young boy allowed his gaze to cover her from head to toe. "She looks like a drowned rat, Father."

Miss Dawson giggled, and her laughter lit up the room like warm sunshine.

But embarrassment flushed through Chase, and he leaned with pointed finger to his son. "Apologize to Miss Dawson at once."

" 'Tis not necessary, Admiral. Your son speaks the truth." She knelt, her gown sending a squishing echo through the room, and smiled at William, whose face instantly brightened. "We shall get along marvelously, shan't we, William?"

William displayed a row of gleaming white teeth and started to say something but then eyed Chase and slammed his mouth shut. Chase's heart sank at the boy's obvious fear of him. He longed to be a good father, longed to pick the boy up in his arms and coddle him, but whenever he came close to doing just that, something deep within him stiffened into severity.

"Mrs. Hensworth, take William to his room and prepare him for dinner," Chase ordered just as Sebastian entered the room.

"Miss Dawson's chamber is ready, sir."

"Thank you, Sebastian." Chase bowed toward the new governess as she rose and watched William leave.

"He's a lovely boy, Admiral."

"He needs discipline."

A shadow of disapproval showed in her eyes before she shifted them away. Chase cleared his throat. Who was this woman to judge him? What did she know of losing a spouse, of trying to raise a child on one's own? He pursed his lips and gestured for her to follow Sebastian. "After you are settled, we shall discuss William's tutelage."

She nodded, gathered her skirts, and followed Sebastian from the room.

A chill overcame Chase at her departure, and he stepped toward the fire. Despite the occasional hints of strength in her eyes, she appeared too fragile, too skittish to be of any use to him or William. The boy needed a strict, regimented upbringing, especially when Chase was away at sea—a condition he hoped to find himself in very soon. For Admiral Dawson's sake, he would give her a week to prove herself a competent governess. Then if she failed, he could dismiss her with a clear conscience.

Dominique stepped through the open door into the room Sebastian indicated and listened to the click of the butler's shoes retreating down the hallway. A tall woman dressed in a simple white frock that gathered below her chest with a blue ribbon, adjusted the bedding on a Spanish-style carved oak bed centered in the chamber. Three candles offered the only light in the room besides the dreary haze that filtered in through a tall window to the left of the bed. Below it stood a small writing desk, and to the right of the bed, an elegant chest of drawers. On her left, a dressing closet extended outward into the room.

"Oh, beg your pardon, miss. I didn't hear you come in." The woman turned around and curtsied. Dominique shivered and tried to smile, sending the maid rushing over to her.

"Why, you're soaked through." She led Dominique over to the tiny coal grate in the corner. "I've just lit this, but it will give you some warmth." Scurrying back across the room, she closed the door. "I'm Larena Scott. I'll be your chambermaid." She grabbed Dominique's valise from a tall-backed chair by the door and placed it on the bed. "Allow me to assist you out of these wet clothes, miss, before you get sick."

"Thank you," Dominique managed to stutter. "I'm Dominique Dawson," she said through chattering teeth as the maid began unbuttoning her dress.

"Pleased to meet you, Miss Dawson."

Dominique hadn't realized how truly cold she was until this moment. Perhaps it was her alarming meeting with the admiral that had kept her mind from her physical discomfort. His rough demeanor had surprised her, for the only other admiral she'd known was her father, and he'd possessed a gentle and loving disposition. In fact, Admiral Randal had been nothing but rude to her from the moment he'd slammed the door in her face. No, rather 'twas from the moment he left her standing on the docks in the rain. Of all the nerve! What sort of gentleman treated a lady thus?

When Larena finished with the buttons, Dominique slid behind the elaborately beaded dressing screen, gathered the folds of her muddy gown, and hoisted it over her head. She laid it on top of the screen and then removed her wet petticoats, tossing them beside her dress.

"I see you've passed the first test," Larena said from the other side as she gathered Dominique's soiled clothes.

"Test?" Dominique fiddled with the lace of her stay, unable to loosen the knots. "Would you help me, Miss Scott?"

The maid circled behind the screen and tugged upon Dominique's stays. "Yes, I fear the admiral tosses out most of the governesses who come for the job after only a few moments' time." She chuckled and helped Dominique remove her stays before giving her privacy again. After a few seconds, a wool robe appeared over the top of the screen.

Renewed fear increased Dominique's uncontrollable shivers. She'd never considered that the admiral might dismiss her. If he did, she would fail in her mission before she'd begun, and then what would become of Marcel? She tried to calm her pounding heart. She must not show her fear, not even to the maid. "I can't imagine why he retained me. He told me more than once that he perceived me to be too weak to manage his son."

"Did he, now? And all while you were standing there shivering." Larena clicked her tongue. "Where has that man's chivalry gone? Out to sea with the rest of him, I suppose."

"Why is he so angry?" Dominique gathered the wool robe the maid had flung over the screen and tightened the sash around her waist. She might be able to understand his animosity toward her, for clearly he disliked her, but not toward his dear son. She'd never forget the dejected look on poor William's face after his father berated him.

"Oh, he's always that way, miss. Don't take it to heart. He's usually far meaner with the ones he likes."

Dominique made her way to the grate and huddled by the coals, longing for a hint of warmth to reach her from the embers just beginning to glow red.

"I suppose he must like me a great deal, then." Dominique smiled despite the tight ball of fury and fear battling in her chest.

"Well, 'tis no wonder with that figure."

Dominique flung a hand to her chest and stared at Larena, aghast. "Oh my, I did not mean to imply that I think the admiral's intentions are in any way dishonorable."

Larena moved to Dominique's open valise. "Well, why not?" The maid shot her a knowing glance, her eyes glittering with mischief. "He is a man, after all." She finished pulling out Dominique's clothes and laying them across the bed. "A handsome one at that."

"I suppose," Dominique remarked as if she hadn't noticed, but visions of the admiral forced their way into her mind. The wavy ends of his mahogany hair tied behind him, those dark brown eyes that reminded her of chocolate she had tasted once in Paris. He was tall, broad shouldered, and his masculine presence had filled the room. She'd been struck by the sharp edges of his face—even found them pleasing at first—until his mouth opened and anger spewed out of it like dragon's fire.

"You *suppose*? My dear, the men in France must be very handsome, indeed."

Heat burned Dominique's cheeks while a sudden alarm tightened her throat. "You don't imagine that's why he's keeping me, do you?" Her mission would be precarious enough without having to dodge the advances of her employer.

"No, my dear." Larena grinned. "Put that thought out of your head. Though he doesn't appear it all the time, there's one thing the admiral is, and that is a gentleman."

A knock sounded on the door.

"I know him well," she continued as she went to answer it. "I've been a chambermaid in the Randal home for nine years. I was Mrs. Randal's lady's maid."

The plump lady Dominique had seen with William entered. "The admiral is having a few guests for dinner tonight. He requests your presence promptly at seven o'clock, Miss Dawson."

Dominique's heart skipped a beat. Why would he invite a governess to his dinner party?

Lorena smiled in her direction. "Miss Dawson, this is Mrs. Hensworth, the housekeeper."

"Pleased to meet you, Mrs. Hensworth, but I cannot possibly attend." Dominique smiled. "I'm utterly exhausted from my trip, and"—she thought of another quick excuse—"the only proper gown I have is covered with mud."

Mrs. Hensworth's cheeks swelled into chubby red balls as if Dominique had just told her she intended to kill the king of England. "But, miss—"

"Never mind, Mrs. Hensworth." Larena gestured for her to leave. "Please tell the admiral Miss Dawson would love to come." With a sigh, the housekeeper wobbled away, and Larena shut the door.

Dominique shook her head. She was not quite ready to begin her career of espionage. Not yet. "But I can't—"

Larena took her by the hand and led her to the dressing closet, where two elegant gowns hung side by side. "The last governess left these. They are quite lovely. She was about your size, too."

Dread slithered up Dominique's back, not only because her excuse had just vanished, but because of the abandoned wardrobe. "Why would she leave such beautiful gowns?"

Larena shrugged and turned away.

"What happened to her?" Dominique's nausea returned. She thought of the harsh manner in which the admiral had treated his son. It seemed the Randal home was truly a mausoleum, after all—a cold vault of contention and heartache.

Larena began hanging up the remainder of Dominique's clothes. "The admiral dismissed her."

"For what reason, may I ask?"

Larena's bottom lip curled. "She lied to him about a personal engagement." Lifting the wet, muddy clothes from the floor, she headed toward the door. "I'll have these laundered."

"Still, why would she leave her gowns?"

"I believe she was most anxious to leave. The gowns were being cleaned at the time." Larena opened the door, stepped out, then shot her gaze back to Dominique. "I like you, miss. I hope you stay a long while, but I should warn you, there is nothing the admiral finds more detestable than a liar."

CHAPTER 3

Dominique laid a tentative hand on Sebastian's arm, halting him before they entered the drawing room. She pressed the folds of her silk skirt, then tugged her white gloves higher on her arms as she listened to the feminine giggles and male intonations seeping through the closed doors. Although her neckline was a bit lower than she liked, the lavender gown was quite lovely and did fit her well, almost too well.

Again she wondered why the admiral had invited her to his dinner party. Did he suspect her true purpose here? Her insides felt as though they were being squeezed in a wine press. All she wanted to do was run back upstairs, hide in her room, and pray for God's deliverance.

She drew in a deep breath and let it out slowly, trying to still her racing heart, then nodded at Sebastian. Not one flicker of emotion melted the stony expression of the butler as he swung the double doors open wide and stepped aside, allowing her entrance. Dominique swished forward, took a quick scan of the strange faces that swerved her way, and prayed her wobbly legs would not give out beneath her.

"Miss Dominique Dawson," the butler announced before retreating and closing her inside the enemy camp.

Dead calm oozed through the room, a chill following in its wake as all eyes scanned her—the two ladies draped over the ottoman glaring at her as if she were an enemy, and the three men standing by the fire studying her as if she were a sweetmeat ready to be devoured.

Dominique swallowed.

"Ah, Miss Dawson. I almost forgot." The admiral broke rank and approached her with a forced smile on his handsome lips.

Warmth radiated within Dominique at the sight of him in his evening attire. *But wait. Did he just say he forgot? I did not have to endure this night, after all?* Dominique wondered if it was too late to turn and bolt from the room. Perhaps they would think her only a moment's apparition and soon return to their banter.

Admiral Randal's black leather boots drummed a warning on the wooden floor as he sauntered toward her. This man was dangerous. Dominique could tell by the way he walked, by the way he looked at her, and by the way her heart seized at the sight of him. His movements were like liquid gold—smooth, assured, and rich. She allowed her eyes to flicker over him, taking in the white breeches that clung to his muscular legs, then sweeping up to his broad chest, where a linen shirt peeked out from beneath a black double-breasted tailcoat. A white muslin cravat circled his neck in a cultured bow.

Then he was beside her. A whiff of sweet cigar smoke tickled her nose as he turned to face his guests. "Miss Dawson is William's new governess."

"Governess? Whatever happened to Miss Lewis?" the elegant blond on the ottoman barked with disgust.

"I'm afraid Miss Lewis didn't work out as expected." The admiral rubbed his chin.

The handsome man standing by the fireplace inclined his head toward the older gentleman. "You go through as many governesses as Lord Markham here goes through mistresses." He chuckled, but the sound faltered on his lips beneath the admiral's stern glance.

"Miss Dawson, may I present Lady Irene Channing." Admiral Randal motioned toward the first lady on the ottoman, by far the most beautiful woman Dominique had ever seen. She had high, exquisitely carved cheekbones, haloed by honey-colored ringlets that bobbed when she spoke. Her eyes, glittering sapphires when gazing at Chase, turned to ice when they landed on Dominique.

"A pleasure, milady." Dominique curtsied, but Lady Irene gave her only a curt nod in return.

"Mrs. Katharine Barton." The admiral pointed to the woman beside Lady Irene. "My sister."

The attractive woman patted her cinnamon-colored hair and flashed a cool smile. "Miss Dawson."

Katharine resembled the admiral, the same dark brown eyes, the strong set of her jaw, the aura of self-assurance—and the same cold demeanor.

From the corner of her eye, Dominique saw the younger of the two men leave the fireplace and head her way.

"Enough of the formalities, Randal. I cannot bear the wait." He took Dominique's gloved hand, placed a gentle kiss upon it, and, while doing so, raised his blue eyes to hers. Sparks of roguish playfulness danced within them as candlelight reflected off his golden hair—the color of a sandy beach on a summer's day. When he rose, he did not release her hand, but a slow smile graced his lips beneath a slick mustache. Not quite as tall as the admiral, he filled out his waistcoat nicely, and Dominique could tell this was a man who broke many hearts.

"And this is Mr. Percy Atherton." The admiral cleared his throat. "If you please, Percy, quit your groveling." He nudged Mr. Atherton away from Dominique.

Lady Irene offered the young man a sly grin. "You must forgive Mr. Atherton, He's an indefatigable ladies' man, I'm afraid. Aren't you, Atherton?"

Percy bowed toward the beauty and gave her a look of feigned grief while pressing his hand over his chest. "But what am I to do after you have repeatedly rejected my advances?"

The older gentleman by the fire chortled. "I fear Parliament has turned your brains to mush, Atherton."

The admiral chuckled. "Nay, I believe they were mush long before he was elected."

The ladies laughed, and Dominique glanced between the men, expecting a fight to break out. Frenchmen would never take such an insult, even in jest.

But when Mr. Atherton faced her, there was no trace of anger on his features. "Don't listen to them, Miss Dawson. They are just jealous of my power."

"Power?" The older gentleman snorted. "Upon my word, if you would pull yourself away from your cricket matches, your parties, and your ladies long enough to actually attend Parliament and vote on important issues, then perhaps our envy would be deserving."

Atherton lengthened his stance and was about to protest when the admiral touched Dominique's elbow and gestured toward the older gentleman. "May I introduce Lord Markham, Lady Irene's father and an old family friend."

"I prefer you not use the term *old*, if you please, Randal." He laughed. "And it is my pleasure, Miss Dawson." He nodded toward Dominique with the politeness of his class. A stately gentleman in his late forties perhaps, he wore an elegant burgundy silk dress coat. Gray streaked his slick ebony hair, and a brass-hilted cane hung over his right arm, which he gracefully leaned upon the mantel. Yet for all his courtliness, something malevolent permeated the air around him.

In the face of such distinguished people—a lady, a lord, a member of Parliament, and an admiral—Dominique suddenly felt as small as a child, and like a child, she wished she could run behind her mother's skirts and hide.

But her mother wasn't here anymore.

And she never would be again. Dominique was all alone in the world.

"Never alone, beloved."

Oh Lord, was that You? I need You now more than ever. Once again, all eyes were upon her. Her fear scattered all rational thought from her brain as she tried to think of something clever to say. Thankfully, Sebastian interrupted the awkward silence with the announcement that dinner was ready.

Lady Irene rose and sashayed toward the admiral with a feline grin upon her pink lips. Lord Markham quickly intercepted and escorted his daughter through the doors. On their heels followed Mr. Atherton and Mrs. Barton. Admiral Randal straightened his coat and extended his elbow toward Dominique. The top of her head reached his shoulders, and she glanced up at him, admiring his strong jaw shadowed with the evening's stubble. When his brown eyes drifted down to hers in a questioning look, she lowered her gaze and placed her fingers into the crook of his elbow, ignoring the heat that instantly flooded her.

What was happening to her? It had to be fatigue or hunger. . . or perhaps sheer terror. No man had affected her like this before—especially one she hardly knew. But then, she had never before entered a man's home as a spy.

The admiral led her down the stairs and into a glorious dining hall, wainscoted in oak, the upper portion of the walls painted a deep royal blue. Framed paintings of battleships upon the sea decorated the walls, while thick velvet curtains dressed the front windows and elaborate pilasters guarded the four corners. He pulled out a chair for her next to Lord Markham then took his seat at the head of a rectangular table crowned in white linen and bejeweled with glimmering candles in silver holders. Royal Crown Derby tableware sparkled in the light of a crystal chandelier hanging above them.

Immediately servants brought in wave after wave of steaming platters laden with green beans, mutton, boiled rabbit, bread rolls, and potatoes. Pitchers of wine, punch, and strong beer were poured into crystal glasses. Dominique's stomach rumbled as the smell of butter, cream, and spicy meat wafted through the room. She had not eaten since that morning, and the little she had partaken of before she'd set sail had been sacrificed into the deep waters of the channel.

Without a word of thanks to God for the bounty spread before them, they dove into their food like hungry hounds chasing after a fox. Bowing her head, Dominique said a silent prayer before joining them. Despite the cold reception she was receiving—particularly from Lady Irene, seated across from Lord Markham, and Mrs. Baron, seated at the end of the table opposite the admiral—Dominique knew she would have no trouble filling her stomach with such delicious food. For a year after their mother died, Dominique and her brother had lived off naught but bread and pork stew, and sometimes not even that.

"Are you a religious woman, Miss Dawson?" Lord Markham asked, obviously having observed her prayer.

Dominique swallowed the bite of rabbit in her mouth. "I am, milord."

"Anglican, or perhaps Dissenter?" He raised a crooked brow.

"I was raised Anglican, milord."

"And now?"

"I continue with the church, but. . ." Dominique bit her lip. "I subscribe to the teachings of John Wesley."

"Wesley!" Lord Markham nearly choked on the chunk of mutton he had just tossed into his mouth. "That fanatic."

"Some say so, yes." Dominique shifted in her seat, unsure whether she had the right to argue with a lord. "But I believe he is correct when he instructs God's children to read the Holy Scripture for themselves and to spend much time in prayer. Only by these things can God transform our hearts through His grace."

A stunned silence closed every mouth in the room, and Dominique felt the blood drain from her face.

Finally, Katharine chuckled. "I'll wager you did not know, brother, that you have brought a religious zealot into your house." She leaned toward Dominique. "You see, my dear brother no longer believes in the existence of God." Her eyes glowed as if she had achieved some major victory.

Chase took a sip of wine and eyed Dominique with concern. "It matters not to me what you believe, but I'll not have you teaching these fables to my son. Is that clear?"

Dominique clasped her hands together in her lap. "Yes, Admiral." She looked away under his intense gaze. *Oh Lord, where have You brought me? Are there no allies in the faith among these people?*

When she raised her eyes again, Percy's gaze raked over her from across the table. "I believe in God." He grinned. "I just don't think He has much to do with His creation."

"My sentiments exactly." Lord Markham shoved a spoonful of potatoes into his mouth.

Lady Irene gave a delicate sigh that sent her curls quivering " 'Tis good that He doesn't pay much attention to us, for I find His rules far too restrictive. Who can live by them?"

Dominique's blood boiled. She knew she should say something to defend her Lord, to help these people see who He truly was, but she felt so alone, so outnumbered, and before she could form a response, the moment passed.

"I fear my daughter has trouble remembering any rules, save those that have to do with her feminine charms and lavish appearance," Lord Markham commented.

Lady Irene swallowed and lowered her gaze.

"Pray tell, Percy," the admiral said. "What's this I hear about proposed cuts to His Majesty's Navy?"

"You've heard correctly." Percy grabbed his glass and leaned back in his chair nonchalantly. "And I quite agree with it. Why waste money on the navy in peacetime?"

"Peacetime? Egad, man. You call this abominable Treaty of Amiens peace?" the admiral said, his nostrils flaring. "Why, you know as well as I that Napoleon is using this pretense of cease-fire to gather his troops and strengthen his navy."

"I know no such thing. I don't think Napoleon, as the new First Consul of France, wants war any more than we do, especially not with Russia on our side."

Dominique's nerves tightened as she listened intently, hoping for any morsel of information she could use.

Admiral Randal slammed down his knife, startling her. "Russia has declared armed neutrality. They will not fight with us against France."

"You do not know that. Nor does Napoleon." Percy sliced another bite of rabbit and turned toward Lord Markham. "What say you, Markham?"

"I fear I have to agree with the admiral." Lord Markham dabbed his lips with the edge of the tablecloth. "Napoleon may be an impertinent cur, but he is not daft."

Dominique quietly slipped another roll from the platter, noting the other two ladies were hardly eating at all. A hearty appetite, especially under duress, was one thing she had inherited from her mother.

"Well, what more should I expect from a retired captain?" Percy threw up his hands. "And you Whigs like to stick together, I see. But now that we have finally relieved Parliament of Pitt and his Tories, we may see some real progress."

The admiral chuckled. "Surely you don't mean from the new prime minister, Addington. He's a buffoon." He tossed back the last of his wine and poured himself another glass.

Lady Irene cleared her throat and raised her shoulders. "I think he's done a fine job. William Pitt was completely inept at fostering any kind of peace with France."

Lord Markham pinched his lips in disdain. "What do you know of it, Daughter? Keep your feeble mind on your lace and perfumes, and leave politics to the men." He smiled at Chase and Percy, eliciting their agreement.

Lady Irene slunk into her chair, and for the first time that night, Dominique felt sorry for her.

"Come now, gentlemen." Mrs. Barton pushed her half-eaten dinner aside. "Let's not talk politics, shall we?"

Ignoring her, Percy faced the admiral. "We all know you prefer war to peace."

"I do not prefer war." Admiral Randal's imperious gaze bore into Percy. "But I do prefer the sea to the idle, nonsensical chatter I find on land."

Lady Irene leaned forward, her voluptuous bosom threatening to escape from her gown. "I sincerely hope you do not consider all chatter nonsensical, Admiral." She smiled sweetly. "I, for one, am glad to see you home for a change."

Dominique's eyes widened at Lady Irene's tawdry display. Yet perhaps the admiral and the lady were courting. A close relationship between them would certainly account for her seductive dalliance. But the red flush that crept up the admiral's face said otherwise.

"Notwithstanding the extraordinary beauty I find in London," he said, giving Lady Irene a half smile then averting his eyes, "I find I am most at home on board my ship."

"See, I told you, dear," Mrs. Barton remarked to Lady Irene. "You are wasting your time with my brother. His first love will always be the sea."

Her expression soured as she directed a stern gaze to Chase. "But what of William? Is the boy to grow up with neither mother nor father?"

The admiral clenched his jaw. " 'Tis why I have hired Miss Dawson." He gestured toward Dominique, who had just finished her bread roll and was spooning another pile of potatoes onto her plate.

"Quite an appetite for so slight a lady, Miss Dawson," Lord Markham remarked.

Dominique set down the spoon and felt a blush rising.

"What do you expect?" Mrs. Barton snorted.

"I find her charming." Mr. Atherton winked at Dominique.

"You would find a female dog charming, Atherton." Lady Irene's lips curled in a sardonic grimace.

"Are you making me an offer?"

With a huff, Lady Irene wrinkled her face before turning toward the admiral. "Why not hire a man to teach William? Wouldn't it be more proper?"

"William has a male tutor, but the boy needs a woman's touch."

"But really, Randal, and no offense to you, Miss Dawson"— Lady Irene cast a lofty glance at Dominique then lowered her voice to a whisper—"why have the governess dine with us? Why, she is no more than a servant."

No offense? Dominique felt the food in her stomach sour. So far she had been ignored, belittled for her faith, ogled as if she were some trollop, and now humiliated. What was next?

The admiral's face darkened. "Because, my dear, I choose for her to, and that is enough."

"Still your tongue, Irene," Lord Markham scolded. "We are in Admiral Randal's house, and it is up to him whom he invites to his table." His sultry gaze traveled over Dominique. "Besides. . .I find her quite refreshing."

A chill slithered across Dominique, and she glanced at the

M. L. TYNDALL

admiral, who, with furrowed brow, glared at Lord Markham.

The servants entered to clear the plates, returning shortly with plum pudding and champagne.

Mr. Atherton, who poured what Dominique thought was his fourth glass of wine, took a sip and grinned at Lady Irene. "You're jealous of any woman as attractive as you are."

Dominique allowed the compliment to salve her shrinking self-esteem.

"Why, you insolent fop!" Lady Irene hissed and started to rise, but at a shake of the admiral's head, she sank back into her chair.

"He does have a point," Lord Markham said.

"Enough!" the admiral barked. "We had need of another female for dinner. Besides, Miss Dawson comes highly recommended. Her mother is of noble heritage, and her father was a great admiral."

Dominique's eyes met the admiral's. Was he defending her, or was he merely trying to prevent his drunken guests from killing one another? A spark of warmth glimmered in his brown eyes, but a cold sheen quickly smothered it as he shifted his gaze away.

Lord Markham pointed his spoon at Dominique. "A real lady should not have to work, nor bother herself with intellectual pursuits. You should be under the care of a wealthy gentleman."

"Father, I believe you already have enough mistresses to support at the moment."

Atherton slapped the grinning Lord Markham on the back. "Quite true, quite true."

Everyone but Dominique laughed.

Mrs. Barton turned toward Dominique. "May I ask who your mother is?"

Dominique's palms moistened. "Who she was," she corrected Katharine and hesitated as she swallowed a knot of fear. Surely mentioning her French heritage would give these people more ammunition against her. It was obvious none of them wanted her here. She scanned each pair of eyes firmly planted on her—including the admiral's, whose stoic gaze gave her no indication of how best to respond.

But why should she be ashamed of the most wonderful woman

she had ever known? She would not, no matter how frightened she was of the consequences. "Marguerite Jean Denoix, daughter of Edouard, vicomte de Gimois," she pronounced with authority.

"French!" Katharine spit out. "I thought I heard the enemy's putrid tone in her voice." She slammed down her glass of champagne, tipping its contents onto the white tablecloth in a golden pool.

Dominique drew a shaky breath.

"A lovely accent." Mr. Atherton toasted her with his glass and took another sip.

"Chase, how could you? How could you bring a Frenchwoman into this house?"

"For one thing, Katharine, this is my house. And for another, as I have said, her father was Admiral Stuart Dawson, a hero of the Battle of the Nile." He rubbed his hands together as if that fact alone would resolve any further conflict.

"It matters not who her father was," Katharine shouted, her eyes aflame. "Everyone knows that French deceit and lubricity are passed down through the women."

"I beg your pardon." Dominique rose to her feet.

"Sit down, Katharine," Mr. Atherton slurred, flapping his hand in the air. "You obviously mistake her for the French strumpet your husband ran off with."

"Percy!" Admiral Randal gave his friend a scorching look, eliciting only an innocent shrug from Percy.

Lord Markham howled in laughter.

Dominique began to wonder if she was having a bad dream. She'd never witnessed such crass behavior. She raised her gaze to the admiral's. Would he defend her honor? But all she saw was a hard, imperious gleam as he shifted his eyes between her and Mrs. Barton. A sudden shiver coiled up Dominique's back. How much power did the admiral's sister wield?

The admiral clenched his jaw as if trying to control himself and faced his sister. "I can assure you, Katharine, her loyalties lie with Britain, and that is the end of it."

"I care not where her loyalties lie! 'Tis her morals that concern me, especially around young William."

M. L. TYNDALL

"How dare you!" Tears burned behind Dominique's eyes.

"I will not stand to have this French"—Mrs. Barton spit the word with contempt—"woman near you or near William!" She locked her fierce gaze upon the admiral. "I insist you release her at once!"

CHAPTER 4

Gathering her skirts, Dominique rushed up the stairs, heat flushing her cheeks. She had been born and raised here in England just like the admiral, his sister, Lord Markham, and Lady Irene. She was just as much British as they were. Why did a slight accent and a French mother evoke such hatred—especially from Mrs. Barton? Was it true her husband had run away with a Frenchwoman? Even so, what did that have to do with Dominique?

She reached the top of the stairs and pressed a trembling hand to her full stomach, now groaning and churning its contents into a nervous brew. *Why am I so weak? Why didn't I stand up for myself?* She had simply stood there, facing the darts of fury and hatred shooting from Mrs. Barton's eyes and the priggish look of contempt on Lady Irene's face, and she hadn't said a word. To make matters worse, when she had looked to the admiral for the assistance one would expect from a *true* gentleman, his disapproving glance crushed any hope of a chivalrous rescue.

She hadn't even defended her Lord when His name had been defamed. Gripping the baluster, she squeezed the unforgiving iron until her fingers ached.

The disappointment on the admiral's face and the censure simmering in his eyes were enough to convince Dominique that he would release her first thing in the morning. He had probably expected someone more like her father—the great Admiral Stuart Dawson. Always so strong, so decisive. *Oh Lord, what good am I?*

How will I ever save my brother now?

Dominique glanced around the gloomy hallway. Closed doors receding into the shadows surrounded her in a gap-toothed leer, all save for the drawing room doors toward the front of the house, under which flowed a glittering lake of light.

Exhaustion weighed heavy on her eyelids, and she forced them apart. Taking in a deep breath, she flattened her lips in resolve. So she had only tonight to gather what information she could. Perhaps she could obtain something of value that would appease her cousin enough to stay his hand against Marcel—and against her—when she returned.

Feminine voices filtered up from below, and Dominique spun to see Lady Irene and Mrs. Barton exit the dining room and head for the stairs, cackling like two hens. No doubt they were heading toward the drawing room for after-dinner tea while the men talked politics and war. *Politics and war.* Dominique bit her lip. That would be a conversation worth listening in on.

She surveyed the gloomy shadows. There wasn't time to dart up the next flight of stairs to her room. Dominique swung her gaze below. With each step Lady Irene took up the stairs, the candle in her hand chased away the darkness that shielded Dominique from view.

Tiptoeing across the wooden floor, Dominique slipped into a hallway to her left and flattened against the wall as a circle of light splashed over where she had just stood. She held her breath. The two ladies reached the top of the stairs and made the turn toward the front of the house.

"I'll warrant you've nothing more to fear from that French trollop." Mrs. Barton's grating voice rang through the hallway. "I've no doubt my brother will dismiss her tomorrow."

"I do hope you are right. The sea is enough competition for me." Lady Irene gave a faint sigh.

"Never you fear, dear. I'm sure if we put our heads together, we can come up with a way to force my brother to fall madly in love with you."

Both ladies giggled as a flood of light illuminated the staircase for a moment before the darkness overtook it again with the slam of the drawing room doors.

French trollop, indeed. Dominique peeked around the corner to make sure the women were gone and then emerged from her hiding place. Lady Irene could have the admiral for all she cared. From what she'd seen, they deserved each other. Clutching the banister with one hand and her dress in the other, she inched down the stairs toward the dining room. The admiral's baritone voice bellowed from within. The other men's voices seemed muffled in comparison. Dominique searched the entrance hall to make sure no servants were about. Her heart thumped against her ribs as she eased next to the closed doors.

Chase inhaled a draft from his cigar, savoring the spicy flavor, then pensively blew a circle of smoke into the dining room as the footman poured three glasses of port.

"That will be all." He waved the young man away and turned toward his remaining guests. The ladies had finally withdrawn to the drawing room for tea, thus giving him a moment's reprieve from his sister's shrewish tongue and Lady Irene's shameless flirtations.

Sauntering toward the marble fireplace, Chase stretched his hands toward the glowing coals, pondering the ghastly behavior of his dinner guests—and of himself. He had not only allowed Miss Dawson to be slandered but had not stepped in to defend her, making himself equally guilty. Why? He supposed he was testing her as he did every new crew member aboard his ship. Weak and skittish behavior would not be tolerated—especially in time of war. Of course, he knew this was a home and not a ship, and she was a woman, not a midshipman, but his son's upbringing was no less important than the defense of the British Empire.

Lord Markham took a sip of his port and turned his chair toward the fireplace while Atherton snatched the two remaining glasses and offered one to Chase. "Quite an amusing dinner party, Randal."

Chase grunted. "I pray, Atherton, that for once you would

control your drinking, along with your tongue."

"Pray? To whom do you pray, my dear friend?" Atherton's eyes glinted with humor. "Yet I believe credit is due your sister for turning the evening on its heel."

When Miss Dawson had fled the room, Chase had considered following her, if only to apologize for his sister's behavior, but then thought better of it. The woman needed to toughen up if she were to survive in London society, not to mention take on the task of instructing his son. Why had she sat there and allowed Lady Irene and his sister to insult her? With her having been born and bred into nobility, he expected more from her. At least she'd been brave enough to admit her mother's French heritage. Yes, there had been strength smoldering within her fiery eyes when she'd said her mother's name so assuredly.

"One never knows what to expect with my sister in the room." He sampled the port, enjoying the sweet, rich flavor and the warmth as it slid down his throat. "But you didn't have to ignite her temper with your explosive remarks."

" 'Twas Miss Dawson who ignited my blood." Percy grinned with a flick of his brows.

"Ah, yes, a lovely creature." Lord Markham took a puff from his pipe. "Well chosen, Randal, well chosen."

Chase wondered what the source of Lord Markham's regard was. "For her brains or for her—"

"Brains? My word!" Lord Markham interrupted with a snort. "Why place your admiration on something so slight when there are far more ample things to admire?"

Percy chuckled. "Indeed."

Shame curdled in Chase's belly as visions of Miss Dawson's lovely curves formed in his mind—the same visions he had no doubt his friends were entertaining. "I recommend neither of you waste your attentions, nor your debased affections. I fear I must let her go."

"Why would you dismiss such an alluring governess, Randal?" Percy downed his port and grabbed the decanter from the table. "Can't stand to have a beautiful woman in your house again? Or are you forever under the thumb of your peevish sister?"

Lord Markham brushed crumbs from his silk coat. "If you insist on releasing her, you might as well have a go with her first."

Chase slammed down his glass on the mantel and faced his lordship. "On my word, Markham, have you gone through all the female servants in your own house that you now take liberties with mine? I tell you, I will not stand for it."

"Settle down, man. You've been far too long at sea." Markham raised one shoulder and tossed a patronizing look at Chase. "What purpose does an attractive governess serve other than to warm your bed at night?"

"The purpose for which I hired her—to teach my son." Chase bunched his fists and began to wonder why he considered this licentious man his friend. Though Miss Dawson did present a tempting bouquet of innocence and charm, he had no intention of bedding her or any other servant. Nor did he intend to ever allow himself the luxury of loving a woman again. He spun around to face the fire, his eyes weary of looking at Lord Markham. "You would do well to curb your appetites, Markham. What kind of example does your philandering provide for your daughter?"

Lord Markham grunted. " 'Tis best she learns early on that women are put on this earth for man's pleasure, and the ones blessed with beauty should use it to secure position and fortune."

Percy pulled a chair up to the fire and plopped into it, nursing a new glass of port. "Surely we are no better, strutting our wealth and power like peacocks in an effort to procure the most winsome females."

Chase plucked the cigar from his mouth and swung about, pointing it at Lord Markham. "Is that what you've put your daughter up to with me?"

"Nay," Markham guffawed. "Begging your pardon, but there are far more influential and wealthy men a lady of her appearance and breeding could attract. You know as well as I, she's had her eye on you since you were children." He leaned back in his chair with a smug look. "I've told her to quit throwing herself at you, but she seems confident she'll make the catch someday."

"Nothing against your charming daughter, but I had a wife once, and I don't intend to take another." Chase laid an arm atop the mantel and gazed into the fire.

Percy rubbed the back of his neck. "I daresay, Randal, you must get over Melody. 'Tis been three years, for God's sake. Surely you have needs."

The sound of his wife's name blasted through the room with the force of a cannonball before crashing into his heart, pulverizing it once again. Chase bit down on his cigar against the pain.

"I'm not suggesting you marry the woman, just enjoy her whilst she is here," Percy continued.

Lord Markham straightened in his chair, his face purpling. "What are you saying, Atherton?" he demanded with a scowl.

"I was referring to the governess, not Lady Irene." Percy raised a palm to ward off Markham's fury.

"She is too timid," Chase offered, trying to scatter the memories of his wife. Melody had been so strong, much stronger than Chase ever was and much stronger than this new governess.

"I'll agree she seems a bit shy and reserved, but, egad, seducing her would be most enjoyable nonetheless," Lord Markham added with a salacious grin.

"Enough talk of this! I've made up my mind. The woman goes."

The last thing Chase needed was further complication in his life. After all, he hoped to be relieved of his duty on the Admiralty Board soon and return to sea. And he didn't want to leave a fainthearted governess in charge of William, especially one to whom his sister was so opposed. The sooner he found a suitable governess and the sooner Sir Thomas Troubridge recovered to resume his place on the board, the sooner Chase could pursue his career in His Majesty's Navy—and leave this house. Visions of Melody plagued him from every corner, from every room. Even the walls echoed with the sound of her laughter, joyous sounds at first, but soon they transformed into the tormenting screams that had haunted the house as she lay in her bed and died in agony.

He could not sleep, he could not eat, and worst of all, he drank too much. Then there was William, the spitting image of his mother. Chase could barely tolerate the boy's presence, and he hated himself for it. Yes, Chase had to leave this house as soon as possible.

Percy let out a sigh then tightened the corners of his mouth. "I still say 'tis a waste to let her go."

Lord Markham sipped his port. "Perhaps I could use a governess."

"You have no young children."

"And your point?" A twisted grin alighted upon Lord Markham's lips.

Chase shook his head. "I daresay you are indeed the scoundrel your reputation warns. I suppose I must have her whisked away before you have the opportunity to dishonor her good name." As a vision of the alluring governess filled his mind, Chase realized it might be best for everyone concerned that she leave as soon as possible.

Markham laughed and tipped his pipe over a plate, tapping out the ashes.

Tossing his half-smoked cigar into the fire, Chase headed toward the door. "Shall we join the ladies in the drawing room?"

As he reached the entrance hall, a shadow flashed in the corner of his eye and disappeared into the darkness with a swish of silk. He rubbed his eyes. Too much port, no doubt.

Dominique's pulse battered her ears. She dashed around the marble statue at the bottom of the stairs just as heavy boots hammered into the hall. Squinting against the darkness, she rushed into the cover of the murky shadows toward the back of the house, praying no one had seen her. Soon, however, the men's boots echoed like claps of thunder up the stairs as they went to join the ladies. Letting out a sigh, she leaned against a set of thick double doors and laid a hand upon her heaving chest. *Lord, I can't even listen in on a conversation without being petrified to death. What kind of spy am I?*

But what a conversation she had heard! Certainly not the political and military secrets she had hoped for. Heat flooded her face at the remembrance of what the men preferred to do with their governesses and her in particular. Thanks be to God, the admiral did not seem to harbor their same sentiments. And what they thought of women—'twas scandalous. Why, she'd never heard such depravity among gentlemen. Perhaps she'd been too sheltered most of her life. But she had found out one thing. The admiral did indeed intend to dismiss her.

After the footsteps faded upstairs, Dominique slowly turned around and ran her hands over the doors. This had to be the admiral's library or perhaps his study. In either case, it might be the place where he would keep any important naval documents he had in his possession.

She pressed down on the handle. Locked tight. Frustration spurred on by fear and exhaustion took over her frayed nerves, and she rattled the handle, praying for a miracle that would suddenly pry open the wooden slab like the parting of the Red Sea for the Israelites, but no divine intervention occurred.

"What are you looking for, miss?"

The shrill voice popped out of nowhere. Dominique jumped and turned to see the housekeeper. "Oh, you startled me, Mrs. Hensworth." Dominique's nerves constricted into tight balls. "I was. . .um. . .I was um. . .looking for the library. I thought a book would help me sleep."

Even in the darkness she could see the skepticism skipping across the housekeeper's expression. "The admiral keeps his study locked."

Dominique stared at the ring of keys jangling from the woman's sash. "You wouldn't happen to have a key, would you?" she asked in her most innocent tone, all the while hoping the quaver in her voice would go undetected.

"Only the admiral carries the key to this room," Mrs. Hensworth announced with finality. "Now you'd best be off to bed before he finds you loitering about."

It seemed more like a warning than a suggestion, making Dominique's choice all the easier. "Of course. Thank you."

Leaving the suspicious housekeeper behind, Dominique crept up the stairs, cast a wary glance at the drawing room, out of which bubbled laughter and light, and then took the final flight up to her chamber. Now what would she do?

She'd no sooner opened the door to her bedchamber than a thought occurred to her. Surely the admiral did not carry the key upon his person, especially not at a formal dinner party. *And definitely not in those tight breeches.* She flung a hand to her mouth as if she'd said the scandalous words aloud and quickly repented of the direction of her thoughts. Nevertheless, he must keep it somewhere in his chamber, and with him occupied with his dinner guests, now would be the only time she'd have to search for it before he put her on a ship tomorrow bound for France.

The thought of entering a man's bedchamber sent a tremor of unease down her back, not to mention the sheer terror at being caught within, but what choice did she have? Turning on her heels, she rubbed her moist hands together, ignored the fear pricking her skin, and slunk down the dark passage that surely led to the master chamber. When she found the door unlocked, she froze, listening to her rasping breaths and questioning the wisdom of her actions. But she must go on. For Marcel.

Once she slipped inside and eased the door shut behind her, the scent of leather and shoe polish wafted around her. With the curtains drawn back, a shimmer of light—from the moon or perhaps a streetlamp—filtered into the room, allowing Dominique to make out the shapes of the four-poster bed on the far wall, a chest of drawers, a writing desk, a lounge, two armchairs, and a washstand, all circling a small fireplace still hot with red embers. She hesitated, listening for any noises outside, then crept across the floor, tripping over a carpet as she made her way to the writing desk—the most likely place for a key. Shuffling through the objects that sat upon it, she came across a taper perched in a brass candlestick and longed to light it but didn't want to alert any servant passing by outside. She gently fingered each object: the stiff features of the quill pens, crisp parchment, neat stacks of books, the smooth metal of a pocket watch. Then she inched her trembling hands down to the single drawer beneath the desk's surface.

Scraping sounded in the hall. A hollow boot step thundered

like an approaching storm. Blood iced in Dominique's veins. The clank of the door latch echoed through the room, and in walked Admiral Randal.

CHAPTER 5

Dominique dove behind the velvet curtains and forced her hand over her mouth to still the ragged breathing she was sure could be heard all the way downstairs.

Oh Lord, please help me. Make me invisible.

The door finally closed, and steps hammered across the wood floor, softening on the carpet and then pounding again. The next instant, light flickered as the admiral must have lit a candle from the coals in the fire.

Dominique shriveled against the wall, forcing herself not to touch the drapes and cause any noticeable movement. Her head began to itch, then her nose, her back—her whole body became one massive prickling irritation. *Oh, why now?* She tried to swallow, but her mouth had gone dry as a desert.

A masculine "Humph" sounded, followed by a clank that had to be the admiral setting the candlestick down on the writing table, not two yards from where Dominique stood.

More boot steps, another candle lit, and a flap of fabric told Dominique she'd landed in the predicament she feared second only to being caught snooping. The admiral was undressing. Even though the curtains blocked her view, she squeezed her eyes shut. Perhaps he would put on his nightshirt and go straight to bed. Perhaps he was a sound sleeper, and she could then sneak out. She bit her lip. Perhaps she was deluding herself that such a man—an admiral in His Majesty's Navy—would not know when an intruder was in his bedchamber.

The creak of a chair told her the admiral had sat down. He groaned, and then a loud thump sounded on the floor, followed by another one. More footsteps, muffled this time, floorboards creaking. . .then silence enveloped the room and wrapped its cold fingers around Dominique's heart.

Where was he?

Mustering an ounce of nerve, coupled with an extreme desire not to stand behind the suffocating drapes all night, Dominique lightly pulled back the heavy velvet and peered out.

Admiral Randal suddenly emerged from the dressing room, wearing only his breeches.

Dominique shrank back, but not before a tiny gasp escaped her lips. She'd never seen a man's bare chest before. Heat radiated from her belly as a flash of tanned skin bulging with corded muscle sped across her mind.

A slight chuckle. More footsteps, this time approaching her hiding spot. Dominique squeezed her eyes shut again and pressed her lips together until they ached. The footsteps halted. She sensed a strong masculine presence hovering on the other side of the drapes—like a panther ready to strike.

Light showered over her. A slight breeze cooled her skin, and she knew he had moved the curtains aside.

"You may open your eyes now, Miss Dawson."

Ever so slowly, Dominique pried her eyelids apart and stared down at unclad feet the size of bear paws. She slammed them shut again and raised her chin until she was sure her vision would be beyond the view of his narrow waist and the huge expanse of his bare chest. When she dared to open them, it was to a sultry gaze and a half smile, not the fury she would have expected from an admiral who had caught a thief in his room.

Her rapid breathing filled the silent air between them, and Dominique thought her heart would surely beat through her chest. The smell of wine and brandy swirled around her like a heady perfume.

"Well, well, well, Miss Dawson. This is the last place I would have expected to find you." Sarcasm tainted his voice.

"I beg your pardon, Admiral. I seem to have gotten lost." Dominique started toward her right, hoping to make a dash for the door, but his arms rose like muscled drawbridges on either side of her, pinning her in place. A spicy, masculine scent combined with the odor of alcohol spun around her in a dizzying tempest.

Gathering tiny shreds of her remaining courage, Dominique shot her gaze to his eyes, pools of black amidst the shadows tumbling over his face. "I insist you let me go at once." Memories of the men's flippant discourse in the dining room of using governesses as bed warmers shot arrows of terror through Dominique. That and the admiral's sensuous gaze that now scoured her from head to toe.

"You insist?" He chuckled, drawing in a deep breath of her as if she were a bouquet of flowers. "Perhaps my friends were right about you." He tore one hand from the wall and brushed a heated finger over her cheek, causing a shiver to run down Dominique—a shiver she couldn't be sure arose from her fear or the other strange sensations tingling within her. The admiral had not participated in the men's depraved talk—at least what she'd heard of it. In fact, he had seemed incensed at their lewd insinuations, but truthfully, Dominique didn't know this man at all.

And she was in his bedchamber.

Alone.

And he was half naked.

" 'Tis been a long while since I've had a woman in my chamber—a very long while." His words circled her like a hungry shark.

When he cupped her chin in his hand and began to caress her lips with his thumb, Dominique did the only thing she could think to do. She opened her mouth and bit the rude appendage as hard as she could.

He roared and took a step back, shaking his hand in the air, and Dominique pushed him aside and dashed for the door. But she made it only a few feet before his hefty frame filled her vision once more. He flattened his back against the door, arms crossed over his chest, and grinned at her like a cat who had just trapped a mouse—a large and ruthless cat.

Dominique halted, her eyes shifting over the room for another escape, her mouth as dry as cotton, and her legs as shaky as her trembling hands. She fixed him with a level stare. It was enough she would return home empty-handed. She would not return home sullied.

"You forget yourself, Admiral. Contrary to what your friends may think, I am your governess, not your mistress."

His eyebrows arched mischievously. "Yet I find you in my bedchamber in the middle of the night."

Oh Father, now what should I do?

Visions of wallpaper, mahogany furniture, and flickering candlelight began spinning around her in a whirlwind. Raising a hand to her brow, Dominique inhaled deeply, trying to stay the oncoming dizziness, when her legs suddenly gave out.

As soon as Chase saw the woman start to swoon, he darted toward her and scooped her up in his arms. She went limp for a second but soon recovered and began to twist and turn like a bowline caught in the wind. He laid her gently in a chair then knelt beside her. Shame weighed heavy upon him. He'd had far too much to drink tonight, and that coupled with a yearning for his wife had made him foolishly toy with this young beauty before him. Yes, indeed, it *had* been a long time since a woman had graced this chamber, not since his beloved Melody had filled the room with her joyous laughter and enticing whispers of love. Chase rubbed his eyes against the emotion that burned behind them.

"Are you all right, Miss Dawson?"

Her breathing came in heavy spurts. "I believe so, yes."

"May I get you some water?"

"No, thank you." Her gaze skimmed over his chest; then she snapped her eyes away. "Admiral, I beg of you, if you are to keep me here, please don a shirt."

Chase stood with a huff of guilt. So she was as innocent as she seemed. For a few brief, intoxicating moments, he had hoped otherwise. He'd hoped that perhaps she had come to offer him the comfort only a woman could bring—if only to appease his loneliness, if only to make the pain go away for one night. But now he found he was thankful her intentions were pure, for he knew he would despise not only her, but also himself, when dawn shone its light upon his betrayal of Melody's memory. Grabbing a white cotton shirt from the dressing closet, he threw it over his head and turned just in time to see Miss Dawson push herself to near standing, then quickly plop back into the chair.

He supposed he should apologize for frightening her, but she owed him an explanation, as well. What was a man to think after a night of drinking and listening to the libertine talk of his friends, especially regarding trysts with governesses, and then to find this particular one—and a rather alluring one at that—prowling about his bedchamber? Egad, the temptation was too much.

His thoughts drifted to Admiral Stuart. He owed the man his career, if not his life. What would he think of Chase's behavior toward his only daughter? He shook his head. Everything made sense on his ship; everything fit into its proper place, its proper time, for its proper function. But not on land, not in his home, and especially not with women. "I must apologize for my behavior, Miss Dawson."

She eyed him suspiciously and wiggled her cute little nose. "Please let me return to my chamber."

"Rest assured I will do just that, mademoiselle, but first, I insist you grace me with the tale that brought you into my room in the middle of the night. You must admit your presence is rather unconventional." Unconventional and foolish, to say the least. If this had been Percy's room or, worse, Lord Markham's, this poor girl would be fighting for her virtue right now instead of defending her actions.

Dominique glanced around the room. Her amber eyes glittered like gold in the candlelight. "I'm afraid I must have been walking in my sleep, Admiral."

He cocked his head, examining her as she shifted uneasily before him. "Do you always sleep in your gown?" He nodded toward the lavender silk that fell in a delicate circle around her feet.

"Oh." She pressed the folds in her lap. "Yes, well. . .I was so tired I must have fallen asleep before I could change."

Chase paced before her. "So am I to understand that you walked all the way here from your chamber, opened and closed my door, and hid behind my curtains all while sound asleep?" Surely this girl did not consider him so daft as to fall for such a fanciful yarn.

"Believe what you will, Admiral. That is what happened." She stood and lowered her gaze.

"Mr. Atherton put you up to this, didn't he?"

Miss Dawson's eyes widened. "Whatever do you mean?"

"I fear he's forever trying to arrange"—he rubbed his chin—"shall we say, *diversions* for me."

"What are you implying, Admiral?" Her trembling hand flew to her throat.

"How much did he pay you?"

"I beg your pardon!" Miss Dawson's face contorted into a churning puddle of fury that nearly made him laugh. "How dare you imply. . ." She dashed to her right, attempting to bypass him, but he threw one arm up, halting her in her path.

"Not quite yet, Miss Dawson." Chase allowed his gaze to wander over her trembling form, amazed at how petite she was—almost too petite. He preferred a more robust woman, strong and solid, not like this fragile thing before him.

She began to sway again. He held out a hand to steady her, but she waved it off. "What does it matter? You intend to release me in the morning anyway."

How could she possibly know that? Chase furrowed his brow. "Do I perceive we have a spy in our midst?"

Miss Dawson's rosy face blanched to a shade whiter than fresh snow in the country. Her chest rose and fell like the rapid firing of a carronade. Finally, she swallowed and raised her gaze to his. "Anyone with any sense could infer your intentions to dismiss me from the conversation at dinner." Her voice trembled.

Chase regarded her with skepticism. He could understand her fear when she thought his intentions had been dishonorable, but why now? Was she that afraid of being dismissed? "I must apologize for my sister's behavior. She has reason to dislike the French—Frenchwomen in particular."

"So I gathered." The corners of Dominique's mouth tightened. "Am I free to go, Admiral?"

Chase stepped aside and gestured toward the door; then he held out his hand. "Would you like some assistance?"

"I can manage, thank you." She slipped past him in a whiff of lilacs, teasing his senses. He beat her to the door and opened it.

"Perhaps I should escort you back to your room." He gave her a sly grin.

"I'm sure I can find my way, Admiral."

"Since you were asleep when you found your way to mine, I wouldn't presume so, Miss Dawson." He bowed and offered her his elbow.

She gave him a nervous glance then accepted his outstretched arm. He felt the quiver from her delicate fingers run up to his shoulder, and he chastised himself again for teasing her into a fright. He scanned the hallway for any servants and was thankful when none appeared. He certainly wouldn't want to tarnish Miss Dawson's reputation.

"You never explained how you ended up behind my curtains," he said as they neared her door.

"I told you. I walk in my sleep. When I heard the door open, I woke up, panicked, and jumped behind them."

Chase had no choice but to believe her. What else could she have been doing in his chamber? Stealing? On her first night here? He kept no valuables in his room worthy of the risk—a fact she would have already discovered if she were indeed a thief.

And it was obvious she hadn't come there for a romantic liaison. But as he glanced at her, at the gentle sway of her hips, at her rich chestnut hair dangling in loosened ringlets over the swell of her bosom, he found himself regretting that fact. And then loathed himself for it. He swallowed hard, trying to squelch the unwelcome rush of warmth through him. He had never so much as looked at another woman, not since Melody had. . .not since she had departed.

Releasing Miss Dawson at her chamber door, he gazed at the graceful shadow of her body and felt heat radiating from her. What was it about this little waif that enticed him so?

"Thank you for a most entertaining evening, Miss Dawson, more entertaining than I've had in quite some time, to be sure."

Moonlight filtered through the front window of the house and danced around her in a halo of light that sent golden flecks shimmering in her hair.

Chase's lips went dry. What was wrong with him that her presence affected him so?

"I fear your entertainment has been at my expense." She took a step back, creating a chilling gulf between them. "Can I expect your coach to drive me to Dover in the morning, or will you leave me to find my own means of transportation again?" Fury spiced her voice, even amidst the fearful tremble, and he found the combination oddly alluring.

Chase knew he should get rid of her. Every ounce of his festering heart screamed to dismiss her at once. But for some reason, he could not. "I fear my judgment has been a bit hasty. I find you intriguing, Miss Dawson. Perhaps you are not the weak little sparrow I first assumed you to be."

She raised her thick lashes and glared at him, eyes glowing with indignation. "If your interest lies in my warming your bed, Admiral, then I fear you will find many a cold night ahead."

"Nay, that is not my where my interest lies." His lips quivered with the effort of not grinning at her like a besotted schoolboy. "But I thank you for your concern regarding the warmth of my bed."

A flush of maroon flooded her face, visible even in the shadows, and she dropped her gaze.

Why did I say that? Why did he enjoy taunting her? Chase cleared his throat. "I believe I shall give you another chance to prove yourself. But I must warn you, Miss Dawson. 'Tis best to stay out of a man's bedchamber at night. Most would not be as chivalrous as I."

"I shall keep that in mind, Admiral." She turned and began to fumble with the latch of her door and finally opened it, casting a suspicious glare at him the whole while.

He couldn't tell whether or not she was pleased about not being dismissed.

"Until tomorrow, then." He clasped his hands behind his back and nodded.

"Yes, Admiral, thank you." The thick oak slab nearly struck his nose.

Unaccustomed to having doors slammed in his face, he spun on his heel and stomped down the hall. Confusion waxed through him at the unusual events of the evening and the most unusual Miss Dawson.

He exhaled mightily. Perhaps he should have dismissed her as he had planned. But in all fairness, for what reason? She'd not yet had a chance to prove herself as governess. And he could not bring himself to believe she was a thief—not the daughter of the great Admiral Stuart Dawson. Regardless, he would have Sebastian keep an eye on her just in case.

It wasn't so much her weakness, nor her presence in his chamber, that disturbed him. She'd awoken something within him, something long dead, something he preferred to keep protected behind thick walls.

And it terrified him.

Perhaps the best thing to do would be to avoid her as much as possible. To throw himself into his work. Yes, he must stay away from Miss Dawson at all costs.

CHAPTER 6

Chase leaned back in his chair. The aged oak creaked beneath his weight as he glanced over the naval officers and noblemen who flanked the long mahogany table centered in the Admiralty boardroom. He rubbed his temples where a headache brewed and then glanced at the dark oak wall clock hanging next to the doorway. Only eleven o'clock. How was he to endure another six or seven hours of this brazen and fruitless pontification? At the head of the table, leaning forward in his big armchair, the First Lord of the Admiralty, Admiral Sir John Jervis, Earl of Saint Vincent, pounded his fist on the table, shaking the feathers of the silver quill pen idly resting in the hand of the First Secretary, Sir Evan Nepean. The First Lord then pointed his bony finger at William Eliot, the second Earl of St. Germans.

"I tell you, sir," he yelled, his pendulous jowls swinging. "The Naval Academy at Portsmouth is naught but a sink of vice and abomination!"

Lord Eliot offered a retort, but Chase refused to give it any credence. The man was a politician and therefore not qualified to decide naval policy. That civilians were allowed to sit on the Admiralty Board baffled Chase—men like James Adams, who sat across from him, a look of utter boredom tugging on his sallow skin, and William Garthshore, who would be asleep at Chase's right if it weren't for his ongoing battle with a nagging fly droning about his head. At least there was Admiral John Markham, who, with elbows firmly planted on the table, bravely entered into the argument with all cannons blazing. And of course Sir Thomas Troubridge. Although Chase admired Admiral Troubridge, he couldn't help but be angry at the man for suddenly becoming ill and forcing Chase into this landlocked hell.

"What say you, Admiral Randal?" Admiral Jervis, or "Old Jarvie" as he was called by most seamen, turned a sharp eye upon Chase, blasting him from his mindless thoughts.

Chase sat up in his chair and rubbed his chin, hoping his lack of attention had not been evident. "Truth be told, your lordship, I am more concerned with Napoleon at the moment than with our Naval Academy or the conditions of our dockyards, as horrendous as they might be."

"Here, here, good man." Admiral Markham gave Chase an approving nod.

"Indeed?" Lord Jervis raised an eyebrow long since deprived of its hair.

"He has invaded Switzerland," Chase began, feeling his ire rising, "and refused our admonitions to withdraw. He persists in pursuing his French empire overseas in Haiti, the territory of Louisiana, and India. And now this scathing report in his *Moniteur* insulting our forces in Egypt and claiming he can easily retake the land. Why we tolerate his threats and blatant affronts to our honor is beyond me."

Garthshore abandoned his skirmish with the fly and turned toward Chase. "Addington believes the Peace of Amiens will hold, Randal." He sniffed and withdrew a handkerchief from his coat pocket. "Napoleon will not risk a war with us when he knows he will surely lose—especially upon the sea." He blew his nose, and a whiff of stale brandy reached Chase's nostrils.

"I beg to differ with you, sir." His upper lip twitching, Chase sat rigid in his chair. "Prime Minister Addington is weak, a proponent of a wishful peace that will never exist as long as that French madman taunts us from across the channel. Anyone with any sense can see that Napoleon is using this time to build up his fleets." Chase faced the Lord Admiral and slammed down his palm on the table. "If we do not act now, he will succeed, and then we may very well lose the war at sea."

Lord Jervis blew out a spray of spittle onto the table. "Napoleon victorious against His Majesty's Navy? Absurd! It will never happen."

"Very well." Chase shrugged, trying to mask the fury roiling in his belly. "I am but one voice among your many worthy ones." He gestured in mock deference at the men circling the table.

"You are not the only voice of reason, Admiral Randal," John Markham added. "And Troubridge will have the same opinion upon his return; I am sure if it."

Oh, do give Sir Troubridge a speedy recovery. Chase made the silent supplication to no one in particular, since he no longer believed in God.

"I trust, Randal"—Lord Jervis shot an accusing glance his way—"that you have taken the necessary precautions in your home?"

"I have, indeed." The subtle accusation that an enemy lurked among his household staff made Chase shift in his seat, more determined than ever to prove the report false.

"And the charts are in place?"

"They are, your lordship."

"Very well." Old Jarvie peered down his superior nose at the men surrounding him. "Then we have naught to fear and would therefore be remiss if we did not use this time of peace to address the poor conditions aboard our ships. We must provide vaccinations against the pox for all our seamen and see that our ship's doctors have the appropriate medicines. What good would a shipload of sick men be should war break out with France again?" His mouth curved in a taunting smile directed at Chase while Garthshore and Adams chuckled like obedient puppets.

Slumping back in his chair, Chase folded his hands across his navy coat and returned to his perusal of the room—anything to pass the time and avoid enmeshing himself in an argument that would surely result in his losing his temper and possibly his career along with it.

Against walls painted the blue, gold, and white of the Admiralty, brass candle lanterns surmounted by royal crowns flanked a painting of Horatio Nelson. Chase wondered what the naval war hero would think of the nonsensical ramblings that went on behind his back while he risked his life patrolling the dangerous seas. Chase clamped his jaws together. He would do anything to join Nelson upon those seas this very moment.

Across from him, a massive oval compass mounted on a map of the world hung above a marble fireplace, whose simmering coals only added to the heated exchange in the room. His gaze shifted to the right of the compass and around the room at the maps and charts lining the walls. Pins marked the location and size of the British fleets across the world. What Napoleon wouldn't give to have one glimpse of the information within this room—and duplicated on documents locked securely within his study. In the French First Consul's power-hungry hands, that information could very well turn the tide of the war that Chase knew would soon resume.

His thoughts drifted to his new governess. It had been nearly two weeks since he had seen Miss Dawson, yet the time had done nothing to erase her from his mind. Ever since that night he had caught her in his bedchamber, he'd been quite successful at avoiding her company. Whenever he had heard her gentle steps in the hallway or her laughter flowing from a room, he had turned the other way, unwilling to face the odd feeling that welled within him in her presence. But what was the cause of it? Though certainly attractive and educated, she possessed no other extraordinary qualities. In fact, she reminded him of a timid sparrow flittering here and there, startled by the slightest movement. So unlike Melody. His wife had faced life—and death—with a stalwart courage he rarely saw, even among his crew at sea. She had never backed down from a challenge, always stood her ground in defense of herself and her family.

Yet he could not deny there was something within Miss Dawson's shimmering amber eyes that attracted him—contradictions that baffled him, a hope despite her circumstances, a peace that defied her outward nervousness, and a strength that belied her weakness. Miss Dawson was a mystery, indeed.

Tonight he would make a point of speaking with her—if only to find out how William was doing. Yes, for William's sake, of course.

"No, William, try again," Dominique urged the young boy as they sat together on the sofa. "The word is *maison*. It means house. Maison. Like the one you live in." She gestured around the morning room in which they sat—the coziest room in the pretentious town house, and her personal favorite. Cushioned high-backed chairs, armed settees, and the plush arch-backed sofa she sat upon with William made it a comfortable place for family gatherings—except it was always empty. So in the past week, Dominique and William had taken over the room for their studies.

The young boy gazed up at her, a perplexed look on his angelic face. "May son," he uttered with all seriousness.

Dominique giggled. "Very close. Much better. We'll have you speaking French in no time. Now try another one." She took the tablet in her lap and wrote *garçon*. "Garçon. It means boy."

"Like me?" William flashed her a set of sparkling white teeth.

"Yes, just like you, William." She smiled and couldn't resist putting her arm around the boy and drawing him near. He smelled of fresh linen and innocence. How could he have become so dear to her in only two weeks? Yet there was something special about William. His exuberance for life, his unconditional need to give and receive love. And even though he had lost his mother and then apparently several governesses after her, he had opened his heart to Dominique in a way no one ever had, child or adult. He reminded her so much of Marcel—naive, untainted by life's cruelties, and filled with enthusiasm for everything around him.

"Gar sin," the boy shouted, his face glowing with pride.

"Close, William. Watch my mouth as I say it. It sounds like gar *sohn*." She pointed to her face and exaggerated the correct position of her lips. "Practice this shape, then try again."

While William contorted his tiny mouth into all sorts of shapes, Dominique gazed out the french doors that led to the small garden in the back of the house and thought of the admiral. Evening shadows crept over the last rays of the sun, and she tugged her shawl up over her shoulders. Only a few embers still glowed in the fireplace, and she wished one of the servants would come and spark the coals—and her courage along with them.

She had not seen the admiral in two weeks, though she had heard the creak of the floorboards as he wandered the halls at night. She had nearly run into him once on her way to check the door to his study. Well past three in the morning, she'd thought everyone would be asleep, but after inquiring of Larena the next morning, the chambermaid informed Dominique that the admiral rarely slept through the night.

Which made Dominique's task all the more difficult.

However, he seemed to be avoiding her, as well. After that horrifying and embarrassing night when he'd discovered her in his bedchamber, he had left early each morning to the Admiralty, only to return late in the evening, taking his supper in his chamber. Why, he'd not even spoken to his son. And of course, every time she got up the nerve to check the door to his study, it was locked. They'd had no visitors. She had heard nothing about naval plans, and she was beginning to think she was wasting her time while Marcel's was running out.

"Garçon," William spouted with glee.

"Very good, William. You sound like a true Frenchman."

"What's this I hear?" a screeching voice blared from the doorway, and in stomped Mrs. Barton in a flurry of lace. "Did you say a *Frenchman?*" Her normally creamy skin flushed a deep red, and her dark eyes sent out more sparks than a crackling fire.

Dominique's stomach clenched. "I'm teaching William French, Mrs. Barton." She rose and pressed the blue and white folds of her skirt, mainly to keep her hands from shaking. " 'Tis important he knows more than one language."

"Teach him Latin, then." She snorted and stalked to the fireplace. "And what on earth are you *still* doing here?"

"He needs to know a spoken language, milady. French would be quite useful."

William tossed the tablet to the side and scooted to the edge of the sofa, his eyes wide.

" 'Tis all right, William." Dominique gave the boy her most comforting grin.

The boy timidly looked at Mrs. Barton. "Auntie, why are you so angry with Miss Dawson?"

"Never you mind, child. I'm not cross with you." She snapped off her gloves and warmed her hands by the fire. "I declare, where are those lazy servants? This fire needs tending. Why, they should all be dismissed at once!" She glared at Dominique, her chest heaving with fury, and then at William.

William, whose normal disposition was warm and inviting, remained frozen in place on the sofa, his pleading eyes shifting to Dominique.

Mrs. Barton adjusted her chignon in one of the gilt oval mirrors that flanked the wooden mantel, then swerved about. "I asked you what you are still doing here. My brother informed me you were to be dismissed."

Dominique drew a shaky breath. "I suppose you will have to ask him."

"Ask me what?" The admiral's baritone voice charged into the room even before his masculine frame filled the doorway.

Dominique's heart jumped at the sight of him in his uniform. A blue coat with a stand-up, gold-fringed collar stretched over his broad chest. Long lapels, edged with gold braid and nine buttons— her face heated as her gaze lingered to count them—ran down to his white breeches, where a service sword hung at his side. A gold-fringed epaulette, complete with one embroidered star, perched on each shoulder. William slipped off the couch, hesitated, then rushed to his father and grabbed onto his breeches.

Instead of brushing the boy aside, as Dominique expected, the admiral patted William on the head but offered him no other acknowledgment. His dark, rich gaze scanned over Dominique with a flicker of unknown emotion and then landed on Mrs. Barton. He cocked a curious brow. "Are you frightening my son again, dear sister?"

Mrs. Barton cocked one hand on her hip. "Why have you retained this French trollop?"

The admiral's posture stiffened. He gave his sister a stern look before pulling on the tapestry ribbon hanging to the right of the door frame. A bell jingled somewhere in the house, and soon the house-keeper's footsteps clapped down the hallway. "Please take William upstairs," the admiral directed Mrs. Hensworth.

"But, Father, can't I stay with you?" The blond-haired boy tugged on his father's navy coat.

"Not right now, William. Go with Mrs. Hensworth."

Dominique's heart sank at the dejection that dragged the hope from William's expression.

After William left, the admiral marched toward his sister, hand gripping the silver hilt of his sword. "I will not tolerate that language in front of my son."

Katharine flattened her lips. "I am sorry, Chase, but you know how I feel."

"And you will apologize to Miss Dawson at once."

Dominique blinked. *Is he standing up for me?*

"I will *not*." Mrs. Barton's eyes simmered with indignation. She shot a spiteful glance toward Dominique.

"You will"—the admiral crossed his arms over his chest—"or you will not be welcome in this house."

"Surely you do not mean that, Chase." Abruptly she wilted and began to blubber, but Dominique got the impression it was only a charade. "You would choose this. . .this Frenchwoman over your own sister?"

"Nay. But I choose not to have my employees suffer the brutality of your tongue. In addition, I choose for you to behave as the lady you claim to be—if not in Miss Dawson's presence, at least in your nephew's."

"My word, Chase, has she mesmerized you with her French charm?" Mrs. Barton flung a hand at Dominique as if she were dismissing her very existence, then sashayed behind her, circling her in a ring of disdain. "That is what they do. They lure you in with their tantalizing perfumes and sweet words. 'Oh,' " she mocked in a theatrical yet poorly executed French accent, " *'je brûle du désir. Oh, je t'aime, mon chou.'* "

Anger surged within Dominique, overtaking her fear. How dare this woman accuse her of such slanderous behavior?

The admiral snapped his fiery gaze her way. "That's enough, Katharine! Apologize or leave this house at once."

Dominique wanted nothing more than to cross the room and throttle Mrs. Barton silent. But instead she closed her eyes.

Oh Lord, help me to love this woman who hates me without cause. Help me to see past her anger into her wounded heart.

Dominique opened her eyes to find the admiral plunging toward his sister, fury pouring ahead of him like waves surging over the bow of a ship.

" 'Tis not necessary, Admiral." Dominique spoke up, stopping him in midstride.

The admiral flexed his jaw and gave her one of those looks that surely sent his crew darting off to do his bidding. "It is necessary, Miss Dawson, because I say it is necessary." Disapproval flickered in his eyes. "How can you allow this assault on your character without at least accepting an apology?"

"I told you the French are weak," his sister hissed.

Dominique swallowed and, after a quick glance at Mrs. Barton, leveled her gaze upon the admiral. "Because, Admiral, she does not truly means what she says. Her words spring from a wounded heart. How can I fault her for that?" Dominique offered Mrs. Barton a tentative smile. "I forgive her."

Her pronouncement struck both the admiral and Mrs. Barton dumb. They stared at Dominique as if she had just declared herself deity. She shifted her stance under their perusal as the seconds went by. Finally, the admiral shook his head and faced his sister, feet braced wide as though he stood on the deck of a warship, face implacable. "Nevertheless, Katharine?"

Mrs. Barton brushed a curl from her forehead and continued to gawk at Dominique. "My apologies, Miss Dawson," she gritted out between clenched teeth.

"Accepted, Mrs. Barton." Dominique retrieved the tablet

William had left on the sofa. "Now if you'll excuse me." She started for the door when the admiral grabbed her arm with a gentle yet iron-hard hand, sending a jolt through her.

"I have something to discuss with you."

The smell of cigar and spice drifted over Dominique, and she turned aside, hoping he didn't see the hot blush rising on her face. "Very well." She took a step back, her nerves resurging like a plague. What could he possibly wish to talk to her about?

The admiral cocked his head toward his sister. "Was there a purpose for your visit other than harassing my governess?"

Standing slightly behind the admiral, Dominique couldn't help but admire the way his mahogany hair curled at the tips as it protruded from its tie.

Mrs. Barton's lips formed into a pout that reminded Dominique of a Yorkshire terrier's. "Yes, there is. I've come calling nearly every night this week, and you've not been home." She slapped her gloves against her hand. "This is the Season, you know, brother. And Lady Billingsworth is throwing a ball tomorrow night. Please say you will do me the honor of escorting me and a friend?" She placed her fingers on his arm and gave him a beseeching look. "And bring Mr. Atherton along if you'd like."

"A friend, hmm? Might that friend be Lady Irene?"

"What difference does it make?" She patted her hair.

"Katharine, you know I do not enjoy those parties."

"It will be fun, Chase." She clung to his arm as if she weren't going to let go until he agreed. "You are unattached and handsome. You should get out and enjoy yourself. Maybe if you did, you would not miss the sea as much as you do. Oh, do say you'll come." She sidled closer to him. "Please?"

"Why is it so important to you that I attend?" The admiral rubbed his chin.

"Because I care about you. And you shouldn't be alone."

The admiral hesitated, glanced at Dominique over his shoulder, a mischievous look in his eyes, then faced his sister again. "Very well," he grunted. "I will come by for you at ten o'clock."

"Yes, lovely." She slid on her gloves in victory. The viper that had surfaced earlier was completely masked behind the sweet smile she now gave her brother.

"I should hope this is not one of your tricks to match me with some debutante."

"Of course not, Chase." She gave him a coy look and, without so much as a glance at Dominique, swept through the door.

Dominique found herself alone again with the admiral, a condition that always seemed to unnerve her.

He turned to face her, his intense gaze piercing her own as if he were probing for an answer to an unasked question. "Please accompany me to my study, Miss Dawson. I should like to discuss William with you, as well as offer you an advance on your wages."

His study? Dominique's heart stopped. "Of course," she muttered in a strangled voice then cleared her throat.

"Are you ill, Miss Dawson?" The admiral frowned and motioned to the door.

Dominique squeezed by, trying to avoid brushing against him. "Nay, Admiral."

"Because if you are sick, I do not want you around William."

"I assure you I am well." *So kind of you to be concerned.*

The admiral breezed past her with a "Humph" and led her the short distance across the hall to his study. The oak door stood like a giant sentinel, staunchly guarding the grand treasure within. Dominique had come to loathe it, for every time she had tried to gain entrance, it seemed to be laughing at her, taunting her, as if it enjoyed keeping her from the one thing that could save her brother's life.

Until now.

After retrieving a key chain from a pocket within his coat, the admiral opened the door with ease. And just like that, Dominique entered in after him, giving the barricade a smug look as she passed. He lit a lantern perched upon an oak tambour desk stationed against the far wall, and the room instantly became a trove of treasures. Rows of books lined the shelves that guarded the sides of the room. Atop them stood vases, odd statues, and bric-a-brac from distant lands—China, Egypt, and India, from the looks of them. A plush

Winston carpet did little to warm the wooden floor before a marble fireplace that sat frigid and empty. The room reflected every bit its master: dark, cold, and mysterious.

Tossing the key onto the desk, where it landed with a clank, the admiral began sifting through a pile of documents as if she were not there. Dominique's eyes locked upon the iron key. It lay attached to a gold chain, on the other end of which was clasped a pocket watch. She took a step forward. Her fingers itched to grab it. She shifted her gaze between it and the papers on the admiral's desk—papers stamped with the seal of the British Admiralty. She must get either those documents or that key, and this might be her only chance. If only she were two feet taller and one hundred pounds heavier. Then she could knock the admiral unconscious, grab what she needed, and flee this unnerving house.

And save her brother's life.

She gazed across the room, searching for something with which to strike the admiral, wondering if she possessed the courage. A brass candlestick sat on a small table between two chairs in the center of the room. If she could reach it unnoticed, if she could knock him cold before he turned around. . .

She eyed his towering figure and broad shoulders, and her resolve weakened. Perhaps she should try another approach. If she could play the coquette, feign affection for him, perhaps get close enough to him to distract him so she could steal the key or shuffle the documents beneath her dress. . .

Sacre bleu, was she daft? She had no idea how to flirt with a man, and the idea of doing so terrified her more than assaulting him did. Suddenly she felt his eyes upon her, and she froze as their gazes locked. Did he know what she'd been thinking?

He narrowed his eyes. "Quit dawdling, Miss Dawson, and come in. Have a seat." He waved a hand toward the set of stuffed leather chairs flanking the small table—chairs of inquisition. She imagined chains popping out of nowhere to wrap around her hands and feet, and she hesitated, trying to quiet her fitful breathing before she slid into one of them.

Above his desk, a massive falcon sculpted from iron hung

on the wall. Its beady black eyes pierced her like arrows, as if the creature knew she was an enemy.

"Do you like my falcon, Miss Dawson?"

Dominique nearly jumped off the chair, unaware the admiral had turned and was staring at her again. "Oui. I mean yes. 'Tis most imposing."

He glanced aloft, his chin upraised in pride. "A gift from the officers on the HMS *Rampage* when I was their captain."

Dominique pressed her clammy hands together in her lap. "Why a falcon, may I ask?"

"A nickname they gave me. The Iron Falcon. I suppose it has stuck with me through the years." A shadow of a smile graced his lips.

"It suits you."

The admiral chuckled. "I'll warrant you did not mean that as a compliment, Miss Dawson." She opened her mouth to respond, but he waved her silent. "But I shall accept it as one."

Dominique supposed she meant it as neither a compliment nor an insult, but simply a statement of fact. As far as she knew, falcons were harsh, strong predators, and that certainly matched her impression of the admiral to this point.

Leaning back onto his desk, he crossed his arms over his blue coat and regarded her. A tiny purple scar etched the top of his right cheek. Why hadn't she noticed it before? A sword wound, perhaps. He scowled, flattening the scar into a point that made him look all the angrier, and Dominique could see how his imperious gaze would surely make a person confess to anything—even things they had not done.

Yes, I'm a spy sent here by Napoleon to steal your precious naval secrets! The words screamed within her head. She shifted in her chair, uncomfortable under his intense scrutiny, but finally determined to meet his gaze with her own. Unfortunately, her eyes landed on his chest instead, and memories of the night in his bedchamber filled her mind. Her breath caught in her throat.

Something flickered in his gaze. Concern? Desire? Did he know where her thoughts had taken her? Was she that obvious? Oh, the shame. Heat rose up her face, but it was he who averted his eyes to the open door as if looking for an escape. He began fingering one of the gold buttons on his coat and then shifted his stance. Dominique wondered what had caused his sudden discomfiture. Surely it wasn't her.

He swung around to face his desk and opened a drawer. "About your pay, Miss Dawson."

With his back to her again, Dominique realized this might be her one and only chance.

Oh Lord, please give me strength and please forgive me for what I am about to do.

When she grabbed the candlestick, it slipped in her slick hand, and she clutched it tighter then rose and ever so slowly crept toward the admiral—silent as a mouse save for the thundering of her heart.

With his back still to her, he muttered something about the agreed fifteen pounds a year, but his words jumbled together in muted tones beneath the mad rush of blood roaring through her head.

She halted behind him, knees quaking. Her fingers gorged with blood. Gripping the candlestick with both hands, she hefted it as high as she could. Then, squeezing her eyes shut, she tensed her arms, readying herself to swing with all her might.

CHAPTER 7

Chase went through the motions of searching through his desk drawer for the coin purse he'd set aside for Miss Dawson, all the while wondering why he suddenly felt like a schoolboy with his first crush. Preposterous. Why, he was grown man—a once-married man. An admiral, for the love of Nelson. And she was naught but a feeble girl who refused to stand up for herself. All he wanted to do was ask her if he could escort her to the ball tomorrow night. It was a simple question, but every time he gazed at her creamy skin and full pink lips and allowed his eyes to rove over the curves of her delicate frame, the words refused to form on his lips. Why? 'Twas a brilliant plan, really. He could temporarily appease his sister, divert any schemes she had at matchmaking, and leave the party early with Miss Dawson—who no doubt would not protest separating from his company.

He heard her moving behind him, soft steps matching the rhythm of her deep breathing, but he didn't want to turn around, didn't want her to see the effect she had on him, not until he could clear his mind and his vision of the sweet innocence sparkling in those amber eyes.

Well, was he a cowering pup or a man? He steeled himself to face her.

"Ah, here it is." He grabbed the purse and swung around, instantly barreling into a warm, soft body. The satchel plunged to the floor in a violent jangle of coins.

A woman screamed. Something heavy crashed to his desk then clanked to the floor. Chase stumbled backward. Streaks of blue and white flashed across his vision. He reached out and grabbed Miss Dawson before she could tumble to the floor.

He held her trembling body close to his, uninterested in what had caused the clumsy collision. The aroma of sweet lilacs teased his nose. She moaned. Chase enfolded her in a strong embrace, pressing her soft curves against him and relishing the feel of a woman in his arms again. She was so small, so slight, and a longing to protect her welled up within him, a feeling so intense it frightened him.

A fist struck his chest, jerking him back to his senses.

"Let me go!" She writhed in his grasp.

He held her tighter. "Be still, Miss Dawson; you nearly fainted. I do not wish you to fall." But truth be told, as she continued to struggle, he was enjoying her lithe movements against him.

"I will not fall, *tu imbécile!*" Small palms pushed against his chest with more force than he thought possible. She kneed his right thigh, sending a dull ache through his leg.

"As you wish." Chase released her.

She took a bumbling step backward, swayed, and held a hand to her forehead. Tiny ringlets of chestnut hair dangled to her shoulders, and her face, drained of color, appeared ghostly. He grasped her elbow to steady her and led her to the chair. She slid into it, avoiding his gaze.

He couldn't help but chuckle. "Did you call me a fool, Miss Dawson?"

She cast him a smoldering glance, which caught him off guard and pleased him at the same time. So she did have some fire within her, after all.

"My apologies, Admiral," she said, her voice quavering.

Chase's heart dropped in a sudden aversion to her quick redress.

"But you *were* behaving a fool." She lifted her chin.

"Indeed?" He smiled. "Well, this fool was merely trying to save you from falling and breaking a bone in my house." He cocked his head. "What use would a bedridden governess be to me?"

The word *bedridden* slipped off his tongue before he realized the unintended implication, especially in light of her recent visit to his bedchamber. He cleared his throat, hoping she hadn't picked up on the innuendo, but the shudder that ran across her shoulders proved otherwise. Yet strangely, her reaction of innocence delighted him. He could not begin to count the women who had shamelessly thrown themselves at him since his wife had died, Lady Irene among the worst of them. How refreshing to find a woman untainted by the licentiousness that ran rampant in society.

The memory of her curves folding against him sent a sudden rush of heat through him. "Nevertheless," Chase began, unbuttoning his coat, "I must admit I enjoyed our dance, Miss Dawson."

Her face blossomed into a deep maroon that matched the rug beneath her feet, and Chase enjoyed watching the rapid rise and fall of her chest.

"It was not my desire to fall into your arms, Admiral. I pray you do not read any more into it than was intended."

"Then pray tell, what *was* intended?" Chase shrugged off his coat and tossed it onto a chair. "You place yourself quite often in the most unintentional and inappropriate situations, Miss Dawson." He gave her a sideways glance. "A lesser gentlemen would get the wrong impression."

"I did not need your help." She sniffed and pressed a hand over her stomach. "I did not ask you to hold on to me."

Chase flattened his lips against a wave of guilt at where his thoughts were taking him and felt a bit like a giant ogre.

Turning toward the desk, he picked up a candlestick from the wooden floorboards and held it toward Miss Dawson. "Yours?" A million thoughts scuttled through his mind. How did it get on the floor? They had not been close enough to the table to knock it from its perch. Miss Dawson must have been carrying it. But why? Out of all the reasons barking for attention in his mind, the only reason that made sense was that she intended to strike him with it.

Impossible.

"It is. . .I was. . .bringing it to you"—she pressed the backs of her fingers to her nose—"to show you. . .to tell you—" Her eyes shifted over the room, scanning his desk intently but never landing on him.

"To tell me what?" Chase flexed his jaw in irritation.

"It is similar to one my mother used to own." She blinked furiously and looked down.

"Hmm." Her unwillingness to look at him during this painfully concocted tale made the hairs on the back of Chase's neck stir. "So you felt the need to sneak up behind me with it?"

Her sharp gaze finally found his. "How was I to know you were going to swing about so violently?"

"I always swing violently, Miss Dawson." He offered her a playful grin. " 'Tis what admirals do, you know." He set the candlestick down and leaned back on his desk. "Do you expect me to believe that you were so desperate to show me my own candlestick that you rushed up within inches behind me?"

Sebastian appeared in the doorway and straightened his pristine black waistcoat. His gaze drifted from Chase over to Miss Dawson. "I thought I heard a scream."

"Nothing to concern you, Sebastian. Miss Dawson and I were discussing candlesticks and improper intentions."

The butler raised one incurious brow, bowed, and marched back into the dark hall.

Chase allowed his gaze to wander over Miss Dawson. She did not answer his question but sat with the poise of a lady, her hands folded in her lap. Brown lashes like a young doe's feathered over her cheeks, which had returned to their golden glow. Her hair, falling in a disarray of curls from their tussle, only added to her beauty. She bit her bottom lip, draining the normal rosy color in one spot, and fidgeted in her chair. Still she did not look at him, and he found himself yearning for one glance from her magnificent amber eyes.

"Was there something you wished to discuss with me, Admiral?" The tone of her voice made it obvious she wished to leave.

Scanning the floor, Chase retrieved the money purse and handed it to her. "An advance on your wages, Miss Dawson. I thought you might need the money."

She took the velvet satchel and nodded. "Thank you. Will that be all?" Her gaze flickered again over his desk, and he wondered what she found so fascinating about its contents.

"How are you and William getting along?"

"Splendidly, Admiral. He is a fine lad."

Of course, Chase already knew that William had taken to his new governess. Every night he had come home that week, he'd heard the boy's laughter bubbling through the house. One particularly lonely night, Miss Dawson's and William's voices, accompanied by a harpsichord, had floated through the rooms like a healing balm, infiltrating the diseased walls and eradicating the death and sorrow festering within them—if only for a moment. Music and laughter, two things that had not graced this house in years. Yet why did the sound of them make Chase so uneasy?

Shaking off the uncomfortable thoughts, he withdrew his sword and laid it upon his desk. "Does he obey you? If not, you may call upon Sebastian when I am not home." He rubbed his chin, regarding her.

Miss Dawson brushed a curl from her forehead and finally offered him a direct gaze. "There is no need, Admiral. I am perfectly capable of handling your son. And if I may be so bold, I believe you misjudge him. He has a kind disposition." She hesitated. "He longs for his father."

"He has a father."

"But not one who is present."

Chase felt a twinge in his jaw. "I must do my job, Miss Dawson, or William will not have the food, clothing, or tutoring he needs. He is a child and does not understand such things."

"He understands more than you know, Admiral."

Chase slammed his fist on the desk.

Miss Dawson jumped. "My apologies. I misspoke." Her voice barely audible, she rose from her chair.

Cursing under his breath, Chase veered around. Guilt pricked his conscience. Clearly her comments had been borne out of a concern for William. Suddenly he thought better of turning his back on her again and spun around to find her grabbing her shawl and starting toward the door.

"If I have your permission, I will take my leave now," she mumbled.

Without thinking, Chase grabbed her arm, halting her. She raised her eyes to his, uncertainty and fear flickering within them. For moments, they stood gazing at each other in silence. He wanted to take her in his arms again, to comfort her, to wipe away the tears that now pooled in her eyes. Why? Confusion and fear churned in his stomach.

"I fear you have formed a wrong opinion of me, Admiral." She tugged her arm from his grasp and took a step back. "Perhaps like your sister you believe Frenchwomen to be naught but wanton playthings." She drew a shaky breath.

Chase grimaced, regretting his touch upon her not only because of its effect on him but also because he clearly had frightened her again. "I assure you, Miss Dawson, I do not share her views." He sighed, unsure how to make her see he was not the knave his actions portrayed. He searched her warm eyes, so different from the cold, angry sheen that covered his sister's gaze.

"May I ask why you forgave my sister so easily? Her behavior toward you was beyond reproach." The gracious act still baffled him. Why, if they had been men, a duel would have resulted from such a scurrilous affront.

She pressed her shawl against her chest. "Who am I not to forgive others when I have been forgiven so much?"

Chase grunted. He assumed she meant by God. "And what horrid things could someone so young have done that required forgiveness?"

" 'Tis not so much what we have done, but the condition of our hearts, Admiral. A wrong motive can be just as evil as a spiteful act."

Forgiveness. Chase had been taught about God's forgiveness at church all his life, but he had never felt he was forgiven, had never witnessed anyone else receive forgiveness in a way that changed him, and had never really seen true forgiveness in action.

Until that night.

He narrowed his eyes upon Miss Dawson, wondering why she fascinated him so much. "And what might your motives be?"

Her face blanched, and she shifted her eyes to the floor. "To care for William, Admiral."

"Yes, of course." Clasping his hands behind his back, he began to pace as thoughts of his sister brought back his promise to attend the ball. He stopped and studied Miss Dawson. Her gaze darted to the door. It appeared the little sparrow yearned to fly away. He moved to block her path then gave her a reassuring smile.

Attending the ball would not be so unpleasant if he could escort Miss Dawson. And it would serve another purpose, as well. Though he could not imagine any foul play on her part, her suspicious behavior did give him some pause, and this way, he could keep a weather eye upon her all evening.

"One more thing, Miss Dawson, and then you may go."

"Yes?"

"I wonder if you might do me a favor."

A line of wariness creased the corner of her lovely mouth. "Perhaps."

He chuckled at her hesitancy. "As you know, my sister has badgered me into going to the ball at Lord and Lady Billingsworth's tomorrow night." His throat went dry, and he swallowed, wondering at his sudden nervousness. "I smell a trap, and one I fear only you can help me avoid."

"*Moi?* I do not understand." Her delicate brows crinkled together.

Chase leaned toward her. "Would you do me the honor of attending the ball with me?"

Miss Dawson's face reddened again so quickly it reminded Chase of red and white signal flags being raised and lowered on his ship.

"But how could that help?" she stuttered, tossing a hand to her chest. "I mean to say, *non*. Absolutely not. I could not possibly." She moved to circle around him.

He stepped in her path again. "You would be doing me a grand service."

She gazed up at him, her eyes shifting between his. "But your sister—surely she loathes me enough without inciting her further? And besides, what would people think?"

"People? They would see naught but Admiral Randal escorting his governess to a dance. They will think what they will, regardless of what they see." He shrugged. "What does it matter?"

Miss Dawson pursed her lips and glanced away. "Nevertheless, I cannot. Now if you please." She made a move to get by him. "May I go?"

Chase stepped aside, disappointment expelling a huge gust from his lips. She swept past him in a whiff of lilacs and moved down the hall with a superior gait that belied the timid girl she portrayed.

Suddenly she froze and turned around. Chase thought to make a dash into his study, not wanting her to know he had been staring at her, but he couldn't tear himself away from the vision of her standing in the dark hall with beams of moonlight dancing around her like angels.

"Very well, Admiral. It would be my pleasure to attend the ball with you."

He studied her, wondering at her sudden change of heart but afraid to press her any further. "Very good." He bowed and watched her turn and fade into the darkness. Elated at her acceptance, he wasn't foolish enough to think that she had agreed because of any affection for him.

No, something else was going on with this intriguing French-woman, something mysterious, something even dangerous, perhaps. Had she intended to strike him with the candlestick? He shook his head and gave a quick snort. It made no sense. Nothing about the woman made any sense. She fascinated him. And what was even more fascinating to him was that he now looked forward to this ridiculous dance with great anticipation.

Yes, this ball would prove to be very entertaining, indeed.

CHAPTER 8

Dominique pulled her blue muslin pelisse tighter around her neck against the morning mist swirling around her. Only in London did the fog seem to possess the unnatural ability to move through fabric as well as skin. Yet riding atop the chill, pleasant memories bounced over Dominique—memories of her mother lovingly insisting she and Marcel bring extra cloaks whenever they intended to visit the city.

As if reading her thoughts, Larena glanced up into the gray sky. "We may actually get to see the sun today, miss."

Following her gaze, Dominique saw nothing but a bowl of soot capping the city, save for a few light cracks where the sun's rays attempted to slice through the pudding-like fog.

"But what difference does the weather make when we are going shopping?" Larena's crimson curls bobbed beneath her bonnet as she walked next to Dominique. " 'Tis most exciting, isn't it? Shopping for the ball tonight?"

"Yes, I suppose." Dominique attempted a weak smile. Larena had jumped at the chance to accompany her down Bond Street—where all high society shopped—to the Grafton House, the only draper's shop Dominique could afford. Apparently dress shopping was not one of the chambermaid's normal activities, but why would it be when no lady had lived in the Randal home these past three years?

Her exuberance was almost catching—almost—for Dominique

wasn't entirely sure she'd made the right decision in agreeing to accompany the admiral. The thought of the upcoming evening caused a tightness in her chest that had kept her up most of the night and made her ravenously hungry that morning. For breakfast, she'd consumed three poached eggs, two pieces of toast smothered with jam, sausage, and five cups of strong tea, and now she found she was hungry all over again.

Horses clattered over the cobblestone streets, pulling elaborately painted phaetons and landaus that carried their well-dressed passengers to whatever grand events were happening that day: a horse race or cricket match or perhaps just a stroll in Hyde Park.

Dominique edged around a peddler selling muffins, and her stomach rumbled at the sweet smell of fresh-baked dough. She pressed a hand over her complaining midsection and decided not to embarrass herself further by eating any more in front of Larena. They passed a window filled with clusters of tightly wound hair in every imaginable color and style. Dominique twirled a finger around one of her own chestnut locks as she examined the wigs, amazed at the variety and the prices.

"If I may be so bold. . ." Larena gave Dominique an inquisitive glance as they continued on their way. "You should be honored the admiral asked you to the ball. He hasn't escorted a lady to a dance since. . .well, since his wife died, I suppose."

"I *am* honored." Dominique sidestepped a young lad racing down the street with an orange in his tight grip. An older gentleman followed quick on his heels, yelling, "Thief! Thief!"

She turned and watched them coil their way through the crowd. "Poor thing. He's probably starving."

Larena tilted her head and gazed at Dominique before they started forward again.

"I do not wish to give people the wrong impression. I'm only going as a favor to the admiral," Dominique stated.

"A favor? Is that what he's calling it?" Larena's lips curved upward, lifting a small freckle at the corner of her mouth.

"Yes, and that is all that it is." Dominique raised a stern brow at her chambermaid, but her thoughts quickly turned to the feel of the admiral's arms around her. That had been all she had thought about during her long, sleepless night. She had closed her eyes only for a second, not wanting to witness the candlestick bashing his head, when suddenly she'd found herself locked in his embrace—a warm, strong embrace that for a brief moment made her feel safe, secure, and cared for. A feeling she'd not enjoyed for a very long time.

A gentleman approached, lifted his top hat at the ladies, and allowed his gaze to scour over Dominique as he passed. She recognized the look, the same hunger she'd seen in the admiral's eyes—or was it? The admiral's gaze had held something deeper, and the warm sensation it produced in Dominique frightened her. She must avoid him; she must do what she came to do and leave as soon as possible; and she should definitely not go to a dance with the man. But what choice did she have? If she didn't go, he would be at the ball with the key to his study in his pocket, and she would spend another night alone in his home, banging her head against the oak barricade. Since her attempt to pummel him unconscious hadn't worked, she saw no other option than to feign an affection for him that would bring her close enough to somehow remove the key from his person. And what better way to accomplish that than a dance?

Larena said something, but Dominique couldn't make it out amidst the cacophony of sounds clamoring in the streets. Well past eleven o'clock, the city seemed to instantly burst with life. Bells of street peddlers rang through the streets, echoing off the brick walls of the exquisite shops lining the avenue: jewelers, tailors, candle makers, booksellers, tea dealers, watchmakers, and purveyors of every imaginable luxury that London society could afford. A German band began to play inside a tavern, horses whinnied, children laughed, and the constant grinding of carriage wheels over the cobblestones only added to the orchestra of madness.

"There's Grafton House, miss." Larena pointed to a small store several yards ahead and across the street. A wooden sign hanging from an iron post projecting from the front read GRAFTON HOUSE DRAPERS.

Dominique nodded as the rich aroma of roasting coffee filled her nose like sweet nectar, and she glanced back over her shoulder at a quaint café.

"A coffeehouse. They are quite popular now," Larena said. "Would you care for some?"

"Nay, but it does smell delicious." No sooner had she said the words than the stench of rot and sewage ripped the succulent aroma from her nose. Coughing, Dominique turned to see a woman emptying a chamber pot from her second-story window into the alleyway below. It splattered onto the street, sending a spray of sludge into the air. Turning her gaze back onto the main street, she pressed forward.

Brave flickers of sunlight broke through the fog, showering the scene with sparkling highlights and brightening Dominque's spirits along with them. Gentlemen decked in tailored coats and breeches, with flowing silk cravats bunched about their necks and top hats perched on their heads, strolled about with canes in hand as if they owned the world, perusing the females as they passed. Ladies flounced by them in promenade gowns, fluttering fans and parasols through the air—though why they would need either on a day like this, Dominique could not fathom. Yes, this was the Season in London about which her mother had always spoken. The time when all the nobility flocked to the city from their country estates to see and be seen.

A tall gentlemen, impeccably dressed, nodded with an approving smile as he passed by on Dominique's left. Another one, across the street, held a monocle to his eye and studied her as if she were a specimen in a laboratory.

Dominique gritted her teeth. She hated being on display.

"Seems you are drawing a bit of attention this morning, miss."

"Indeed." Precisely what she did not want to do, either on the street, in the house, or anywhere in London, for that matter.

"When did you have your coming out?" Larena asked as they wove around three giggling ladies.

"Coming out?"

"Yes, your coming-out party."

Dominique cringed as memories fell on her like a sudden weight. "Five years ago." Had it been that long? "I had just turned eighteen." She remembered the excitement of having her first silk gown tailored, of the maids fawning over her before the event, bedecking her curls with jewels and applying rice powder to her face and salve to her lips, the proud look on her mother's face, and of course, the attention she received from the young men at the ball.

"You must have been quite a hit."

"I can't really say. 'Twas the best and worse evening of my life."

"Whatever do you mean?"

"We received news of my father's death late that same night." Dominique sighed as her heart shriveled, reliving the agony. "And my mother moved us back to France within a month."

"I'm very sorry, miss." Larena gave Dominique's arm a gentle squeeze. Her blue eyes warmed in concern. "Perhaps 'tis just as well. By the looks you're getting today, you'd have been married off your first season, to be sure."

They passed an art gallery on their right, its windows stuffed with magnificent oil paintings lined in rows next to huge bronze sculptures. Horrified, Dominique tore her gaze from a statue of a naked man. She cleared her throat. "Do you disapprove of marriage?"

"I disapprove of slavery, miss, which is what most marriages are."

Dominique blinked. She'd heard some women call their marriages drudgery but never slavery. "Is that what you thought of the admiral's marriage?"

"Nay." Larena shook her head and stared ahead of them. "I discouraged Melody—I mean Mrs. Randal—from marrying the admiral, but truth be told, they were quite happy together. He loved her very much."

A strange twinge startled Dominique. Somehow she couldn't picture the admiral loving anyone—or being happy for that matter.

"Do you never hope to marry, then?"

"I'm already eight and twenty, miss. Well past marrying age

for a woman." She adjusted her shawl. "Besides, I have more than proven that I can take care of myself. I don't need a man to rule over me."

The words shot from Larena's mouth with such spite that Dominique wondered what had happened to make her so opposed to what most women considered a blessed privilege. Yet her independence ignited envy within Dominique. If she had been able to take care of herself and her brother, they would not have had to depend on Cousin Lucien—and she would not be in this horrid predicament.

"You're far more courageous than I am," she admitted as she stopped next to an apple cart and gazed across the busy street, wondering how they would ever cross it safely.

The maid studied her. "Perhaps you simply have not been given the chance to prove yourself."

Ah, but she had been given the chance.

And she'd failed miserably.

After her mother had died so suddenly last year, Dominique, who hadn't a clue how to fend for herself, had been reduced to dragging her brother through the streets of Paris, begging for morsels of food. It had proven to be the most shameful and terrifying time of her life, and she believed they both would be dead—or worse— if Cousin Lucien hadn't rescued them. No, she had proven herself incapable of being anything like Larena.

Dominique felt a tug on the bottom of her pelisse and looked down to see a young costermonger, a boy no older than William. "Please, miss, would you buy an apple?"

Smudges of dirt marred his pale complexion. His unkempt hair sprouted in all directions. He scratched his chest through a hole in his ragged clothes and swept his bare feet through a puddle, then held the red fruit out to her with an empty, pleading look in his eyes.

Dominique knelt and smiled as her heart split in two. A vision of Marcel as dirty and unkempt as this young lad crept through her mind. He'd been the one who had done most of the begging— especially toward the end when Dominique had all but given up.

"I'd love to buy an apple. How much?"

"Two pence, miss." He coughed to the side, a raspy, moist cough that sent a chill down Dominique's spine. He raised his glassy green eyes to hers, a tiny flicker of hope skipping across them.

Dominique opened her purse and dug out a shilling then placed it in the boy's other hand, closing his fingers around it. When he peeked at the coin, his eyes widened, and his lips parted in a generous smile. "Thank you, miss."

"And you eat the apple for me, will you?"

"Aye, miss." Without hesitation, he chomped on the ripe fruit. Juice dripped off his grinning lips before he scampered away.

Dominique rose and scanned the street again. Seeing an opening betwixt phaetons, she grabbed Larena and ventured forth.

"I've never seen the likes of that, miss—not from a lady." Larena shook her head as they skirted around a pile of fly-infested manure.

Dominique tossed her hand to her nose against the putrid smell as they reached the other side and stood in front of Grafton House.

Larena's brow crinkled, folding her freckles together. "Now you won't have enough for a decent overskirt."

"Perhaps not, but that boy and his family will eat tonight."

Larena's eyes moistened, and she turned aside as Dominique opened the door to the shop.

After an hour of sifting through a multitude of fabrics and listening to Larena's endless opinions on the fashions of the day, Dominique finally purchased a lovely maroon satin overskirt, embroidered in golden lace. Since she couldn't afford a new gown, this would do nicely to dress up one of the gowns the last governess had left. She'd tried it on before they'd left the house that morning, and it fit wonderfully. Although the neckline was a bit lower than she felt comfortable with, it was not as risqué as most of the gowns she'd seen. She certainly didn't want to give the wrong impression. Even with the new overskirt, it would be a plain dress by comparison to the more expensive gowns, but it suited her, and she hoped she wouldn't bring shame to the admiral.

When she stepped from the shop, her purchase flung over one arm, she found her mood had vastly improved. Perhaps it was the patches of sun that now lit the bustling street as she and Larena made their way through the crowd.

"Do you know where St. Mary Woolnoth is located?" Dominique scurried beside Larena, who had quickened her pace.

"I believe the church is on Lombard Street." She flashed Dominique a grin. "Not too far from here. I can show you the way another time if you'd like. But we must get home to prepare you for the ball. We haven't much time."

Truth be told, Dominique would much prefer a visit to see the Reverend John Newton. Although she had met him only once, her father often spoke of him as the man who had "opened the eyes of his soul" to see the truth of God. Her father told her that if she ever found herself in London in need of help, she could always go to Rev. Newton. And Lord knew, she needed help—desperately.

"May I ask why it interests you?"

"My father and the rector were good friends, and I wish to visit him while I'm in town."

"Well, you shall have plenty of time to do that, miss. I do believe the admiral intends to keep you in his employ. Surely he cannot help but see the change in William already."

"Truly?" Dominique had no idea if she was benefiting William. The boy seemed to enjoy her company, but then, he would enjoy anyone's company in light of his father's continual absence.

"Can you not see it?" Larena's wide eyes were aglitter. "Why, I've not heard that boy laugh in years. And sing?" She shook her head, sending her red curls fluttering in the breeze. "Not since his mother died. You are just what William needs. And it warms my heart, Miss Dawson." She gave Dominique's arm a tender squeeze. "Truly I've come to love that boy as if he were my own."

Dominique's heart felt strangely heavy. As soon as she could get her hands on the information Lucien wanted, she'd have to leave—leave dear sweet William all alone in the world again without a mother, and from what she'd witnessed, without a father, as well. Surely they would find another governess for William, and no doubt a lady far more suitable than she. She tried to console herself with that thought as they toiled through the crowd. She raised her face to the sun, relishing its warmth while trying to avoid the leering gazes of the men who brushed past her.

The sound of angry male voices up ahead startled her.

"How dare you? I will not stand for such an affront, sir," one man bellowed.

"You'll not only stand for it; you'll take it like the weasel you are and scurry away."

Someone chuckled, and a crowd began to form around the men, who had obviously carried their altercation out into the street from a club up ahead.

Gentlemen nudged ladies behind them in a protective gesture while inching forward, craning their necks for a better view of a grand diversion in their otherwise humdrum day.

Larena halted, her face pinched in alarm. The crowd pressed in on them. "We should not go any farther until this is settled." She squeezed in front of Dominique and craned her neck to watch the fisticuffs.

Strong fingers gripped Dominique's arm.

A short, burly man dressed in a silk overcoat and gaudy purple cravat dragged her away from the mob. Her throat clamped shut. She tried to scream. No sound came from her lips save a few feeble sputters.

The man gave her a stern look before he pushed her down a narrow alleyway. He slammed her trembling body against the cold brick wall. A rough hand that smelled of tobacco and fish stifled her scream under a crushing hold to her mouth. Terror gripped her in a cold sweat.

"*Avez-vous les documents?*"

Wide-eyed, Dominique shook her head as the man lowered his hand from her mouth. Perspiration trickled down the back of her gown. She could no longer feel her heart beating.

"*Pas encore,*" she replied in a squeaky voice. Her gaze darted to the street. People dashed by, rushing to view the altercation. She could still hear the men fighting. Yet she could not call for help.

If she did, this man would surely expose her for the spy she was.

If anyone heard them speaking French, they'd no doubt be brought before the constable. *"En Englais, monsieur, s'il vous plaît."*

He scowled. "Do you have the documents?"

"Not yet," she repeated in English. "I need more time." Dominique rubbed her sore arm and met the man's slick, narrow gaze. His hair hung in greasy strands to his shoulders. The stink of human waste rose from the ground around him like a poisonous vapor.

With an evil sneer, the man dropped his other hand from her arm. "You have been here two weeks, mademoiselle."

"He keeps the documents behind a locked door."

A rat scampered through the puddles of sludge around their feet, and the man kicked it aside with a fiendish snicker. His sinister gaze locked on her. "Your brother's blood cries out to you, mademoiselle. Do not forget him."

"His blood?" Panic pounded in her chest. "Is he all right? Is Marcel all right?" She felt light-headed again. *Oh please, Lord. Don't let me faint. Not here, not with this man.*

"For now." He slid a finger over his oily mustache and sneered at her "You must bring me something to ensure his safety." He glanced toward the street. "By Monday night."

"But I cannot." Dominique sobbed. "That's only two days. I need more time." How could she possibly accomplish in two days what she'd not been able to do in two weeks?

"Tuesday morning at the first hour. There's a tavern, the Last Stop, on Cecil Street, off Strand. Come alone."

"Miss Dawson." Larena's worried voice filtered through the crowd that now seemed to be dispersing.

Dominique's knees nearly gave out, and she gripped the wall behind her lest she topple to the ground. The cold, moist brick bit into her hands like sharpened gravel. "But, monsieur, I cannot possibly get away that late at night."

"J'en ai assez!" he barked. "If you do not come with something we can use, your brother will pay for your disloyalty with his blood."

CHAPTER 9

Chase poured himself another swig of brandy, grabbed the glass, and tossed the golden liquid to the back of his mouth. It slid down his throat like fire and plunged into his belly, radiating a pleasant numbness to his agitated nerves.

"Sir, should you be partaking quite so much before the dance?" Sebastian asked.

Chase spun on his heel and glared at the butler as the slender man brushed off Chase's navy frock and ensured the gold buttons on the cuffs were snug. He knew the man was right, but ever since dinner that evening—dinner he had reluctantly consumed in the company of both his son and Miss Dawson—he had been unable to stifle a rising tide of trepidation.

The conversation had flowed well enough, and the food had been delicious as always, but Miss Dawson's alluring smile, the ease of her intelligent conversation, and the way she interacted with William had caught Chase off guard. The boy beamed in her presence as if a part of him had been brought back to life, that part within Chase that he preferred to remain dead and buried.

Unfamiliar confusion stormed through him as he stomped across his bedchamber. He hated these blasted balls, should be furious that he'd been finagled into going, should dread the whole event. Then why did he find that a small part of him sparked with anticipation? The unwelcome sensation kindled a burning fury, and that, coupled with extreme unease, had led to his drinking.

Why couldn't he be out upon his ship where life was simple and straightforward? He hunted the enemy and then blasted that enemy with his cannons. Here in London, he had no idea whom his enemy was. Everything was muddled beneath pretensions, etiquette, peerage, and treacherous courtship rituals. Even his own feelings betrayed him.

"Why did you never marry, Sebastian?" Chase huffed as he plopped into a chair and shoved his foot into a leather boot. Sebastian had been with him for seven years, but Chase felt he barely knew the man. He had only recently learned of his butler's French heritage on his mother's side, something that, as a British admiral in wartime, he should have known. He cursed himself for his negligence and eyed Sebastian with suspicion. Yes, indeed, why hadn't the man taken a wife?

The butler raised one gray eyebrow and disappeared into the dressing closet, reappearing within seconds, a white silk cravat in hand. "I have always believed, sir, that marriage is naught but a prison that serves only to keep a man from achieving success."

"Indeed?" Chase thrust his other foot into his boot, surprised at the butler's declaration and wondering if it were more of an excuse than the truth.

Sebastian cleared his throat, his cheeks purpling as if he were suddenly afraid of Chase's anger. " 'Tis only my personal belief, sir. I know it was not the way of things with you and Mrs. Randal."

"Never fear, Sebastian. I do not fault you for it. In fact, I find myself quite in agreement with you these days." Chase stood and tugged the hem of his blue navy waistcoat, wondering why his thoughts had drifted to marriage in the first place.

Sebastian gave him a curious look. "But surely you did not. . ." He dropped his gaze. "Forgive me."

"You may speak freely, Sebastian."

"Surely you did not believe so with Mrs. Randal?"

Chase cringed at the second reminder of his wife. Why did everyone in the country have to mention Melody? Wasn't every inch of this house enough of a reminder? Even this room—this room they had shared. His gaze took in the massive Italian oak bed, and a sinking feeling consumed him. He needed another drink. His eyes shifted to the bottle of brandy sitting on his desk, beckoning him. No, he must keep his wits about him tonight. He would need them to guard against the conniving chicaneries of his sister.

He gave Sebastian a stern look. "Mrs. Randal is gone. Do not mention her again." Chase snatched the cravat from Sebastian and flung it about his neck as the butler's jaw tightened. Sebastian took a step back, and a distant, impassive expression descended on his features. Perhaps Chase had been too harsh. He examined his butler. Tall, slender, always impeccably attired in a white ruffled linen shirt beneath a double-breasted black waistcoat and dark wool breeches, Sebastian had the bearing of a stately prince. And although his butler was now fifty and well past the age of marrying, Chase had always wondered how the successful, well-groomed man had been able to resist the more alluring gender. "Did you ever have a lady love, Sebastian?"

"No," the butler replied staunchly, stepping forward to fold the neck cloth in the usual Gordian knot. "My aim has been to oversee the home I am employed in with the utmost efficiency, and to do so affords me little time to pursue other activities." He stepped back to examine his work, and the lines around his mouth folded into a frown. "No, this will never do. . .never do." He hurried forward and engaged in another battle with the silk cloth.

Chase raised his chin, allowing the man to work. Sebastian had done a fine job, especially since Chase had fired his steward recently, forcing Sebastian to take over those duties, as well. But had Chase ever complimented the butler on his exemplary work? Had he ever spoken to him outside of an order? Chase opened his mouth to voice his long-overdue approval, but the high-strung butler kept fidgeting with his cravat, jerking Chase's neck and sending annoyance rather than approbation speeding through him.

He hated being fussed over, even by Sebastian, who prided himself on every detail of the Randal home—including the faultless attire of his master. Though Chase didn't know the man well, surely Sebastian's loyalty for so many years precluded any possibility of duplicity. The light scent of cedar rose from the aged man as Chase examined a fleet of gray hair atop his head surrounding a last stubborn squadron of brown. Was the man happy with his choice?

"There is something to be said for achieving success in one's career," Chase began as Sebastian finished with the cravat and held out Chase's frock. "But do you ever long for anything more?"

Sebastian snapped his head back. His brows sprang up, and Chase wondered whether he was surprised at the question or at the fact that Chase had bothered to ask. "More, sir?"

Chase thrust his arms into the coat then eased it over his shoulders. Had the man wanted love? He harrumphed. "Family."

"Nay, sir, I came from a rather large family." Sebastian handed Chase his pocket watch and key. "Ten children in all. We had barely enough to eat. My mother died trying to take care of us while my father was away at sea. No, sir." He shook his head and scratched his bushy gray sideburns. "I find family, even love, vastly overrated."

Even love. "Your father is a seaman?" Chase realized he knew nothing about his butler.

"Yes, sir. Was. A petty officer aboard the HMS *Bristol.*"

"Indeed, I had no idea. But you said *was?*"

"He died of the scurvy, sir." A flicker of malice cooled Sebastian's gaze.

Slipping the watch and key inside his topcoat pocket, Chase studied his butler, curious at his quick change of manner. Did he harbor bitterness about his childhood, and if so, toward whom? In Chase's employ, the man had never lacked for food or shelter, but in all those years, Chase had yet to see him smile.

Leaning forward, Sebastian adjusted the collar of Chase's frock and handed him his service sword.

"What are your thoughts about Miss Dawson?" Chase asked as he strapped on the sword.

"William seems quite fond of her. But she is a bit skittish, sir, and she often has the cook up in arms."

"Really. How so?"

"She seems to be consuming large quantities of food, sir."

Chase chuckled. "You must be mistaken, Sebastian. The woman is as tiny as a mouse."

As Chase examined himself in the gilded looking glass perched by the dressing room, a wave of disgust passed over him. He looked like a navy dandy. He would much rather be wearing the uniform he wore aboard ship than this frock with the stand-up, gold-fringed collar matched in opulence by the gold bullion of his epaulettes. In fact, he would much rather be walking across the weathered deck of his ship at this moment than walking out onto a dance floor at Lady Billingsworth's ball. But he had already given his word to his sister, and a gentleman never goes back on his word.

Chase shrugged off the sudden concern about his appearance.

"You look splendid, sir." The butler took a step back and nodded. "You'll have all the ladies swooning, to be sure."

"That is not my desire, Sebastian." Yet Chase wiped an unintended smile from his lips as his thoughts drifted to Miss Dawson.

Inhaling a deep breath of the misty, chilled air in front of the Billingsworth house, Chase proffered his hand to assist Miss Dawson from the landau. She laid her delicate gloved fingers in his, and her eyes met his briefly. Volumes spoke from within their amber depths, and Chase felt weakened in their wake.

When Miss Dawson had descended the stairs that evening, a heated clot had formed in Chase's throat. It wasn't the simple but elegant dress she wore or the way she had arranged her hair in a bouquet of chestnut curls around her face. No, there was an aura about her, a sweet spirit that drifted over her—a vulnerability, an innocence that pulled on him with the force of a summer squall, and he'd suddenly regretted inviting her. What had he been thinking?

Percy hopped out of the carriage, gave Miss Dawson one of his lascivious winks, then turned to assist Lady Irene and Chase's sister. Chase perused the petite governess beside him, only to enjoy the blush rising on her cheeks from Percy's blatant flirtation. He found her naïveté both refreshing and charming.

Miss Dawson had barely said a word during the carriage ride to the Billingsworth house, not when they'd stopped at his parents' massive estate, nor when his sister had uttered a rude exclamation upon finding her in the landau, nor when Lady Irene snubbed her with her disapproving silence, nor even when Lord Markham had allowed his drooling gaze to feast upon her during the whole journey. She'd simply smiled and endured their cold mannerisms and surly remarks with a grace that confounded Chase. Was it weakness. . .or something else?

After showering Chase with her most seductive smile, Lady Irene glared at Miss Dawson with a tilt of her pert nose before taking Percy's arm and proceeding to the front of the house. Couples donned in their finest attire milled about on the square and exited from other carriages that pulled up all along the gravel courtyard.

Lord Markham burst from the carriage, shaking it on its hinges. A waft of strong wine emanated from him. His glazed eyes scanned over Miss Dawson before he offered his arm to Chase's sister. "Would you do me the honor, Mrs. Barton?" He gazed at the towering white pillars of one of the largest town houses on Grosvenor Square. From the windows, orchestra music floated on shimmering light that drifted down upon new arrivals. "Looks to be a fine party, eh, Randal?"

Chase snorted. "We shall see."

"Really, Randal, quit being such a boor. You have a beautiful lady on your arm and an evening of wine and dance to enjoy. Have fun for a change." Lord Markham led Katharine to the back of a crowd that had formed at the front entrance.

"You've been silent this evening." Chase glanced at Miss Dawson. Disappointment gnawed at him when her features were lost in the shadows. Then she turned toward the house. A wash of candlelight flickered over her face, and he had a strong urge to caress her cheek. Her eyes glanced over the scene as if distracted before they landed on him again.

"Better to be silent than to say something I would regret, Admiral."

"Hmm. A good philosophy, I'll wager. And certainly one which present company could use some instruction upon." He chuckled, and her responding smile seemed to scatter the darkness around them. He took her arm and caught up to his sister and Lord Markham, feeling a sudden lightness in his step.

Katharine turned to Chase, ignoring Miss Dawson at his side. "How could you offend Lady Irene so?" she hissed.

"Offend?" Chase snickered. "You invited me to this soiree. You never said I couldn't invite a guest."

Lord Markham bellowed his greetings to people he knew as he made his way toward the door.

"You know as well as I that I intended for you to escort Lady Irene," Katharine whispered.

"Precisely why I invited Miss Dawson."

"You are incorrigible."

"So I am told." Confident he had thwarted her latest matchmaking scheme, he grinned. But then he felt Miss Dawson stiffen at his side. He sobered his tone. "I do not wish to guide Lady Irene's affections down a course that leads to naught but an empty dock."

"You should give her a chance, Chase. She'll make a good wife. And she adores you so."

Miss Dawson's grip tightened on Chase's arm. "I assure you, Mrs. Barton, I am only here as a favor to your brother. I have no intention of coming between him and Lady Irene."

Chase snapped his gaze to Miss Dawson. She'd said the words with a conviction that suddenly dampened his newly improved mood.

"You assume too much, Miss Dawson," Katharine retorted with a smirk. "I assure you that you pose no threat to Lady Irene."

Miss Dawson gave her a curt grin and looked away.

Dominique gazed across the floor where couples had just begun a cotillion to start off the evening dance. A small orchestra played at the back of the huge gala room filled to near bursting with ladies in shimmering gowns and lords in pristine evening wear. Draped across the walls, garlands molded from stucco surrounded impressionist paintings of flowers and fruits. Long mirrors paneled one side of the room, reflecting the glittering light from a multitude of cut-glass chandeliers. Chairs and taborets padded with velvet lined the walls where ladies already took their seats. Dominique gazed up to see a domed ceiling frescoed in bright colors that added to the magnitude and gaiety of the scene. Several people crowded around a buffet against the far wall where lemonade and wine punch were being served to refresh the guests after dancing.

Dominique had never seen anything quite so magnificent. Her plain gown so paled in comparison with the beautiful attire of the ladies surrounding her, like a sparrow among so many peacocks, that she longed to slip into the shadows. She glanced around for the admiral, but he had been stolen away by a group of navy men wishing to discuss something of import. She must convince him to dance with her so she could snatch the key from his coat and leave as soon as possible.

A group of noblemen, sharp in their evening wear, stood in a regal cluster beside her, discussing politics while allowing their sultry gazes to devour every lady who passed by, occasionally feasting upon Dominique as if she were the hors d'oeuvre.

Several gentlemen had already requested she reserve a dance for them. She'd agreed, unsure how to respond to the attention she was drawing, and as she stood surrounded by so much opulence, she suddenly felt more out of her league than ever. Butterflies fluttered a wild dance in her stomach as a nervous hunger consumed her. *Lord, what am I doing here? I don't belong among these people. And where is the admiral?*

Mr. Atherton gave her a saucy nod from the dance floor as he escorted Lady Irene through the regimented steps of the cotillion. Mrs. Barton huddled with a group of ladies by the banquet table, their sharp eyes periodically darting her way in disapproving glances. A head of gray hair dislodged from the crowd and seemed to be bobbing in her direction.

Dominique cringed. *Lord Markham.* Something about the man

sent a cold shiver down her back. *Please, Lord, do not let him come my way.* But she'd no sooner shot up the prayer than the beast appeared beside her.

"Miss Dawson, I daresay, your beauty shines like the sun among these many paltry stars." He waved stubby jeweled fingers over the glittering sea of alluring females.

Dominique tensed. "Thank you, milord, but I'll wager you say that to all the ladies." She tried to move away from him, but he sidled up beside her, brushing his arm against hers.

"Ah, I see the admiral has been telling tales about me." He leaned toward her and grinned, blasting her with a puff of wine-laden breath that stung her nose. "Perhaps they have piqued your interest, mademoiselle?"

"My only interest, milord"—Dominique forced a steely tone into her voice—"is in being a governess to the admiral's son."

"Yet I fail to see how you can do that from a ball, and especially when you display yourself in so tempting a fashion." His bloodshot eyes fixated upon the swell of her bosom, and Dominique turned aside and splayed her fan over her chest, horrified. Was her gown too provocative? A blush rose up her neck and onto her face. She glanced down at her dress, then at the gowns of the other women standing nearby. No, by far she wore the most modest attire in the room.

Lord Markham must have misinterpreted her embarrassment as a playful attempt at flirtation, for his thick fingers grabbed her arm and turned her about. "Perhaps you need some air, mademoiselle? A stroll outside may do you some good?"

Was he mad? The last thing she intended was to place herself alone with this salacious hound. "No, I'm quite happy here, thank you." She tugged on her arm, but his grip tightened.

He raised a cultured brow and wrestled with his cravat as if overheated. " 'Tis a bit stuffy, wouldn't you say? I would enjoy some cool air. Won't you join me?"

The words sounded more like a command than a request. "I do believe some cooling off will do you good, milord, but no, I respectfully decline your offer. Now please release me at once."

Lord Markham's eyes hardened as he wrenched her closer to him. "Now you listen—"

"What's this, Markham, stealing my lady?" The admiral's baritone voice had never sounded so pleasing. He erected his strong presence like a tower of defense between them. One glance at Dominique's face, and the smile that graced his handsome lips melted into a thin line.

Lord Markham released Dominique and tossed a jovial chuckle toward the admiral. "We were just about to dance."

"Yet as her escort, I believe the privilege of the first dance falls to me, does it not?" The admiral furrowed his brow as he glanced between them.

The tight ball of nerves in Dominique's stomach began to unravel, but the thought of dancing with the admiral and trying to steal his key caused it to wind back up again.

"Of course." Lord Markham nodded. "Won't you save a dance for me, Miss Dawson?"

Dominique dropped a curtsy and gave him a tart smile but did not grace him with an answer.

With a snort, he marched away.

The admiral's concerned gaze landed on her. He studied her for a moment then cocked his head. "Are you all right, Miss Dawson? I believe you have gone white again."

She watched Lord Markham slither through the crowd like a snake seeking his next victim. "Yes, I'm fine." She forced a smile.

The admiral followed the direction of her gaze. "Forgive him; he means no harm."

"I'm not so sure." Dominique stared into the admiral's soothing brown eyes—eyes that were usually guarded but that now held a warmth that sent her heart fluttering.

"He will not touch you." He said the words with the same authority he must wield upon his ship, and she knew he meant them. His protectiveness cloaked her like a warm blanket. She watched the rise and fall of his chest beneath the gold buttons of his blue waistcoat and remembered how he'd stolen her breath away that evening when she'd first seen him at the bottom of the stairs, waiting for her. Why, she'd barely noticed poor Mr. Atherton standing beside him until she neared the front door.

She shifted her gaze under his continual perusal and scanned the resplendent room and the lords and ladies ensconced in their bright dance. Was she really here? At a wonderful ball with a handsome admiral? She felt like a princess in a fairy-tale dream. Would her life have been filled with such glorious parties if her parents hadn't died? She shook her head.

Whom was she trying to fool? She was no princess. Never would be.

She was but a pauper on a pauper's mission to save her brother's life. There was no one to protect her or her brother—save God. She waved her fan through the air, trying to dry her eyes, not wanting the admiral to see her distress. Raising her gaze to his, she hoped to draw upon the strength she saw there, knowing all the while that this man who stood beside her declaring his protection was the same man she must steal from, the same man she must betray. She had to get that key from him tonight, or all would be lost.

As they waited their turn to follow the lead couple in the dance, Chase found he could not keep his eyes off Miss Dawson. She was like a beacon of light on a stormy night that drew him to shore despite every effort to sail in the other direction. The closer he came to the light, the brighter things appeared. Yet he was well aware of the jagged rocks that dotted the shallow water as he neared her, threatening to tear his ship to pieces. . .and his heart along with it.

He could not bear that pain again.

She looked around the room, uncomfortable in the silence. Then her eyes met his.

"May I ask you something, Admiral?"

"Of course."

"Why are your parents not in attendance? Why did you not go in to see them when we picked up your sister at their estate?"

"A rather bold question." But he supposed that was one of the things he liked about her.

"Forgive me." She lowered her lashes as they stepped forward in a movement that brought them even closer.

Chase flexed his jaw. "My parents and I have had a parting of ways. We have not spoken in years."

She gave him a look of astonishment as they stepped around each other and then back again. "I'm sorry."

"They disapproved of my marriage. My wife was a common seamstress."

"Yet even now. . .after. . ." She bit her lip as she stepped back in line.

"Yes, even now. . ." He waved a hand to dismiss the topic, unsure why he'd even disclosed it. The last thing he wanted was her pity.

She turned from him and approached the man to his left as Chase stepped toward another lady. The sudden separation caused an ache that soon dulled when she reappeared in front of him again, a tender smile on her lips. Candlelight danced over her hair in a display of reds, browns, and golds. Her rosy cheeks matched the color of her lips, and he found his gaze drifting down to them, wondering at the feel of them on his, wondering at their taste, wondering. . .

And much to his astonishment, she slipped even closer to him.

Grabbing her arm, he dashed from the dance floor, dragging her behind him.

"What is the matter?"

"I thought you might be in need of refreshment," he lied. "And I do not wish to monopolize your time."

His sudden change in demeanor caused her forehead to wrinkle in the most amusing way, and he shook his head, forcing himself not to gaze upon her. Everything she did, every movement, every expression, delighted him.

Skirting around him, she grabbed a glass of lemonade as Lady Irene flounced their way. Her hair sparkled like spun gold. "Won't you save a dance for me, Admiral?" She stepped in front of Dominique as if she weren't there and puffed out her chest in a creamy, bountiful display. Sapphire blue eyes shot a silent appeal.

"I would be honored," Chase said with more exuberance than he felt. Despite his annoyance with Lady Irene's brazen request, he needed a distraction from Miss Dawson. He needed to get his mind off her and find what was left of his reason. What better way to do that than to spend time with Lady Irene? "Yet I see you are not in want of admirers." He motioned toward the cluster of men she'd left standing across the dance floor looking rather like a pack of sick puppies, but realized too late his comment could be construed as jealousy.

"But none so important to me as you," she cooed.

Obviously she had taken it as such. Chase shifted his gaze to Dominique, who met his eyes briefly before glancing away.

"Ah, there you are, love." Percy approached Lady Irene with well-practiced elegance. "I should have assumed I would find you with Admiral Randal."

"I am not your love, Atherton." Lady Irene gave him a scathing glance.

"Oh, my heart. Cut to the quick once again." He winked at Dominique then flapped his hand toward Chase. "Take her away, Randal. I make a poor escort for such a comely enchantress."

"Don't listen to him. He's done naught but dance with every beautiful lady here and left me quite on my own." Lady Irene drew her lips into a pout that Chase knew was supposed to captivate him, yet he found his glance angling around her, searching for Miss Dawson.

Percy reached her first. Out on the floor, a Scottish reel had begun. "May I have this dance?" He extended his arm toward Miss Dawson. She set down her lemonade and glanced at Chase.

He waved them on, battling a rising fury in his gut.

"Now I can have you all to myself, Admiral." Lady Irene slid her gloved hand into the crook of his arm, a look of satisfaction on her face. But Chase soon found his gaze locked upon Percy and Miss Dawson. The lecherous man fondled her delicate waist as he led her to the center of the floor.

"Ah, see." Lady Irene grinned. "They appear well matched, don't you think?"

Dominique had not danced a reel in years, not since her presentation at court five years earlier. She was amazed that she remembered the steps so well, but perhaps it was Mr. Atherton's exquisite skill that sent them floating over the floor as if their feet never touched the polished marble beneath them. The handsome member of Parliament curved his lips in a wolfish smile, and she wondered why she felt none of the unease in his presence that she did whenever Lord Markham gave her an equally seductive grin.

"He is quite taken with you, you know." He managed to shout above the melodious combination of flute, violin, and piano that filled the room.

"I beg your pardon. Of whom do you speak?" Dominique took his hand and pirouetted around him.

"The admiral, of course."

Dominique drew her lips in a tight line, remembering the abrupt way the admiral had pulled her from the dance floor. She must have insulted him with her impertinent questions, or perhaps he'd grown bored of her company or she'd taken the wrong dance step. Either way, he clearly had no interest in her, especially given the way he'd brushed her off on Mr. Atherton as if he longed to rid himself of her company. Though her heart felt as though it had suffered a blow, 'twas for the better. His attitude certainly helped her to stifle her own wayward emotions and concentrate on the task at hand—getting the key from him. She must do it tonight. "I fear you are mistaken."

Out of the corner of her eye, she saw the admiral in close conversation with Lady Irene on the outskirts of the dance floor. He laughed and leaned his ear toward her every word. They were suited for one another. Lady Irene's gold-trimmed ivory gown flowed around her in a sweep of shimmering silk, the jewels hanging from her neck and ears glittering with the same shine as the golden curls framing her face. What did Dominique have to compare with her? Besides, Lady Irene had loved the admiral from childhood.

"I've known Randal for years, Miss Dawson. I am not mistaken," Mr. Atherton whispered in her ear.

"I believe 'tis obvious his affections are toward Lady Irene," she retorted as he guided her through the line of dancers.

"Bosh. . .pure bosh, Miss Dawson. Look at his face."

Dominique allowed Mr. Atherton to spin her around until she found the admiral just a few yards from them. Their eyes met. His were ablaze with an emotion that startled her—not a happy emotion, nor an amorous one. It seemed more ravenous than anything.

Mr. Atherton led her away.

"He's always in a bad humor," she said.

"Not when he was dancing with you." He smiled with a lift of his eyebrows.

After the dance finished, Dominique was barely able to catch her breath before another gentleman, a Lord Wilbert Hensley, stepped in for Mr. Atherton. She remembered him as one of the men who had requested a dance earlier that evening. After their dance, several more gentlemen took their turns spinning her around the floor. All the while, she spotted the admiral perched in different spots about the room, glaring at her with the beady eyes of a falcon. She wondered where Lady Irene had gone off to.

Finally, out of breath, she refused the last gentleman and made her way off the floor for some lemonade. The admiral appeared at her side. "I trust you are enjoying yourself?"

"Yes, thank you," she returned, baffled at his accusatory tone. She sipped the cool liquid and tried to avoid the admiral's gaze as the sour taste puckered her mouth. "And you?" She studied his topcoat pocket, where she believed the key to his study was hidden. She must focus on only that, not on the towering strength of his presence, not on the strong cut of his jaw, and not on the regard that more oft than not flickered across his gaze.

"Truthfully, I hate these affairs." He glanced across the room. His jaw flexed, sending a ripple over the slight stubble that shadowed it while his mahogany queue brushed the back of his navy jacket. "Would you like to get some air?" He offered his elbow.

Nodding, she set down her glass and took his arm. This might give her the opportunity she had been looking for.

A blast of cool air struck her as they inched through the crowded door and took the stairs down to the courtyard.

Confusion raked over her. "You don't have to watch over me simply because you are my escort. I am sure you would rather spend your time with some of the other ladies. I see the way they look at you."

"You do?" He chuckled as he escorted her around a carriage and across the cobblestone street. They came to an iron fence that enclosed a small garden. Dark, fuzzy shadows of trees and bushes stretched before them like sinister watchmen—or spies.

"I am grateful you came, Miss Dawson." He shifted his boots on the gravel. "What I meant to say, of course, is you have helped me out of a jam with my sister's matchmaking schemes. Consequently, I do not intend to leave you at the mercy of London's worst knaves."

Knaves? "All the men I danced with appeared to be naught but gentlemen, Admiral." Was he jealous?

"Yes, they do appear so, do they not? But you are quite naive concerning the ways of London society."

She glanced up at him, but he refused to meet her gaze. He stared out across the darkness as if searching for something. Music drifted over the town house, along with bursts of laughter and voices raised in chaotic banter. Above the admiral's tall frame, inky blackness blanketed the sky. She tried to envision her hand sliding up his chest, searching for the key to his study, and shivered.

He finally faced her. "Are you cold, Miss Dawson?"

"No." An idea sped through her mind. "I mean yes, I am a bit." She rubbed her shoulders.

The admiral unbuttoned his topcoat and slipped it from his shoulders. "This will have to do. I have left my frock inside."

The warmth from his body poured from his coat over her arms and down her back like hot bathwater, sending a tingling through her legs. Spices and cigar smoke swirled around her, intoxicating her with his scent. She tugged the coat over her chest and ran her fingers over the pocket, feeling the lump within. She must pull it from its hiding place before she gave the coat back to him. But how?

She darted her eyes wildly about. Her nerves coiled together in frozen thickets. A crazy idea popped into her head.

"Upon my word, look, a shooting star!" She pointed at the sky behind him, and as soon as he turned, she plunged her hand into his pocket, groping for the cool feel of a silver chain. Her finger entangled in a loose thread. She tugged on it, but the fiber seemed to wrap around her like a spider's web ensnaring its prey. The more she pulled, the more entwined she became.

The admiral spun back around.

CHAPTER 10

Terror spiked through Dominique. The admiral's eyes narrowed in confusion. With her hand still entangled in his topcoat pocket, she twisted and bent over, forcing herself to cough as vigorously as she could. With continued hacks and barks that she prayed sounded authentic, she stumbled toward the fence. Her searching fingers touched the chain. Cold silver circled around her hand. She yanked it from the pocket, ripping the fabric. Had he heard the ripping sound? Clenching the prize, she blundered forward. What should she do with it? He would surely see it in her hand.

"Miss Dawson, are you all right?" His concerned voice sounded behind her.

Boot steps crunched the gravel. Dominique leaned one hand on the cold iron fence and did the only thing she could think to do. She stuffed the pocket watch and key down the front of her gown. The icy metal snaked behind her petticoats and in between her breasts, sending a chill through her. She spun to face him, holding a hand to her mouth.

Skepticism coursed through his eyes. "Are you ill?"

"Nay, forgive me, Admiral. I am not sure what came over me." Her breathing came out hard and ragged.

"Perhaps 'twas this fanciful star you saw?" He lifted a mocking brow. "A shooting star, Miss Dawson? In London? We are lucky to see the sun during the day, let alone a star at night."

She swiped the back of her hand over her forehead "On my

word, I could have sworn I saw something." She sighed, hoping to divert the cause of her obvious fear. "It frightened me."

He enfolded her hand in his. Warmth spread through her gloves and up her arms. The chain shifted and slid beneath her stays, jangling as loudly as a gong. But he did not seem to hear it. "You are quite safe, I assure you." He gave her a reassuring smile that stole the remaining breath from her.

Her gaze flickered between his chocolate brown eyes, and she wished with everything in her that what he said were true.

"You appear to be coming down with something. Perhaps we should venture in from the cold?"

She nodded, distracted by a myriad of thoughts as she plotted her next step. She must somehow leave the ball without the admiral and make her way home. If they left together, he would surely take notice of the missing key, and once they were home, she'd have no opportunity to search his study. Even at night, the admiral never seemed to sleep. And his unexpected roaming through the house would not afford her the time she required.

"I must admit, I am feeling suddenly weak," she said as they braided their way through the crowd and climbed the stairs to the house. She wasn't lying. The close proximity of the admiral and the taut feel of his muscles beneath her hand had a dizzying effect upon her.

"Perhaps I should escort you home, Miss Dawson." He halted and started to turn around. "Frankly, I have no desire to remain any longer."

Alarm pricked her heart. "No. . .no." She tugged on him. " 'Tis far too early, and you promised your sister, remember?"

He groaned in acquiescence.

"Perhaps I simply need some refreshment."

"Yes. I daresay 'tis been at least an hour since you last ate." He chuckled and gave her a sly look.

Dominique gritted her teeth as a flush of embarrassment flooded her face. Squinting against the bright candlelight, she squeezed through the door as the admiral bowed right and left to acquaintances who addressed him. Music and laughter wove among the aromas of strong perfumes and sweet cakes. Slipping off the coat, she handed it back to the admiral with a smile. His gaze wandered over her in a tender caress, giving her pause. Wasn't it only a few hours ago that he had abruptly dismissed her to dance with Mr. Atherton?

Donning his topcoat, he led the way to the buffet against the far wall, and Dominique prayed he would not notice the missing watch and key. Plucking a glass of punch from the table, she scanned the sea of dancers flowing back and forth in waves of sparkling colors.

Mr. Atherton stood across the way, drink in hand, leaning against a door frame with one booted foot crossed over the other. Though favoring the lady who addressed him with an occasional nod or smile, it was obvious his interest lay elsewhere. Dominique felt sorry for the woman, who seemed to be trying her best to attract the handsome member of Parliament. His gaze locked upon Dominique's, and he smiled. Perhaps she could feign a sudden illness and convince Mr. Atherton to escort her home. She glanced up at the admiral. A scowl twisted his features as he noticed their exchange.

"I'm so furious, I could. . .I could—ah!" Lady Irene clenched her fists until her manicured nails bit into her skin, while managing to smile sweetly at the passing Lord and Lady Hemmings. She turned a cold eye on Mrs. Barton, who stood beside her. "I thought you said I'd have him all to myself tonight."

"Indeed, that was my plan." Mrs. Barton patted her pearl-laden coiffure. "How was I to know he would invite that French tart?" she spat through her teeth. "I thought he would have released her by now."

Lady Irene eyed the petite beauty standing beside the admiral. The young governess smiled at something he said then took another sip of her punch. "My word, but if that girl isn't always eating or drinking something. She'll no doubt end up a fat cow someday," she snickered then moaned in despair. "Look at the way he looks at her." She allowed her gaze to wander over Chase, the broad expanse of his shoulders perfectly filling out his gold-embroidered uniform, his handsome Roman face, the commanding way he stood amidst the crowd. Yet he gazed down at that infernal governess as if she were the only woman in the room. A deep yearning consumed Lady Irene. "Why doesn't he look at me that way? What is she compared with me?"

"You are the most fetching woman here, Irene," Mrs. Barton snapped. "Force his attentions upon you. He's a man, after all."

"I have poured every ounce of my charms upon him tonight, but to no avail," Lady Irene sobbed. "He never even noticed my new gown." She swirled around, her mood brightening for a second as she delighted in the sweep of ivory silk. "I spent a fortune to have it tailored just for this evening."

"You mean your father spent a fortune." Mrs. Barton's eyes glinted with humor.

"What difference does it make?"

"Never you mind, dear." Mrs. Barton patted her arm. "Men are such fools. And my brother the chief of them. He does not know his own mind. He will be no happier with her than he would with a common strumpet from the docks."

Lady Irene snorted. "She is no better than that, to be sure. An orphan with no dowry. A woman who must work to provide for herself. Why, she has no right to even be at this soiree." A gentleman approached Lady Irene with an expectant gaze, but she waved him off. She had no time for admirers when her very future was at stake.

"She'll no doubt grow bored and run off with the first man who catches her eye—and break my brother's heart." Mrs. Barton's normally poised face hardened beneath flaming cheeks. "I must do something." Her fiery gaze shot to Lady Irene's. "We must do something. I will not have my family name sullied by another French miscreant, I tell you. I will not."

Lady Irene found Mrs. Barton's fury both contagious and exhilarating, but it did nothing to ease her fears. Where every man swooned over her attentions, the admiral showed no interest. "But what can we do?"

Mrs. Barton tapped her fingers across her chin. "In time she will prove herself every bit the tramp we know she is." A shrewd grin twisted the corners of her mouth. "We must simply hurry along the inevitable. We must force her to compromise herself in front of the admiral. Then he will see that I have been right all along."

Lady Irene nodded, not understanding what Chase's sister had in mind, but a sudden excitement lifted her hopes. "I'm so grateful to have you as my friend, Mrs. Barton."

" 'Tis I who should be grateful to you. I know you'll make a good wife for my brother. We just have to do a bit of orchestrating to help him see that, as well—and before the night is through. Now I have a plan." She pursed her lips. "We must first speak with Mr. Atherton." She lowered her voice to a whisper and leaned toward Lady Irene. "This is what you must do."

Dominique set down the empty glass and glanced at Mrs. Barton beside her. Only minutes earlier, the admiral's sister had approached them in an agitated flurry, informing the admiral that Vice Admiral Hyde Parker wished to speak to him immediately in the parlor. After excusing himself, the admiral had marched in haste from the room, leaving his sister behind. Dominique couldn't understand why the woman who hated her so much remained by her side. She wished she could excuse herself, as well, so she could find Mr. Atherton and move forward with her plan to leave the ball. She scanned the room, looking for him, but he was nowhere in sight. Her heart felt as though it would burst through her chest. She had to leave as soon as possible. *Father, please provide a way.* Although she hadn't truly felt God's comforting presence since she had arrived in London, she hoped He still heard her prayers. Perhaps He disapproved of her mission. Her heart sank. If God were against her, then surely she would fail. *Lord, please don't let Marcel die. Please tell me what to do.*

"Miss Dawson, I must beg your forgiveness." Mrs. Barton faced her with what appeared to be the beginnings of a smile on her lips. "My behavior toward you has been most unbecoming." She coughed and seemed to be choking on her words. " 'Tis plain my brother is fond of you, and I hope we can start over and be friends."

Dominique studied Mrs. Barton's brown eyes—so much like her brother's—hoping to find sincerity there. Could it be the woman truly wished to be friends? Dominique had not had a close friend since childhood, and the thought of having one now—of not feeling so alone—brightened her spirits.

"Oh, there is Lady Irene." Mrs. Barton waved the young beauty over, and Dominique felt a sudden twinge of queasiness. Perhaps Mrs. Barton had overcome her hatred of the French, but Lady Irene? Even as she approached, the forced smile on her lips belied the contempt shooting from her icy blue eyes.

Lady Irene flounced beside Dominique in a puff of French *parfum* that nearly overwhelmed her. "Lovely gown, Miss Dawson," the woman said without looking at her.

The hairs on the back of Dominique's neck bristled. "So nice of you to say."

"The punch must be delicious. I believe you've had three glasses, have you not?" She picked up one of her own from the table. "I do so love a sweet wine punch, don't you?"

Dominique wasn't sure what to make of Lady Irene's sudden need for idle conversation—especially when she had barely said a civil word to her since they'd met—so she simply nodded.

After casting a suspicious glance at Mrs. Barton, Lady Irene tipped her glass to her pink lips and grinned as if she knew a big secret.

Dominique spotted Mr. Atherton by the door. "If you will excuse me." She nodded at both Lady Irene and Mrs. Barton, thankful she had a reason to escape the awkward situation.

"But, Miss Dawson." Lady Irene suddenly shifted and bumped into Dominique, leaning her full weight against her.

Dominique struggled to keep from falling while the blond beauty continued to bumble forward.

"I must tell you. . .I must. . ." Lady Irene stuttered.

Before Dominique realized what she was doing, Lady Irene barreled into her again and tipped her glass onto Dominique's gown.

Maroon liquid slid down the silky fabric, the stain expanding as it went. The crowd of people around them ceased conversing and pointed with stifled gasps.

Lady Irene covered her mouth. With wide, laughing eyes, she stared at Dominique.

Mrs. Barton nudged Lady Irene aside. "How could you?" She retrieved a cloth from the table and patted Dominique's gown. "How clumsy of you. Look what you have done. Oh, you poor dear. I know just what to do. Follow me."

Still in shock from the assault, Dominique stared at Lady Irene as Mrs. Barton escorted her from the room into an entrance hall, then up a flight of marble stairs and into a small chamber on the second floor. "Lady Billingsworth has prepared this lovely room just for such emergencies," she prattled.

Dominique gazed over the room. A pine dressing chest with swing mirror stood against the far wall, and two porcelain washbasins sat atop marble consoles to her left. A leather chaise sat in the center of the room along with two high-backed sofas.

"Take off your gown, and I will use this water to clean it." Mrs. Barton gestured toward the carved oak screen perched next to another door on her right. "Never fear, I'll have it as good as new."

Dominique's stomach tightened. "Why are you being so kind? You've made your feelings toward me quite clear."

"As I told you, I wish to make amends, my dear."

"Please do not take me for a fool." Dominique clasped her hands together. "Lady Irene's mishap was obviously deliberate."

"Yes, I'm sure it was. My apologies for her behavior. I'm afraid her jealousy gets the best of her at times."

"And you did not put her up to it?"

Mrs. Barton's jaw dropped. "Of course not. What purpose would that serve?"

"Why, to be rid of me for the evening, of course."

"Then do not leave." Mrs. Barton shrugged and waved her gloved hand through the air. "I will clean your dress, and I assure you it will be fit enough to return to dance. Or perhaps I could ask Lady Billingsworth if she has a spare gown in case of such an accident."

She smiled. "I am sure she has. She thinks of everything."

Dominique studied Mrs. Barton. Perhaps she was trying to help. Her smile and mannerism seemed sincere, but something in her eyes gave Dominique pause. She sighed. She was so out of practice in society, she could hardly tell when someone lied to her.

"I do appreciate it, Mrs. Barton, but I should go home." Dominique blinked and lowered her gaze, still confused by the woman's sudden kindness. "I know you wish your brother to remain. Won't you ask Mr. Atherton if he'll be so kind as to escort me?" Although Dominique was certain Lady Irene had soiled her gown on purpose, she perceived it as a blessing in disguise, for she now had a perfect excuse to leave the ball.

"Perhaps 'tis best, my dear. But please, allow me to scrub your dress before the stain sets in. It would be a shame to ruin your new gown."

Dominique reluctantly slid behind the dressing screen and removed her dress, handing it to Mrs. Barton.

She heard the click of the woman's mules over the floor and then a splash of water. More clicking. Dominique hugged herself against the sudden chill creeping over her bare arms and glanced down at her petticoats. Pristine white and fluffy lace. At least the punch had not soaked through her dress. Pressing her fingers over her rigid stays, she felt the key still snug within.

Silence enveloped the room. No sound of water, no click of heels, and no more of Mrs. Barton's incessant sighs.

"Mrs. Barton?"

Nothing.

Dominique peeked out from behind the dressing screen and allowed her gaze to drift over the room. No movement. No sound. "Mrs. Barton?" She eased from behind the screen and inched toward the center of the room, peering into the dark corners. A chill struck her.

Mrs. Barton was gone—and so was her dress.

With a crash, the door beside the dressing screen burst open and in flew Mr. Atherton, tottering across the floor with a drink in hand.

Horrified, Dominique froze and stared at the young member of Parliament who stood between her and the dressing screen. A rush of shame heated her, and she flung her hands up to cover her chest and arms.

Mr. Atherton instantly sobered. His jaw dropped, and he gaped at her as if he'd never seen petticoats before.

"How dare you?" Dominique finally managed to say, her eyes darting to the dressing screen.

"My apologies, miss." His look of shock dissolved into one of roguish cupidity. "I was told I would find a collection of exotic liquors in here, but I believe I have discovered something even more tantalizing."

"You will avert your eyes this instant, Mr. Atherton," Dominique stormed, her chest heaving.

"Alas, I cannot." He grinned and took a slow sip of his drink. "I fear the good Lord has graced me with very little self-control." He sauntered toward her.

Dominique took a trembling step back.

Mr. Atherton raised his handsome brow. "But since we find ourselves alone, and you"—he took her in with a sweep of his sultry gaze—"already without your clothes." He shrugged playfully. "Why waste the moment?"

As he continued his approach, Dominique saw no maliciousness in his eyes, and her fears subsided. "The moment you seek will never occur, Mr. Atherton." She nodded toward the open door behind him. "Now if you will please leave."

He spanned the distance between them and gave her a crooked grin. "Of course. I did not mean to frighten you."

"On the contrary, I believe you rather enjoyed doing just that."

He took her hand, raised it to his lips, and placed an innocent kiss upon it.

The other door squeaked on its hinges. Dominique released a huge sigh. Mrs. Barton must be returning with her dress—finally. She tugged on her hand, but Mr. Atherton would not release it.

Admiral Randal, hand on the hilt of his sword, marched into the room.

CHAPTER 11

Chase halted in midstride. His gaze swept over Miss Dawson, noting her bare arms and formfitting petticoats, then darted to Atherton, who had turned to face him. His friend jerked one hand away from the governess, while the drink in his other one slipped and shattered on the floor in a burst of glass and golden liquid. Chase's heart shriveled.

"I was told you were in some distress, Miss Dawson." He stared at her, taking liberties with his gaze and enjoying the way she flushed. He knew a gentleman should avert his eyes, but the pain in his heart forbade him to behave like a gentleman at the moment. He turned to Percy. His friend stared at him wide-eyed and began shaking his head. "But I see Mr. Atherton has things quite under control." Chase regarded his longtime friend and clenched the polished hilt of his sword. "Atherton, you have my permission to escort Miss Dawson home. She informed me she did not feel well, and I can see why. She has no doubt caught her death of cold."

He spun on his heel then stomped from the room as Atherton shouted, "You misunderstand, Randal," behind him. He bounded down the stairs two at a time, ignoring the complacent look on his sister's face as he passed her.

"I am sorry, Chase, but I thought you should know." Her smug voice followed him into the ballroom and trailed him like an annoying insect through the throngs of giddy people. But her words fell muffled on his ears. He no longer cared what she had to say.

He reached the buffet, searching for a drink. Nothing but lemonade. He needed something stronger. A sword of betrayal cut him in half as visions of Miss Dawson's disrobed body standing beside Percy in the chamber—alone—blasted through his mind. Now their flirtatious exchanges and the way she had gazed at him during their dance began to make sense. The scar on Chase's cheek burned, and he rubbed it. He had thought Miss Dawson was special—different from the ravenous women who used their seductive charms to win men of power and wealth—men like Percy Atherton.

What a fool he had been. He slammed his fist on the table, sending spoons and bowls clanking and drawing curious glances from those nearby. Why did her betrayal affect him so? After all, he was not seeking to court her. The last thing he wanted was to marry again. He had allowed the romantic allure of the evening to infect him, and like a disease, it had rotted away his sense of reason. That was it. And nothing more. He hung his head. How he longed to go back to sea.

A soft hand lay upon his arm, and he looked up to see Lady Irene, her usually provocative gaze now demure. She looked much more beautiful than he remembered.

"Is something wrong, Admiral?" Her long lashes fluttered above a look of genuine compassion. "Can I be of some help?"

Chase swallowed against another vision of Miss Dawson in her lacy petticoats. "Yes, I believe you can, milady. May I have this dance?"

A cold drizzle pelted Dominique as she stepped from the curricle Mr. Atherton had rented for their ride home. She tightened her shawl around her, but it did nothing to prevent the chill from shooting icicles through her skin. What had begun as the most glorious evening of her life had ended in shame and disaster. She glanced down at her stained gown that Mrs. Barton had tossed at her with a snort after the admiral had left, then down to the puddles forming around the edges of the stones that made up the walkway.

She started to gather her skirts but dropped them. Perhaps it was more fitting that she allowed them to drag in the mud along with her heart.

"I'll walk you to the door," Atherton announced, hopping out behind her.

"That won't be necessary. I am sure Sebastian will be up awaiting his master's return."

After instructing the coachman to wait, Mr. Atherton smiled and offered her his elbow. "Nevertheless, miss."

Atherton hadn't spoken a word during the ride to the Randal home, and despite his many blatant *affaires de coeur*, Dominique sensed his discomfort at the evening's turn of events. Somehow the value he placed on the admiral's friendship endeared the gallant rake to her, and she felt sorry that he had most likely lost that friendship.

"I cannot impress upon you how sorry I am for what happened, Miss Dawson," he began as they made their way over the moist walkway. "I had no idea you were in that chamber. Mrs. Barton informed me the room contained Lord Billingsworth's collection of fine brandies, you see. . .and, well, I could hardly resist a sample of them for myself." One of the corners of his mouth tipped in the beginnings of a grin. "And then I saw you."

Dominique's chuckle faltered on her lips. Truly, she did believe his motives for entering the room to be pure. For all his faults, he hardly seemed the type to barge in on a woman's boudoir and force himself on a lady. Though he had toyed with her, he had accepted her refusal with honor and certainly would have left the room had not the admiral entered at just that moment.

"I do not fault you, Mr. Atherton. I fear I was duped by the admiral's sister. I thought she wanted to make amends for her behavior when instead she wished to tarnish my reputation and ruin my employment."

"Ah, yes—dear, sweet Mrs. Barton. The vixen." He spat the word with a harsh chortle. "Never fear. I shall set things straight with the admiral come first light."

Dominique's thoughts sped to the images of the admiral

dancing across the marble floor with Lady Irene when she and Mr. Atherton had left for the evening. Why had the sight of them enjoying themselves caused every ounce of Dominique to cringe? Isn't that what she wanted—the admiral otherwise engaged, allowing her to come home and get the documents she sought. . . to save Marcel?

"Nay, Mr. Atherton. Clear your own name if you must, but it matters not to me what opinion the admiral forms from such a foolish incident. Besides, he seemed quite taken with Lady Irene when we left." A vision of the admiral and Lady Irene going through the steps of the Roger de Coverly on the dance floor slithered once again through her mind.

"Oh, bosh, and you well know it." Mr. Atherton led her up the stairs and dashed beneath the covering, doffing his top hat. Flickering light from a lantern hanging by the door played upon his handsome features.

"I thank you for the escort home, Mr. Atherton."

"My pleasure, miss." He bowed and leaned toward her with a devilish grin that made her see why all the ladies swooned at his feet. "Truthfully"—he raised his brows—"I believe Mrs. Barton's insidious plan will topple back into her lap. Did you see the admiral's face? Egad, what a sight!"

"Yes." Dominique did not find the same pleasure in the remembrance, for not only shock, not only anger, but pain had burned within the admiral's eyes. A pain she had inadvertently caused. "He was angry, to be sure. I thought for a moment he would slice you in two with his sword."

"Nay, 'twas far more than anger. Jealousy, Miss Dawson. Pure raging jealousy—and the fact that he felt it will surely assist him in recognizing his feelings for you."

"Mr. Atherton, let me make myself clear. I neither elicit nor desire the admiral's affections."

"Indeed?" He scratched his chin, a taunting look in his eyes.

Dominique huffed. "Why are you so intent on forcing a courtship between us?"

"Because Randal has been alone far too long. And because I've never seen him shine so brightly as he does when he is with you—not since Mrs. Randal."

Though the statement made her heart skip, she shifted her wet slippers over the cold stones and her thoughts to another topic—the conversation she'd overheard in the dining room. "May I ask you a question, Mr. Atherton?"

"Of course." He leaned his shoulder against the front wall of the house and folded his arms across his chest.

"Do you never wish to marry?" Dominique felt her stomach tighten, surprised at her own boldness. She glanced at the coachman perched atop the curricle. No doubt he could hear every word they said, but she hoped his presence would not deter Mr. Atherton from speaking the truth.

"Ah, but you are changing the subject, Miss Dawson." He chuckled, a playful glimmer skipping across his blue eyes. "Marry? I fear I would get bored with one woman. Marriage is so restrictive. A man like myself must have freedom."

"But there is a price to pay for such freedom, is there not?"

"A price?"

"You will never enjoy having a companion through life, someone who understands you, who knows you, who loves you and promises to stay with you, come what may."

"If such a love exists, miss, I have yet to see it." He shrugged. "The notion is overrated, I'm afraid."

Dominique clasped her hands together. She knew she ought to get inside as soon as possible and retrieve the documents, but something in Mr. Atherton's eyes, a weary emptiness, gave her both pause and the incentive to continue. Besides, the admiral was no doubt occupied with Lady Irene and wouldn't be home for hours. "Do you believe in God, Mr. Atherton?"

He gave her a quizzical look. "Yes, of course. And I thank Him for providing so many wonderful things for my pleasure." He grinned.

Dominique swallowed. *Lord, please give me Your words.* "Is that the only purpose of your existence, to please yourself?"

He snapped his head back and laughed. "Am I to assume you

find my lifestyle frivolous, Miss Dawson?" He pressed a hand over his heart. "This vexes me greatly."

Pleased to see he took her question in good humor, she forged ahead, asking, "Have you no grander purpose in life, no higher calling?"

"I give my opinion at Parliament. It is enough." He waved a hand through the air.

Dominique shook her head. "Truly, if I lived to please only myself, I would find life infinitely boring, not to mention restricting, yet you seem to find freedom in it. It baffles me, sir."

"Indeed. And I am equally baffled by your sudden temerity. You had me fooled into thinking you were meek and cowardly."

"Forgive me." Dominique lowered her lashes. "I have overstepped my bounds."

He leaned toward her, and the aroma of spicy wine wafted around her. "I meant it as a compliment." He snapped his top hat upon his head and took a step toward the stairs. "I have made a decision, Miss Dawson, and I won't take no for an answer. We shall play a coquettish game, you and I, and drive the admiral mad with jealousy." His eyes glinted with amusement. "Then he will see his true affections for you."

Horror gripped Dominique. "I beg you not to, sir, for my sake." If she could obtain the information she needed tonight, she would leave within days. She cringed. But if she failed and must stay longer. . .A sudden heaviness tugged on her heart.

Mr. Atherton chuckled and tipped his hat before sauntering down the glistening pathway. "We shall see, Miss Dawson. We shall see."

Dominique slid the iron key into the lock of the admiral's study, and with a quick twist and a clunk, the bolt released its tight grip. A candle in one hand, she pressed on the handle with the other and lightly pushed the door. The hinges creaked through the dark, sleeping house like warning bells. Dominique froze. When Sebastian had admitted her into the house, he'd informed her that the rest of the staff was asleep. Only he remained awake until the admiral returned.

"Oh Lord, I pray You close Sebastian's ears," she whispered, though unsure whether God would answer the prayer of a spy.

Once she'd slipped inside the study, she closed the door and leaned against it, trying to calm the rapid beating of her heart. Her head grew light, and the room began to spin. She pressed a hand to her chest. If she were caught in this room, no foolish excuse of sleepwalking would save her this time. She would be sent to the gallows for treason. This was it. She had to either steal the documents and betray the country she loved or scurry like a frightened mouse back to her room and allow Marcel to die.

Images of his cheerful face flowed before her in happy memories from another life. After their father had died, their mother had been too grieved to offer her children any comfort, and Marcel and Dominique had become inseparable. Then when poor Mama had abandoned them, as well, they had clung to each other for dear life.

She pictured his curly brown hair and beaming green eyes— eyes just like their father's—smiling at her, encouraging her when they'd had no food to eat for days. Being the eldest, Dominique had assumed the role of protector and provider, but Marcel had been the strong one. Though barely sixteen at the time, he possessed more courage than most grown men she'd known. "Don't cry, Dominique. We shall make it. We will find food. We will again be a great family." At the time, she'd attributed his hope to youthful naïveté, but now she began to realize he had his father's strength and courage—neither of which she had inherited.

She scanned the admiral's study. Save for the tiny circle of light afforded her by her candle, most of the chamber loomed over her in monstrous shadows. Blood hammered through her temples. She closed her eyes as one final image of Marcel jarred her from her terrified stupor. He staggered, held from behind. His wide, pleading eyes gaped at her as a knife pricked his throat, releasing a trickle of blood.

"I will save you, Marcel. This time I'll be the strong one," she whispered.

Forcing herself from the door, she crept across the room to the admiral's desk. She set the candle down, listening for any movement in the hallway. Only the sound of her ragged breathing reached her ears. Lying atop the imposing desk were piles of neatly stacked papers. She began to sift through them, deciding to take only the most important documents from each pile so as not to draw immediate suspicion. But how was she to know which ones contained the most valuable information? With a sigh, she examined a document covered with charts and figures that made no sense to her. She would have to do her best—and she would have to hurry.

Minutes later, she emerged from the room with a stack of nearly fifty papers, all stamped with the Admiralty seal and, from what she could surmise, containing lists of various fleet sizes and locations, firepower, battle strategies, commanding officers, and number of crewmen. As she made her way up the stairs to her room, she prayed it would be enough to procure Marcel's freedom. After stashing the documents in her valise, she tiptoed across the hall to the admiral's bedchamber and deposited the key chain on his writing desk, hoping he would assume he had forgotten to take it to the ball. Before leaving, she paused to gaze across his dark room, the huge oak bed, the chest of drawers as tall and broad as its owner, the rectangular window framed in maroon velvet curtains. Heat engulfed her as she remembered the way the admiral had caught her hiding behind them, his bare, muscled chest gleaming in the candlelight, and the way she had felt so close to him. She breathed in his masculine scent and caught herself smiling, wishing for a moment that she could remain William's governess. But her smile faded as quickly as it had come. She could entertain no further thoughts of the admiral or of his precious son. Soon she would be gone and never see either of them again.

Chase entered the house, tossed his frock at Sebastian without a word, and tried to shake off the brandy fogging his thoughts. He had indeed found a stronger drink than the lemonade, but he was now beginning to regret his overindulgence. He had hoped the liquor would keep his thoughts off Mr. Atherton and Miss Dawson, but it had only increased his anxiety. As much as he enjoyed Percy's company, Chase didn't trust the man—especially not with a beautiful woman—and he regretted sending them off together.

"Did Miss Dawson arrive safely?"

"Yes, sir, nearly an hour ago."

Chase released a long-held sigh. He wanted to ask the butler if Mr. Atherton had brought her to the door and what exactly had transpired between the two, but all he asked was, "No other problems, then?"

"I believe Master William had a nightmare earlier, sir. He was screaming." Sebastian's tone was as dull and colorless as the shadows drifting across his face.

Chase knew William had dreams about his mother from time to time, though he had never been home to experience one firsthand. "Did Mrs. Hensworth attend to him?"

"I believe Miss Dawson came to his aid. He is asleep now, sir."

"Very well." Chase took the stairs up to William's room just to make certain he was all right. Besides, Chase wasn't sure he wanted the unscrupulous Miss Dawson so close to his son anymore, not until he determined just what had occurred between her and Mr. Atherton at the ball.

As he approached the boy's nursery, gentle snores reached Chase's ears. Tiptoeing around the corner, he leaned against the door frame and peered inside, allowing his blurry gaze to wander over the shadows in the room until it alighted upon one that melted his heart. Stretched across the chaise lounge that sat next to William's bed lay Miss Dawson, her chestnut curls tumbling over her silk robe. Beside her, William pressed against her bosom, his chubby little arms around her waist. Both of them were sound asleep. Hazy light from the window drifted over them in an ethereal glow that reminded him of a holy portrait of Madonna and child. Chase rubbed his eyes, fighting back an unusual burning behind them. He had not seen William care for any woman this way—not since the boy's mother was alive.

Chase tore off his topcoat and tossed it in the corner of his dark bedchamber, slamming the door behind him. He tried to shake the vision of William so peacefully asleep in Miss Dawson's arms, her hand over his forehead in a gentle caress. He did not want to think kindly of her right now, not after her wanton display with the charming Percy Atherton. He felt like spitting but instead ripped through the buttons of his waistcoat and flung it to join his topcoat. Stomping to the fire, he grabbed a bronze poker and jabbed at the smoldering coals, remembering the two of them leaving the ball arm in arm. No doubt that was Miss Dawson's plan all along, and he had been too foolish to see it. All the ladies clamored for Atherton's attention—charming, personable, intelligent Percy. The sort of gentleman who always knew the right thing to say at the right time and who with one look could cause the staunchest female to swoon.

Chase held none of those engaging qualities. He was a navy man, more comfortable at the helm of his ship than at a society gathering. He lacked the social graces of a London dandy—was too harsh and authoritative with women, he had been told, and had no idea how to pay a lady a compliment. Melody had never expected one. She had been content with Chase as he was. It was one of many things he had dearly loved about her. And he had believed Miss Dawson possessed a similar quality, but perhaps not. He hung his head. No, there would never be another woman for him besides Melody.

He had left the party early despite the rather resonant and avid protests of his sister and Lady Irene. They normally stayed at those ridiculous balls until well past one in the morning. Chase was in no mood to tolerate any more of the bombastic chatter of his peers, nor to escort the doting Lady Irene across the dance floor. When Miss Dawson had left, she had taken all the enjoyment of the event with her, leaving him with only emptiness inside and the haunting vision of her in her petticoats standing by Atherton's side, their hands interlocked. He wanted to remember that scene, for it kindled the anger burning within him, and forget the tender one he had just witnessed between her and his son. He wanted to be angry with her. He wanted to dismiss her. He wanted to strangle the strange feelings rising within him whenever she was around.

Kneeling, he stabbed at the coals until warmth radiated over him. He knew his sister had some involvement in the scandal, but he did not know to what extent. Certainly she was not conniving enough to force Miss Dawson to disrobe in front of Atherton. That he could be sure the governess had done quite on her own. Nevertheless, he could not shake the feeling that something was amiss.

Blast! He stood. He would dismiss Miss Dawson first thing in the morning. He would not stand for a woman of questionable morals governing William, no matter the boy's growing affections for her.

Dropping the poker in the rack, he forged into the darkness toward his dressing room and plunged into the bedpost, jarring his forehead upon the hard oak. Swearing, he groped his way to his writing table and felt across the grainy wood for the candle. His fingers landed on something cold and round. His pocket watch? Couldn't be. He remembered dropping it in his topcoat pocket. He picked it up. The smooth silver chilled his fingers as they slid over the watch, the chain links, and finally the cold iron key. Finding the candle, he made his way back to the fireplace, lit the wick, and stared at the watch and key in his hand. His thoughts took him back to the moment Sebastian had handed it to him as he was preparing for the ball.

Or had he?

Perhaps that had been another evening—a different time. He'd had a few glasses of brandy. The scar on his right cheek itched, the memory of the betrayal behind its acquisition adding to his discomfiture. He rubbed it. It was not like him to be so careless. Better to check his study just to be sure.

Flinging open the door, he headed down the stairs, candle and key in hand. Once inside his study, he waved the flickering light over the room. Nothing appeared out of place. He sat down at his desk and began scrutinizing each pile of documents he had so carefully laid out.

A grim smile curled upon his lips.

The rat had taken the bait.

CHAPTER 12

Pain throbbed like war drums in Chase's head. He squeezed the bridge of his nose and grimaced as he took the stairs down to the dining room. Why the headache? He had not overindulged more than usual the night before, though he had most assuredly wanted to. Perhaps his body finally had mutinied against him for continually denying it the sleep it required, for he had wandered the halls again until well past three in the morning before crumpling to his bed in a heap. Only one thing would give Chase satisfaction this day—dismissing his tart of a governess. But not before he ascertained whether she'd pilfered the documents from his study.

As he took the last step, hoping for a cup of the coffee whose exotic fragrance taunted him from the dining room, the annoying cackle of laughter pierced his skull. Turning toward the irritating noise, he made his way toward the back of the house to the morning room, intending to silence the offenders immediately.

But as he neared the open door, William's hearty laughter both warmed his soul and sent a spike of guilt through him. The boy never laughed like that with Chase. But why would he? Miss Dawson's soothing voice followed in the wake of his son's gleeful outburst, eliciting another giggle from him.

Chase cast a disgruntled gaze past the edge of the door.

Miss Dawson sat on the wooden floor beside his son playing a game of jacks, her gold satin skirts encircling her like a halo. She leaned over and planted a kiss upon William's head and wiped the hair from his face. The lad gazed up at her, his eyes sparkling with more love than Chase had seen in them in years. A huge smile broke upon William's lips. "Can we play again, Miss Dawson? I know I can beat you this time."

"Oh, you can, can you?" She laughed. "Well, perhaps one more game before church."

Chase allowed his gaze to remain fixed upon William—something he rarely did. The boy's thick blond hair shifted like sand in every direction whenever he moved his head. Those vivid forest green eyes bursting with energy and life. The exact replica of his mother. A dark heaviness settled on Chase. He turned to leave, unable to bear the sight, when his boot scuffed over the wood, alerting them.

"Father!" William looked up, his dimples deepening beneath rosy cheeks. He sprang to his feet.

"Sacre bleu," Miss Dawson uttered with a glance over her shoulder. She scrambled to rise as William darted toward his father. Refusing to turn around and face Chase, she struggled to her feet and pressed down the folds of her skirts. "Forgive me, Admiral. I was told you arose late on Sunday."

William reached Chase and was about to grab ahold of his breeches when Chase gave him a stern look. The boy froze, but hopeful exuberance glittered in his eyes as he looked up at his father. "William, a gentleman always assists a lady to her feet."

William's gaze darted to Miss Dawson, and he took off again with greater zeal. Although she was already standing, he grabbed her arm and tugged it as if to aid her with the last step. Yanked off balance, she tipped to the side, flapping her arms through the air, then stumbled, let out a tiny shriek, and began to topple backward.

In two strides, Chase reached her and wrapped an arm around her waist, hoisting her effortlessly off the ground. A wayward jack lay on the floor where her feet had been. He carried her to the rug in the middle of the room. Her hair tickled his chin as waves of lilac caressed him like gentle swells upon the seashore. Something deep within him stirred. She felt as light as a feather in his arms, and her body's warmth seeped through her gown onto his skin and, like a spark to dry coals, enflamed him. He plopped her down—albeit a bit too hard—and backed away. Egad, he had intended to dismiss her, not fondle her.

"See, I helped her, Father, didn't I?"

Chase exchanged a glance with Miss Dawson, who gave him a lopsided smile before she looked at William and broke into a chuckle.

"Yes, you did." He rubbed the boy's head, stifling the laughter that threatened to rise and join theirs, afraid of the effect it would have on him.

William beamed, appearing to rise in stature, and within Chase burned a longing to be a real father to this boy he loved so much.

Chase raised his gaze to Miss Dawson. A crimson flush burned her cheeks, and he wondered whether he had the same effect on her as she did on him. But no, he shook the thought from his mind. More than likely, 'twas remembering the sordid incident of last night that shamed her.

As well it should.

But why had thoughts of it vanished from his mind the instant his arm had wrapped around her? He silently cursed himself. Why did he allow this woman, this mere strumpet, to affect him so ardently? It was not like him at all.

He crossed one arm over his waist and rubbed his chin with the other, studying her, enjoying the way she shifted uncomfortably and dropped her gaze under his perusal.

Guilty. Yes, guilty.

His sister had been right all along.

"Admiral, about last night," she began in a timid voice he could hardly hear.

"I do not wish to discuss it." He held up a hand. "William, please pick up your jacks and put them away."

"Yes, Father." Keeping an eye on the couple, the boy plodded to the haphazard pile on the floor and knelt.

"But I believe you misunderstood what hap—"

"You mistake me for a dimwitted buffoon, Miss Dawson," he

stormed. "I know what I saw, and that is the end of it." His voice blasted through the room louder than he intended. William's frightened gaze met his and then skittered to Miss Dawson as if he were looking for protection.

Miss Dawson's chest rose and fell in rapid convulsions.

A tense moment of silence hovered over the room. The woman was far too skittish. Chase should be glad he had put her in her place, but instead he felt like a fiend—a fiend who enjoyed bullying women and children.

Miss Dawson slowly raised her eyes to his in a trembling effort that must have taken all of her miniscule courage. "Will you be joining us at church?"

"I do not attend anymore." He shook his head, angered at the introduction of a topic that only annoyed him further.

"May I ask why?"

With narrowed eyes, he shot her a look of warning. "Though I fail to see how it is any of your business, I no longer believe in God."

William uttered a tiny gasp.

"Je suis désolée." She glanced at William, her hands clasped before her.

"I am not sorry, Miss Dawson." He saw her flinch at his understanding of her French. "But at least I am no hypocrite."

Miss Dawson bunched her fists at her sides. "I beg your pardon."

Chase turned to his son, who had placed all his jacks within the leather pouch and stood staring at him, fear darting across his eyes. "Away with you now, William. Go find Mrs. Hensworth and have her ready you for church."

"But I am rea—"

"Now!"

The happiness of the morning drained from William's face and formed a puddle of despair at his feet, where the boy now stared as if praying it would jump back upon him. Slowly he scuffed across the room, avoiding Chase's gaze but casting an apprehensive glance at Miss Dawson over his shoulder before he left. Chase grimaced and swept his gaze to Miss Dawson.

"Are you implying that I am a hypocrite, Admiral?" she snapped.

"I am, indeed, Miss Dawson." He tugged on the lacy cuffs of his white shirt and sauntered to the window. Rebellious rays of morning sun had broken through the barricade of fog and sifted through the panes of the french doors, providing a warmth against his sudden chill. "You attend church, espousing a belief in God and His moral code, yet clearly you do not live out those same rules elsewhere." He did not turn around, desiring neither to see the effect of his harsh words on her face nor to have her witness the emotions he tried so desperately to hide upon his.

"Since you will not afford me the courtesy to explain myself," she responded behind him, her voice shaky, "I fear my only answer to your accusation is that you are also a hypocrite, sir."

Chase spun around—incredulous at her comment, angered, even, but at the same time amazed. Did she never fail to surprise him? Finally, he let out a coarse chuckle.

"Continue." He waved her on. "I anxiously await your explanation for such an affront."

Miss Dawson bit her lip and glanced down. "If you do not believe in God, then surely you do not believe there are such things as morals."

"And why would I not?" He clasped his hands behind his back, not daring to draw any closer to her, fearing the caldron of conflicting emotions fuming within him, fearing he would close her mouth with either the press of his hand or the press of his lips.

"If there is nothing outside of ourselves, no divine authority, then who is to say what is right and what is wrong? By whose standard do you judge me?"

Her words struck a chord of reason within him. He furrowed his brow. "I suppose by the code of our society."

"And who is to say that is right?" She placed a hand over her stomach then raised her tremulous gaze to his. "You are angered and most likely want to dismiss me because you found me in my petticoats with Mr. Atherton." She gulped and hesitated, and

Chase wondered whether the memory shamed or thrilled her.

"Regardless of what you believe happened," she continued, "you judge me on the basis of what society says is correct behavior for a lady—though I daresay the same behavior is not held as a standard for men."

Chase snorted and rubbed his chin, astounded by her sudden dive into philosophy. He had not thought her intelligent enough to consider such deep matters. For that matter, he had never taken the time to ponder these things himself.

Miss Dawson locked her gaze firmly upon his for the first time during the conversation. "Therefore, if you do not believe in God, then you have no right to judge my actions, Admiral, as long as they have done neither you nor your family any harm." The words were incisive, but the tone was as soft as the cooing of a dove.

Harm? He'd barely been able to sleep a wink last night, but that was not for her to know. Yet he could not deny the woman made sense. How could he judge her, indeed? Or anyone, for that matter? Without God, was there any right and wrong other than what men dictated according to their whims? Then why was he so furious with her? "I have no right, you say?"

She swallowed and wrapped her arms around her stomach.

Ignoring her obvious dismay, he continued. "Egad, woman, I have every right. My concern is for my son."

"Do you intend to dismiss me?" she asked without looking up.

"I am considering it." Chase braced his hands on his hips and sighed. "If only for William's sake." But he knew that was a lie. From what he had witnessed, Miss Dawson had done wonders for his son.

"I assure you I have no intentions of showing William my petticoats."

Chase swung back toward the window, hoping to hide his traitorous grin. He ran a hand through his hair. Truth be told, her behavior did not match that of a woman caught in a tryst; it was more that of a woman scorned, a woman mistreated.

A woman misjudged.

Regardless, he liked the effect it had on her, for it emboldened her tongue. He faced her again and sauntered toward her.

"Speaking of Mr. Atherton, when did you arrive home last night?"

"As you are aware, Admiral, we left the ball around midnight. I arrived home twenty minutes after that."

"Did Mr. Atherton walk you to the door?" *Kiss you? Take liberties he should not have?* He knew the overdressed fop had probably tried.

Miss Dawson shifted her stance and played with a tiny ringlet that had slipped from her bun. "Yes, he walked me to the door. But he behaved the complete gentleman, if that is what you wish to know."

"Why should I wish to know that?" He huffed with a shrug of his shoulders. "Since you were so late to your bed, Miss Dawson, I'm wondering if I might ask you a question."

She nodded, casting a glance at the door as if she wished to flee.

"Did you hear or see anyone roaming about the house at that late an hour?"

Her eyes widened then lowered. Was that a shudder that ran through her? "No. Why do you ask?"

"Something was stolen from my study."

"Stolen?" Miss Dawson spun around and skittered to the fireplace. "How could that be?" She held her hands out to lifeless coals then quickly snatched them back. "Don't you keep your study locked?"

Chase regarded her skeptically, wondering how she was privy to that information. "Yes, that is what makes it all the more puzzling." He approached her. "And I carry the key on me at all times."

"Indeed?" Miss Dawson wrung her hands together, still staring into the cold fireplace.

"In fact, I had it with me last night." He closed the gap between them, careful not to make a sound. He wanted to see the truth in her eyes when she faced him.

She turned around and flinched. "Perhaps you were mistaken and left it in the house." She shifted her gaze over the floor by their shoes as if searching for something. A gurgling sound rose from her stomach.

Guilt poured from her every movement. Chase had seen it dozens of times before when he had questioned disobedient crewmen. "You seem quite agitated, Miss Dawson. If I were a gambling man, I would wager you to be the thief."

She flung a hand to her breast. "Me?" Her chest heaved. "Forgive me, Admiral. I am simply terrified." Finally, she lifted her gaze to his, her lips quivering. "The thought of a thief rummaging through this house at night, why, it frightens me so."

Of course. Chase chided himself. How could he have suspected this timid sparrow of such a crime? He longed to take her trembling hands in his, longed to assure her of his protection. Instead, he clasped his own behind his back. "It is I who must beg your forgiveness, Miss Dawson. I should not have mentioned it."

She nodded and looked away.

"Rest assured you are quite safe within these walls."

Thanking the altar boy, Dominique slid her hand over the cold banister and inched down the stairs leading from the right of the sanctuary to the church offices below. The service at St. Mary Woolnoth had encouraged her. Hearing the Word of God read aloud reminded her that she needed to spend time reading the Bible on her own. Each powerful word had stormed through her, charging her with supernatural strength—a strength she very much needed.

Guilt pressed upon her like a heavy burden. She had lied to the admiral. Right to his face. What kind of person did that make her? But what choice had he given her? If she had told him the truth, he would have arrested her. As it was, she had just one day left before she turned over the documents to the Frenchman—before she could save Marcel.

The sermon had not been given by John Newton, the current rector of the church, and as soon as the service had concluded, Dominique inquired as to his whereabouts. Much to her solace, she discovered that although he was not feeling well, he was willing to see her. She must speak to him. She must discover if God found favor with her present course or whether she was out of His will and doomed to failure. More than anything, she needed comfort from someone who cared.

After sending William and Mrs. Hensworth home, she asked the footman to wait outside while she headed downstairs.

Now as she emerged into a huge dark hall lit only by candlelight flickering from an open door at the end, she wondered at her sudden nervousness. Perhaps it was due to her not having seen Mr. Newton in years. How could she know whether he could be trusted? How much should she tell him?

The musty smell of aged wood, mold, and incense emanated from the nearly one-hundred-year-old church walls, enhancing the feeling that she walked toward her own inquisition. Resisting the urge to turn around and dash from the church, she made her way forward, remembering her father's words. *"John Newton is a dear friend who will never turn you away."* Dominique needed a friend, a friend who could offer her godly advice—especially after the admiral had accused her of stealing documents from his study. He seemed to believe her tale of fabricated fear, but how long could she keep her secret from such a cunning officer?

Stepping into the light of the doorway, she paused. A frail man sat hunched over a tiny desk in the corner, scribbling on paper. A candle, half melted in its brass holder, sat beside his fast-moving hand. Other than the desk and chair, the humble room contained another chair, a bookcase against the far wall, and a small coal stove. A brass-hilted cane was propped against the wall next to the reverend as if it held up the structure. No paintings or ornamental carvings decorated the plain white walls save for a large wooden cross, which hung over the desk where he sat. He dipped his pen in a bottle of ink and continued his work.

Dominique cleared her throat.

He glanced over his shoulder and squinted. "Ah, my dear." Setting down his pen, he rose and adjusted his black rector's robe before scuffling toward her. Gray hair, neatly combed but thinning, hung to his shoulders, and although his face was etched with too many rivulets of time to count, he beamed at her with the enthusiasm of youth. His back bowed slightly forward as he stood before her, and Dominique found herself wishing she could reach out and straighten him, if only to make him more comfortable.

Brown eyes beneath hooded lids scanned her with naught but joy radiating from them. "I can't see very well anymore, I'm afraid, but I can tell you've grown into a lovely young woman." He chuckled and gave her one of the most genuine smiles she'd ever seen, then boldly took her hands in his gnarled ones. She sighed as tension seemed to flow out of her.

"Why, last time I saw you—when was that? Ten years ago?— you barely reached my chest."

"Yes, Mr. Newton, I am three and twenty now."

"My word, how time flies. Come, come." He pulled her inside. "Have a seat. Pray tell, what have you been up to all these years? Surely you must be married now and have little ones of your own."

Dominique slid into a chair as sorrow squeezed her heart. "Nay, I'm afraid not." The hope of marriage and children no longer shone brightly in her future.

"Waiting for someone worthy of you, no doubt?" Mr. Newton clutched his chair by the desk and dragged it over to hers. He sat with a moan and gazed at her, concern crinkling the corners of his eyes. "I never heard from you and your mother after your father was killed." He said the word so brashly, with such finality, that it startled Dominique—not that she hadn't accepted her father's brutal death at sea long ago.

"We moved to France."

"Ah, and how does your lovely mother fare?"

"She died last year, Reverend." Dominique returned the favor of honest communication. "From a horrid fever." She swallowed a lump of pain as the sound of her mother's agonizing screams rang through her memory.

"Oh, my poor dear. My poor dear." He took her hand in his and rubbed her skin with his bony fingers. "What of your brother? Who takes care of you?"

"I do." Dominique squared her shoulders. "I am employed as a governess in the Randal home." Instantly her shoulders sank.

What was she so proud of? She was nothing but a spy—and a liar.

"Indeed? Admiral Chase Randal?"

"Yes. Do you know him?"

"By reputation only. I've spoken with sailors who've served under his command." He nodded and placed her hand onto her lap. "A harsh but fair man, I'm told. Lost his wife a few years ago. What a shame."

"Yes. He seems quite bitter about it. I believe he has rejected God because of the tragedy."

"Then that is a real shame, indeed. But perhaps having a godly woman as yourself in his home will help him receive the love and comfort of God."

Dominique shook her head as guilt washed over her. "As much as I would wish it, Reverend, I fear my presence does no one in the home any good. They are a worldly group, and as many times as I try to forgive, to turn the other cheek,"—she thought of the slander and abuse of Mrs. Barton and Lady Irene—"as many times as I expound on the Lord's mercy and goodness,"—she thought of Mr. Atherton—"they pay me no mind, even so much as laugh at me. I am far too weak and intimidated to be a good witness." *And too much of a liar.*

"I doubt that, child," Rev. Newton said. "You are most likely doing far more good than you realize. God has placed you there for a reason."

Dominique offered him a grateful smile, but she doubted the Almighty's reason was her strong witness. And she doubted it was to spy for France, either.

"So you are all alone, miss?" The reverend's eyes misted, and Dominique got the impression he could feel her pain from where he sat. "Where is your brother?"

"That is why I have come." Dominique raised a hand to her nose, trying to stifle the burning in her throat and eyes. "I am in trouble."

"What trouble, child?" Mr. Newton took her hand again and looked at her with the genuine concern of a father.

No adult since her mother had died had expressed such heartfelt

regard for her welfare. Overcome, Dominique released the tears
that had filled her eyes, and one by one they streamed trails of fear
and sorrow down her cheeks.

"Can I trust you, Reverend?"

"Of course."

"What I mean to say is. . .is. . .can I trust you? Can I trust you if
I tell you something that may go against your good conscience?"

Rev. Newton took her other hand and held them both together
in a warm caress. "Whatever you disclose to me stays between me
and God, I assure you of that." He smiled. "Now what has you so
vexed, my dear?"

"They have M–Marcel." She muttered her brother's name
through sobs.

"Who does?"

"The French."

Releasing her hands, Rev. Newton reached inside his black
robe. He pulled out a handkerchief and handed it to Dominique.

She dabbed at her face. "They will kill him if I don't give them
what they want."

The lines on the reverend's face tightened, and he shook his
head, the loose skin on his jaw quivering. "How can this be? What
could they possibly want from you?"

"I cannot tell you." Dominique desperately wanted to, if only
to relieve herself of the burden she carried all alone. But how could
she admit to treason? It would not be fair to share the weight of
guilt with such an innocent man.

His scraggly brows rose.

"I do not know if God is with me. I don't know why He's put
me in this situation." She squeezed her eyes shut. "Who am I to be
called to such a task?"

"You are a precious child of God." Mr. Newton squeezed her
hand in his, and despite the bony, rough feel of his skin, an unusual
warmth flowed from the touch of one so old.

"I don't believe so." She gazed at the blurred figure through
her tears.

"But God does, my dear. If He has chosen you for a task,

whatever that task may be, He knows exactly what He is doing."

Dominique sniffed and dabbed her nose, then released a sigh, trying to settle her breathing. "Please tell me what God wants me to do. I don't have much time left. If I do what they ask, I betray. . . all who are dear to me. If I do not, I have as good as murdered my brother."

The reverend leaned back in his chair. No shock or indignation burned in his eyes from her mention of betrayal. Instead, he seemed to have gone to a different place, a peaceful place that flooded his eyes with a deep, inexhaustible love. She longed to join him there and never return.

He labored to rise, plodded the few steps to his desk, and grabbed a black book before returning to his chair. "I cannot give you the answers you seek. But I can point you to Someone who can." He set the book gently in his lap and gave her a knowing grin.

"I have prayed to God, Reverend." Dominique shook her head. "I hear nothing. No peace comes upon me. No answers, and still I am frightened."

"Do you think the mighty men of old were not frightened?" Mr. Newton opened the holy book. "Do you remember Joshua? He was called to the task of leading all of Israel into the Promised Land. He had seen miracle after miracle in his lifetime, yet still God had to tell him three times. . . ." He glanced down, flipping through the pages, then lifted the book to within an inch of his eyes. "In Joshua 1, verse 6, God tells Joshua, 'Be strong and of a good courage,' then in verse 7, 'Be thou strong and very courageous,' and then in verse 9, 'Have not I commanded thee? Be strong and of a good courage; be not afraid, neither be thou dismayed: for the Lord thy God is with thee whithersoever thou goest.' " He placed the book back on his lap.

Dominique swiped at a wayward tear as despondency pressed upon her heart. She'd heard these stories before—wonderful, miraculous stories—but they applied to other people, more powerful people than she. "Joshua was a strong warrior. Who am I compared to him?"

"You have missed the point, my child. He was no different

than you or I. Just a man with human weaknesses." Rev. Newton coughed to the side then leaned toward her, his eyes aglitter. "The Holy Scripture is filled with examples of men and women who possessed no special qualities on their own. Moses stuttered, Abraham lied about his wife, Jacob was a swindler, Paul murdered Christians, Peter denied Christ. And what of Gideon? God called him to save the Israelites from the hands of the Midianites. He replied to God that he couldn't perform such a task, for he was the least in his family and from the weakest clan."

"I know just how he feels." Dominique sniffed and forced down a cynical chuckle.

"Yet God used him and an army of only three hundred to crush thousands of Midianites." The reverend slapped his palms together as if to demonstrate the rapid deliverance of God then raised one hand to the sky. "Glory to His name."

His exuberance, however, did nothing to break through her shield of fear. That was all well and good for people following God's direction, but where did it leave Dominique? "But what if the task I must do is wrong, Reverend? What if it goes against God's will? Surely He will not help me then."

Rev. Newton scratched his jaw. "If you feel you have no choice other than to do this deed, then you must ask Him what to do and then believe He will show you. You must believe, child." He smiled. "Trust Him, no matter what you see happening around you."

Dominique nodded. She had asked for direction many times before, but no answer ever came. Did she truly believe God would guide her? Maybe her lack of faith had been the problem all along.

Rev. Newton patted her hand. "Jesus *is* your strength. Once you realize that, you will not seek it within yourself."

"Thank you, Reverend." Dominique forced a smile, enjoying her time with someone who truly seemed to care. And although fear still gripped her heart, she now had a plan. She would go home and spend the night in prayer—and then *believe* God would guide her. He must give her a clear answer by tomorrow night. For if He didn't, she would have to make the most daunting decision of her life: betray her country or see her only brother die.

CHAPTER 13

Darkness overtook Chase, finally capturing his thoughts and locking them in the hold of his mind, giving him a brief repose from their tormenting afflictions. But it didn't last long. He tossed his sweat-slick body over the down coverlet and moaned. A trickle slid down his neck onto the pillow. Light formed in the darkness. Melody appeared beside him on the bed—their bed—her sweet face aglow like an angel's, her hair shimmering in a waterfall of gold around her. She smiled and gave him that look, that look that is such a rarity even betwixt married couples, that look of love, of knowing, and of complete acceptance.

"*I miss you,*" Chase said in his dream, longing to reach up and touch her, but afraid she would disappear if he did.

"*Love our son, Chase.*"

"*I am trying, dear.*" He sighed.

She slid her fingers through his hair as she always used to, and although he couldn't feel her touch, the effect of it enfolded him like a warm blanket. He closed his eyes. When he opened them, she was gone, and ebony darkness slapped him in the face. He bolted up in bed. Panting, he mopped the sweat from his brow and neck with the sheet and jumped to the floor.

Another dream. Always the same. Always a taunting memory of the love he would never have again.

Plodding to the fireplace, he lit a candle from the coals and made his way to his desk. Perhaps another glass of brandy would soothe his thoughts enough to sink them into the depths of sleep—well below the dreams storming upon the surface.

After downing the biting liquor and finding no comfort in it, he eased into his breeches and stepped out into the hall. Wandering through the shadows of the sleeping house was the only thing that seemed to becalm him at night. He lumbered down the dark passage, his mind still tormented with the dream, and struck his toe on the hard leg of a pedestal table. Pain shot up his foot, and he cursed under his breath as the vase teetered on the tabletop. Thankfully it didn't fall. He would have that blasted table removed first thing in the morning, for it wasn't the first time he'd slammed into it during his nightly excursions.

Floorboards creaked as he made his way to the stairwell. Leaning on the railing, he gazed past the first floor, down to the entrance hall below. Muted light from street lanterns spilled in from the windows, sending shadowy monsters crouching to the corners. His nightly friends. Kindred spirits, if you would. For wasn't he just like them? A monster, a restless shadow roaming the empty house searching for. . .What was he searching for? He gripped the wood railing, fingering the intricately carved grooves, and shook his head. He didn't know.

To his left, past the stairs, the dark rectangle of Miss Dawson's door broke through the gloom. Chase rubbed his eyes. He hadn't seen her since that morning. After she'd returned from church—*late*—he'd remained in his study and had not joined her and William for the noon meal or for supper. Then, after inquiring of Sebastian, he'd learned that she'd gone to her room, professing a stomachache, and had not emerged since. 'Twas no wonder with the amount of food she ate. He snickered.

His thoughts drifted to the conversation he'd had with Mr. Atherton earlier that day. The pompous man had paid a call simply to inform Chase of Miss Dawson's innocence in the scandalous incident at the ball. Chase gritted his teeth as a cord of distress tightened around him. The embarrassing mishap no longer bothered him, for he had already suspected foul play on his sister's part. What grated him now was that Mr. Atherton had the audacity to ask Chase for permission to court Miss Dawson. Of course, it was her decision. Chase was not her father. Besides, why should he care whom she bestowed her favors upon?

The *tick-tock* of the grandfather clock in the entrance hall clipped over his nerves. A horse and carriage rumbled by on the street.

Chase blew out a sigh as he remembered the other equally distressing event—the missing Admiralty documents. But he was taking care of that. Yes, that mess would soon be cleared up, and the culprit would be caught and receive his due punishment.

A flutter of soft words floated over him, muted yet melodious and pleading. He shook his head, thinking he'd finally gone mad. Was he now hearing the voice of his dead wife when fully awake? Holding his breath, he listened and turned toward the source. Miss Dawson's door. The hint of a glow sliced the darkness underneath. He inched forward, cringing at the creaking of the floorboards, and leaned his ear against the oak barricade. Fervent words poured from within. To whom was she talking? Who would dare to be in her chamber at this hour?

Perhaps he had been wrong about her, after all. The bile of jealousy rose in his throat, tempting him to burst into the room and expose the shameless lovers. But if he was wrong, he would risk appearing a complete scatterbrain. Hesitating, he slid his moist hand around the polished handle and eased it down. The latch clicked, but Miss Dawson's voice did not cease from within. Pushing ever so slightly, he opened the door just a crack. Did he dare peek inside? Surely it was not proper, but he had to know who was in there with her. He peered through the opening.

Miss Dawson knelt beside her bed, hands clasped before her and head bowed. A lustrous glow covered her in golden light, shimmering over her white nightdress and setting her long tresses aflame. Chase swallowed. The light seemed to come from above her, and Chase craned his neck to find its source but could not determine it through the narrow opening. An open book sat upon her fleece coverlet, and she laid one hand upon it as she continued whispering.

Praying.

She was praying. Amazement sped through him, and though he knew he should afford her privacy, he turned an ear toward the opening.

"Father, I seek Your wisdom. I seek Your favor this night. Please reveal Your will to me. Please strengthen me as You did the men of old. Forgive me for my weakness and especially for my lack of faith. If only I could believe. . .if only I could believe You are with me." She laid her head into her hands and appeared to be sobbing, and Chase resisted the urge to run in and comfort her. What was distressing her so much?

"Lord, please watch my brother. Please protect him and keep him safe until I can see him again."

Chase huffed. Her brother. How selfish of Chase not to realize she must miss him terribly.

She gazed up, and the tears slipping down her cheeks sparkled in the light. "Father, please bless little William."

Chase blinked and tried not to move.

"Help him to grow up loved and nurtured and knowing You. Provide a woman who will love him and fill the gaping hole left by his mother's death."

Warm regard and a burgeoning affection burned Chase's throat. She was praying for his son.

"And the admiral." She bowed her head once again.

Chase leaned closer.

"Please comfort him in his loss. He seems so. . .so lonely, so empty, so cold. Help him to open his heart once again to his son and to You."

Of all the—lonely? Empty? Cold? Chase jerked and accidentally bumped the door. A tiny creak echoed through the darkness. One peek inside told him Miss Dawson had heard it. She stood, wrapped her arms around her chest, and headed his way.

Dominique crept toward the doorway. Had she left it open? Her heart climbed into her throat as she pushed the door aside and squinted into the shadows of the hallway. Nobody. 'Twas probably just the wind. She closed the door and latched it, then returned to her prayers. Picking up her Bible, she read aloud the two verses the Lord had shown her: ' "The Lord is my strength and my shield; my heart trusted in him,' " and her favorite, " 'Fear thou not; for I am with thee: be not dismayed; for I am thy God: I will strengthen thee; yea, I will help thee; yea, I will uphold thee with the right hand of my righteousness.' "

She sighed. The promises of God—if only she could believe them. She had been praying for hours but felt no surge of power or strength, and her faith seemed as faulty as ever. She began to shake whenever she thought about the task she must perform the following night. *What kind of spy am I? What kind of Christian am I, Lord?*

Closing the Bible, she laid it back on the side table and crawled into bed. . .and waited. An idea popped into her head from God. At least she thought it was from God; she hoped it was from Him—for it was the only thing she knew to do.

Creeping out of the kitchen door in the basement of the house, Dominique flipped the hood of her cloak over her head and tightened it around her neck. A light mist sprinkled over her, glazing the stairway as she cautiously made her way up to the street. Her heart hammered a vicious beat within her chest. She had never ventured out in public without benefit of escort, and she suddenly felt naked. Even after her mother had died, Marcel had always been by her side. Through the dirty, perilous streets of Paris, he had always been there. But not tonight; tonight she not only must make her way through the dangerous streets of London alone, but also must negotiate with a murderous villain for her brother's life.

Blood pounded in her ears as she opened the iron gate and stepped onto the street. First things first—making it to the tavern in the middle of the night without being accosted. Then she would worry about her meeting with the French contact. She patted the documents folded in the pocket of her cloak and heard their reassuring crackle. Hard to believe that a wad of papers could save someone from certain death.

Hugging the iron fences lining the street, Dominique avoided the circles of light cast onto the cobblestones from the brass lanterns. An odd chill crept up the back of her neck, and she stopped and looked behind her. The dark silhouette of a man halted then slid behind a town house across the street. Strange. Perhaps one of her neighbors returning from a soiree. Shaking off her uneasy feelings, she pressed onward. Lights appeared ahead, jostling as if they floated in midair. The clomp of horses' hooves soon followed, and Dominique dove into the shadow of a bush near the walkway. A carriage ambled by, its passengers blasting a ribald ballad from the windows. *Drunken noblemen.*

Resuming her course, she picked up her pace and tried to remember the streets she'd memorized from the map of London Larena had shown her. Dominique had said her interest stemmed purely from curiosity about the layout of the massive city, and the chambermaid had happily complied, pointing out where she grew up near the east docks and where her family now resided and, of course, the Mall, the Queen's Palace, and Piccadilly.

Sweet Larena, such a strong, independent woman. Dominique wished she could send her on this frightening errand in her place. She'd probably relish the adventure of it, instead of quaking in her shoes like Dominique. Yet Dominique feared for the chambermaid. Larena believed in God, had attended church with Dominique, but she trusted the Almighty no more than she trusted men. Dominique bit her lip. Yet did *she* really trust God? Surely the quivering of her knees proved otherwise. How could she be sure God was with her in this traitorous task? Did He care about nations and their wars or only the hearts of men? Confusion stormed through her, multiplying her terror.

Making her way down several small streets, Dominique tried to avoid the larger thoroughfares where people would no doubt still be bustling about, attending soirees and men's clubs. As she left the quiet neighborhood behind, the city twinkled with lights as far as she could see. Bursts of laughter and song rose from the distance.

Approaching Broad Street, Dominique hovered beneath a birch tree and waited for two coaches to pass. Several gentlemen decked in black trousers and coattails sauntered her way. Holding her breath, she tried to still her trembling as they passed within twenty feet of where she hid. Memories resurged like demons— memories of her nights spent on the streets of Paris, hiding in the shadows, clinging to Marcel. Finally, their gleeful voices, slurred with alcohol, faded into the night. When no one was in sight, she dashed down the main street for a block then turned down Andrews. She flitted from shadow to shadow as music and laughter from Leicester Square, a few blocks to her right, teased her ears, making her feel all the more alone on her treacherous errand. Gathering the collar of her cloak in her moist fist as if it could protect her, she pressed on.

Turning a corner, Dominique kept her gaze downward as she prayed and forced her wobbly legs to keep moving. Coarse voices halted her. A huddle of slovenly men littered the porch of a tavern a few feet ahead. Dominique peered about wildly, looking for an escape. It was too late to turn around. Saying a silent prayer, she inched her way across the street away from the men. But one of them saw her. He elbowed his friend.

"Look what we have here, gents. A lady out for a bit o' fun."

The other men turned around and staggered to the edge of the porch. "Where? I don't see nothing."

Gathering her skirts, Dominique darted for a cluster of warehouses across the way. Maybe she could hide among them and make her way to the Strand through the back alleys. *Oh Lord, protect me. I must live to save Marcel. Please, Father.*

"There she goes! Let's be after her!" Deep voices roared behind her.

The clacking of boots on cobblestone, accompanied by heated grunts, chased her through the night. A cold sweat pricked her skin. Her hood flew off her head and flapped behind her. The misty air struck her face like a slap of death. Vulgar laughter and jests stabbed her ears. She glanced over her shoulder. The grinning mob closed in on her. Images of another assault—a man in a dark alley in Paris—filled her terror-stricken mind. She could feel his cruel hands upon her, the grip of a madman determined to get what he wanted.

Oh Lord. Not like this.

Dominique dashed forward and slammed into a large man. She bounced off his thick chest as if he were made of brick. Stunned, she shook her head and jerked to the side to weave around him, but he reached out with one hand and held her in place.

Her heart sank. He was with them. She was trapped.

"Let me go!" she screeched and tried to yank loose from his grip, which, although tight, did not pain her arm.

The crunching of boots behind her ceased. Dominique's breath stuck in her throat. Squeezing her eyes shut against an onslaught of dizziness, she awaited her fate.

But instead of anxious voices in pursuit, instead of lewd comments tossed her way, only curses and grunts of disappointment spilled from the mouths of her attackers.

Dominique dared a glance over her shoulder. The odious gang of men scratched their bearded faces and peered into the night as if she did not stand nigh ten feet before them.

She gazed up at the man who held her, wondering how one man could frighten off a band of twenty ruffians. His oversized top hat hid the features of his face beneath its shadow, while black clothing concealed his body. He did not look at her but kept his gaze locked on the drunken men.

"Where'd she go?" one man shouted.

"Why, if I'm not the King's uncle, I ain't seen that before."

"She just disappeared."

"Told ye we shouldn't 'ave drank that tawdry brew."

Another laughed. Then one by one, they turned and swaggered away.

The dark-clad man released her arm.

Dominique's mind scrambled through a thousand explanations for what had just happened but finally settled on a cloud of impossibility that floated through her mind, leaving her cold.

What did this man intend to do with her now? "I owe you a huge debt, sir. I am most grateful." She hoped to appease him with her appreciation.

He only nodded.

She should have been frightened, but for some odd reason, she felt more peace than she had all evening.

Flipping her hood back atop her head, she started down the street. He made no move to stop her, and she breathed a sigh of relief. Yet one glance behind told her he followed her.

She swung her face forward again. Odd. She did not hear his footsteps—even now.

"There's no need to follow me, sir. I'm quite all right," she shouted back at him while continuing to walk.

He said nothing.

"One o'clock on a misty morning and all is well," a charlie cried in the distance. Where had he been when the band of villains had chased her? Then again, she hadn't really needed him, had she?

Dominique quickened her pace. She was late. Would the French rat wait for her? Dampness broke out on her palms.

As she neared the Strand, the stench of human excrement and rotten fish nearly drowned her. She gagged and pressed a handkerchief to her nose. The Thames. She was almost there. Her breath came in rapid spurts. She turned down Chandois, hoping to avoid the crowds on the Strand for as long as possible. No such luck. A phaeton sped by, its iron wheels squealing over the stones. She ducked beneath the overhang of an inn. The large man in black halted on the street. When she proceeded, he fell in behind her.

Why was he still following her? Blood drained from her face. Perhaps he'd been assigned to spy on her. Perhaps the admiral suspected her. Clutching her cloak, she swerved around. "Sir, I beg you. Please leave me be."

Still he said nothing. But this time he did not stop. With a brief nod, he glided past her and proceeded across Bedford Street up ahead—the same direction she planned on going. Movement caught Dominique's eye, and she glanced to her right. The shadow of a man slid into the gloom of a cluster of trees. She swallowed. The night seemed to be crawling with villains. Dominique hastened behind the dark man who had saved her, keeping her distance.

No sooner had she passed over the street than two men appeared out of nowhere, kicking dirt up with their boots. Their chortles rang in the air like sirens. Dominique froze beneath the halo of a streetlamp. She had no time to dash into the shadows. The towering man in black appeared alongside her and stood in silence. How had he retreated so quickly? Dominique gazed up into his shadowed face but still could not make out his features.

As the men passed by, one of them looked straight at Dominique. She returned his gaze, waiting for him to say something, waiting for him to pounce on her. He moved so close beside her, she could make out the color of his eyes—ocean blue. But no sooner had their gazes met than he turned to his friend and continued his story as if she weren't there. Dominique glanced at the large man. Her breath caught in her throat as a warmth that belied the cool night blanketed her. Who was this strange man who cloaked her in invisibility? Why didn't he speak to her? Why couldn't she see his face? She pressed a hand over her pounding heart and opened her mouth to ask him, but he proceeded forward in silence.

After turning down Southampton, she followed the man across the Strand to Cecil. Halfway down the avenue, the Last Stop loomed like an eerie fortress. The man in black halted at the foot of the stairs.

How did he know where I was going?

Guttering lantern light cast dark fingers onto the porch and stairway, beckoning poor souls to the debauchery within. To her left, the Thames licked the docks as if anticipating her demise. Movement flashed in the corner of her eye, and she stared down the gloomy street. The dark shadow of another man lumbered toward her then abruptly turned and disappeared across the avenue.

Sucking in her breath, Dominique inched up the steps, casting a glance over her shoulder. The man in black stood like a statue. He wouldn't go in with her. Why? The sudden loss overwhelmed her and sent her head spinning again. Raising her hand to her forehead, she shoved herself through the doorway.

The putrid stench of stale alcohol and tobacco struck her, stealing her breath. A rat scampered across the wooden floor and wove around a maze of tables and chairs before disappearing into a dark corner. Dominique tightened her cloak under her chin and scanned the room for the Frenchman. A tall, bony man with huge eyes and a hook nose stood behind a counter, pouring drinks into mugs. Three sailors lined the bar, their backs to her. To her right, two men at a table entangled their arms in a fierce wrestling match as a group formed around them, shouting and thrusting fists in the air. The Frenchman was nowhere in sight. Was she too late? What would happen to Marcel now?

"Scads, gents, 'tis a lady!" a muddied voice blared her way.

All eyes shot to her. Even the two battling men halted, though they did not release their stranglehold on each other's arms.

The door opened behind her, admitting the stench of the Thames in a chilly blast that fluttered her skirts. One glance over her shoulder told her a willowy man in tan pantaloons and blue topcoat had entered. Ignoring her, he slid into the shadows of the tavern toward the right. Not the Frenchman.

She faced forward, allowing her eyes to search the corners of the tavern one last time.

One of the sailors at the bar sauntered toward her. His brown trousers hung loosely on his thick frame. A red jacket barely covered his stained, checkered shirt. A seaman, not an officer, not a gentleman. But she wouldn't expect to find a gentleman in such a place. "Can I help ye, missy?" A blob of spittle perched at the corner of his lips like a cannonball ready to fire.

"Quit your slobbering. She's with me." The Frenchman emerged from the shadows on her left and took her by the elbow. She winced under his clawlike fingers as he led her to a corner table by the back wall. Grunts of disappointment followed on their heels. Dominique felt as if she'd escaped a pit of vipers only to be thrust into a lions' den.

"I knew you would come." He kicked out a chair and plopped down. The light from a lantern perched in the middle of the table set his features in a sinister glow. Amazingly, he hid his accent well beneath a forced Irish brogue.

"Of course, monsieur; you have my brother," Dominique replied.

"*Asseyez-vous.*" He motioned toward a chair beside his. Spilled ale pooled atop the table and dripped over the side. Something brown and crusty oozed over the wooden seat.

"I'll stand."

"Do you have the documents?"

"Oui." She glanced around cautiously, hoping no one had heard her French. "Yes."

He held out his hand.

Reaching into her cloak, Dominique grabbed them and tossed them his way, praying she had chosen only those papers that gave away the least damaging information. She'd spent an hour sorting through all the documents, carefully choosing these five.

As he perused them, his gleeful expression soured. "*C'est tout?*" He rubbed his lips. "Is this all you have?"

"No, I have more." Dominique's knees began to quake. "I have all the information my cousin will ever need to defeat the British at sea." She clenched her jaw, hoping that wasn't true, praying she'd never have to give up everything to this slimy rat.

The burly man shot to his feet, plucked a knife from his belt, and stepped toward her.

"It is not with me, sir," Dominique stuttered, trying to still her pulsating breaths.

He halted, and his dark eyes slithered over her.

She forced herself to meet his gaze, hoping her terror was not as evident to him as it was to her. God had shown her that it would be foolish to give them everything they wanted. As long as she held on to the most vital information, she had the power. But for some reason, as this greasy man eyed her like a snake, she felt as powerless as a mouse caught in a trap.

She swallowed an explosion of fear. "And you will not get the rest of the documents until you bring Marcel to me alive and well."

"How dare you threaten me?" He booted a chair aside and

shoved his face into hers. The odor of ale and sour meat filled her nostrils and stifled her breath. "I ought to drag you back to His Excellency and let him kill both you and your brother."

"But then you wouldn't get the rest of the information you desire, would you?" Her voice came out in cracked pieces, but her intent was clear.

He snarled, and Dominique shrank back, momentarily closing her eyes, expecting him to strike her.

"Lucien will not like this, I assure you."

"Nevertheless, you will relay to him my terms."

"He is not a man to take terms, mademoiselle." The Frenchman took a step back and slid a finger over his oily mustache. "*En fait*, he will most likely kill Marcel and be done with you British dogs." He spat to the side.

Dominique gasped. Her legs trembled, and she grabbed onto the back of the chair to keep from falling. She must keep her wits. She must maintain her control. *Lord, help me*.

"I don't believe you, sir. Lucien needs information only I can give him. He will do as I say." She nodded in an assurance that was sorely lacking within her. "You will bring Marcel back to this same spot in two weeks, and I will return with all the information Lucien demands."

"Who are you to demand anything from His Excellency!" His bark silenced the crowd for a moment before they resumed their carousing. "You," he continued in a seething whisper, "will bring the rest of the documents to me tomorrow night, or as sure as I stand before you, Marcel will die."

CHAPTER 14

After Dominique fled the horrible tavern, the man in black led her all the way home, never once looking back. When she arrived at the Randal house, he had simply kept going. She crept to her bedchamber and eased the door shut. Even at nearly two o'clock in the morning, the creak of wooden floorboards echoed through the house. Who would be up at this hour? Leaning against the door, she rubbed her forehead and tried to make sense of an evening that now seemed more like a nightmare than reality.

Tossing off her moist cloak, she fell onto her bed and noticed her open Bible upon it. Had she left it there? She couldn't remember. Lighting a candle, she glanced over the pages. Her eyes latched upon one verse that glowed brighter than the others: "For he shall give his angels charge over thee, to keep thee in all thy ways. They shall bear thee up in their hands, lest thou dash thy foot against a stone."

Dominique froze. Her hands began to shake. She set the candle down upon the night table and stood beside her bed, wrapping her arms around herself. "Lord, could it be? Did You send an angel to protect me?"

Even as she said the words, all the tears she had withheld during the harrowing evening, all the tears brought on by her fears and heartache, filled her eyes and poured down her cheeks. She fell to her knees, trembling, and leaned her head in her hands, humbled by the love of God.

Warmth bathed her as the terror of the night spent itself in gut-wrenching sobs. She had done it—she had done what she'd set out to do, but she had not been alone. God had been with her. He had protected her. He had sent an angel to watch over her. Why, she could not understand, especially when her task reached beyond legal boundaries.

"I believe You, Father. I believe You are who You say You are. I believe You are all powerful and that You are with me." She rocked back and forth, praising Him and basking in the knowledge that He loved her and would never leave her.

No sooner had the fearful storm within Dominique begun to quiet than the Frenchman's threat rose like a black thundercloud upon her peaceful waters. He had said Lucien would kill Marcel if she didn't bring all the documents to him tomorrow night. But how could she? What motive would they have to keep him alive if she delivered everything they desired?

A knot formed in her throat. Had she not just declared her faith in the power of God? And yet not a second later, she shriveled in fear.

Forgive my weakness, Lord. Please tell me what to do.

But she already knew. She must hold out and stick to her plan. She must remember that now she had a card to play in this treacherous game of life and death. But what she didn't know was how she would survive the following night—how could she force herself to sit and do nothing, all the while thinking that at that very moment she might be causing Marcel's death?

A tap on his chamber door jarred Chase from his half sleep and sent him fumbling to answer it. He admitted the tall midshipman and quickly shut the door behind him. Though a waning candle still flickered on his desk, Chase could barely make out the young man's features. "What news, Franklin?"

The man shifted his boots across the floor. "He went to the Chaucer down by the river." Chase knew the tavern, one of the nicer taprooms where untitled men congregated to have a drink or perhaps solicit female companionship. "Ah, yes, to meet someone, perhaps?"

"I cannot say, Admiral."

"You cannot?" Chase's ire rose like a flame. "You are being paid to say, Franklin. Did he or did he not meet someone?"

"He spoke with several people."

"Did he hand off the documents?"

Franklin shook his head. "I never saw him hand anything to anyone save for a shilling to the barmaid for a drink."

Chase rubbed his chin.

"Permission to speak, Admiral."

"Yes, of course." Chase waved a hand through the air.

"Are you sure you are correct in your assumptions? I watched your butler for more than two hours, and truth be told, he appears to be naught but a lonely old man in need of a drink and some companionship."

Chase huffed and massaged the back of his neck. "That will be all, Franklin. Keep a weather eye out every night as instructed."

"Aye, aye, Admiral." Franklin saluted and marched from the room.

Chase began to pace. As much as he hated to place suspicion upon Sebastian, as much as he had denied the Admiralty's insinuations that someone in his own home was a spy for France, Chase could come to no other conclusion. The old butler fit the description given the Admiralty by their sources abroad: British born but with French ties; someone close to Chase—a servant, a relation; someone with access to his study; and someone with a need to improve his station in life.

Chase hung his head. He had hoped with everything in him that he had been wrong. But then the documents had gone missing. Who else could it be? He allowed his mind to scan the list of household servants once again. None with the brains, none with the motive and access, and none with the ties to France like Sebastian. Save Miss Dawson—Chase chuckled at the thought of an admiral's daughter spying on Britain. Hogwash. Pure rubbish.

Katharine pushed her way past Sebastian as soon as he opened the door. Lifting her skirts, she gave Lady Irene, who sped in behind her, a smug grin and headed up the stairs.

Sebastian grunted. "Mrs. Barton, allow me—"

"Never mind, Sebastian, I will find him," she shot back over her shoulder.

Laughter drew her to the drawing room, and without so much as a knock or an announcement, she thrust open the doors and burst inside in a swish of lace. What she had to tell her brother could not wait another minute, nor could it wait for propriety. But the vision displayed before her halted her in her tracks and sent icicles through her veins.

Candlelight flickered across the room, setting it aglow with a golden warmth that kept out the descending gloom of evening. Miss Dawson presided on the flowered divan, William snug by her side, their smiling faces pressed within a book. Across from them sat Chase, one leg perched upon the other, reading the *Spectator*. A sensation of rapport, of affection, swept over her—a sensation of family. Something she hadn't felt in quite some time.

It only incensed her further.

After she had exposed the tawdry woman's promiscuity to Chase, he dared to sit in the same room with her? She had heard he had not released her yet, but this was beyond reprehensible.

Grabbing Lady Irene's hand, she brought her alongside. "Chase, I must speak to you immediately."

The enchanting scene was shattered, and they raised their heads, seeming just now to notice her. William's beaming blue eyes widened. The young boy stood, bowed, but made no move to greet her as he usually did. No doubt the French vixen had poisoned the young lad's mind against his own aunt. He quickly reassumed his seat beside her.

Chase set down his paper and gave her a look of annoyance as he stood. "Good evening to you, dear sister, Lady Irene." He bowed. "A pleasure to see you both." The smile that lifted his lips did not reach his eyes. "Now pray tell, what has you so overwrought?"

Katharine ground her teeth together. Why did he always have to patronize her? "I must speak to you alone, if you please." She shot a fiery glance at Miss Dawson, who merely looked back at her with those fawn-colored eyes of innocence. *Innocent, indeed.*

"You may speak freely here." Chase folded his arms across his chest.

Lady Irene tensed beside her. "If I may, Admiral. I believe you should hear what your sister has to say. 'Tis a matter of grave importance."

"Ah, no doubt." Chase nodded and cocked a brow. "Some new scandal is afoot? Or perhaps some poor beau failed to swoon at your feet, Lady Irene, as expected when you graced him with one of your sultry glances?" He snorted, and Katharine heard Lady Irene groan beside her. "Or perchance you wish to invite me to another ball? The last one was quite entertaining, to be sure." He sauntered toward the windows, where a setting sun splattered blood red over the panes.

" 'Tis none of those things, Chase, I beg you." Katharine's news pranced upon her tongue like a herd of wild horses longing to be released from their corral. Raising her chin, she glanced at Miss Dawson, and a smug triumph cushioned her rapidly beating heart. Surely now her brother would release the French miscreant and find a wife among the *haut ton*, a loyal British noblewoman who would treat him as he deserved—someone like Lady Irene. She gave her friend a victorious smile. Chase would no doubt thank Katharine later, when he realized she had saved him from certain devastation.

The admiral spun around. "Very well, I shall listen to you, sister, but mark my words, if this is another of your conniving plots to sully Miss Dawson's reputation, I will not stand for it."

Katharine blinked. So he knew about her part in the incident at the ball? No doubt that loose-lipped fop Atherton had failed to keep his mouth shut. Well, no matter, it wouldn't make any difference—not after Chase heard what she'd come to tell him.

"Ah, yes." He moved to the fireplace and leaned against the mantel. "Mr. Atherton explained the situation quite clearly to me. And I believe you both owe Miss Dawson yet another apology, do you not?" He nodded toward the governess, who had turned a bright shade of scarlet to match her wanton heart. "You not only ruined her gown, but caused her a great deal of embarrassment, as well."

Chase straightened his blue waistcoat and shifted his stern gaze betwixt her and Lady Irene. Why did he always have to wear that blasted navy uniform? Fear squeezed Katharine's stomach at the thought of losing him. Aside from their aging parents, Chase was all she had left. How she longed to see him happily married and settled in London. But not with this Frenchwoman, who would surely break his heart and send him sailing out to sea.

William shifted in his seat and whispered something in Miss Dawson's ear. Setting the book down, she took his hand in hers and held it in her lap. Katharine cringed at the affection between them and elbowed Lady Irene, motioning with her eyes toward the boy. In spite of Lady Irene's protests, Katharine had instructed her friend to warm up to the lad, to converse with him, read to him, play with him, whatever it took to prove herself a worthwhile mother in Chase's eyes.

Lady Irene slid onto the divan beside him and offered him one of her sweet smiles reserved for her favorite gentlemen.

It did not have the same effect on William. Cringing, he sank back into Miss Dawson as if a giant viper were after him. He wrinkled his nose against what Katharine assumed was Lady Irene's overabundant perfume.

"William, what are you reading?" she asked.

The boy gave her a sour look and glanced up at Miss Dawson. She nodded at him with a smile.

"*Tom Thumb*," William whispered, staring down at his book.

"Oh, *Tom Thumb*!" Lady Irene screeched and bounced up and down on the divan, shifting her gaze to Chase to see if he noticed her exuberance. Her outburst seemed to frighten William further, and he inched closer to Miss Dawson. Katharine sighed. Clearly she needed to spend more time on Lady Irene's mothering skills.

Chase's brow wrinkled; then he looked at Katharine. "Enough of this. I await your apology."

Miss Dawson slowly rose. "Admiral, I beg of you. There was no harm done. Let us simply forget the incident."

Katharine narrowed her eyes upon the governess. Very clever. *See how she plays the charming saint, the forgiving victim.* Fury burned within her. And one glance at her brother told her 'twas obvious he'd fallen for the ruse. He gazed at Miss Dawson, and she at him, and in that brief second what Katharine saw in their exchange sent spikes of terror to her bones. She must act, and she must act quickly.

"Chase, I beg you." She gave him her most pleading look—the one that always seemed to win him over. "May I have a word with you in private?"

No sooner had the admiral and his sister left the room than a chill struck Dominique. When she looked up, it was to Lady Irene's icy blue eyes boring into her from the other side of the room.

"Mr. Atherton tells me you are very committed to Christian principles." She tilted her head and allowed her gaze to wander over Dominique as if she were studying her through a microscope.

"That is true. Are you not?" Dominique clasped her hands in front of her, uneasy in the presence of this high society lady who obviously harbored only hostility toward her.

"Humph. I suppose." She tossed her head, sending her golden curls quivering, and glided across the room. "You aren't one of those Methodists, are you?" She scrunched her nose.

William tugged on Dominique's gown from where he still sat on the divan. "What is a Methodist, Miss Dawson?"

Dominique smiled at him. "I will explain later, William." The last thing she wanted was for the young boy to witness any more quarrels. He had already heard far more caustic words that evening than was prudent for one so young. Her thoughts sped to the admiral and Mrs. Barton, and fear swirled in her stomach. Whatever she had wished to discuss with him, it involved Dominique; of that she could be sure. The woman had never looked so supercilious before, as if she gloated over some assured victory.

"The Methodists," Lady Irene began, "dare to say that people of high rank and good breeding are no better than the common wretches that crawl on the earth." She reached the window and gazed out, her peach gown aglow in the last rays of sunlight. "Absurd."

As much as she wanted to, Dominique couldn't leave without responding to this grossly inaccurate belief that ran rampant through the British society. "I believe we have all sinned and fallen short of the glory of God, milady." She extended her hand to William, thinking it best if she left Lady Irene to her ill-humored musings. "Come, William, let us retire to your room."

Mrs. Hensworth appeared in the doorway. "There you are, William." The plump housekeeper's gaze scanned over Lady Irene and ended in a smile when it reached Dominique. "I'll take him upstairs, miss."

William peered up at Dominique with eyes as big as blue saucers. "Can we go to the park tomorrow, Miss Dawson?"

"Of course we can." Dominique brushed the hair from his forehead and felt a burning of affection fill her eyes.

"Thank you, Mrs. Hensworth." Dominique kissed William on the cheek, eliciting a chuckle from the boy, and watched as he followed the housekeeper from the room. She must leave this house soon, for she feared if she did not, she would have to leave her entire heart behind.

"Now if you will excuse me." Dominique nodded toward Lady Irene.

"Why are you not cross with me?" Lady Irene turned from the window and gave Dominique an inquisitive stare.

Dominique searched Lady Irene's exquisite eyes but found only anguish behind the sparkling blue. Her thoughts sped to her own source of anguish, Marcel. "Because I know what it is like to want something so badly that you would do most anything to get it."

The woman returned her gaze with disdain. "Men do not desire women who cling to such prudish religious restrictions, not in our society, and especially not a man like the admiral. He needs a woman with more. . .more. . .shall we say, lively passions." She sashayed to the fireplace and tugged off her gloves.

A rush of blood heated Dominique's face "Lady Irene, I assure you I was not speaking of the admiral. I have no interest in him." She took a step out the door, hoping for a quick exit.

"But I fear he has interest in you." Dominique heard a strain in Lady Irene's voice. Her eyes shimmered in the firelight. Withdrawing a handkerchief, she turned her face away. "I cannot for the life of me figure out why. You with your strict religious rules. How tiresome. Why, the admiral hates organized religion. He no longer even believes in God."

Dominique's heart both leapt and sank in the same moment. Leapt at Lady Irene's suggestion of the admiral's affections and sank at the poor girl's misery—and at the admiral's. Anguish consumed Dominique at the thought that both Lady Irene and the admiral—unless their hearts softened toward God—were destined to live hopeless lives, only to spend eternity without Him. Yet didn't her own faith waver from day to day? How strong was her belief? Dominique swallowed. Sorrow stiffened her jaw. She started toward Lady Irene, hoping to comfort her, but the woman raised her handkerchief in the air and waved her back.

Desperation set in. Dominique wanted to tell her how wonderful God was, how much He loved her, how she did not have to search for love and acceptance solely in the arms of a man, but Dominique's taut nerves coupled with the hatred emanating from the woman bound her tongue in knots.

"I do not have to live by a set of rules," she finally managed to say. "I simply want to please my Father in heaven because He has been so good to me." Dominique returned to the doorway then stopped. "Besides, I find His laws often bless me more than restrict me. He created them for our well-being."

A shudder ran across Lady Irene's shoulders, but she did not turn around. She was listening at least, and an idea came to Dominique. "Just like the admiral forbids William to run out in the street where he could be struck by a carriage, God's laws are for our own protection, because He loves us."

"Nonsense." Lady Irene sniffed. "I have not followed them, and I am perfectly fine."

"Then I will pray He continues to bless you regardless of your lack of appreciation for those blessings, milady."

Lady Irene spun around to bestow a vicious stare upon Dominique. "Please leave."

Dominique scurried down the hall and up the stairs, her heart breaking for the young noblewoman. *Oh Lord, open her eyes to Your truth.*

As she closed the door to her chamber, alarm hit her like a dense fog. Her heart began to sputter. She flung open her window, hoping the cool air would revive her senses and her faith, but only a sooty chill invaded her room, wrapping icy chains of fear around her. She began to pace, her dinner souring in her stomach even as her nerves forced it to hunger for more. In less than five hours, she was supposed to meet the French contact at the Last Stop.

Or—as he had threatened her—Marcel would die.

But she wasn't going.

"So what is so important that you barge in on my Tuesday evening repose and further insult my governess?" Chase leaned back on the desk in his study and examined his sister.

Katharine flounced to a padded wooden chair near the center of the room and floated into it, her rose-colored muslin dress billowing out around her. She threw a hand to cover her heart as if she had just walked across town. "I fail to understand how you can sit in the drawing room with that *woman* as if she were your wife and allow her to become so affectionate with William."

Chase clamped his hands on the edge of his desk. "Is that what you have dragged me here to discuss? Egad, but you have the brazen impudence of an old seadog." With a shake of his head, he started toward the door. "Enough is enough, dear sister."

"No, Chase, please." She shot to her feet and grabbed his arm. "That is not what I wish to speak to you about. Hear me out, I beg you."

He stopped, crossed his arms over his chest, and glared at her, trying to remember the winsome, doting girl of his youth. They had both suffered much since then, but she had endured more humiliation and heartache than most women could bear in a lifetime. He knew she truly wanted the best for him. Regardless, he was tired of her false accusations, tired of her interference, and tired of her pushing Lady Irene upon him. Oh, how he longed to go back to sea and be done with these trifling family squabbles.

"Miss Dawson betrays you."

Chase turned to leave.

"She left this house late Monday night."

"Whatever are you talking about?" He faced her, amazed she would lower herself to such levels, amazed that she hated Miss Dawson so much.

"She left around midnight and made her way to a tavern down by the Thames off Cecil Street."

"With whom?"

"Alone."

Now he knew his sister lied. Most women would never dare venture out at night without protection, Miss Dawson chief among them. She cowered at the slightest rise of his voice. "Am I to believe that my timid governess went out in the middle of the night without an escort to a dangerous part of town?"

"Yes, Chase. 'Tis true." Katharine wrung her hands together, her brown eyes searching his as if challenging him to find falsehood within them.

"How do you know this?"

"I had her followed."

"Whatever for? Why, this is pure rubbish!" Chase marched to his desk, searching for his brandy but finding none. He refused to allow his sister's words to take root in his growing trust for Miss Dawson.

"Please, Chase, you must believe me. I've always known something was amiss with her." Her skirts rustled as she approached. "Women sense things about each other. I had to know. I had to protect you. So as soon as I received word she had left the house, I sent one of my footmen to follow her." Her voice cracked.

"And how, pray tell, did you receive this word?" None of this made sense, and Chase knew if he persisted, he would eventually expose the hole in her ship of lies.

"It matters not." She flapped a glove through the air then raised one brow his way. "Suffice it to say, there is at least one other person in this house who has sense enough not to be fooled by the strumpet's charms."

Chase grimaced and turned his back to her. "What did she do at this tavern?" Why was he playing along with her deception? Why did his stomach suddenly fold in on itself?

"She spoke with a man and then left."

Chase felt the blood race from his heart. If his sister were telling the truth, if Miss Dawson had met a man at a tavern, then one of only two things could be true: Either she had a lover, which defied everything he knew about her and struck a sudden blow to his heart, or she was the spy he had been warned about, an impossibility for an admiral's daughter. Therefore, he had no choice but to assume further duplicity on his sister's part.

"And she came home unscathed?" He flattened his lips, turned, and ran a thumb over the scar on his cheek. "I know this city at night. 'Tis not a safe place for a woman. Someone like her would not have made it very far without being assaulted—or worse."

"I do not know how she accomplished it, Chase, but I promise you, I am not lying." Katharine laid a gloved hand on his arm, and he saw no insincerity in her eyes.

"This is preposterous." He jerked away from her.

"If I can prove it to you. . .if I can have her followed again and bring you proof, will you believe me then?"

"Why do you hate her so? I have no plans to marry the woman." Even as he said it, he could not deny the growing feelings within him. Nevertheless, soon he would be back upon his ship—away from Miss Dawson, away from his sister, away from this madness and back to war where things made sense.

Katharine tugged at a lock of cinnamon hair that had escaped her bonnet. "I tell you, she is not the innocent she pretends to be. She is half French, after all." Her eyes pooled with tears. "And my concern is not only for you, but for William."

"Very well." Chase gave her a look of warning. "Gather your proof and bring it to me. But mark my words, if it does not unequivocally establish the truth of your accusations against Miss Dawson, you will formally apologize to her and promise me that you will henceforth leave her be. Is that clear?"

Katharine nodded.

Yet even as he said the words, Chase ignored the gnawing feeling in his gut that his sister would not have offered to prove a lie.

CHAPTER 15

Around the edge of the canvas, Marcel's boyish face grinned at Dominique.

"Marcel, you must be still." She dipped her brush into the tan paint and applied it to the canvas, shifting her eyes back and forth between the portrait and the ten-year-old boy flailing his legs out in a chaotic dance over the velvet padded chair.

He huffed and scrunched his face until it looked like a tight ball of yarn.

"How is it coming, dear?" Madame Marguerite Jean Denoix, Dominique's mother, floated into the room on a cloud of turquoise silk and raven curls and curved her rosy lips into a smile that said, *You are so precious to me.*

"Marcel won't be still, Mother. I cannot paint his portrait when he changes position and expression whenever I look at him."

"Marcel?" Mother arched her motherly brows his way.

"But, Mother, 'tis finally sunny outside, and I wish to go take Vaillant to the park."

"You can go horseback riding when your sister is finished with this session. You know she needs to practice her painting."

Marcel's expression soured but immediately brightened as he gazed toward the door of the parlor.

"What is this I hear about horses?" Admiral Stuart Dawson strode into the room, garbed in his Admiralty blues trimmed in gold, his long tawny hair slicked behind him. Dominique's heart leapt with pride. But his gaze did not land on her or on her brother. His dark blue eyes alighted upon her mother and remained there as he closed the distance between them.

Dominique's mother faced her husband, and in that moment the tender exchange within their gazes spoke of a love most people only dream of. Her father leaned and whispered something in her mother's ear before placing a gentle kiss on her cheek, sending a deep rose blossoming over her mother's normally peach-colored complexion. She gazed up at him, her eyes sparkling.

Marcel hopped from his chair. "Father, can we take the horses out? You promised to teach me how to jump."

Dominique grunted. "Father. Marcel will not stay seated."

"Pray tell, madame." Her father crossed his arms over his chest and wrinkled his brow at his wife. "Where did these bickering children come from?"

Her mother giggled. "I believe they are ours."

"Indeed?"

Marcel tugged on his father's arm. "Please, Father. The sun is shining, and you said—"

"Let us see what your sister has produced, shall we? If it resembles you in the slightest, then perhaps I'll take you riding."

Dominique cringed. She hadn't wanted anyone to see the portrait until it was finished, especially not her father. And it certainly didn't look like Marcel, not yet, anyway.

"Hello, precious." Her father kissed her forehead then stood back and rubbed his chin. "Ah, yes. Quite good, my dear. I can see the resemblance."

She eyed the splattering of paint on the canvas and knew it looked nothing like Marcel, but somehow that made her father's compliment warm her heart all the more.

"Yes, indeed." He glanced at his wife. "I believe we may have another Rembrandt right here in our midst."

Her mother nodded with a smile. "Oui, she has talent. She takes after her *grand-mère*, Madame Camille."

Marcel cocked his head and wrinkled his nose at the picture.

"That is not me. It looks more like that old cook aboard Father's ship, Mr. Gregory."

"Oh, it does, does it? Well, perhaps I need to add this, then, to complete it." Dominique dipped her brush in a puddle of dark brown and with two quick swipes drew a curled mustache onto the portrait.

Silence enveloped the room as all eyes widened. Her father raised a fist to his mouth and cleared his throat. A slight giggle slipped through her mother's lips, and she looked away. Then suddenly they all broke into laughter and fell into each other's arms.

Even within her deep sleep, Dominique felt herself smile. She tossed to the other side of her bed and tried to plunge back into the sweet memories of another life long since passed.

Marcel's face appeared out of the shadows. Black grime smudged his gaunt cheeks. Rips banded his once-pristine linen shirt, and the lace at the cuffs hung in tattered strips. "I found us something to eat." His blue eyes glowed with promise as if they were sitting down to dinner over roast pork and potatoes. " 'Tis not much, but it will help get us through the night." He held out two pieces of moldy bread and a half-eaten apple.

Dominique took a scrap of bread and forced a smile. She swallowed against a burst of shame and studied her brother. At seventeen, he should be pursuing a noble education, learning how to wield a sword with the other young upstarts, and flirting with young ladies in satin gowns and bouncing curls. Instead, he scoured the streets like a vagrant, an orphan begging for morsels of rotten food—not like the son of a British admiral, not the like the descendent of French nobility.

He flung a torn burlap sack across her shoulders. "This may help ward off the cold." He blew on his hands and rubbed them together, gazing up into the strip of starry sky above them. "At least it will not rain tonight."

"Thank you, Marcel." Dominique glanced around the dark alleyway deep in the heart of Paris and inched closer to the barricade of drums and crates they hid behind. A rat scampered toward them and stopped, sniffing at the food in their hands. Marcel booted it away and sat beside her, wrapping his arm around her back and pulling her toward him.

Dominique coughed and held a hand to her nose against the stench of waste slithering through the alleyway. She supposed she should be used to it by now, but tonight it seemed to solidify in the air around them, just like the despair that threatened to swallow her whole. Her thoughts drifted to her mother, her death still a festering wound putrefying Dominique's heart. She had promised to take care of her brother but had failed miserably. What was to become of them now?

"Do not fret, sister." Marcel bit into the apple. "I will take care of you. I will find a way to restore our fortunes—never fear."

His optimism under such duress only added to her shame. As the eldest, at one and twenty, she should be the one taking care of her brother, not the other way around, but after four months of living on the street, she had neither the energy nor the desire to press onward. When she had been accosted in the alley last week by a man promising to buy her and Marcel dinner, she had nearly forfeited her virtue and would have if Marcel had not fended off the beast. After that, Dominique had lost the will to go on. And if it were not for Marcel, she would curl up in a hole somewhere and allow herself to die.

The gloomy alleyway faded, and her rags transformed into a glorious gown of royal blue velvet. Marcel, decked in a ruffled white shirt and dark pantaloons, stood before her. "I promised I would take care of you, did I not?" He flashed a perfect set of white teeth and ran a hand through his curly dark hair. At that instant, Dominique thought him very handsome, even if he was her brother.

Over his shoulder, Cousin Lucien's slick smile reminded Dominique of a snake about to strike.

A burly arm shot from behind Marcel. Candlelight gleamed off a steel blade.

"You will do as I say, or your dear brother will die," Lucien hissed.

Marcel's deep blue eyes bored into her, fury and fear brewing within them. The blade cut into his throat. A trickle of blood spilled down his neck and stained his white shirt, blossoming like a deadly rose.

"Marcel! Marcel!" she screamed. "Marcel, I will save you, I promise."

"Marcel!" She wrestled against what felt like a thousand sweaty hands. "Marcel!"

"Dominique." The deep voice intruded on her nightmare, softly at first, then louder and louder. "Miss Dawson." Strong fingers gripped her arm. "Wake up."

Dominique bolted upright. Her ragged breath came in spurts that matched the rapid beating of her heart. Nothing but darkness surrounded her. No sound but her own breathing. She pressed her hands against the moist sheets on her bed.

"Dominique." Someone touched her arm, and she sprang from the bed, peering into the shadows. Milky light filtered through the window, outlining the large figure of a man standing on the other side of her bed. He skirted around the oak bedpost.

" 'Tis me, Miss Dawson, the admiral."

She shrank back from him and rubbed her eyes, forcing back the haunting images of her past. *The admiral?* What in the name of all that was holy was he doing in her chamber? Terror heightened the wild beating of her heart.

He halted before the foot of the bed. His face was lost in the shadows. "Forgive me. I did not intend to frighten you, but you were screaming the name Marcel."

"Screaming?" she whispered and tried to shake the fog from her mind.

The admiral took another step, and the dark shadow of his arm rose toward her. A memory, one now fresh in her mind, stormed through her—a memory of another man in a dark alley of Paris coming at her in the night. She screamed and jumped back. "Stay away!"

He froze. His heavy sigh filled the room as he retreated and stumbled into the desk by her bed. He moved to the coal grate and knelt. Dominique eyed the door. Could she run? Ridiculous—the admiral wouldn't hurt her, would he? Then why was she so frightened? Snatching her robe from the back of a chair, she flung it over her shoulders and pulled it tight about her. Did he know what she was doing here? She drew a deep breath. *Do I truly know?*

Candlelight flickered over his handsome face from the other side of the room. His bare feet thudded on the wooden floor as he made his way back to her—slow, measured footsteps as if he were afraid to wake her. And when she gazed into his chocolate brown eyes, she found only concern within them.

He set the candle down on the high-back dresser, where it cast a circle of flickering light around them, highlighting his broad chest that peeked from behind an unbuttoned shirt he must have donned in haste. A pair of trousers hung loosely on his hips. "Are you all right, Dominique?"

"Yes," was all she could muster amidst the conflicting emotions raging within her, especially at the sound of her Christian name upon his lips.

"You were screaming." He ran a hand through his loose mahogany-colored hair that reached just below his shoulders.

"I was?"

"Quite loudly, I might say." His lips curved in an enchanting smile.

Dominique hugged herself and lowered her gaze. "Forgive me for waking you." She didn't know what else to say. His close presence in her bedchamber at night, coupled with his evident care for her, played havoc with her already reeling emotions.

"I was not asleep." He touched her elbow, and the smell of brandy and spice washed over her like a heady perfume.

"You are trembling." His dark gaze latched onto hers.

Dominique swallowed and eased down into the chair he led her to, thankful for the support beneath her. Her head was beginning to spin, and the last thing she wanted was to swoon into the admiral's arms again—especially against his bare, muscled chest.

He squatted beside her chair. His eyes softened as they met hers. Gone was the harsh commanding sheen, the cold protective barrier that always shielded his gaze. Was it the alcohol that lowered his defenses? Dominique tightened her robe about her chest and felt her breath catch in her throat under his intense perusal.

He raised his hand, all the while keeping his gaze upon her, and gently brushed a finger over her cheek, sweeping away a loose curl. She closed her eyes beneath his tender touch, ashamed that she did not move away, ashamed that she allowed him to be so familiar, but somehow unable to pull herself from him.

"What frightened you so?" His deep, sultry voice slid over her like warm butter.

Dominique snapped her eyes open and shifted in her chair. She tried to awaken from the spell he cast upon her, no doubt conjured by his strong, protective presence and the tender emotional state left to her from her nightmare. She gazed over the chamber, anywhere but into those caring brown eyes. His sword lay on the foot of her bed. He had charged in here to protect her, no doubt believing some villain named Marcel was accosting her. His chivalry only added to the warm tingle that now radiated through her.

How could she betray this man—this strong, courageous, honorable man? Twice she had found herself alone in a bedchamber with him, completely at his mercy. Yet he had never made an inappropriate move toward her, had always behaved the gentleman. She raised her gaze to his, unable to avoid searching his unguarded eyes. Heartache and betrayal cried out in agony deep from within him, but kindness and love also took residence there. He had a good heart.

And she would destroy it.

She would betray him and not only ruin his career, but leave his heart shattered once again.

Yet what choice did she have? Right at this very moment she was supposed to be meeting the Frenchman—would be meeting the Frenchman if her plans hadn't changed.

And she fully intended to meet him again. Betray her country and betray this man.

To save Marcel.

"Who is Marcel?" Chase asked.

Dominique lowered her gaze. "My brother."

Chase rubbed the back of his neck as relief swept through him. *Her brother. Of course.* When he'd first heard her screaming, he'd thought the worst. Grabbing his sword, he had burst into her room to fend off the attacker. The fury that had enflamed him at the thought of someone hurting Miss Dawson both surprised and frightened him. But once he realized she was only dreaming, the second-worst thing occurred to him—that this Marcel was a lover, that his sister had been right.

Why did he feel so relieved to be wrong? What difference would it make to him? He allowed his gaze to wander over her. The white lace of her nightdress curled around the edges of her silk robe. The glow from the candle, as if seeking something worthy of its light, shimmered over her in caressing waves. Her chestnut hair trickled down her shoulders onto her lap, and Chase swallowed a longing to run his fingers through the silky strands. 'Twas the brandy again, no doubt. He must curb his drinking when Miss Dawson was around.

"If I may ask, where is your brother?" He silently cursed himself for not inquiring before—for not ensuring that the son of his friend, Admiral Stuart, was also under good care.

She lifted her swimming eyes to his. "He is in France."

No place for the son of a British admiral. "How old is he now?"

"Eighteen."

Chase shifted his weight onto his other foot and leaned an elbow on his knee. "May I ask how he provides for himself?"

"A distant cousin took us in after. . ." Dominique pressed the back of her hand to her nose.

"I see." Chase yearned to take her hand in his, to offer what comfort he could, but he only looked away, allowing her a moment. "Then why does he need saving?"

"I beg your pardon?" She swiped a tear threatening to escape from her eye.

"You were screaming that you would save him."

His statement seemed to blast through her resolve, opening a floodgate of tears that now streamed down her cheeks.

Against all propriety, he took her trembling hand in his. "Forgive me. I have upset you again."

She allowed his tender grip at first then suddenly jerked her hand away. Wiping her face, she averted her gaze. "My apologies, Admiral. I am not sure what has me so overwrought. Perhaps I am simply tired." She gazed at him, her amber eyes brimming with emotion—fear, sorrow, but something else that caused Chase's heart to flip. "As I have said, Admiral, 'twas a bad dream, nothing more."

Chase rose and took a step back. What was he doing lurking about a woman's bedchamber at night—especially this woman's? He should have left as soon as he discovered she was only having a dream, but the picture of her writhing upon the bed in agony had wrapped a cord around him and held him in place. He drew a deep breath, hoping to quell the peculiar yearning within, and decided to address the problem at hand. "We should send for your brother immediately. He should not be in France."

Dominique blinked. "But he has no land, no title, no trade. What would he do here?"

"I would hire him. A footman, perhaps?"

She opened her mouth, no doubt to protest, but he held up a hand. "I know 'tis beneath him, but it would get him out of our enemy's territory before they muddle what is left of his reason with their warped philosophies. Perhaps I could get him a commission on board one of my ships."

Miss Dawson's chest rose and fell as rapidly as a fire bellows, and he couldn't tell whether she was grateful or whether he had frightened her again. She folded her hands in her lap and gazed up at him. "You are too kind, Admiral. I don't. . .I do not understand. You barely know me. You do not even know my brother."

He flattened his lips. She was right. He had only known her but a month, but truth be told, he felt as though he had known her all his life. "Your father saved my life once." He raised his brows. "I owe him."

"Is that why you offer to help Marcel—as payment on a debt?"

She snapped her gaze to his, harshness replacing the sorrow. "That is why you hired me?"

"At first, yes." He looked away, not wanting to face the sudden anger in her eyes, much preferring the tenderness of only a moment ago. "But I find you to be very good for William." *And for me.* He shook the thought from his head as rapidly as it had come, not ready to admit the effect she had on him, not ready to taint the memory of his wife with these unwelcome and befuddling feelings.

"We are descendents of French nobility, sir, and as well you know, also of British Admiralty." She tossed her quivering chin in the air. "We will not be subject to your charity."

Chase stared at her wide-eyed and couldn't help but chuckle. She had shocked him once again. One minute she behaved as a frightened, timid sparrow; the next, strength welled up in her that reminded him of a lioness protecting her young.

She stood. "I'm sorry to disturb your evening, Admiral, and though I am grateful for your concern, you should not be in my chamber."

But despite the harsh tone of her voice, he knew fear still held her captive. He sensed a distress that went beyond simple concern for her brother, and he longed more than anything to come to her rescue—to becalm her fears and remove all her difficulties.

She began to sway. He reached for her arm. "Why won't you let me help you?"

"There's nothing to be done, I'm afraid." Her tears returned, glistening in the candlelight, and he felt a shudder course through her.

He took a step toward her and pulled her into his arms. To his surprise, she melted against his chest, her soft curves folding into him as if they were made for each other. Sobs wracked her body. He ran his fingers through her hair, allowing her to release her sorrow. He didn't know how to comfort her, didn't know how to help her, but one thing he did know: His sister was wrong. This frightened woman was innocent of any wrongdoing.

Her sobs quieted, and he cupped her chin and lifted her face. Glittering eyes met his as their breath intermingled. No deceit, no malice, nothing but a chaste yearning for love and comfort beamed from within them.

Without giving it a thought, he lowered his lips to hers. Soft and warm, they met his in a moist caress. Heat flamed inside his belly. He drew her against him as their kiss grew hungrier.

She pushed off his chest and jerked away from him. Raising a hand to her lips, she glared at him.

Chase clenched his jaw. Why had he done that? Shame spread an icy film across his passions. He had not kissed a woman since Melody—had not wanted to kiss a woman since Melody. Yet as he looked at Dominique, at her quivering lips, at the innocent spark of fervor in her eyes, and as the feel of her surrender still pulsated through him, he would gladly have done so again.

"I have never kissed a man before," she declared, breaking the silence.

"Indeed?" He smiled. "You are quite good at it." He planted his hands on his waist and looked down. What was wrong with him? How had this woman bewitched him? The bulwark he had so carefully erected around his heart began to crumble, allowing his enemies entrance: love, care, concern. But they never came alone. Terror and torment bit at their heels: terror at losing the one he loved and the torment of already having done so.

"I would ask you to leave, Admiral." She wrapped her arms around her chest.

He stepped toward her. "Forgive me, Domin—Miss Dawson. I have no excuse for my behavior." He sighed. "I fear I have only frightened you further, which was the last thing I wished to do."

"A condition you can rectify by your absence, sir," she retorted in a shaky voice.

"Not until I know you have calmed." He reached toward her, his only hope to reassure her of his noble intentions, not wanting to leave her with the impression she had anything to fear from him.

In a flash of white lace and silk, she leapt for the bed, grabbed his sword, and thrust it out before her. The tip of the blade wobbled inches from his chest. Her face scrunched in determination in the candlelight, but her eyes darted furiously between his. "For the last time, I beg you to leave."

Chase grinned and retreated, forcing down a sudden burst of indignation. "I surrender, Miss Dawson." He chuckled with arms extended. "I am your humble prisoner." He gave her a mock bow. Perhaps he should just leave as she requested, yet his pride would not allow a woman to get the best of him. How dare she hold a sword to him in his own house? Especially when he'd come to her chamber to save her.

Fear skittered across her eyes, melting his fury. She was truly afraid of him—or of something, and he found he could not allow that. He did not want her to think that he meant her any harm.

The sword oscillated before his chest as the muscles in her arms were no doubt straining beneath its weight.

In a quick move, he shoved the blade aside with his forearm, slicing his shirt and the skin beneath. While she fumbled to recover, he grabbed the hilt from her hands with ease.

He held it, point down, by his side. Her rapid breathing filled the room as she stared at him aghast.

"I must say, I have never quite had that reaction after a kiss." He gave her a devilish look then tightened his lips.

"What do you intend to do?" she asked as if just realizing she had held a sword to her employer and was now alone with an angry man.

"I intend to leave, as was always my plan." He grimaced and snapped the hair from his face. "I am not the sort of man to force himself on a woman."

"And yet you did."

"I believe your response indicated otherwise." He gave her a half smile, pleased when he saw her face reddening.

"I was distraught. . . ." She shifted her stance and gazed over the room. "I had a nightmare."

"Sleepwalking again, Miss Dawson? Or perhaps this time sleep kissing?"

"How dare you?" She squared her shoulders.

"Rest assured, Miss Dawson, I will dare not attempt it again." He bowed and sauntered from the room, closing the door behind him.

Chapter 16

The rasp of heavy fabric and the glare of sunlight startled Dominique from a fitful sleep. She sprang up in bed, momentarily dazed as memories from the night before shoved their way into her consciousness. A spark of terror brought her fully awake as a voice rang from her right.

"Sorry to wake you, miss." Larena finished tying the curtains aside, then turned and smiled. "But you planned to take William to the park before his tutor arrived."

"I did?" Dominique stared aghast at the red-haired woman. "Yes, of course." She rubbed her eyes against visions she hoped came only from a nightmare. One glance over the room, and her heart squeezed. The admiral had been in her chamber last night. She pictured him standing by the foot of her bed, his shirt open, his hair in wild disarray around his shoulders, a handsome smirk on his face.

And she'd kissed him—passionately.

Panic sliced through her. *Sacre bleu.* She'd drawn his sword on him.

"What troubles you, miss? You look as though you've seen a ghost."

"Far worse, I'm afraid," Dominique gasped.

"Is something amiss?" Larena approached the bed as Dominique tossed her legs over the side. "Did something happen last night?" The chambermaid's round face pinched. "I thought I heard voices, but then again, this house is full of voices at night, so I paid them no mind."

"The admiral," was all Dominique managed to say as a clump of shame and horror rose to constrict her throat.

"Yes, what about him?"

"I had a dream, a nightmare." Dominique shuddered as the harrowing vision of Marcel with a knife to his throat replayed itself in her mind. "And the admiral came."

"To your chamber? Oh dear." Larena moved to sit on the bed then hesitated.

"Please." Dominique patted the quilt beside her. "Yes. I must have screamed, and he thought I was being attacked."

Larena sat down, and a tiny smirk danced across her lips. "Oh, to be sure." She gave her a sideways glance.

"You couldn't possibly think he had other intentions?" Dominique wrung her hands together in her lap, remembering the way he'd pulled her into his arms, remembering the way she had surrendered so readily. Heat flushed over her.

Larena patted her hand. "I know the admiral to be a decent man." She nodded reassuringly but then offered Dominique a sinister wink. "But a fair warning to you: He is a man nonetheless."

"He kissed me," Dominique blurted, unsure why she disclosed so much to Larena. She supposed she needed a friend, a woman who could tell her that these new, overwhelming sensations within her were silly and trivial, a part of the frivolous dalliance betwixt the sexes.

Larena stood. "I am all astonishment, miss. 'Tis so unlike him." She adjusted her cap and stuffed a curl back into it. "I told you about depending on men. Even the good ones are not to be trusted." She stomped to the grate, poked at the embers, then shoved more coals into the opening.

"I do not mean to impugn the admiral." Dominique feared she had misspoken, tarnishing the admiral's reputation with his staff. "I believe him to be a good man, a lonely man, perhaps. He did not mean to kiss me, I am sure."

Even as she said it, a warm quiver raked over her. Why had

she succumbed so easily to his seduction? Why had she fallen into his arms like a common hussy? Those arms, so strong and warm, surrounding her like iron guards. She had felt safe, almost loved, for the first time since her father had died. Though she greatly admired the admiral for his intelligence and commanding spirit, she had witnessed another side of him last night, a tender side that made her heart burn within her.

"Miss, your face is as red as a beet. Do you have a fever?" Larena scanned the room then plucked Dominique's robe from the bottom of the bed and tossed it over her shoulders.

Dominique laid the back of her hand over her cheek. A fever. That must be it. There was no other possible explanation for her behavior. "Perhaps I *am* coming down with something."

"Taking advantage of a poor frightened girl—he should be ashamed of himself." Larena clicked her tongue. "If only Melody could see him now."

Melody. His wife. Dominique wondered what sort of woman had caught the admiral's heart. "What was she like?"

"Melody?" Larena disappeared into the dressing closet. "She was a wonderful lady." Her voice bellowed from within. Moments later she emerged with garments in hand. "You would have liked her."

"Am I anything like her?" Perhaps that was why the admiral had kissed Dominique. Yes, it made perfect sense. A lonely dark night, a bit of brandy, and a woman who reminded him of his wife. Any explanation besides the one that kept making her heart leap. Because she didn't want her heart to leap. She didn't want to care about the admiral or about William or Larena or about any of these people. In two weeks she would have to betray them all, along with her country.

"Nay, miss." Larena laid a chemise, petticoat, and stays on the end of the bed and studied Dominique. "She was taller than you, larger boned. Her hair glowed like sunshine on a clear day—the envy of all London, I might add. Her eyes were sparkling blue like William's. Yes, she was a strong one, but then, she would have to have a formidable constitution to put up with the admiral." She chuckled. "Smart, too. She wrote poetry and read voraciously.

Milton, Alexander Pope, Fielding." She smiled off into the distance then waved a hand through the air. "Well, what can I say? Before she married the admiral, and afterward, as well, all the gentlemen in town adored her."

Dominique sank onto the bed. She was nothing like Melody. "He misses her terribly, doesn't he?"

"I doubt he will ever be the same." Larena placed her hands on her round hips. "Now don't be getting your hopes up, miss. That man will only hurt you. He is not to be depended upon, at least not anymore. He will sail right out to sea the first chance he gets and leave you and William behind without so much as a by-your-leave."

"I have no hopes, Larena, but to be the best governess for William." *And to save Marcel.* Dominique hung her head, realizing what a fool she had been to allow her naive feelings to steal her thoughts and intentions away from her real purpose here—if only for a moment.

Larena nodded in satisfaction. "I am most pleased to hear it. No sense in entangling yourself with a man when you have proven that you can provide for yourself."

Dominique remembered her earlier conversation with the chambermaid. "Surely there has been someone in your life whom you depended on, someone you trusted?"

Larena shook her head, sending her fiery curls springing around her freckled face.

"Your parents, perhaps, your father?"

"My father was a brute of a man, a cobbler by trade. He beat my mother and wasted his wages on harlots and drink. My mother died more of a broken heart than the consumption."

"I am sorry, Larena." Dominique took the chambermaid's hand in hers. "We have the loss of our mothers in common, at least."

"Aye, that we do, miss."

"But not everyone will disappoint you." Dominique swallowed as she said a silent prayer. "There is Someone you can depend on who will never let you down."

"And who might that be?" Larena cocked a disbelieving brow.

"God, of course."

Larena withdrew her hand and snorted. "Begging your pardon, miss, but how can you say that after what has happened to you?"

Dominique stood and moved to the grate, holding her hands up to the heat that now flowed from it. "I don't understand the tragedies that have befallen me. But somehow deep inside, I do know God is with me, and He will never leave me."

She heard Larena sigh as her slippers scuffled over the floor. "I have emptied your chamber pot and brought you up some fresh water."

"Thank you, Larena." Dominique's stomach rumbled as she turned to see the chambermaid approaching the door. "I hope I haven't missed breakfast."

"Oh no, miss, there are biscuits and tea in the morning room." Larena opened the door and smiled.

"Is the admiral about?" Dominique dreaded running into him—especially after last night. She would not blame him for dismissing her at once after she'd nearly run him through with his own sword.

"Nay, he left before dawn, miss."

Mrs. Hensworth appeared at the door. "Mr. Percy Atherton is downstairs, miss, requesting that he escort you and William to the park."

Dominique strolled down Rotten Row, one hand squeezing William's slender one and the other laid discreetly upon Mr. Atherton's arm. "A lovely day."

"Yes, with a promise of sunshine, I do believe." Mr. Atherton gazed up into the gray mist that swirled above them.

"I do appreciate your escort, Mr. Atherton, but 'twas not necessary. My chambermaid or one of the footmen would surely have accompanied us." Yet she really did not mind Mr. Atherton's company. For some reason, she did not fear the reputable rogue, but after what had happened last night, she had no desire to upset the admiral, nor did she want any part of Mr. Atherton's silly charade of jealousy.

"But what better way to get more acquainted, my dear?" Mr. Atherton tossed his shock of sandy hair behind him as a lady, who passed on their right, batted thick lashes at him from above a fan spread across her cheek.

"Acquaintance of yours?" Dominique grinned.

Mr. Atherton raised his brows. "She seems familiar, but I cannot recall her name." He glanced at her over his shoulder then faced forward with a shrug. "Who can keep track?"

"Mr. Atherton"—Dominique sighed—"I had hoped you would have given our conversation the other night some deep consideration."

"Our game with the admiral?"

"Nay. I would like to discuss that with you forthwith, but I was referring to our discussion on a higher purpose for your life."

"Ah." Mr. Atherton yanked on his cravat as if it choked him. "God and all that. Yes, I believe I have given it a *moment's* thought." His lips curved beneath his slick mustache.

"You are a rogue, indeed, Mr. Atherton." Dominique giggled.

"At your service." He nodded. "But pray tell, since you preach this grand purpose with such fervency, do favor me with a description of the task God has give you."

Dominique could tell by the twist of his lips that he intended to trap her with his question. "You are not here by accident, Mr. Atherton. When you submit to God, you become a part of His kingdom, and He leads you daily down the path He has preordained for you to follow."

"I already serve a king, and I daresay he is quite a buffoon."

"I do not speak of His Majesty, George III; I speak of the King of kings, the all-wise and all-powerful Creator of the world. I assure you, you will not find Him a buffoon." Dominique paused, expecting a retort, but he simply strode along, gazing into the distance.

"He cares more for your character than your image," she continued. "He cares more for your inner strength, your goodness, your patience, your self-control than He does your wealth, title, or outward appearance. His plan encompasses all of eternity, not just our time on this earth."

Mr. Atherton remained quiet.

"Miss Dawson, Miss Dawson." William tugged on her arm. "When can we stop and have our picnic?"

"Soon, William; we are almost there." She gave his hand a squeeze and smiled at the youthful glow on his face. It had been a wonderful idea of Mrs. Hensworth's to take a small basket of biscuits, apples, and cheese down to Serpentine Lake at Hyde Park. Dominique couldn't remember the last time she'd enjoyed an outing at the park. Years ago—a lifetime ago when the world had been different and Marcel hadn't been much older than William.

Her nightmare surged to the forefront of her mind, sending a chill over her. She tightened her shawl around her shoulders, her heart collapsing at the thought that her dear brother might already be dead. *No. Lord, please do not let it be so.* She had to believe her plan had worked. She had to believe they wanted the information she possessed more than they wanted her brother dead. If her hunch was correct, then no doubt the slimy Frenchman would make himself known to her soon in order to confirm their upcoming meeting. She must be on the alert for him whenever she was about in public.

"Are you quite well, Miss Dawson?" Mr. Atherton asked. "You are trembling."

"Just a bit cold." Dominique gazed over the long walkway beside the park. Pink and white cherry blossoms budded on trees lining the row, emitting a sweet scent that attempted to mask the smell of horse manure saturating the air.

Despite the early hour, several of London's high society strolled about in their finest morning attire. Out on the main thoroughfare, horses pranced by, gentlemen perched atop them like kings gazing down upon their subjects. A gentleman with a lady on each arm eased by them on their left, his eyes grazing over Dominique. Two ladies in muslin carriage gowns giggled up ahead, flashing their fans over their lips as they flirted with a man on horseback who had slowed to smile in their direction.

" 'Tis Father," William announced, pointing in the distance.

Dominique gazed up to see the admiral astride a silky black

steed trotting toward them, his imperious gaze locked upon her. Her stomach constricted into a tight ball as he reined in the high-spirited horse beside them. Muscular thighs filled out a pair of tawny pantaloons that were tucked within his black Hessian boots. He adjusted his brown riding coat and pierced her with his gaze yet said nothing. A sudden heat swept over her, and she loosened her shawl and lowered her eyes, wondering where his thoughts took him—to their kiss or to the blade she'd pointed at his chest?

Mr. Atherton leaned toward her ear. "Now we shall have him."

Have him? Dominique cringed. Did she wish to have him? Certainly not in the way Mr. Atherton referred to. Her face heated. What was she thinking? She didn't wish to have the admiral at all.

"Father." William released Dominique's hand and barreled toward the admiral, stopping to clutch the stirrup. "Can I ride with you, Father?"

The admiral's stern gaze shot over Mr. Atherton, then Dominique, like a carronade taking aim, and finally landed on his son. "Nay, William. Not now. I must be off to the Admiralty."

He leaned on the pommel and tightened one corner of his mouth. "I was not aware you were escorting Miss Dawson this morning, Percy."

"We are having a picnic, Father, by the Serpentine," William announced with exuberance. He tugged on the stirrup, sending the horse clomping to the side. "Can you join us?"

"Blast it all, William. Step back," the admiral barked as he settled down the agitated animal. "As I have told you, I have business to attend to."

William lowered his sun-flecked lashes and kicked the dirt before scampering back to Dominique. She pulled him into an embrace and felt a shudder run through him that sped straight to her heart. Fighting back her embarrassment at seeing the admiral again, she leveled a harsh stare upon him. Why did he have to be so insensitive with the boy?

The admiral's face softened. "Another day, I promise, William."

The boy peeked past Dominique's skirts and nodded at his father.

"I trust you have no objection to my becoming better acquainted with Miss Dawson?" Mr. Atherton gave her a feigned look of adoration and placed her gloved hand back in the crook of his elbow.

The steed snorted, although Dominique couldn't be sure the grotesque sound hadn't come from the admiral. His normally handsome face twisted into a purple mass.

"Upon my word, Percy, do as you please." He glanced down the lane as if bored with the conversation then shifted in his saddle. "I would caution you, however, not to kiss the lady when your sword is within reach." His dark eyes traveled to Dominique, a roguish grin lifting his lips.

Dominique's breath quickened. She smiled down at William then gazed over the cherry trees and brushed a hand across her muslin gown—anything to avoid looking at the admiral.

Mr. Atherton's brow wrinkled as he glanced between them. "Indeed, I shall keep that in mind. However, there's a play at the Drury this weekend. I'd like to take Miss Dawson. Why don't you escort your sister and Lady Irene, and we can make an evening out of it?"

Dominique nudged Mr. Atherton with her elbow. Certainly the last thing she needed was for him to further infuriate the admiral.

The admiral's face swelled and reddened again. He turned aside and coughed.

"Unless you prefer I take Miss Dawson alone?" Mr. Atherton faced Dominique. "Yes, perhaps that would be best, my love. Then we shall become even better acquainted."

"I would be delighted," the admiral shouted in a tone that bore no resemblance to delight. "Now if you will excuse me." Without so much as a nod or a good-bye, he kicked the stallion's sides and charged down the road.

Chase stomped into the boardroom at the Admiralty, unable to focus on anything save the vision of Miss Dawson's hand upon Percy's arm as they strolled down Rotten Row with his son. How dare she kiss Chase with such passion the night before and then be so familiar with another man the very next day? *Women.* As fickle and unpredictable as the sea—but unlike the sea, they used trickery and deceit to gain control over men. The sea might someday take his life beneath its violent waves, but he would be a bird-witted sop before he would allow another woman to sink his heart beneath waves of despair. Did he fault Melody for dying? Perhaps he did, along with God and the rest of the world for taking her so quickly from him.

Yes, he must get back to sea.

He examined the faces of the Admiralty Board—staunch, aged faces circling the table, all eyes leveled upon him.

Late again.

"Nice of you to join us, Admiral Randal." Lord Elliot snickered.

Chase plunged into his chair.

"And in a far worse humor than usual, I might add." Mr. Garthshore chortled from his right.

Chase sighed and examined the pompous admirals and politicians all decked in their finest. The First Lord of the Admiralty, Admiral Jervis, sat hunched over some documents.

"What news of Troubridge?" Chase asked. "Has he recovered yet?"

"Anxious to leave us so soon?" Admiral Markham leaned back in his chair and steepled his hands together in front of him.

"You know I prefer the sea," Chase mumbled.

"I fear you shan't be leaving us anytime soon, Admiral Randal." Old Jarvie raised his face from the parchment before him. "Not until you uncover the spy in your midst." He tossed down his pen and stood. "It is preposterous to think a French spy could make his way into your home. This does not bode well for your future in His Majesty's Navy."

Chase grimaced and gulped down a burst of angry fear. "I have yet to determine if there even is a spy in my home, sir. Perhaps your informant was misled."

"Yet you told us some of the Admiralty documents are missing, did you not?"

"Yes." They had gone missing. That much was true, but he still found it difficult to believe he had not seen through Sebastian's or any of his staff's betrayal. Memories of another betrayal shoved to the forefront of his thoughts—a betrayal long ago when Chase, as a new post captain, had assumed command of the HMS *Indomitable*. Young and naive, he had not expected his best friend and first lieutenant to attempt a mutiny against him. The scar on Chase's cheek began to burn, and he rubbed it. Since then, he had vowed never to trust anyone again. Now this—under his own roof. What was wrong with him? Had he grown lax since Melody's death? Perhaps it was that flighty little governess who had muddled his brain.

Lord Jervis pushed back his chair and began to pace. "Finally, that bumpkin Tsar Alexander has realized Napoleon means what he says and is mobilizing his forces. We may be able to form a coalition with him against France soon. And we have received word that Napoleon is amassing troops in northern France in hopes of crossing the channel for an invasion." He halted and slammed his fist on the table, sending a rumble across it. "If we are to defeat him in the attempt, it is imperative that he not realize the enormity and power of our fleet." He glared at Chase. "It is imperative that he greatly underestimate our forces."

Chase glanced at Lord Jervis, the tightness of the man's lips, the cold cruelty burning in his eyes, his unyielding jaw, and for the first time, Chase believed his career in the navy was in serious jeopardy. This man had the power to cause his ultimate dismissal, and if that occurred, Chase would have no reason to live.

"You told us you suspect your butler?" Old Jervie continued, his narrowed eyes aflame. "Why, pray tell, have I not heard of his arrest?" Lord Jervis gripped the edge of the table, the skin on his jaw shaking from rage.

"If he has the documents, he has not handed them off yet, milord. I'm having him followed as we speak."

"I should hope so, Admiral Randal. Your loyalty is at stake. If you cannot catch a simple spy in your own home, how can we continue to entrust you to command a fleet of our finest ships?"

Grunts of agreement bristled over Chase.

"You will discover and capture the spy." Lord Jervis picked up his pen and pointed it at Chase. "Or as surely as I am the First Lord of the Admiralty, you will be court-martialed for treason."

CHAPTER 17

T hank you, Sebastian." Katharine eased out of her Spencer and handed the coat to the butler. "Where is the admiral?"

"In his study, I believe, Mrs. Barton." The slender man raised his bushy eyebrows and nodded. "Would you care to wait in the drawing room while I inform him you are here?"

High-pitched, mismatched voices floated down from above through the front hall in a sweet melody Katharine had not heard in years.

"What is that noise?" Though somewhat pleasing in an odd sort of way, Katharine found that it tweaked her nerves.

"That is Miss Dawson and William singing upstairs," Sebastian remarked, folding her coat over his outstretched arm.

Ah, that devious cat. Katharine clenched her jaw. That was why the tune disturbed her. 'Twas the sound of the siren's call luring her brother and her nephew into a deadly trap. She gave Sebastian a look of annoyance. "Is this a common occurrence?"

"Yes." Sebastian dared to look her straight in the eyes as if in challenge of her acrimony. "It has been quite nice to hear music in the house again."

Katharine narrowed her eyes. "Yet I did not ask for your opinion, did I?"

The butler did not respond, but he also did not lower his gaze.

Impudent servant. Grabbing the banister, Katharine headed upstairs, hearing Sebastian's footsteps behind her. "You are dismissed,

Sebastian. I am family and can find my way around this house without escort."

"Very well." She heard the man huff his retreat down to the hall.

Purpose drove her onward as she slinked up the stairs like a cat on the prowl. She had arrived a few hours before they were to attend the play with one goal in mind—to spy on that French tramp, to gather some ammunition against her while she was unawares, while she was alone and not putting on a righteous act in front of Chase.

As she neared William's chamber, his cheerful, melodious voice, interrupted only by deep laughter, floated from within. Is that not what she had always wanted? A good mother for the lad? Someone who would love him and take care of him just as Melody would have wanted? She clutched the polished wood of the banister and paused. Despite the sound of William's happiness, she mustn't forget this Frenchwoman was an imposter, a vixen, a liar, and no matter what Katharine saw or heard, Miss Dawson's involvement in this family would end up only in heartache. Good heavens, she had already caught Miss Dawson venturing out at night doing God knows what, more than proving she was not who she said she was. And Katharine could not bear to see her brother suffer the same agony, the same degradation, the same humiliation that she had experienced when her own husband betrayed her at the hands of a Frenchwoman.

A vision of Gage, her husband, flashed before her. Tall, handsome Lord Barton—Colonel Barton, as he preferred to be called. Decked in his military reds, the tips of his brown hair curling from under his cocked hat, and those flashing green eyes that tore straight into her soul. Just the thought of him still sent her heart skipping—despite his betrayal. She still had the letter he had mailed her from France—the one telling her he had fallen in love with a Frenchwoman and was never coming home. Her eyes misted as she took the last flight of stairs to William's bedchamber. Not only had Gage betrayed her, but he had betrayed his country, as well, and he had defamed both of their families' names. She would be dead and buried before she would ever allow that to happen again—especially to her brother and his son.

Halting outside the open door, she listened to the playful chatter and intermittent songs emanating from the room. She peeked around the corner. Miss Dawson and William sat side by side on a couch, a plethora of open books spread out on the table before them.

"How about this one?" Miss Dawson pointed to one of the books.

"I do not know that one."

"Never you fear. You follow the words, and I will try to remember the tune. Shall we?"

William grinned and gave Miss Dawson a look of such adoration it startled Katharine.

"All hail the power of Jesus' name, let angels prostrate fall!" Miss Dawson began in a booming voice that was slightly out of tune.

Katharine ducked behind the door frame and leaned against the wall. Religious songs. No doubt hymns from some dissenting church. As she listened to William join in the chorus, a vision of the stained glass, tall columns, and massive baroque canopy of St. Mary's Cathedral loomed in her mind, along with the reverence, the awe she had felt standing in the presence of God while the choir sang His praises. She had not attended church in years, and a sudden emptiness stretched like a vacuum within her.

One more peek revealed Miss Dawson with her arm around the shoulders of a beaming William as they flung their hands through the air, conducting an invisible orchestra.

Why couldn't Lady Irene be the motherly type? Katharine had encouraged her on many an occasion to spend more time with William, to take him to the park, to read to him, but the young beauty never seemed interested. Truth be told, William had always cowered in the noblewoman's presence.

Katharine shook her head, trying to jar the deceiving thoughts firing into her resolve. She would not be counted among the fools taken in by this woman. Miss Dawson had gone out that night— alone—to a questionable tavern to meet a questionable man.

Although the woman had not braved the act again, Katharine was sure that at some point the French strumpet would return to the slime from which she had come. How could she not? It was her nature.

Their song ended in a burst of giggles that grated like knife blades down Katharine's back.

"Miss Dawson, do you like Mr. Atherton?" William asked.

Katharine leaned her ear toward the door. Mr. Atherton and Miss Dawson's excursion to the park was all over town, and tonight they would attend the play together. Perhaps she could discover Miss Dawson's true feelings for the flagrant member of Parliament.

"He is a kind man and a good friend of your father's," the governess replied.

"He is very funny, don't you think, Miss Dawson?"

"Yes, he is quite amusing, William."

"Do you like him more than my father?"

"I like them both very much."

"But you like Mr. Atherton more? You are going to the play with him tonight." There was a hint of sorrow in William's voice.

A long silence ensued.

"Mr. Atherton and I have much to discuss," Miss Dawson finally said. "Shall we sing another song?"

As the duo began another hymn, Katharine clenched her fists. *Much to discuss?* Mr. Atherton never discussed anything with a lady past arranging a tryst. Surely Miss Dawson could see that Chase held some affection toward her—misguided as he may be. That she not only played the flirt with his best friend but dared to flaunt it right before his eyes was proof enough of her insidious ways.

Withdrawing from the door, she slipped down the hall, determined more than ever to catch Miss Dawson in one of her nefarious night excursions.

"Enter." Chase heard the door to his study open as Sebastian stepped inside.

Chase studied his butler. How could this slight man who had been a loyal member of his staff for seven years be a spy? But there was no other explanation for the missing documents. And Chase's career, his future, and the very future of Britain were all teetering precariously on the yardarm of this man's deception. The stakes were too high to gamble upon—too high to allow for the slightest error.

Anger thrashed within him. Perhaps he should just have Sebastian arrested on the spot to appease Lord Jervis. Yet a search of the butler's quarters had revealed no documents, no evidence of traitorous activities. And Chase would not condemn a man based on naught but flighty and fearful accusations.

He finished the calculation before him and looked up from his work. "Yes, Sebastian."

The butler cleared his throat. "I thought you should know your sister has arrived, sir."

"This early? The play is not for another three hours." Chase rose and rubbed the back of his neck. "Where is she?"

"She insisted on wandering through the house on her own, sir."

"Oh, she did? Always up to something, that one."

"Yes, sir."

Chase chuckled. He had not expected an answer from his butler but found it amusing the man agreed with his assessment. No doubt, his sister would be found spying on Miss Dawson, waiting for the governess to make one tiny blunder so she could run to Chase and report her infraction. Well, he would tell his sister tonight she had nothing to fear. Miss Dawson had obviously set her sights upon Percy. Why should he be surprised? Percy was everything that Chase was not: charming, agreeable, extremely wealthy, and romantic.

Chase studied his butler. The man had gone out three more times since the last report, always to the same tavern, always only to drink and socialize. It made no sense. What had happened to the documents? Since the night they had gone missing, Sebastian had been followed every time he had left the house.

"Is Miss Dawson in her chamber?" Chase decided to belay

the topic temporarily, hoping to set Sebastian at ease with futile conversation.

"No, sir, she is still with William upstairs." A hint of a grin lifted the old man's thin lips, and the shock of it took Chase aback.

"You smiled."

"I beg your pardon, sir?" Sebastian scuffed one shoe over the floor then brushed a speck from his breeches.

"That is the first time I have seen you smile. And 'twas at the mention of Miss Dawson."

"If I may, sir," Sebastian began, "she is quite good with William and very agreeable." He opened his mouth to add something then slammed it shut.

"Please continue." Chase found he was most interested in Sebastian's opinion of Miss Dawson. After all, the man had probably spent more time with her than Chase had. Perhaps he had some waggish tale to tell that would shed some light on her true character.

"She often speaks with the maids, the footmen, the cook, and the entire staff. She treats everyone with equal importance. Everyone in the house has grown quite fond of her, Admiral." He tugged on his waistcoat. "In addition, she gives half her wages to the beggars who come to the servants' door."

Chase jumped to his feet. "She does? You don't say." Clasping his hands behind his back, he paced. Baffling woman. Why would she do such a thing? The candle on his desk flickered in agreement, sending the sting of beeswax to his nose.

"Yes, sir. I have never seen the likes of it. She has indeed brought joy back into the house."

Chase cursed beneath his breath. Sebastian's opinion of Miss Dawson had only served to endear her more to him. Did the blasted woman ever do anything selfish or deceiving? Egad, what was she, an angel? No wonder his sister could find naught to bring against her.

Confusion curdled in his belly—confusion and terror as the realization struck him that Miss Dawson had most assuredly stolen a piece of his affections. This he could never allow. Already the agony of losing her bared its ugly teeth within him. No. No. No.

She was not right for him. Despite her admirable qualities, she was not Melody and never would be. Weakness, fear, and timidity. These were not the qualities he sought in a wife. *Wife?* What was he thinking? Besides, any woman who pursued Percy certainly did not possess the character and intellect of a lady of quality.

Sebastian cleared his throat. "Will that be all?"

Chase halted and stared at the butler, suddenly remembering why he had asked him to stay. "Speaking of joy, Sebastian." Chase skirted his desk and leaned against it. "Are you content here?"

"Sir?" Sebastian blinked.

"Are you happy in my employ, in this house?"

"I am most grateful for the position." Sebastian lowered his gaze—out of respect or guilt?

"You may speak freely, Sebastian. I truly wish to know." Even as he said it, he doubted the butler would be forthright. Why would he? Until recently, Chase had barely said anything to the man, save to order him about.

Sebastian's forehead wrinkled. "Yes, Admiral."

"Are your wages satisfactory?"

"Of course, sir," Sebastian replied then gave Chase a perplexed look. "May I ask what this is about?"

"It is about loyalty, Sebastian," Chase barked in a voice harsher than he intended. "Loyalty to the Randal home and loyalty to Britain." Frustration stormed through him. He must catch the spy in his midst—if there was one—and be done with this sordid business, or he might never get back to sea.

Sebastian's lip quivered. He snatched a handkerchief from his pocket and dabbed his forehead. "You have always had my loyalty, Admiral."

Chase nodded and crossed his arms over his chest. Clearly the butler was distraught, but for what reason? "I will not stand for betrayal, not on my ship and not in my home." Chase took a step toward him. "I would hope, Sebastian, that as my butler all these years, should you come across someone in my employ who proves to be otherwise, you would bring that person to my attention immediately."

Sebastian nodded, his gaze darting around the room.

"That will be all," Chase said, and Sebastian bowed and exited, closing the door behind him. Pouring a swig of brandy, Chase tossed it to the back of his mouth as he pondered what to make of Sebastian's reaction. Either the man was indeed the spy, and his jitters were a result of his fear of being caught, or he was simply distraught at having his master imply the accusation. Either way, time would tell. Either way, Chase would have his spy soon.

Dominique stepped into the entrance hall of the Theatre Royal Drury Lane and was instantly accosted with a thousand sights, sounds, and smells. The haut ton of London, dressed in their finest, floated across the room in a flurry of conversation and high-pitched laughter—the ladies swishing about in their silk gowns, the gentleman sauntering beside them in their fashionable tailcoats. An orchestra played in the distance. Candlelit chandeliers, hanging from a domed ceiling gilded in gold leaf, showered ethereal light over the scene. Adding their sparkling glow, lanterns hung all around them on walls papered in colorful patterns of roses and tiny cherubs.

Dominique thought of the mysterious man who had protected her through the streets of London. He'd looked nothing like the fat little baby angels decorating the walls. Had he really been an angel? Why had she begun to doubt the miracle she had believed so adamantly only a week ago? *Oh Lord, please help my weak faith to grow.*

Blasts of French perfume coupled with the reek of strong drink struck her nose as they made their way through the crowd. She gripped Mr. Atherton's arm a little tighter and took a deep breath. This was her first play. She should be beset with excitement, but despite the splendor, her insides were a jumbled knot. It had been a week since she had given her ultimatum to the Frenchman, and she had not seen him since. With the passing of each day, terror grew like a deadly disease within her, eating away her faith, her hope, and her resolve until she had begun to believe Marcel must truly be dead.

What little hope that fought to remain within her now prodded her to keep her eyes alert for the Frenchman's repugnant face. Despite her terror, she would happily tolerate the sight of him if only he would make contact and confirm their arrangement.

"Quite a splendid affair, wouldn't you say?" Percy leaned toward her and spoke above the clamor.

"Indeed, yes." She tried to smile, but everything inside her wanted to scream. Not only for Marcel, not only for her betrayal of her country and friends, but for the man whose footsteps she heard stomping behind her.

The admiral.

He had barely said two words to her all evening, even when she had been forced to endure a dinner with him and his sister. Dominique had expected Mrs. Barton not to speak to her, although the woman's frequent looks of disdain spoke volumes enough, but the admiral? Perhaps he was still angry about the sword. At least William had been present to offer her some jovial conversation.

And of course, the tension had done little to stop her voracious appetite from consuming everything on her plate and then some. She pressed a hand to her churning stomach, where it seemed those last two helpings of roast beef were beginning to protest.

Adding to this quagmire of stress, Lady Irene and her father, Lord Markham, had joined their party, making any hopes of a pleasant evening nigh impossible. Lord Markham had already spent considerable time allowing his licentious gaze to slither over Dominique as if she were next in a line of tasty treats he had reserved for himself. Lady Irene, a picture of loveliness in her shimmering jewels and flowing lace, had fawned over the admiral all evening. Dominique's only consolation was seeing the admiral's face bunch into tiny knots of annoyance at the lady's constant pufferies.

"Have you ever seen one of Cibber's plays, Miss Dawson?" Mr. Atherton asked.

"No, I am afraid not."

"I daresay you are in for a treat."

"I doubt she has seen any plays, have you, miss?" Lady Irene chirped from behind them.

"Quit being such a shrew," Mr. Atherton shot over his shoulder, giving Dominique a sly smile. Though she heard no retort, she could just imagine Lady Irene's face a red mask of fury.

"Ah, there he is. Come, my dear," Lord Markham announced. "I see Lord Wichshur, the man who asked for an introduction." He tugged his daughter's arm from the admiral's and dragged her off through the crowd toward a particularly handsome man standing off to the side, conversing with two other well-dressed gentlemen.

"I wonder what all the fuss is about." Mrs. Barton came alongside Mr. Atherton and stared after them.

"No doubt another potential amour, dear sister." The admiral accidentally brushed against Dominique—or was it an accident? A tingle warmed her arm, and she gazed up at him. His chocolate brown eyes found hers for a moment, and the adoration that glowed within them startled her.

"I know Lady Irene," Mrs. Barton huffed. "Her heart has always been completely yours, Chase. Never fear."

"*Fear* is not the term I would use." The admiral cocked a brow at his sister.

Dominique turned her face away before he could see the smile that unavoidably appeared on her lips.

"I have met the man," Mr. Atherton announced, still staring at Lady Irene and Lord Markham as they halted before their victim. "He is a duke in possession of a huge estate in Bedfordshire—a massive land holding. Worth quite a bit, from what I hear."

"You should be jealous, brother." Mrs. Barton smirked.

"Jealousy is not an emotion I feel very often." His dark gaze snapped to Dominique and lingered there again, warming her with its intensity.

"Speaking of. . ." Mr. Atherton tilted his head toward the admiral. "Perhaps you would like to escort Miss Dawson to her seat. I feel the need for some liquid refreshment."

"Speaking of what, Percy?" The admiral snorted as Mr. Atherton took Dominique's gloved hand from his arm and placed it onto the admiral's.

"I beg your pardon?" Mr. Atherton leaned an ear toward the

admiral. "You really should speak up, Randal. I cannot hear you over the clamor. Nevertheless"—he waved a hand through the air—"if you will excuse me."

Before the admiral could protest, Mr. Atherton scurried away.

"Very well, then, ladies, shall we?" The admiral offered his other arm to his sister.

Without looking at Dominique or saying another word, he led her and his sister up a curved staircase and down a hallway, nodding at acquaintances along the way. Then, brushing aside a set of heavy velvet curtains, he ushered them into a first-level seating box, as yet devoid of any patrons.

Dominique smiled at him as he escorted her to a chair toward the front, but he did not return her regard, and she found herself hungering for another glance from those deep brown eyes. She quickly chastised herself for the desire.

Instead of sitting, the admiral moved to the wooden railing and gazed down upon the milling crowd below. A large, curtained stage spanned the end of the massive room toward Dominique's right, and across the way, four long rows of seating boxes stacked one upon the other reached all the way to the arched ceilings above. People began filling them, some taking their seats while others hung over the edge, waving at acquaintances below. Dominique carefully scanned the crowd for any sign of the Frenchman.

"I wonder where Lady Irene and Lord Markham are," Mrs. Barton said to no one in particular just as Mr. Atherton stumbled in, drink in hand. He winked at the admiral and took a seat beside Dominique, then ran a hand through the stylish tawny curls at his collar. The admiral's gaze scoured over them before he stomped out of the box.

"Now where is he off to?" Mrs. Barton said.

Dominique cringed at the look of pain she'd seen on the admiral's face. Was she the cause? Was it Mr. Atherton's silly game? No, she did not wish to believe that, for then she would have to admit the admiral was indeed jealous, and if he was jealous, that meant he must harbor some affection for her. Dominique threw a hand to her chest. Why did her heart leap at the thought? Perhaps she should ease his pain by disclosing the true nature of Mr. Atherton's flirtation. But no, if she did, and the admiral did care for her, then he would be free to pursue her, and she could not allow that to happen—she could not allow it because deep down she feared she would not be able to resist him. Besides, how could she entangle herself with a man she intended to betray? It would only cause both of them pain and end in disaster. And the admiral had suffered enough in his life. Dominique would not be the cause of more pain than she was forced to inflict upon him by her deception.

As soon as she exchanged the documents for Marcel, she and her brother must leave London and start a life somewhere else—far away from the admiral and far away from William. Just the thought of it made her heart shrivel, but she had no choice.

The curtains parted, admitting Lady Irene and Lord Markham. Dropping into her chair, Lady Irene let out a dreamy sigh and smiled as she withdrew her fan and waved it over her flushed face.

"Whatever is the matter, dear?" Mrs. Barton leaned over the seat between them and placed a hand on her arm.

"Why, nothing is the matter. Nothing save I have just been introduced to the handsomest, wealthiest, and most eligible man." Her blue eyes sparkled like the sea on a sunny day.

Katharine gave an unladylike snort, pursed her lips, and snapped her hand back. "What is he to you? What of my brother?"

"He is trying to arrange it so he can sit with us. Is that not marvelous?" Lady Irene replied as if she had not heard Mrs. Barton at all.

"Yes, marvelous." Mrs. Barton withdrew a handkerchief from her reticule and dabbed at her neck.

That Lady Irene had switched her affections so easily did not surprise Dominique nearly so much as it seemed to shock Mrs. Barton. Perhaps now the two of them would cease their conniving matchmaking and their continual assaults on Dominique's character.

With a grunt, Lord Markham squeezed past Mrs. Barton and slid into the chair on the other side of Dominique. She faced forward, her heart dropping into her stomach, only further agitating the moiling caldron within. She had hoped the admiral would sit beside her, for no other reason than that she always felt safe by his side—and tonight she needed to feel safe. Lord Markham, however, had the opposite effect. He brushed his leg against her skirts, sending an icy chill over her. "You are truly a bright rose among many weeds, Miss Dawson."

She smiled, nearly choking on the bile rising in her throat, and turned to Mr. Atherton for protection, but the young member of Parliament was absorbed in a flirtatious exchange with a lady in the seats below them.

Finally, she heard the familiar thud of the admiral's boots and sighed. The scent of spice and brandy wafted over her shoulder as he sank into the chair behind her. Though she could feel Lord Markham's gaze snaking over her, Dominique forced herself not to look at him, not wanting to acknowledge his interest, not wanting to give him the slightest excuse to continue his crude dalliance.

As if knowing she needed some comfort, the admiral leaned toward her from behind. She knew it because she sensed his strong presence long before he spoke. "You look quite lovely tonight, Miss Dawson." His warm breath caressed her neck and sent delightful ripples down her back.

Dominique turned her head slightly to respond, shocked by his compliment, but he had already retreated. Was it the brandy that spoke for him? Why would he say such a thing when he had ignored her most of he night?

One by one, the lamps were blown out, and the theater began to dim. As the orchestra started a new concerto, people scrambled to their seats, and the chattering ceased. Dominique settled into her chair, grateful that at least for the duration of the play, she could escape from these maddening people around her and from the maddening feelings within her and even from the maddening task before her.

But no sooner had that comforting thought begun to soothe her mind and the first actor appeared onstage, than out of the corner of her eye, she saw a man slink in through the curtains and take a seat in the left corner. She felt the man's gaze upon her and turned briefly to see who it was.

Even in the shadows, she recognized the slick mustache and the sordid smirk beneath it.

CHAPTER 18

Dominique's heart ceased beating. She crumpled in her seat, gasping for air.

"Are you quite all right, my love?" Mr. Atherton asked.

Dominique nodded and brought herself upright. "Please forgive me." She tried to smile and shook out her fan, holding it over her trembling lips. Another glance to her left told her that she had not seen an apparition. The Frenchman sat no more than two yards from her, grinning like a leopard, a spotted leopard about to pounce on his prey.

Another actor emerged onto the stage, his blaring voice echoing through the massive theater, but by the time his soliloquy reached Dominique, it fell muffled beneath the mad rush of blood through her ears.

The contact's presence must surely mean that Marcel still lived! A wave of hope suddenly poured over her heart, becalming the frenzied beating.

Something humorous occurred onstage, and Lady Irene's and Mrs. Barton's laughter blasted over Dominique from behind to join Mr. Atherton's beside her.

She glanced over her shoulder at the man whose piercing eyes were still upon her. He jerked his head back toward the curtains twice and then nodded, a threat etched across his harsh gaze.

How would she be able to speak to him alone? She doubted she could leave the box without an escort and, even more so, doubted she could slip away unnoticed. She shook her head and turned back around. But when she glanced back to somehow relay this information to him, he was already gone.

Horrified, she turned forward. Her fan slid from her sweaty grip and landed on Lord Markham's lap. Without thinking, she grabbed it, accidentally brushing her fingers over his breeches. Instantly she felt his slimy gaze snap in her direction. She did not have time to deal with the lecherous man. Leaning toward Mr. Atherton, she tapped his arm. "Please excuse me. I shall return shortly," she whispered.

Tearing his eyes from the play, he examined her quizzically. "Where are you going?"

With a shake of her head, she slowly rose.

"I shall accompany you," Mr. Atherton huffed as he scooted to the edge of his seat.

"Non," she responded a bit too loudly. All eyes shifted to her. "That will not be necessary. Thank you. Enjoy the play. I shall return presently."

Atherton nodded with a look of apprehension, but fortunately he slouched back into his chair, no doubt believing she needed to relieve herself. Without gazing at the admiral, Dominique barreled through the curtains and out into the hallway.

The Frenchman was nowhere in sight.

Taking a few steps, she clasped her hands together and glanced about wildly. Where had he gone?

Tiny needles of fear pricked her skin. Why would he simply disappear without speaking to her? What sort of heinous game was he playing? Gathering her skirts, she darted to the top of the stairs and peered down into the front entrance where several patrons meandered about in flirtatious conversations. A quick scan of the crowd revealed the Frenchman was not among them.

The hope that had risen at possibly hearing news of Marcel dwindled. With a heavy sigh, she began trudging back to the box seat when, out of the corner of her eye, she saw the Frenchman gesturing to her from deep in the hallway. No sooner had she started to follow him than he turned and trotted away. Even though only a few people ambled about, Dominique had a hard time keeping up with him as she wove between them. Finally, he halted, looked both ways, and slipped behind thick curtains to his right.

Halting before the maroon draperies, Dominique held her breath. *Oh Lord, help me and give me courage.* She wrung her hands together, trying to calm her raucous heart. Brushing aside the velvet hangings, she slid though the opening.

A rough hand seized her by the throat.

The Frenchman tossed her into one of the chairs in the back of the empty chamber and released her. Choking, Dominique rubbed her neck where his thick fingers had threatened to squeeze the life from her and stared up at the stocky man. With a snicker, he adjusted his satin-trimmed, ruby red coat and flexed his hands before him as if he were readying them to attack her again. Dominique sped her gaze across the small room, looking for a possible escape route. It appeared to be some sort of anteroom that led to a much larger chamber stuffed with stage supplies. Lantern light from the larger room flickered through the open door, making the Frenchman appear even more sinister in half shadows.

"What of Marcel?" Dominique found her voice, though it sounded as though a jagged rope were stuck in her throat.

"*Il vit.*" The man spat on the floor. "He is alive, for now, although your *tromperie* cost him a few days *sans* food or water." He snorted. "I tell you I would not want to be locked in His Excellency's prison." His lips twisted in an evil grin. "A most horrid place."

Dominique swallowed but found that her throat had gone completely dry. Visions of Marcel's emaciated body clinging to life amidst rats and filth in some French cell caused the remainder of her dinner to heave into her throat. Somehow she kept from spewing it upon the Frenchman, though the idea was not without some appeal.

"His Excellency was most displeased with your bold demand." He flung his loose, greasy hair behind him and gave her a look of complacent superiority. "I tell you he was quite overcome with fury and thought to have the boy's throat slit *immédiatement.*"

Dominique gripped the sides of the chair until her fingers

ached. "Obviously," she began, speaking slowly so as not to reveal the tremor in her voice, "he has decided against that course." A flicker of victory sparked within her at the way the Frenchman's upper lip curled. She knew Lucien wanted the documents more than he wanted Marcel dead. Her gamble had paid off. *Thank You, Lord.*

"Oui, pour le moment." He raised his hand and stared at his fingernails. "We will meet you at one o'clock in the morning, Tuesday next. Same place."

"And you will bring Marcel?"

He nodded.

"Alive?"

"Naturellement. What do you think we are, *les barbares?"* He gave her an incredulous look then gripped the chair arms on each side of her and shoved his face into hers.

"And *you* will bring all the information we require."

"As I have said." Dominique pressed against the back of the chair and turned away from the man's foul breath.

"Très bien." He released the chair with a snap. "There is one more thing."

Dominique tensed.

"The documents must contain enough valuable information to be worth the purchase of your brother's life."

Sacre bleu. Dominique shook her head and gave the man a gaping stare. What more could they require of a simple girl? A sudden fear gripped her—fear that they could hold Marcel's life over her indefinitely, feigning dissatisfaction with whatever she brought them, a fear that this nightmare would never end. But what choice did she have? If she could at least get Marcel upon British soil, then perhaps they could escape somehow, some way. "I tell you I have retrieved all I can from the admiral's study."

"You'd better hope so, mademoiselle." He eased a finger over his mustache.

"After you peruse their contents, you will let us go?"

"Oui, but of course."

"May I have your word on that?"

"You have my word as a Frenchman." He lengthened his stance and stood regally, looking off into the distance as if posing for a painting.

She didn't think it would matter if she told him that the word of a Frenchman meant nothing to her.

"*Maintenant, allons, allons.*" He grabbed her arm and jerked her to her feet. A spike of pain shot through her shoulder. He gestured toward the curtains. "Return before your people grow suspicious." Even as he said it, Dominique heard her name filtering through the hallway.

The Frenchman slunk into the shadows against the far wall.

"Miss Dawson. Miss Dawson."

The voice was neither Mr. Atherton's nor the admiral's, and the sound of it sent the hairs on the back of her neck springing to attention. She mustn't let Lord Markham or anyone else see her with the Frenchman. She dashed across the antechamber toward the supply room in the back. Her foot struck the hard leg of a chair. It crashed to the floor with a loud thud as a sharp pain rose up her leg.

"Oh, there you are, Miss Dawson."

Dominique slowly lifted her gaze as Lord Markham parted the curtains and entered the room. The reek of alcohol saturated the air.

She shifted her eyes to where the Frenchman had stood, but only the fluttering of curtains evidenced his passing.

Dominique gazed back at Lord Markham, and the look in his eye turned her blood to ice. "How did you find me?"

"Find you? Why, 'twas quite obvious that you wished me to join in your little game of cat and mouse." He staggered and grabbed the back of a chair.

"I beg your pardon." Terror gripped Dominique. "I have no idea what you are talking about."

"Come now, Miss Dawson, let us not play innocent." He licked his fingers and dabbed at the silver-streaked hair on each side of his face. "I've seen the way you look at me, the way your hands grazed my leg when we were in the seating box."

"That was an accident, I assure you." Dominique inched around the fallen chair, hoping to make her way to the other side of the room where there was a clear path to the curtains. "And I look at you no differently than any other man."

"Oh, brava, brava." He clapped. "Your acting is superb. Perhaps you should be onstage, my sweet, rather than those atrocious actors. Nevertheless"—he sauntered toward her—"I find I am up to the challenge."

One glance over her shoulder told Dominique it would be best to avoid the storage chamber, where she would no doubt be trapped. The only way out was behind Lord Markham's massive swaying body. Since his faculties were not presently at their sharpest, she might be able to catch him off guard and dash past him.

As if he read her thoughts, a wicked grin writhed upon his lips. "Splendid. You are going to make this interesting, are you? I do so love games. What roles should we play? The conquering war hero and the captive slave girl? The wealthy lord of the manor and the innocent but seductive chambermaid?" A devilish twinkle flickered across his glazed eyes.

Dominique swallowed and pressed a hand to her roiling stomach. "How about the noble gentleman and the lady who leaves this antechamber untouched?"

"Hmm." Lord Markham scratched his chin. "I daresay that doesn't sound like much fun."

Continuing to edge toward the other side of the room, Dominique kept her anxious gaze upon Lord Markham. Surely this noble gentleman—this earl—would not force himself on a lady. Once he realized her disinterest, he would no doubt stand down. "Lord Markham, I apologize if I have given you the wrong impression, but I assure you, sir, I have no interest in a liaison with you."

A slight grin parted his lips but fell away as his brow wrinkled. A hue as dark as the maroon curtains behind him splattered over his swollen cheeks. "Impossible. Do you know who I am? Do you realize what I am worth, what I could do to improve your station?"

"I find I am quite happy with my present station, milord."

"Who are you but a mere servant, a flighty tart, to speak to me so?" He huffed. "I am not a man to be trifled with, Miss Dawson. You cannot flirt with a man of my position then lure him into a private place, only to leave him cold. It is simply not done!"

"Lord Markham, I—"

"What is this I see around me?" He waved his arms about the room, the lace fluttering at the cuffs of his sleeves. "You fondled my leg, you placed your fan over your lips in that seductive way that said you longed for a kiss, and then you left the box seat. Now I find you all alone waiting for me in this anteroom. You cannot deny it."

Dominique had forgotten about the fan and its many different uses as a coquettish tool. "I know what it must look like, milord, but it is not—"

"No more talk. I will not be denied."

Dominique gulped. From the look in his eyes, she knew he meant what he said. *Lord, help me.* She glanced across the room, praying that her angel would appear once again to save her. But the tall, dark man was nowhere to be seen.

Lord Markham stormed toward her. She bolted for the curtains, scrambling around a chair. Almost there. Almost there. She heard him grunting behind her. She reached for the curtains. One more inch.

Strong arms grabbed her waist and hoisted her off the ground.

Terror stole her breath. Visions of the man in Paris coming at her in the shadows blasted through her mind. At the time, she had believed she would lose her purity in a dark, filthy alleyway in Paris. Now, though her surroundings were better, the result would be the same. No Marcel to come to the rescue this time. No angel. No one knew she was here.

She pounded Lord Markham's chest. Gathering what little breath she could gasp, she screamed with all her might. His hand slammed down upon her mouth. Pain shot to the back of her throat as the scent of brandy stung her nose. He dragged her into the supply room, closed the door behind them, and shoved her to the floor.

She screamed.

Lord Markham gave a low, satisfied chuckle. "No one will hear you in here, Miss Dawson."

CHAPTER 19

Chase shifted in his seat, trying to concentrate on the actors flitting across the stage below him but finding it impossible. Where in the blazes had Miss Dawson gone? She'd seemed quite flustered when she left, her face blanched, her hands trembling as if she had seen a ghost. Perhaps she wasn't feeling well. No doubt her stomach was agitated from all that food she had consumed at dinner. He found himself smiling at the memory then quickly replaced the expression with a frown. He should not be thinking of her at all. She had made her choice.

And that choice sat in front of Chase at the moment, uttering a guttural chuckle at something onstage. Why, Percy didn't seem the least bit concerned about Miss Dawson's absence. What sort of gentleman was he?

Speaking of escorts, Lady Irene's chair sat conspicuously absent beside Chase. But he was not so fortunate as to have her leave the room entirely. He could hear her and her new beau, Lord Wichshur—who had entered shortly after Miss Dawson had left—blathering away in the corner. The odd thing was it delighted him rather than bothered him. His only regret was the obvious letdown to his poor sister, who had given up firing looks of reproach at the new couple and now sat moping in her chair to his right. He had never seen her quite so distraught.

Chase's gaze landed on the empty seat in front of her. The true source of his apprehension was that Lord Markham had gone missing, as well. Although he had left several minutes after Miss Dawson, the thought of him running into her alone in the hallways sent Chase's blood boiling.

Yes, something was amiss.

Chase stood, nodded toward his sister, then placed a finger to his lips to stifle her impending protest. She snapped her mouth shut and faced forward with a huff. Slipping through the curtains, he halted and scanned the hallway, where only a few patrons milled about. A woman's scream, loud at first, then muffled, rang through the gallery like an alarm. The hairs on his arms bristled. A couple across the way froze at the sound but then proceeded with their merrymaking as if they had not heard a thing.

Chase stormed down the hallway, gripping the hilt of his service sword, hoping the screech had not come from Miss Dawson but somehow knowing deep down that it had.

He strained his ears for another cry, any unusual sound that would give him direction. Anger and fear drove him forward in a frenzied search as he scanned every inch of the passageway. *God, if You are there, please help me find her.* He surprised himself by the prayer. The last time he had prayed, it was for Melody to live. When naught but a smug silence had yawned at him from heaven, he had stopped praying altogether.

A door slammed. Chase halted before a small, curtained room on his right. He tore through the heavy drapes and marched into a dark anteroom. Empty. Save for one overturned chair, all seemed in order. He turned to leave. A slight scraping sound scratched his ears. His gaze sped to a door at the back of the chamber. It opened to his touch, and he barreled into the room.

Boxes, stage props, and costumes swept past his vision in a blur of flickering lantern light. A screech, a groan, and a sudden movement caught the corner of his eye, and he swerved to the left.

Lord Markham angled his body toward the wall in a dark corner of the room—at least it appeared to be Lord Markham. He wore the same ostentatious tailcoat as his lordship had been wearing earlier that evening. Chase squinted into the shadows. Markham shoved something against the wall. . .no, not something, someone. Blue silk and white lace fluttered behind him. The woman struggled as Markham flattened his body upon hers, whispering obscenities that putrefied in Chase's ears. Was this another of his lordship's many *affaires d'amour*? No. The woman gasped and moaned as if her mouth were covered. Chase recognized the delicate timbre of her voice.

Dominique!

Fury blasted like cannon fire through Chase—fury such as he had never felt before. He bolted toward them, grabbed the back of Lord Markham's coat with both hands, and tossed him like a rag to a pile of boxes nearby. Lord Markham, arms and legs flailing, crashed into the crates, crushing two of them and spilling their contents onto the wooden floor.

Chase turned to Miss Dawson. Tears streamed down her flushed cheeks from eyes that screamed with terror. The front part of her gown had been torn away. She trembled like a leaf in a storm. He touched her arm, longing to comfort her, but a thump behind him alerted him that Lord Markham had recovered.

"What is the meaning of this, Randal? How dare you interrupt?" The inebriated man struggled to his feet and wiped the dirt from his coat.

Chase clamped his jaw. "How dare *I*? You assault an innocent woman as if she were a common harlot, and you question me?"

"Scads, man." Lord Markham gritted his teeth. "I assure you, she was quite willing. We were but playing a game, weren't we, my dear?" He raised a salacious brow and stepped toward Miss Dawson, but Chase moved between them and crossed his arms over his chest.

"By the look on her face," he hissed, "she does not appear to be a willing participant in this *game* of yours, Markham."

Lord Markham's upper lip extended as he peered down his nose at Chase. "You will address me as *Lord*, if you please."

"I will do so when you begin to act like one."

"What the devil do you mean, sir? How dare you impugn my character?" He adjusted his cravat and wobbled on his feet. Composing himself, he continued, saying, "You who have no title to lay claim to. Why, you are naught but a miserable aging admiral pining away for his dead wife."

Chase felt blood surging to his fists. How he longed to bash that pretentious smirk off Lord Markham's face. He took a step toward him.

Lord Markham flinched then threw back his shoulders. "Mark my words: I'll not be giving my daughter away to the likes of you."

"Yet I do not remember asking for her hand." Chase thought to tell his lordship that he would not marry Lady Irene if she were the last woman in London, but he had no desire to malign her—'twas her father he took issue with.

Lord Markham's sordid gaze weaved around Chase and landed on Miss Dawson. "Do you think to have this lady's hand, then? I would be quick to tame her if I were you, before she has a go with every young stallion in town. Why, she practically begged me to meet her down here."

Chase would stand no more of this man's slanderous impertinence. He slammed his fist against Lord Markham's jaw.

Miss Dawson gasped.

Markham's face snapped sideways, and he reeled backward, trying to catch his balance before he once again tumbled to the floor.

"You will not ever speak of Miss Dawson in such demeaning terms," Chase roared, rubbing his burning knuckles.

Lord Markham scrambled to his feet. His face swelled into a purplish red. Fury stormed in his eyes as he rubbed his cheek. "You will pay for that, Randal."

"Another time, perhaps." Chase grinned but kept his narrowed gaze upon the vermin. "Now be gone with you, you lecherous sot." He dismissed him with a wave and turned to Miss Dawson.

She stood frozen in place against the wall. Her lips quivered as her moist eyes rose to meet his. He heard Lord Markham's footsteps behind him, but he thought the man had enough sense to leave, to know when he was defeated—that is, until Miss Dawson's eyes widened as she glanced over his shoulder.

"Chase." His Christian name upon her lips would have sounded sweet if her tone had not been so urgent.

He flung around just in time to avoid the tip of Lord Markham's sword thrust in his back. Dodging to the left, Chase plucked his blade from his scabbard and leveled it upon his enemy. "You do not want to do this, milord."

"And why not?" Lord Markham huffed. "Because I should fear the skill of the great Admiral Randal?" He twirled the tip of his blade tauntingly before Chase. "I fear you will discover I have acquired my own exquisite skill."

"Though the thought causes me to tremble, milord, you are in no condition to fight. It is my wish neither to hurt nor humiliate you further."

Lord Markham snorted. "Never fear. I will not suffer you to do either." He lunged forward, but Chase sidestepped the attack with ease and pummeled Lord Markham on his back with the hilt of his sword. Markham groaned and stumbled forward before swerving around. He held his blade high and charged toward Chase, growling like a rabid dog.

Chase met the man's sword with his own and their blades clanged together, sending an eerie chime through the room. His lordship advanced again, his face a knot of twisted rage, but Chase met each parry with one of his own. With a snap of his blade, he forced Lord Markham's sword aside. "Enough of this, man."

Lord Markham hesitated. Beads of sweat dotted his forehead, and his breath heaved, but he shook his head and lunged once again toward Chase.

Chase tilted his sword down in defense and then swung it back up, snagging it hilt to hilt with Lord Markham's. Grunting, he forced his lordship back then shoved him, releasing the locked hilts. Markham swore under his breath, staggered, then composed himself and crept forward, his eyes ablaze with cruel revenge.

Chase waited impatiently for his next charge. Enough of this defensive frittering. He should attack Markham and be done with it. Yet despite the man's assault on Miss Dawson, despite the fact that he was an insidious rogue, Lord Markham was an old family friend, and Chase had little desire to actually harm him.

Markham drove his blade toward Chase. With a huff of frustration, Chase hopped aside and, before his lordship could pivot for another blow, jabbed the tip of his sword into Markham's arm, not deep enough to cause any real damage, but deep enough to inflict pain.

With a screech, Lord Markham dropped his sword and threw a hand to the wound. The blade clanked to the ground as the stinging odor of blood permeated the air. He peered beneath his hand with horror then snapped his gaze to Chase, his nostrils flaring. He eyed his blade, not two feet from where he stood, as if he considered snagging it up again to resume the fight.

Chase planted his boot firmly upon Lord Markham's sword and wiped the tip of his own on a costume that had spilled from one of the crates. "Now will you leave?" He sighed.

"You have not heard the end of this, Randal." Pressing a hand over the gash on his arm, Lord Markham raised his chin as Chase retrieved the belligerent man's sword and extended it, hilt forward.

Grabbing it, Lord Markham shot a look of repugnance at Dominique before plowing out of the room.

Easing his sword back into his scabbard, Chase shrugged off his coat and tossed it aside, then ran an arm over the sweat on his brow. He faced Miss Dawson. Her gaze locked upon his, a whirlwind of fear, gratitude, and hope brimming in her misty amber eyes. She took a shaky step toward him.

He must resist her. He must resist the tug she had on his heart. For his own survival, he must resist her.

He couldn't resist her.

He reached out and drew her into his arms.

She fell against him, the warmth of her body merging with his. In that instant, something hard inside of him melted into a soothing balm that flowed through him, enveloping all his wounds. He released a long-imprisoned sigh and caressed her hair as she laid her head on his shoulder and began to sob. Wrapping his other arm around her, he embraced her, giving in to his need to comfort her, to protect her.

And at that moment, he knew.

He knew that he loved her.

Dominique folded herself into the admiral's strength. His heart beat strong and quick against her cheek as she lay upon the fast rise and fall of his chest. Spice and tobacco tickled her nose. She drank in the scent like medicine and sank into him, releasing all the fears, all the tensions, all the nightmares of the past month. Savoring his strength and protection, she allowed her tears to flow unabashedly.

She had thought all was lost. Though she had struggled against Lord Markham with all her strength, he was far too powerful. When he had forced her against the wall, his brandy-drenched breath spewing over her in a poisonous cloud, his hands groping in places no man had ever touched, she had resigned herself to her fate. Raw terror had begun to numb her senses to protect her from what was surely to come. Then she had heard the door open, and in walked the admiral.

The look on his face, the absolute fury of it, resurged in her mind. He had come for her. He had been concerned enough to seek her. But how had he found her? It did not matter. He was here. He had saved her virtue. And as she nestled against him, she thought of no place she would rather be. "Thank you, Admiral," she whispered into his black waistcoat.

Grabbing her shoulders, he pushed her back from him and peered down at her, concern flickering in his eyes. "Did he hurt you?"

Dominique shook her head and looked down, suddenly ashamed of the whole incident. Grabbing her torn gown, she held the severed pieces together over her exposed undergarments.

"I believe I have already seen your petticoats." Chase's chuckle settled over her like a warm blanket. He brushed a lock of her hair from her cheek and caressed her skin with his thumb.

Heat flushed over Dominique. Her heart jumped. She gazed up at him, overcome by the intense emotion she saw in his eyes. He had lowered his shield once again. Behind it waited a man of great strength, as well as great kindness.

His gaze shifted to her lips, and she remembered their kiss, the warmth of his mouth on hers, the feel of his breath on her cheek, his stubbled jaw rubbing against hers, and the new sensations that had burned within her. Confusion twisted around her heart. Her breath quickened. What was she doing? God help her, she wanted the admiral to kiss her again. She wanted to feel his arms around her. She wanted to spend time with him, to get to know him, to fill that empty place within him.

But she couldn't.

She could never allow herself to love this man. She could never allow him to express the tenderness now burning in his gaze—a tenderness that made her weak in the knees and frightened her at the same time. For in a week she would betray him.

Dropping her gaze, she took a step back. "We should go."

"Indeed. You have been through quite a bit this evening." He grabbed his topcoat and threw it over her shoulders, buttoning it down the front. "This should cover your gown until we can pass through the crowds."

Dominique swallowed a burst of emotion. The kindness of his protective gesture made what she had to do much more difficult.

He extended his arm and gave her a roguish grin that melted her heart. "Never fear, milady. I shall have you safe and sound at home in no time."

"Admiral—" Dominique hesitated, feeling suddenly nauseated. She glanced up at Chase and forced out the rest of her sentence, each word stabbing her heart as it passed through her lips. "If you don't mind, I would prefer Mr. Atherton escort me home."

CHAPTER 20

Dominique dropped the spade into the black soil and began hacking away at the clumps of hardened dirt. The scent of fresh earth wafted over her, coupled with the fragrance of sweet roses from a large bush lodged in the corner of the tiny yard. Cracked pots filled with withered plants lined the gravel pathway, and a weed-infested flower bed spread out toward the kitchen door as if begging for help. Dominique sighed and brushed her hair from her face. The tiny clearing at the back of the house was yet one more part of the Randal home that had suffered in Melody's absence.

"You really do not have to do this, miss." Larena sat on a carved stone bench pressed against the back wall, holding small pouches of herb seeds on her lap. " 'Tis the scullery maid's job."

A horse neighed from over the brick wall that barricaded them from the stables and carriage houses beyond.

"I know 'tis not proper, Larena, but I want to teach William how to plant seeds and inform him of the importance of herbs." Dominique stopped to catch her breath, realizing she had not worked outdoors in quite a while—not since she had helped her mother tend to their garden in Portsmouth.

"When do I get to help you, Miss Dawson?" William's bright blue eyes sped to hers as he crouched beside the square patch of dirt.

Dominique gazed at the sundial littered with leaves, then up at the sun, now nearly halfway across the sky, and wondered why on the one day she had decided to work outside, the ever-present veil of fog had gone on holiday. Wiping the perspiration off her forehead with her sleeve, she resumed her task.

"You see, William, the soil must first be prepared by loosening and sifting it before we plant the seeds. That is what you are going to do." She gave him a look of proud excitement. "The most important part."

William grinned, his chubby cheeks dimpling as he inched closer to the raised garden.

"Do not fall in the mud, William," Larena warned, "or Mrs. Hensworth will turn me into a goose for dinner."

"A goose?" William giggled, and Dominique could not help but smile.

She had decided to teach William as much as she could about life, literature, music, and the love of God before she left him—as much as any six-year-old could absorb, that is.

Left him.

Sorrow burned in her throat. She glanced down at the boy as he dipped a finger in the dirt a few feet away and examined the globs that clung to his skin, then looked up at her with that mischievous grin that reminded her so much of his father. She knew without a doubt that she would leave a large part of her heart behind with William.

And with the admiral.

Chop. Chop. Chop. She slashed at the soil, wishing with each forceful blow that she was slicing into herself. For two days she had wallowed in self-loathing over what she had been forced to say to the admiral that night at the Drury. After Mr. Atherton had escorted her home, she had collapsed into bed and wept until morning, wept not just for the frightening meeting with the Frenchman, not just for Lord Markham's terrifying assault—the thought of which still sent her trembling—but for the look on the admiral's face when she had told him she preferred Mr. Atherton to accompany her home.

She could not dispel the vision from her mind. His smile had instantly fled from his lips, his strong cheeks had sunk inward, and his jaw had hardened into a tight mass of twitching muscles. For a second, she thought she saw pain burn within his eyes before he erected the familiar cold shield and agreed to her request without a trace of emotion in his voice.

At that moment, her heart had crumbled into a million pieces, and she was not sure it would ever come back together again.

She had remained in bed the entire next day, excusing herself with complaints of a headache, but truth be told, she had hoped to avoid an encounter with the admiral. Now that it was Monday, she could rest assured that he would be gone most of the day at the Admiralty—and for the remainder of the week, for that matter. Only the evenings would present some difficulty, but Dominique felt confident she could find enough reasons to excuse herself from attending dinner and keep to her room as much as possible. Surely the admiral would not protest after she had spurned his affections so vehemently.

It was not just for him that she hoped to avoid any contact. Truthfully, she did not think she could handle gazing into those brown eyes, not only because of the pain she had caused that might still be lingering there, but because she did not think she would be able to resist him if he opened himself up to her again. She could no longer deny that her affections for the admiral had blossomed and were nigh to a point where they began to smother her reason. And her reason must remain intact—for Marcel's sake.

In less than a week, she would see her brother again, and they could begin their life anew. In the meantime, she must avoid the admiral at all costs, for if fear of her predicament did not kill her, if shame at her betrayal did not, then surely her broken heart would.

She slashed the soil again and again. *Father, why have You put me here—to break everyone's heart, including my own? Why am I so weak, so useless?*

"I believe you have killed it, Miss Dawson." Larena snickered behind her.

Dominique shook the morbid thoughts from her head and stared down at the mutilated soil. "Well, yes. Indeed. It does appear so."

William chuckled. "Is it my turn now?"

"Absolutely." Dominique smiled.

The boy gazed up at her, but his eyes suddenly shifted above her head and brightened. " 'Tis Father!" He waved his plump little hand with exuberance.

Dominique dared to glance over her shoulder. Up above them, behind the french doors of the morning room, stood the admiral, looking quite dashing in his blue navy coat. He did not wave, nor did he smile. Dominique's heart lurched in her chest nonetheless.

She darted her gaze forward. What was he doing home? Warmth flamed up her neck and onto her face, both at his intense perusal and at the memory of being in his arms the last time she had seen him.

"Why, miss. You don't look well." Larena giggled. " 'Tis some grand effect the man has on you, I would say."

"Sacre bleu, Larena. 'Tis the heat is all."

William's gaze shifted between Larena and Dominique. "Do you like my father, Miss Dawson?"

Dominique froze, unsure of how to answer the young boy's bold question, then decided on the truth. "Of course I do, William. I like him very much."

Chase took a puff of his cheroot and exhaled the sweet, pungent smoke in a cloud that obscured his view. He waved it aside, not wanting to lose for a moment the vision of Miss Dawson and his son below.

"What are you staring at?" Katharine lifted her skirts and stormed to the window.

"Of all the. . .Mercy me, will you look at her? Why, she is a filthy mess. Upon my word, that is no way for a lady to behave. Do not say I did not warn you, Chase."

"Personally, I find it quite charming. A woman unafraid to get her hands dirty. Very refreshing, indeed."

"You cannot be serious." Katharine snorted. "Not after all that she has done."

"Do remind me, sister—just what, pray tell, has she done?" Chase cocked a brow in her direction but quickly returned his gaze to the garden below. He watched as Miss Dawson knelt on the stone pathway and took William's hand in hers, then gently helped him poke a hole in the dirt and drop a seed therein. The boy's wide smile and beaming admiration as he looked at Miss Dawson sent a flurry of emotions through Chase: adoration, appreciation, and a deeply embedded pain. He rubbed his heart as if he could ease away his agony, but to no avail. He had a feeling the pain of her rejection would never subside and would indeed linger within his chest year after year right alongside the pain of Melody's death. He turned toward his sister. "I have not seen a shred of your supposed evidence against Miss Dawson."

Katharine pursed her lips and swished across the room. "I assure you my man did see her enter that tavern late one night, Chase. That alone should suffice to prove she cannot be trusted. And there is another deception I have discovered. This whole affaire d'amour with Mr. Atherton was a ruse to make you jealous."

Chase froze. He snuffed out his cigar on a tray and faced her. "Indeed?" Nigh impossible. If she had no affections toward Percy, then why had she insisted on his accompaniment home the other night? Especially when it had been Chase who had swooped in to her rescue, when it had been in Chase's arms she had sought comfort and protection, and especially when he had been sure, at least for the briefest of moments, that she returned the affections that burned so ardently within him.

Egad, he had been about to declare his love for her when she opened her lips and spoke only of Percy. What a fool he had been. He had vowed that night never to open his heart to another, yet here he stood, watching the cause of his suffering from the window of his own house like a lovesick puppy.

"However did you discover this mad plot?" He shielded the emotion from his eyes—a skill he had become quite proficient at—and tried to sound nonchalant.

"I questioned Mr. Atherton on the night of the play. The silly fop could never keep a secret, especially not after a few glasses of brandy." Katharine gave Chase a sweet smile and alighted upon the arch-backed sofa like an angel. *More like a wolf in angel's clothing.*

Chase longed to believe it had been Miss Dawson's idea to make him jealous, but he knew better. She was far too honorable and innocent to concoct such a scheme. And for what reason? "Then it was Percy's idea?"

Katharine patted her cinnamon hair and straightened her back. "I suppose, yes, but that does not excuse her involvement in the deception. Of course, you know she means to trap you into marriage."

Chase chuckled. Of that he could be sure his sister was grossly mistaken. "Odd. Yet she spurns my every advance."

Katharine's fiery gaze snapped to Chase as if he had slapped her cheek. "Advance? Please do not tell me you are interested in that French charlatan." Her eyes widened, and she shot to the edge of her seat. "Did you say she spurns you? How dare she slight such a worthy prospect as yourself? I cannot believe it!"

Chase laughed. "I know not whether I am to be outraged at my intentions or at her disregard of them. Besides, where I place my affections is none of your business, dear sister."

"Affect—oh my." Katharine stood and laid the back of her hand over her forehead as if she were coming down with a fever. "It is my business when I see you making a monumental mistake. Would that someone had warned me about Lord Barton before I had agreed to marry him."

"Would you have listened?" Chase rubbed his chin as he remembered expressing some reservations about the engagement to a very stubborn and lovesick sister.

Katharine looked down and fingered the vinaigrette hanging about her neck as if she needed to open it and breathe the sweet contents to keep from fainting. She lifted her gaze, her pink lips curving slightly. "But you have much better sense than I do, Chase. You always have."

"Then there is no need to concern yourself, is there? Come now." Chase touched her arm and gestured for her to sit while he took a seat beside her. "Do not overset yourself. It matters not what my intentions are toward Miss Dawson. I assure you she does not return them." He winced as the verbal declaration pained him once again like a knife in an open wound.

Katharine's brown eyes studied him as if seeing him for the first time. "You are different, Chase. Not quite yourself."

"Really. How so?"

"More compassionate, more kind."

"So I am normally a brute?" He grinned.

"I did not mean—"

" 'Tis quite all right. I know I can be harsh at times." Frankly, he had felt like a crusty old seadog the past few years: peevish, cantankerous, and unpleasant. And he had not really cared to be anything different. What had changed him? He glanced toward the window but was too far from it to see Miss Dawson. From the minute he had met her, something had begun to soften within him—and it had never stopped. Even in light of her rejection.

Katharine touched his arm, drawing his attention back to her. "Now perhaps you will give Lady Irene another chance?"

Chase raised his brow at his sister's persistence. "Surely you are not serious? Why do you keep insisting on this match?"

"Because despite Lady Irene's faults, she will always be loyal to you." She glanced down. "And our family cannot take another scandal, another disgrace." She withdrew a handkerchief as if she were about to cry but only crumpled it in her hands. "I do not want to see you suffer as I did. You have already suffered enough." Katharine lifted her glassy eyes to Chase. "For these past three years since Melody's death, Lady Irene has waited for you, has turned down worthy suitor after worthy suitor in the hopes of securing your interest. Surely you can see she would make a trustworthy wife."

Chase took her hand in his. "Perhaps trustworthiness is not the only quality I desire." He shrugged. "Besides, after what I saw at the Drury Lane and have heard about town since, Lady Irene and Lord Wichshur have formed quite an attachment. Is this the loyalty of which you speak?" He huffed. "I would say her loyalty extends only as far as the suitor's purse and social position."

Katharine snapped her hand from his and rose, sauntering toward the fireplace.

"It is only temporary." Her shoulders seemed to sag with her mood. "Lady Irene grew tired of your constant rejections. She is hurt; that is all. I am quite sure she is just trying to make you jeal— to get your attention."

"By your own admission, then, am I to suppose that a scheme to make me jealous is acceptable when preformed by Lady Irene but not by Miss Dawson?"

"Oh, Chase, you know what I mean." Katharine waved a hand through the air, and Chase thought for a moment that she was crying.

"No, I cannot say that I do."

Katharine swiveled around, her eyes a stormy brew. "And what of this Lord Markham business?"

"Business? Is that what you call it?" Blood surged through Chase. How could his sister not understand the horror of what had happened? "The man assaulted Miss Dawson."

"Do you honestly believe her innocent in the matter?"

"Yes, I do." Rage began to strangle his voice, and he cleared it in an effort to calm himself. "And you may inform his lordship, should you cross his path, that he is no longer welcome at the Randal home. He is fortunate that I do not call him out to the grass before breakfast."

"A duel? Surely you do not mean that." Katharine took a step toward Chase, alarm burning in her eyes. "A duel over *that* woman?"

"She is more deserving of the honor than most." Chase took a deep breath. "Lord Markham attacked Miss Dawson, unsolicited and unprovoked. And that is the end of it."

"She has your brain in a fuddle. She could only betray you. Why can you not see it?"

Chase rubbed the burning scar on his right cheek and closed his eyes. Could Dominique betray him? He could never believe it. "If that concludes your list of her wrongdoings, I suggest you close the subject until you can provide evidence to the contrary."

When Chase opened his eyes, Sebastian's lanky frame appeared in the doorway. "Mr. Atherton to see you, Admiral."

"Show him to the drawing room. We shall be there presently." Chase clamped his jaw. He had no desire to see Percy today, but a sudden thought gripped him. "And, Sebastian?"

"Yes, sir."

"Have Miss Dawson join us, as well."

Dominique bit her lip as she made her way to the drawing room, brushing out the folds of her skirt. At first angry that the admiral had called her away from her gardening, she now felt nothing but fear crawling up her back, pinching every nerve along the way. Surely he could see she was unkempt and in no condition for socializing. Why had he insisted on interrupting her at that moment? What could he possibly want? Whatever it was, it was most assuredly not going to be pleasant. She imagined him angry and bitter and anxious to inflict some punishment on her for her slight of his affections.

She tucked a wayward curl behind her ear and hoped she appeared somewhat presentable. Larena had assisted her in donning a clean gown and washing the mud from her face and hands, but at Sebastian's constant bickering that she not keep the admiral waiting, she had hurried through her toilette and surely had not done a proper job.

Voices drifted from the room as she reached for the door handle, making her all the more nervous because she recognized them. Her moist palms slid on the latch, but finally she lifted it and made her entrance. The admiral's eyes locked upon hers immediately, drawing her gaze to him. He stood next to the fireplace, one arm leaning casually over the mantel, his booted feet crossed at the ankles, his mahogany hair tucked behind his ears in a slight curl. A curve graced his usually stern jaw.

Though she tried to pull her gaze from his eyes, she found she could not, not because of any anger or sternness, but because of the warmth and affection she found within their brown depths.

Where she had expected fury or at the very least pain, she saw only regard and admiration. She shook her head to dislodge the hold his eyes had upon her and surveyed the room. Mrs. Barton sat draped in peevishness on the flowered ottoman, and Mr. Atherton stood by the window, drink in hand, shifting his mischievous eyes between her and the admiral, a catlike grin upon his lips.

"Miss Dawson, thank you for coming." The admiral approached and took her hand in his, laying a gentle kiss upon it. It was only then, with the feel of his warm lips upon her skin, that she realized she had forgotten to don her gloves. Her heart sped, causing her breath to quicken and her chest to rise and fall in such rapid movements she was sure everyone would notice. Yanking her hand from his, she took a step back.

"How may I be of service, Admiral?"

The admiral smiled with a look that said he'd noticed her reaction to him and it pleased him.

Mrs. Barton coughed.

"Please have a seat, will you not?" Admiral Randal gestured toward a chair.

Dominique lowered herself into it but kept to the edge, back straight and hands folded in her lap. She eyed the open door. The Admiral came and stood beside her, a protective gesture that made her heart leap. Why was he being so kind? She could deal with his anger, could deal with his rudeness, even his cruelty, but she could not handle his compassion.

"I am afraid they are onto us, my dear." Mr. Atherton gulped his drink and slammed the glass down before sauntering her way. "The admiral's sister has given us away, I fear, although why"—his blunt gaze swerved to Mrs. Barton—"I have no idea."

"To show Miss Dawson's capability of deceit, of course," Mrs. Barton stated as if it were obvious to all.

"Perhaps it would have been better to forgo this one opportunity to malign Miss Dawson's character in light of the end result?" Mr. Atherton teased her.

Mrs. Barton glared at the young member of Parliament. "The end result you desired was quite in contrast to my own."

"Ah, trifles, my dear, trifles." He gave her a boyish smile and brushed a speck of dust from his waistcoat.

Dominique gulped. So the admiral knew she and Mr. Atherton had been feigning their attachment. Was that the cause of his good humor? She dared a quick glance up at him and found his eyes locked upon her. Lowering her gaze to her lap, she concentrated on her breathing, which had suddenly taken a rapid course.

"And I daresay the plan worked," Mr. Atherton continued. "Wouldn't you agree, Miss Dawson?"

"I do not know what you mean, Mr. Atherton." She gave the admiral a measured look. "And I assure you I was not a part of this scheme."

"I realize this was Percy's doing, Miss Dawson." The admiral's deep voice floated over the room. "This is not the first time he has meddled in my affairs." He grinned and shook his head. "I only wished to hear your part in the charade. Which is why I summoned you here."

Mrs. Barton's gaze scoured over Dominique, yet the usual flare of spite had cooled into a look of curious examination.

Chase inched closer to Dominique's chair, and she looked down, feeling tension emanating from him in hot coils. How could she tell the admiral the truth? That her intention was only to prevent his advance; that although every ounce of her longed for his love, she could never accept it. But she could say none of that. "I have nothing to add, Admiral, save to beg your forgiveness."

Mrs. Barton's brow wrinkled.

A chill raked over Dominique as she remembered what Larena had told her about the admiral's loathing for liars. Surely he would spew his rage upon her and dismiss her immediately.

"I do not fault you, Miss Dawson." His soft words sent a wave of shock through her. "Atherton can be quite persuasive—especially with the ladies." She heard him chuckle but could not bring herself to look at him.

Mrs. Barton opened her mouth as if to say something but then snapped it shut. The harsh lines on her face deepened as she studied her brother.

"Nevertheless," Mr. Atherton interrupted, "as I have said, the plan was successful."

"Whatever can you mean, Mr. Atherton?" Mrs. Barton's lips tightened into a thin line.

"Do you not have eyes in your pretty head?" Mr. Atherton sat beside her on the couch and leaned back, propping his ankle across his knee. "You have only to observe the way they look at each other."

"This is madness." Mrs. Barton shifted in her seat and averted her gaze to the glowing coals in the fireplace.

The chill that had come over Dominique only moments before now transformed into a fire that quickly spread up her neck and onto her face. Not only was it most improper to be speaking of such things in public, but what made it all the more dreadfully embarrassing was that the conversation was about her and the admiral.

She swallowed. What was happening? Why wasn't the admiral angry at her deception? Why was he not denying his feelings? She gazed up at him. Why was he just standing there staring at her with that warmth as if the center of his whole existence rested upon her?

Dominique quickly looked away but saw that their exchange did not go unnoticed by Mrs. Barton. She shifted her sharp gaze back and forth between her brother and Dominique, her eyes finally landing on Dominique, staring at her as if she had some grand malformation. Dominique reached up to check her face, expecting some glob of dirt to be hanging from her cheek. Nothing. When she returned Mrs. Barton's gaze, the hatred had dissipated from her eyes, replaced by a confusion that was soon drowned in a pool of moisture that caused Dominique to blink.

Blood rushed to Dominique's head, and she felt as though she would faint. She sought out Mr. Atherton in the hope that he would make some sense out of the unusual reactions from both the admiral and his sister.

Instead, he flung an arm over the back of the sofa and raised his cultured brows in a look that said, *I told you so*. "I do say, Miss Dawson, your very presence seems to have shut the mouths of both the Randals—a condition I have never seen in all my years of their acquaintance."

Dominique gripped her moist hands together. "I fear you are mistaken, Mr. Atherton. I have done naught but sit here quietly."

William suddenly burst around the corner, sending a wave of relief over Dominique. Mrs. Hensworth was quick on his heels as he ran toward the admiral. "Father, Father. I planted an herb seed all by myself."

"Forgive me, sir." Mrs. Hensworth scurried after the boy. "He got away from me."

The admiral fisted his hands on his hips, and Dominique expected the usual angry reproof, but instead he gave William a look of teasing disapproval.

William froze. He scanned the room, glancing over his aunt and Mr. Atherton before seeing Dominique.

"Miss Dawson." His eyes lit up.

Dominique opened her arms and he ran into them, gripping her around the neck and leaving fingerprints of mud on the muslin fabric of her collar.

Mrs. Barton let out an exclamation. "Chase, really. The boy's manners."

William pulled back and examined his fingers and then her dress. His eyes misted. "I am sorry, Miss Dawson."

Dominique hugged him again. "Never you mind, William. A little mud never hurt anybody."

William slowly raised a timid gaze to his father.

The admiral took a step toward him then halted. The muscles in his jaw tensed, and he rubbed the scar on his cheek. He gazed toward the window then back at Dominique, a troubled look in his eyes. She longed to reach out to him, to ease his struggle, his pain.

Finally, he expelled a huge sigh then approached and knelt beside them. He gave her a skeptical look before turning toward his son.

William shrank back.

Chase winked solemnly at his son. "William, please go with Mrs. Hensworth and have her clean you properly."

The boy tilted his tiny brows at his father then smiled and scooted away from Miss Dawson. "Yes, Father."

Mrs. Hensworth took him by the hand and led him toward the door.

"Father?" William tugged on the housekeeper's arm and turned.

"Yes?"

"Miss Dawson said she likes you very much."

A stunned silence enveloped the room. Dominique clamped her eyes shut in horror.

"Indeed?" she heard the admiral declare.

"Yes. Can she be my new mother?"

CHAPTER 21

Dominique slid farther into the pew of St. Mary Woolnoth and lowered her gaze. Letting out a long-suppressed sigh, she blinked back the tears that had been threatening release all through the Sunday morning service. Now that the parishioners and attendants had left the beautiful sanctuary—all save for Rev. Newton—she unleashed the emotions she had kept so carefully guarded all week long.

"What has you so distraught, my child?" Rev. Newton eased beside her with a slight moan.

"Please forgive me, Reverend." She raised her gaze to his. "It has all become too much for me, I fear."

The many furrows on Rev. Newton's brow deepened. "What has?"

"The deception, the terror, the pain. . .everything." Dominique wrung her hands together. After William's embarrassing question about her becoming his mother, Percy had chuckled, Mrs. Barton had choked until her face reddened, and the admiral had remained in silent perusal of Dominique until she could stand it no more. Upon politely excusing herself, she had fled from the drawing room as fast as her slippers would take her. Since then, she had avoided the admiral with great success, though she often heard him roaming the halls in the middle of the night.

"I do not understand, child." Rev. Newton pressed his bony hand upon hers and gave her a look of concern. "If you would tell me exactly what has you so vexed, perhaps I could pray for you."

"I wish I could, Reverend." She closed her eyes and shook her head. "I have made such a mess of things." Why had she allowed herself to grow so close to William? To the admiral? Even to Larena—who had informed Dominique the other day of how much she valued their friendship—when Dominique knew she must betray them all and leave? And Dominique's very presence had done nothing but distress Mrs. Barton and bring back painful memories of her husband's betrayal. It would have been better for them all if she had never met them.

"You are still in Admiral Randal's employ?"

Dominique opened her eyes and nodded.

"God makes no mistakes." Rev. Newton patted her hand and smiled. Light from a chandelier hanging above them shimmered over his gray hair and swept down upon his black robe, making him appear all the holier. "He has you there for a reason."

"What, I cannot imagine." Dominique gazed at the two massive white pillars that stood like sentinels on each side of the wooden altar and felt insignificant by comparison. "I have done naught but destroy lives. Larena still believes no man, especially God, is to be trusted. Sebastian is the same cold, unhappy man as when I first encountered him. Mr. Atherton continues his destructive ways despite my warnings, and Mrs. Barton and Lady Irene hate me all the more each day. The only one I believe I have impacted is young William." She sniffed. *And now I must leave him and break his heart.*

Rev. Newton regarded her with twinkling eyes, the bags beneath them forming a gentle smile. "You may think you have made no impact, but I am always amazed to discover what a sincere child of God can do simply by being present." He glanced up at the gold cross centered on the retable. "Our Lord does not ask us to be perfect, only willing."

Dominique frowned. "Willing and *able*, I imagine, which is where I fail Him."

"You can never fail Him, and you do not need to prove yourself in battle for Him. He has already won." The reverend grabbed her hand and gave it a strong squeeze that belied his frail appearance. "But what of the admiral? I sense this has something to do with him, as well?"

The admiral. . . Chase. Dominique swallowed against a burning in her throat, unable to deny her intense feelings any longer. "I love him, Reverend. I cannot help myself."

"Ah, yes." Rev. Newton's chuckle echoed through the sanctuary. "Perhaps that is why the Lord has placed you there, my dear?"

She looked at him, wishing that were the case. Wishing for one brief moment she was free to love the admiral and his son without the threat of losing Marcel.

The reverend cocked his head. "Love is never wrong. It covers a multitude of sins and heals all wounds."

"In this case, it will cause only pain."

"Hmm. Then he does not return your affections?"

Dominique rose and began to pace. "No, I believe he may." Her heart leapt at the thought, and a longing to be loved by such a man consumed her. "That is what makes it all the worse."

"This involves the threat on your brother you spoke of before?" Rev. Newton's lips tightened as he grabbed his cane and strained to rise from the pew.

Dominique rushed to assist him. "Yes, I must leave tomorrow night. My brother's life depends on me." A shudder ran through her. How she hoped to deal with such unscrupulous men and escape with Marcel unscathed, she had no idea.

Rev. Newton leaned on his cane and drew his brows into a knot. "I see."

"Where is the strength promised to me in the Bible?" Dominique pressed her hand over her agitated stomach. "I still feel like the same frightened little girl I have always been."

"I never said you would *feel* any differently, my child." Rev. Newton smiled. "God does not promise we will never be afraid. He only promises He will never leave us, and He will protect and help us with the tasks He has called us to do."

"Called?" Dominique huffed. "I cannot imagine that He has called me down this beastly path."

"If your heart is toward Him, He will show you the way." Rev. Newton took one of her hands in his. "You are trembling." He led her back to the pew. "Have a seat and allow me to read you a passage from one of my favorite psalms." Grabbing a Bible from the podium, he opened it and sifted through the pages, finally landing on one near the center. "Yea, the sparrow hath found an house, and the swallow a nest for herself, where she may lay her young, even thine altars, O Lord of hosts, my King, and my God."

Dominique's heart froze. "The admiral calls me a little sparrow."

Rev. Newton lifted his gaze and grinned, revealing a row of aged, yellowing teeth. "Perhaps God is indeed speaking to you." He returned to the Bible and continued, "Blessed are they that dwell in thy house: they will be still praising thee. Blessed is the man whose strength is in thee; in whose heart are the ways of them. Who passing through the valley of Baca make it a well; the rain also filleth the pools. They go from *strength* to *strength*, every one of them in Zion appeareth before God."

He gently closed the Holy Book. "Perhaps this is a journey of strength for you, my dear, one in which God is teaching you to trust in Him." He touched the tip of his cane to his chest and gave her a knowing look. "No matter what you may be feeling inside."

Dominique allowed herself to grin. "You are such a wise man."

"I serve a wise God." He chuckled. "But, ah, you forget, I was once a slaver, a loathsome creature who ne'er had a thought for anyone but himself." He clutched the Bible to his chest. " 'Tis only by God's grace I am still alive."

"I shall miss you, Reverend." Her heart sank at the thought of leaving such a strong spiritual man who seemed almost like a father to her now.

"Will you never return to London?"

"I do not believe I will ever be able to." She looked away. If she succeeded in betraying England as she must do to save Marcel, then without a doubt, she could never return to her homeland.

"Then I shall see you in heaven." Rev. Newton raised his brows, a twinkle in his eye.

As Dominique considered what might happen to her if she

was caught by British authorities—or worse, what Cousin Lucien might do to her anyway—she let out a tiny snicker.

"Perhaps that shall be sooner than we think."

Dominique set the candlestick down upon the oblong table in the middle of the kitchen and glanced around the gloomy room. The pungent scent of roast venison filled her nose like a taunting memory, though she knew the evening's meal would be long gone by now. She must find something to eat—anything to still the turmoil in her stomach. This was her last night in the Randal home. She had not expected to find sweet slumber in light of what she must face the following night, but she had not expected a mutiny within her belly, either. Now forced from the safe haven of her chamber, she had ventured down the service staircase to the kitchen in hopes that some sustenance would quiet her rebellious nerves.

The kitchen, always a bright and bustling place during the day, overflowing with gleeful chatter and succulent smells, appeared a cold gray vault in the middle of the night. Dominique shivered and tightened her robe around her, scanning for the familiar cupboard where she knew the cook stored extra food.

Her eyes landed on the kitchen door, a dark rectangle in the shadows of the room, and visions filled her mind of the ragged children clambering down the steps from the street above, their dirt-encrusted hands reaching out for the morsels of food she often gave them.

Who would feed them now? *Oh Lord, take care of them and of all who are hungry on the streets.*

Careful not to wake up the servants who slept nearby, she crept toward the cupboard. Light from a street lantern trickled through the window in a band of shifting rays that joined the light from her candle in a dance that bounced through the room, illuminating choice spots while leaving others in darkness.

As she reached for the cupboard, the light shifted, and shadows swallowed her hand. She bumped into something hard and cold, sending the interfering object tumbling to the stone floor.

Clang! Clang! Clang!

Dominique stiffened and held her breath until the ringing ceased. Some spy she was.

When she dared to move again, thankfully the rasping of her released breath was the only sound that reached her ears. Leaning down, she retrieved the rebellious copper kettle and placed it on the counter before returning her attention to the cupboard. Grabbing a jar of preserves, she could wait no longer for food and plunged her finger into the succulent jam. She brought it to her mouth, breathing in the sweet strawberry scent. Stifling the moan on her lips, she scooped another fingerful to her mouth.

Something scuffled in the hallway. A strip of light appeared beneath the wooden door.

The jam spurted up her throat in a warm, sour glob, nearly choking her. She set down the jar and blew out the candle, then searched the room for a place to hide.

Too late. The door creaked open. Candlelight filled the room. Dominique froze.

There the admiral stood, dressed only in pantaloons and a white shirt that hung open. Stepping inside, he set his candle down and gave her a most enticing grin. "So I see the little sparrow has finally left her nest."

Dominique shifted her gaze away, chastising herself for not being able to control her hunger. Now she must face the one man she had hoped most to avoid. How could she look him in the eyes, knowing she would soon betray him? How could she look him in the eyes and not betray her deep love for him? "I was hungry."

"A common occurrence, I am told." He chuckled and lifted the jar of preserves from the table, eyeing it suspiciously. "Have you been avoiding me? You have not joined us for dinner."

"I have not felt well."

"Ah, but you have recovered, I see." Chase set down the jar and took a step toward her.

Dominique's insides melted, but she dared not raise her gaze to his. A trace of alcohol swirled in the air between them and mingled with the spicy scent she had come to associate only with

Chase. The room began to spin.

Chase raised his hand toward her, spanning the distance between them. Dominique flinched. He took a lock of her loose hair and fingered it as if it were made of silk, then released it, allowing it to flow across his hand.

All the air in the room seemed to swirl around Dominique.

"You are not *truly* ill, are you?"

Was that fear in his voice? Dominique still dared not look at him.

"It is nothing, I assure you." She raised a hand to her forehead as heat flushed through her. Perhaps she was becoming ill, after all.

Chase grunted and brushed past her. She heard his bare feet treading across the stones until they stopped, and he let out a long sigh. "She told me she was not ill. She told me to return to the sea, to my duties in the Royal Navy, that she would recover in due time."

Dominique raised her gaze. Chase stood with his back to her, staring out the kitchen window, his tall frame a dark, brawny silhouette against the light seeping in from outside. He clenched his fists at his sides as taut ropes of tension stretched out from him.

Dominique remained quiet, examining the raw emotions pouring forth from a man who normally shielded them well.

He snorted and glanced her way. "She *was* quite ill, you know. But she knew how much I loved the sea." He flattened his lips and faced the window again. "By the time I returned, it was too late. She died three weeks later."

Overcome with sorrow, Dominique eased beside him. "It was not your fault."

"Of course it was. I should have been here." He gripped the wooden counter.

"You could not have stopped the disease." Dominique touched his arm. "She did not want you to watch her suffer. I can understand that. Can't you?"

"No," he barked, startling Dominique. "It was my own selfishness that drove me away. I knew in my heart I should have stayed, but I wanted to return to the sea." He squeezed his eyes shut and hung his head. "Did I love the sea more than my own wife? What sort of man does that make me?"

"We are all fallen creatures, Admiral." Dominique thought of her own shame—of the traitorous task she must perform the following night. "Only by God's grace can we hope to become any better."

Chase snorted. "Yes, your wonderful God. If I am so flawed and therefore to be excused, where was He when Melody was dying?" His blazing eyes snapped to hers. The stubble on his chin shifted as he tightened his jaw, and he reminded Dominique of a bull about to charge.

Fighting a rising fear of his anger, Dominique nonetheless placed her hand gently upon his as she said a silent prayer. "He was here with Melody the whole time."

Chase's already stormy eyes began to spark with fury, and Dominique tried to jerk her hand away, but he smothered it between his. His warm fingers began to caress hers. She glanced up at him curiously and found that a softness had replaced his angry gaze.

"You have her same kind heart, her goodness, her charity."

She blinked and looked out the window, anywhere but at those chocolate brown eyes that now gazed so adoringly at her. Did he see her as only a replica of Melody? "I am nothing like her."

"True. In many ways." He leaned toward her ear and said quietly, "In many pleasing ways."

Every nerve in Dominique sparked to life. She swallowed and tried to still her frantic heart while she glanced about the room, at the stove, the cupboard, anywhere but his broad shoulders and the strong chest peeking from behind his open shirt. He reached up and placed a finger under her chin, directing her gaze to his. Once there, she found there was nothing else in the world she would rather look upon.

The candlelight flickered over the tips of his mahogany hair, setting it ablaze about his shoulders with fiery streaks of red.

"It pleases me to see you." His deep voice floated over her, stealing its way through the stony resolve she had so carefully erected around her heart.

Outside, the clomp and rattle of a carriage sounded, along with the rustle of leaves picked up by the wind as if warning her that danger was near.

She should heed the warning and flee from the room, but instead she remained. Chase brushed a finger over her cheek. Dominique closed her eyes, relishing his touch—*Just for this one moment*—soaking the sensations into her memory where she would never forget them. Oh, how she longed to simply fall into his arms, tell him everything, and allow him to make it all go away, to save Marcel, to save her, to love her.

But she couldn't.

"No." Dominique snapped her eyes open. "I beg you. Please do not." Though she had tried to deny what her heart had told her every time she looked in Chase's eyes—that this extraordinary man actually cared for her—she could no longer whisk away the truth. Instead of thrilling her, however, the revelation only made her heart sink further into despair.

He dropped his hand from her cheek, the loss dousing Dominique in an icy bath.

"Forgive me. I will not flatter myself to think you return my affections." He turned to leave but spun back around with a sigh. He took her hand in his. "Tell me you have no feelings for me, that you find my company as odious as you have declared, and I promise to leave you be."

And Dominique could tell from the stern look in his eyes that he meant it. Now all she had to do was say the words—fallacious as they were. Better to hurt him now than give him hope, even for a day.

Sorrow burned in Dominique's throat, closing it so tight she could barely breathe. She gazed into his eyes and knew what this unveiling of his heart cost him—how long it had been encased in bitterness over Melody's death. How could she deny what every ounce of her screamed to proclaim? She lowered her gaze and opened her mouth to offer him a twisted tale of lies, but no words came forth.

At her silence, a chuckle bounded from deep within Chase.

With the tip of his finger, he lifted her chin, and before she realized what was happening, his lips were upon hers.

The world around Dominique dissolved. Chase pulled her against him with the intensity of a man long deprived of love, and Dominique sank into him, returning his kiss with equal fervor. She could not stop herself. It was as if she were under some spell, a spell she hoped never to come out of. Inhaling the spicy scent of him, she snuggled deeper in his strong arms—arms that embraced her as if she were the most precious thing in the world. *Oh Lord, what am I doing?*

Then he withdrew, gently brushed the hair from her face, and cupped her chin before placing tender kiss upon tender kiss across her lips. Dominique could not move. Her heart danced wildly in her chest. She must come to her senses.

She jerked her face aside and tugged from his grasp. "I must go." Turning, she charged across the room, bumping into the table.

"There you go again, flitting off like the frightened sparrow you are." Chase groaned behind her.

She halted. Yes, she was a frightened little sparrow, frightened for Marcel, frightened for her own life, but most of all frightened of the love she felt for this man and the power he had over her. She faced him. *"C'est facile d'être courageux quand vous n'avez rien à perdre."*

He flattened his lips with a snort. "I quite agree. It is easy to be brave when you have nothing to lose. But on the contrary, I have come to realize I have much to lose."

Sacre bleu. He understood her French?

"Yes, I am fluent in French, mademoiselle." He bowed then moved toward her. "I love you, Dominique. Can you not see that?"

Dominique threw her hands to her face and shook her head. No, she did not want to see that, did not want to hear that.

"Forgive me." Turning, she clutched the edges of her robe and dashed from the room.

CHAPTER 22

Ignoring the trembling that made her legs feel like soggy biscuits, Dominique clutched her valise to her chest as she rounded the corner onto Broad Street. The small case held all her worldly belongings, all that she had first arrived with at the Randal home and all she now left with—all save her heart. She knew that part of her would forever remain behind with the admiral and his son.

Oh Lord, please be with them. Please help them understand.

Just thinking of the pain her betrayal would cause them nearly tore her in half. William had now lost two mothers. And Chase. . . Would he ever be able to love again?

Dominique swiped at the tears streaming down her face, trying to stop the deluge that had begun the moment she closed the door to the Randal home and walked away. A brisk wind picked up, swirling leaves at her feet and sending a chill over her damp face.

A carriage approached, raucous laughter pouring from its windows, and Dominique dashed into the shadows of a shoemaker's shop. In the distance, a charlie cried. His deep voice echoed across the dark streets, sounding more like a horn than a human. "Twelve o'clock. Fair weather now, but a storm brews in the east!"

A storm, indeed. The most frightful storm Dominique would ever encounter. She leaned against the cold brick wall and closed her eyes. No matter how hard she tried to quiet her erratic breathing, it only grew more rapid, as if it were competing with the uncontrollable quiver that consumed the rest of her. The putrid stench of horse manure and rotten food pinched her nose as she heard the clip-clop of the carriage retreating down the street. She tightened her grip on her valise. The documents crackled within— the documents that would save Marcel. Sighing, she shook her head. In what kind of world did simple papers determine whether a man lived or died?

The rough brick scratched her glove as she shoved from the wall and stepped out from the shadows. She now must focus on her meeting with the Frenchman and put behind her the pain of leaving Chase and young William. A full moon winked at her from behind a barrage of dark clouds forming overhead.

Oh Lord, give me the strength Rev. Newton read to me of from Your Word. Help me to save my brother.

As she turned back onto the street, a gust of wind slapped her, its inquisitive hands plucking at the hood of her cloak. Thunder growled in the distance, and Dominique wondered if God were answering her. If He was, He sounded angry. A chill tightened across her skin, and she clutched her cloak about her neck and peered into the darkness. Tall black buildings loomed on each side of the street like spectators in some kind of heinous play or perhaps trolls requiring payment or a secret password before they would let her by. The faint sound of an eerie melody, no doubt from some bawdy tavern, snaked around the dark corners, grating her nerves.

Everything within her told her to turn and run back to the safety of the Randal house—the safety of the admiral's arms—but she kept her feet in place and swallowed hard against the terror and foreboding that threatened to keep her from her task. She must find somewhere to hide the documents before she reached the Strand. Pressing forward, she skirted the corner of Chandois Street and spotted a massive tree. Its roots spread across the ground like an old woman's bony fingers. After darting a glance around her to ensure nobody was about, Dominique opened her valise, withdrew the documents she had rolled and tied with a string, and knelt down to the roots. She stuffed the scroll into a knothole at the base of the tree, then covered the edge with rocks and loose branches.

The plan had come to her earlier that day. She must have some leverage—especially with such unscrupulous sorts as these men of Napoleon's.

Oh Lord, am I doing the right thing? She glanced up at the dark, fuming clouds. No answer. Just a chill that shot like an icicle through her heart and the distant rumblings of a storm—a storm that threatened to swallow her and Marcel alive. *Where are You, Lord? Why do I not feel You? Why am I still so frightened?*

Spinning around, she clenched her jaw, trying to compose herself. How could she face the Frenchman in such a state? She must appear strong, in control, or all would be lost. She marched forward, bracing herself against the increasing wind but hoping it would help to dry her eyes. She turned down Andrews Street.

And froze.

Beneath the overhang of a large mill stood the mysterious man in black. She had once believed he was an angel. Now, in light of her fear and heartache, she couldn't be sure of anything.

He stepped out from the building. Though a street lantern hung on its post above him, the features of his face were still lost to her beneath his wide hat.

"Who are you?" she yelled above the rising wind.

He tipped his hat in her direction but said nothing, and despite the power that radiated from him like an invisible shield, she found once again that she feared him not.

Grabbing her skirts in one hand, she dashed past him.

Chase snapped the brandy toward the back of his mouth, felt the burning trail down his throat, then tossed the glass into the fireplace. It shattered against the back bricks and then over the coals, the droplets of liquor igniting small pockets of flames. He rubbed the back of his neck, frustration bubbling within him like some vile brew. Perhaps it was the rising storm outside his chamber window, the wind from which sent a loose window pane chattering in a chaotic frenzy; perhaps it was that he hadn't seen Miss Dawson since the prior night—the night when they had kissed—or perhaps he was just losing his mind, as he'd assumed all along.

Stomping around his bedpost, he grabbed another bottle of brandy, lifted it to his lips, then slammed it down again on his desk. No amount of alcohol could deaden the pain of Dominique's rejection. Lord knew, he had tried. But had she really rejected him? He rubbed the scar above his right cheek and plodded across the Turkish carpet centered on the floor. Nothing made sense anymore. In the kitchen that night, she had responded to his touch, his kiss. He had felt her desire, her affection, seen it in those glowing amber eyes.

And she had not denied her feelings.

But she had not voiced them, either.

Was it him? Was he too harsh, too cold, too forceful? Did he frighten her? What kept her from him? Why, when he had finally opened his heart to another, did she flee from him like a skittish sparrow?

Stopping, he glanced up at the haunting shapes the candlelight formed on the ceiling. *God, if You're there, please help me.*

It was only the second time he had addressed the Almighty in three years—three years, two weeks, and four days, to be exact, the day Melody had died—so when only silence responded, he was not surprised. Even if God existed, Chase doubted his prayers would be heard. Chase certainly would not accommodate such insubordination and insolence aboard his ship. Why would the Creator of the universe be any less demanding?

A pounding on his door startled him from his musings and brought a much-welcomed interruption, no matter the cause. Tonight, to be left alone with his demons was proving to be unbearable.

Midshipman Franklin stood outside his chamber, his eyes alight with excitement, the heels of his boots tapping the floor in anticipation. He saluted.

Alarm shot through Chase. "Yes, Franklin, what is it?"

"The governess has left, Admiral."

"Left? Whatever do you mean?"

"You told me to tell you if anyone in your employ left the house. And she did, sir, just a few minutes ago, alone."

Chase felt his stomach tighten. He had forgotten his additional orders to Franklin. He still had a spy to catch, after all, a duty he had obviously neglected in light of his overwhelming involvement with Miss Dawson. Cursing his negligence, he grabbed his coat, tossed it over his shoulders, buckled on his belt, and took his sword and pistol—just in case.

What in God's name was the woman doing out so late at night, and alone? Terror choked his throat, a familiar terror, the terror of losing someone he loved. Or worse. A terror that his sister had been right all along and he had been played for a fool.

"Lead the way, Franklin."

Dominique rounded the final corner onto Cecil Street. One final glance over her shoulder told her the man—or angel—still followed her. *Lord, I wish I knew for certain if he was Yours. Or am I just dreaming that You are indeed watching over me?*

A gust of wind blew her hood from her head, tousling her hair over her face. She smelled the Thames long before she heard the lap of its rancid waters. Not far from shore, a small, single-masted ship lolled in the high tide, ghostly light winking at her from one of its windows.

She halted before the tavern and examined the name painted on a sign above the door: THE LAST STOP. Dominique sighed. Indeed. Her last stop. Her last chance to save Marcel. Off-key fiddle music scraped against her ears, and she forced her chattering teeth to be still, thankful that her tears had ceased. Perhaps she had no more to shed. Or maybe they had succumbed to the horror that now forced all her blood in a mad dash to her head.

If she could trust the Frenchman's word, then Marcel was inside this tavern. That thought alone sufficed to give her the strength to proceed up the stairs.

A blast of cheap liquor, vomit, and sweat slammed into her as she opened the door. Salacious grins widened upon filthy faces from every dark corner as her eyes adjusted to the glare of lantern light and candlelight scattered throughout the room. The music stopped, and Dominique's heart along with it.

"Well, call me a cuckolded squid if that ain't a lady." A slurred voice slithered over her from her right. "Lookin' for a real man, perchance, *milady?*"

Dominique dared a glance in the direction of the voice as the other men in the room joined in a deep guffaw.

Nothing but formless dark shapes appeared before her eyes, like specters from hell. The flickering lights began to spin around her. Dominique coughed, searching for a breath of fresh air. She scanned the room, peering into the same dark corner where the Frenchman had been before. A buxom red-haired woman sat upon a man's lap, laughing so hard her bosom shook like enormous bowls of jelly. The man was far too scrawny to either hold the large woman or be the Frenchman.

Dominique felt the blood that had pooled in her head turn to ice. Had he changed his mind? Was her brother already lost? *Oh God.* Her stomach cramped, nearly toppling her. She gripped the valise with both hands until her fingers ached.

A man emerged from the shadows, kicking aside a chair with a curse. He focused his red-rimmed, lifeless eyes upon her. The top of his balding head gleamed as he passed beneath a lantern. What remained of his brown hair dangled to his shoulders like dried seaweed.

She tried to move her feet, tried to turn and run, but every muscle within her froze as if in protest that her body had reached its limit of terror for the evening.

So this was it. She would die here and never know what happened to Marcel or the admiral or sweet William.

A wall of cold air struck her from behind. A burning spasm shot through her right arm as strong fingers grabbed her and dragged her from the tavern. She went tumbling down the steps, slipped, and fell. A jolt of pain shot through her knees as they struck the hard wood.

"*Vite. Levez-vous.*" The man yanked on her arm so hard, she felt it would separate from her body. Shards of agony shot into her shoulder and down her back as the man lifted her off her feet and tossed her onto the dirt road.

"Please, you are hurting me."

"Oh, *pardonnez-moi*," the man barked as he hauled her down the street. Dominique glanced over her shoulder for the man in black. He stood across the road beside a brick building, arms at his sides, watching her.

But making no move to come to her aid.

Before she could yell to him for help, two other men emerged seemingly from nowhere and fell in line behind them. The man yanked her down an alleyway beside a small warehouse to their left. He flung her around to face him.

The Frenchman.

"*Vous m'avez trompé.* You tricked me," he snapped between gritted teeth and squeezed her arm tighter.

Dominique winced. His spit splattered over her face, dousing her with the scent of fish and tobacco. He glanced toward the street, flinging his greasy hair behind him.

The beef she had eaten for dinner soured in her stomach and started to rise. "Whatever do you mean? I have brought the information you want." She glanced down at the valise crushed against her chest. "I have not deceived you."

"You told someone."

"*Non, je promets.* I did not." What was he talking about? What kind of game was he playing? Her mind sifted through a thousand possibilities. *Oh God, what am I to do now?*

One of the men chuckled and spit a black glob onto the hard dirt. A ship's horn sounded in the distance.

"My men tell me you have been followed."

Followed? Who would follow her? Did they mean the man in black? "I swear to you I told no one. Where is Marcel? Is he here?" She started to push past him, but he gripped her shoulders and hurled her against the brick wall. Her head snapped onto the hard stone. Something warm and moist oozed from beneath her hair.

"Oui, we have kept our bargain. Unfortunately, you have not kept yours."

Dominique tried to focus on the Frenchman as he spoke, but his face blurred into a nondescript, oscillating mass before her. Only the line of his slick mustache as it moved up and down remained tauntingly clear.

Lightning cracked the midnight sky, outlining the villains with an eerie glow before drowning them in darkness once again. Thunder roared an angry growl. The building behind Dominique quaked.

The Frenchman grunted, glared up at the sky, a boiling mass of dark clouds, then gripped Dominique's arm again and dragged her back onto the street.

"*Le marché est rompu.*" He released her and turned away, heading toward the river. She stumbled back and fell to her knees in the dirt.

No. The deal couldn't be off. He had said Marcel was here. Where were they going?

The ship.

"Wait!" Dominique shrieked, her voice cracking. "I have what you want." Dropping her valise to the ground, she tore it open and felt inside for the stack of papers she had kept separate from the others. Where were they? Groping madly through her things, she took a deep breath, trying to keep her focus. Finally, she felt them, stood, and held them out before her. "*Les voici.*"

The Frenchman slowly turned, a sinister smile angling his greasy mustache. He sauntered toward her, eyes as narrow and cold as a snake's. A gust of wind bristled his hair against his white cravat and brought with it the sting of rain, a threat of the impending storm.

Halting before her, he brushed a finger over the few pages. "Once again, *c'est tout?*" He shook his head with a snort. "Mademoiselle Dawson. You disappoint me. I am done with this game. *C'est finis.*" He waved a hand through the air and spun about.

"Game?" Dominique's anger surged, smothering her fear for a moment. "This is your game, monsieur. You have all the cards."

He continued walking toward the Thames, ignoring her, his two companions keeping in step beside him.

"I have but one card to play," she yelled after him.

Dominique craned her neck to glance around them. Was

Marcel on that ship? Her heart nearly crashed through her chest at the thought. Every muscle within her twitched to make a mad dash past the men, to jump aboard that boat. To find Marcel.

"This is but a portion of what I have!" she screeched, her voice edged with terror. Holding the papers up high, she gripped them tightly against the increasing wind. "When you give me Marcel, I will take you to the rest. They are not far from here." Her heart seemed to solidify into a brick as it jumped into her throat. *Oh Lord, help them to listen. Do not let them sail away.*

The Frenchman turned and charged toward her as if he were going to knock her to the ground. Dominique cringed, squeezed her eyes shut for a second, but held her ground. He snatched the papers, sidled under the light of a streetlamp, and perused them. "You traitorous shrew," he spat, eyeing her with disdain.

Heavy footsteps crunched the gravel behind her. A short, portly man waddled toward them, beads of sweat dotting his puffy face. "They are not far behind. One of them is a navy officer. *Vite.* We must go."

Dominique glanced behind her. Whom was he talking about? Was this part of their plan? A trick to force her to hand over all the documents without getting Marcel?

The Frenchman cursed and drew a pistol from his belt. He pressed the cold barrel to Dominique's forehead. "I should kill you right here."

Thunder shook the sky. The hard metal seemed to burn a circle into her skin. He cocked the pistol with a grin, and she knew from the look in his eye he wouldn't hesitate to pull the trigger. In fact, he might even enjoy it.

She could not die. Not here. Not now. Not like this. And not with so much at stake.

She opened her mouth to speak but could not stop her lips from quivering. Finally, she blurted out, "I promise I have not deceived you. I do not know who follows me. I swear. Please. Please." She started to shake uncontrollably, and the tears she had been so successful at holding back now filled her eyes. "If you give me Marcel, I will take you to what you want." *God, help me. Give me strength*, she prayed silently. Then a thought came to her. "Unless he is dead. Perhaps he is dead," she uttered in a caustic tone that belied her terror. "Then you can forget ever seeing the rest of the documents, monsieur."

The Frenchman lowered the pistol with a huff and dragged her to the edge of dock. "Here is your precious brother, mademoiselle."

"Francois," he yelled, and instantly a bulky man appeared on the deck of the ship, holding a lantern in one hand and towing a smaller man behind him. Carefully he navigated past the rigging to the bow of the ship. When he raised the light above them, Marcel's boyish face emerged like a beacon of hope in the darkness. Though he struggled in the man's grip, he smiled at her. He looked well.

Unharmed.

"Marcel! Marcel!" Dominique cried then broke into sobs of relief.

"Dominique!" he shouted in return. "Do what they say, *ma chérie*."

Wrenching her arm from the Frenchman's grasp, Dominique dashed down the dirt street toward the Thames, everything blurring before her. Desperation overcame fear—overcame reason.

Lightning etched a jagged spike across the sky, and someone pushed Dominique from behind. She stumbled and plunged to the hard wood of a small jetty at the edge of the water where a jollyboat tottered over the waves. Splinters pierced through her gloves into the delicate skin of her palms. She gasped. Thunder growled, sending a ripple over the black water of the Thames. Two men hauled her to her feet, nearly tearing her arms from their sockets.

Ignoring the pain, she glanced up at Marcel. His Adam's apple bobbed beneath an anguished swallow.

"I will save you, Marcel. Do not fear," she sobbed.

"I know." Marcel started toward her, but the burly man clamped his arm around the boy's neck and dragged him, coughing, back to the boat.

She watched as he sank down into the bowels of the ship and felt her heart sink with him.

The men lifted her off her feet and plopped her back down by the Frenchman.

"So you see?" He raised a brow in her direction.

"Give him to me." Dominique choked on her own words, no longer trying to mask her terror or her agony behind a facade of strength. "And I will give you what you want."

"There is not time, *Vicomte*." The fat man shook his head at the Frenchman, then cast an anxious glance over his shoulder. His fat fingers gripped the hilt of a sword strapped to his side. "Unless you wish to have your throat stretched by a British rope."

The Frenchman followed his companion's gaze down the dark street then turned toward Dominique. "I will give you one more chance. The isle of Lihou, off Guernsey, do you know it?"

"Yes." She nodded. She had heard of it. It sat just off the coast of France.

"Two weeks hence. Meet me there. We will exchange your brother for the documents. If you do not have all the papers we want"—he narrowed his eyes and grabbed one of her hands, squeezing it until she winced in pain—"in these dainty hands of yours, you will watch your brother die." He brushed a coarse, smelly finger over her cheek. "And then I will kill you myself. *Comprendez-vous?*" He nodded for the men to board the ship.

Dominique swallowed. "Oui, I understand. I will be there."

The fetid trio dropped into the jollyboat and rowed to the ship. As they made sail and sped off under the stormy breeze, Dominique melted to the ground, unable to control her tears anymore. One by one they dropped onto the already moist dirt, quickly soaked up as if they never existed, as if no one cared. *Why, God. Why?* How could things have gone so wrong when she had tried to do everything so right? She must pull herself together. She must get going. Wiping her face, she slowly rose and took a deep breath. A light mist began to fall.

Picking up her valise and lifting her skirts, she dashed down the street, eyeing the man in black who remained by the side of the road.

A lot of help he had been.

"*You are still alive, beloved. As is Marcel.*"

The voice came from within Dominique and was so gentle, so loving, she knew it was God. *Forgive me, Lord. I know You must have a plan. I just wish You would inform me of it.*

Thunder boomed, shaking the buildings around her. Dominique darted down the street, across the Strand, and onto Andrews. No one was in sight. Why did the Frenchmen believe she had been followed? She glanced to her left, knowing before she saw him that the man in black followed her. The sense of control and power that surrounded him eased over her. Why had he not helped her? *Oh Lord, I do not understand.* No matter. She must retrieve the documents and return to the Randal home—one more time.

A million questions bombarded her. How would she procure passage aboard a ship? How could she convince the captain to stop at the Isle of Lihou? Fear sent her thoughts into a whirlwind. She would have to worry about those things later.

Marcel was alive!

At least she could hold on to that. *Thank You, Lord.* The vision of him standing on the dock flowed over her like a ray of warm sunshine, his curly dark hair blowing in the stormy breeze, the spark in his blue eyes as bright and genuine as his smile. Yes, his smile, even in the midst of captivity and in the face of death. But that was Marcel. Like their father, always the brave one.

Turning down Chandois, Dominique quickly found the large tree, knelt beside it, and uncovered the bundle of papers. Without bothering to stuff them in her valise, she dashed down the street. She must return to the Randal home before she was missed.

A fierce wind tore across her, lifting her skirts and sending the hood of her cloak pounding against her back. The sense of protection and power disappeared, leaving behind a feeling of foreboding. Dominique glanced over her shoulder for the man in black.

He was gone.

She faced forward and ran headfirst into a solid mass of muscle. She bounced off the large man, but his strong arms reached out to grab hers. The scent of brandy and spice sent off warning bells within her. Another man in uniform came up beside him.

A blast of thunder broke through a heavenly dam, and a torrent of rain suddenly poured from the sky as if somehow trying to obscure the happenings below.

The first man snatched the roll of papers from her hands.

Swiping away the rain pooling in her lashes, Dominique slowly raised her gaze to his, knowing before she did whom she would find.

Admiral Chase Randal.

CHAPTER 23

Chase crossed his arms over his bare chest and stared out the window of his chamber. Muted gray shapes formed out of the darkness, their cold, lifeless masses mimicking the numbness that gripped him. 'Twas a new day. Oh, that its light would chase away the night's events as well as it now did the shadows. Chase released a long sigh, wishing with all his might that last night had been just another of his nightmares, even though both the exhaustion tugging upon his body and the agony wrenching his heart told him otherwise.

Dominique had betrayed him. . .had betrayed England. An admiral's daughter. Chase rubbed his scar. Yet there was no denying the evidence. He glanced at the curled pile of papers on his desk, documents stamped with the emblem of the British Admiralty, the very same documents he had planted in his study—to catch a spy. And the very same documents he had found in her hands.

Dominique was the French spy the Admiralty had been looking for all along.

Yet even as he thought it, he found it hard to believe. Her timidity, her innocence, her faith, and even her affection for him, all a charade, all a performance. What an actress she was, better than any he had seen at Drury Lane. He snorted, pushing back a wave of agony, unwilling to express any emotion. Not for a traitor, not for a charlatan, not for a trollop who betrayed her homeland. Why had she done it? For money, no doubt. Chase swallowed hard.

His sister had been right all along.

He stormed from the window, every muscle taut, and slammed his fist into the wall. "Augh!" he growled. A dent marred the paneling, but he didn't care. Shaking his throbbing hand, he cursed under his breath. Now that Admiral Troubridge was recovering, Chase would leave this godforsaken town house, head out to sea, and never return. How could he have been such a half-wit? Perhaps he was not worthy to be hailed as an admiral in His Majesty's Royal Navy if he could be so easily duped by a simple girl. Egad, he had welcomed her into his home, into William's life, into his life, as a favor to her father, a gesture of kindness. And thus he was repaid. The French manner of returning a favor, no doubt.

Chase gripped the back of a chair until blood trickled from the wound on his right hand, feeling like a caged animal. Why? He was not the one locked in his chamber. He should call the marines and have her arrested immediately and thrown behind bars in Newgate. He should. For he well knew that according to the articles of war, he could be hanged for giving shelter and sustenance to the enemy. But for some reason, he could not turn her in, not just yet.

The half bottle of brandy beckoned him from his desk, glittering like liquid gold in the first rays of the sun shooting through the window. He released the chair. No more. The drink had befuddled his mind, especially when it had come to Miss Dawson.

Just the thought of her betrayal sent something hard and black slinking over his heart, encasing it once again. This time it would be forever.

Dominique could not get warm. No amount of pacing, no amount of quilts tossed about her shoulders could drive away the chill that covered her like a morning frost. Flinging the blankets back onto her bed, she rubbed her arms. The smell of the Thames rose from her sodden gown. *Oh, my dear Marcel. What have I done? I have failed you.* Agony constricted her throat. *Oh God, I told You I could not do this.*

Darkness clung to her chamber, defiantly refusing to give up its hold as a new day dawned outside her window. After she had run into the admiral last night, he had grabbed the documents, immediately turned his back to her, and ordered the man with him to escort her back to her chamber and lock her within. That was nigh five hours ago and she had heard no sound in the house save the pattering of mice and whispers of maids. Why she had not been thrown into the corner of some prison cell, she could not say.

Dominique sank onto the bed. The fear that had suffocated her all night had dissipated the moment she had looked up into the admiral's brown eyes, eyes burning with both shock and pain, eyes that tore through her heart like a hot sword.

Then he had turned away.

Why was she no longer afraid? Perhaps terror reaches a pinnacle, a place where it can go no further—where it loses consciousness. If that were the case, then either her fear was finally dead or it would come back to life soon enough. But for now, all she felt was emptiness, resignation, much like a prisoner must feel while being led to the gallows.

All was lost. Marcel would die. And she would be hanged as a spy.

A jingle of keys, a clank, and her door creaked open to reveal Larena carrying a tray of food. The scent of spicy hot tea and creamy breakfast porridge rose like a tantalizing aroma—the aroma of a last meal.

A look of horror paled Larena's face and widened her blue eyes. Even the freckles on her cheeks shrank in fear. "Are you all right, miss?" She set the tray down and scurried to the stove, not waiting for an answer.

"Where is the admiral?" Dominique asked.

"In his chamber." Larena ignited the coals and grabbed the poker, keeping her back toward Dominique.

"Come over to the stove, miss," Larena beckoned her. "You will catch your death."

Dominique stared at the chambermaid poking at the coals, her red curls springing from underneath her cap. " 'Tis what I deserve."

"Oh, what nonsense is this?" Larena replaced the poker and rushed to Dominique, taking her hands in hers.

"Do you not know what I have done?" Dominique snatched her hands back and hung her head. "Why are you attending to me?"

"The admiral instructed me to see to your needs, same as always." She gestured toward the food. "You should eat something."

Dominique shook her head. For once, she had no appetite. At any minute the admiral would burst through that door and have her arrested. What choice did he have? She had been caught spying, and she must pay the price.

"Whatever the admiral believes you have done. . ." Larena sat on the bed and leaned toward her. "Whatever reason he has for locking you in here, it cannot be true, miss. He will come to his senses soon, to be sure."

"Not this time, Larena. I fear he has finally come to his senses, after all."

Larena brushed a strand of Dominique's hair over her shoulder and shook her head. "I have grown fond of you, miss. You are good for him, for William. You belong with them."

"I wish that were true. But I find I am no good for anyone." Dominique squeezed her eyes shut, willing tears to flow, if only to alleviate the burning behind her eyes, but not one drop fell. She had no more tears left. "I have failed everyone."

"You have not failed me. You have befriended me. Been kind to me." Larena set her warm hand upon Dominique's. "My word, you are freezing." She touched her sleeve. "Your dress is wet. We must get you out of these clothes immediately." She stood and began tugging on Dominique's arm.

"I am a spy for France," Dominique blurted out, wanting to stop this outpouring of undeserved kindness from the maid.

Larena froze, her blue eyes stark against the red curls framing her face. "A spy? For France? Absurd. You are talking nonsense."

" 'Tis true. Chase. . .the admiral will turn me over to the Admiralty today, no doubt."

Larena blinked. "I scarce can believe it."

Dominique kept her eyes lowered, almost wishing that the

chambermaid would yell at her, curse at her, or better yet, just leave her be.

Larena took a step back. "Why would you do such a thing?" Her mouth hung open.

"I had no choice. They threatened to kill my brother."

"My heavens, all this time." Larena's pretty features wrinkled. "That is why you came here? Not to be William's governess?"

Dominique nodded and stared out the window, unable to face her. "I should never have come. I have only made things worse."

Silence cloaked the room, save for the crackle of coals and Larena's frantic breathing. Dominique turned to find the maid's face a blanket of white. She twisted her hands together as if trying to remove them from her arms.

"But your faith, your devotion to God?" She took another step back as if Dominique suffered from some sort of espionage contagion. "Because of you, I have begun to pray again and read my Bible. You showed me that God loves me and He is worthy to be trusted."

Dominique flinched. "How could I have done so when my own faith wavered daily?" Yet as she studied the chambermaid's eyes, she could not deny the new spark twinkling within them.

"On the contrary, miss. We all struggle with our faith. Mine has suffered these past years under so much neglect it barely existed—until you came along."

Alarm bristled over Dominique, only adding to her guilt. "Please do not allow my weakness to keep you from pursuing a relationship with God, Larena. What I did has nothing to do with His goodness, His faithfulness, and His love for you."

"Never fear, miss. I know that."

Dominique released a sigh. At least there was one life she had not completely destroyed.

"You lied to the admiral." Larena flung a hand to her mouth as if all of a sudden realizing the magnitude of Dominique's crime. "You would have left William?" She gave Dominique a look of complete reproach. "How could you hurt them so?"

"I am sorry, Larena. I never meant to hurt anyone."

Dominique felt her insides start to crumble. "I love my country. I love William"—she swallowed—"and the admiral. But as it turns out, I love my brother even more."

"You should have trusted God, miss. There will always be wars." She waved a hand in the air. "God is in control of such things. I doubt a few documents in the wrong hands will change His plans."

Heat flushed over Dominique. Such faith put her to shame.

Larena started for the door as if she couldn't get away fast enough, then spun around. "Does the admiral know your reason for spying?"

Dominique shrugged. "What does it matter? He is a man, an admiral. He will only see the crime."

"He will never forgive you, miss." The chambermaid flattened her lips and shook her head, giving her declaration a seal of finality.

Dominique nodded. She had already come to that conclusion, but her heart shriveled at the words nonetheless.

Larena opened the door. "I will pray for you, miss," she said with true concern before closing it and locking the bolt.

Thank you, my friend. I will need it.

"Chase, I daresay you look terrible." Katharine stood aghast as her brother plodded into the drawing room, stubble shadowing his chin and neck, wrinkled breeches hanging loose upon his hips, a white shirt streaked with yellow stains tossed haphazardly over his chest. No navy waistcoat, no cravat, no crisp, clean pantaloons and shiny boots. Certainly not proper attire to entertain company, even if that company was only his sister and Mr. Atherton.

"I am sorry you find the sight of me so despicable." He bowed with a huff. "Perhaps you should leave."

"No," she snapped. "I wish to see you." It had been five days since word had reached her that some travesty had befallen the Randal home. Of course, she had made haste to see what had occurred, only to discover a brother who would not see her, a governess locked in her chamber, and a houseful of gossiping servants. Obviously the French tart was involved in some scandal—as Katharine had predicted. She just hadn't known what it was, nor its effect on her brother—not until now. She barely recognized the man standing before her.

Mr. Atherton poured himself a glass of port. "Really, Randal, 'tis not like you to be caught in such a state."

Katharine took a step toward Chase, drawing in a whiff of his scent. Spice, sweat, and tobacco tickled her nose, but no alcohol, yet she could think of no other explanation for his condition. "Have you been drinking?"

"To my great dismay, madam, I have not." He gazed at her with eyes devoid of any spark. "I find I have developed an aversion to it."

Percy stormed toward the open door. "For God's sake, Randal, where is Sebastian? You are no doubt quite ill. We must call for the physician at once."

Chase sank onto the couch, not a glimmer of a smirk at Percy's sarcasm gracing his lips.

Katharine eased beside him, assessing his mood and tempering her inquiries. "Chase, pray tell, what has happened? Why is Miss Dawson locked in her chamber? Why have you not seen me in five days?"

"Is that why you disturbed my rest? To bombard me with questions?"

"Rest? Good heavens, Chase, the servants tell me you have neither eaten nor slept all this week." Katharine examined his sallow skin, sunken cheeks, and the dark circles around his eyes, and a dull ache pressed upon her heart. He had seemed so happy the last time she'd seen him.

Percy took a seat on a chair across from them and eyed Chase. "You really do appear the wastrel."

Chase raised a brow. "Very well, I believe we have all confirmed that my appearance is lacking. Is there anything else you both wish to discuss?"

Katharine laid a hand over his. "What is it, Chase? What can we do?"

M. L. TYNDALL

He shook his head but did not reply as he stared off into the room, eyes transfixed on nothing in particular. Finally, he shifted his haunted gaze her way. "Alas, my pride forbade me to tell you what I must tell you now, that you were correct in your assessment of Miss Dawson."

As she suspected. Though she should have felt elated that her suspicions were confirmed, Katharine felt only despair as she looked at the sorrow tugging upon her brother's face and the emptiness in his eyes. "Whatever do you mean?"

"She is the spy the Admiralty was searching for in my house." He tore his gaze from her.

"Spy? For the French?" Katharine gasped as his words flew through her mind, searching for a perch to land upon. She had thought Miss Dawson was hiding something, but never this. "I cannot believe it."

"Nor can I." Percy shot to the edge of his seat, brows furrowed. "There must be some mistake."

"No mistake, I assure you. I caught her with documents in hand."

"This is balderdash!" Percy sprang to his feet. "I am sure she can provide an explanation. Did you ask her?"

"I do not chitchat with spies."

"So you have not heard her explanation?" Mr. Atherton shoved his reddening face toward Chase.

Chase glared at him, his eyes simmering like burning coals.

Mr. Atherton flicked the remaining port down his throat then slammed the glass on the table. "Surely there is some reason for her treachery. You have come to know her, Randal. We all have. I have found nothing cruel or deceitful in her. Quite the opposite. Egad, she is so faithful to her God and her beliefs, I could not even tempt her." He gestured toward himself as if he were God's gift to the female gender. And dressed in a green velvet coat, complete with gold embroidered trim, grazed by the curled tips of his blond hair, Katharine could see his point.

"She had us all fooled," Chase said listlessly. "Can you not admit to it?"

"I, for one, will admit to no such thing." Percy brushed a speck of dust from his coat and began pacing. "And I am ashamed that your loyalty falters so easily under the slightest suspicion. Look what she has done in this house." He gestured out the door. "Look how William loves her, how the boy has come to life again under her care and tutelage. Even the servants adore her. She has affected the whole house. Not to mention the change in you. I have never seen you so happy. Egad, man, are you blind? If she had Admiralty documents in her possession, upon my word, there must be a reason for it."

As Katharine listened to Mr. Atherton's soliloquy, she could not help but see the truth embedded in his words. The house had indeed changed since Miss Dawson's appearance—and for the better. Why had she not seen it before? She had been too caught up in her hatred of the Frenchwoman who had stolen her husband. . .yet Miss Dawson was not that woman. She was nothing like the thieving tramp Katharine had imagined the woman to be like.

And Chase. She glanced his way as he sat on the couch beside her, hands fisted across his chest, a caldron of anger and sorrow. Had he not become a better father, happier and more excited about his life than she had seen him in years? So unlike the dark, empty man who sat before her now.

He turned to her. "Why so quiet, Katharine? I would expect you to be gloating in your victory, wagging your superior finger at me with an 'I told you so.'"

Did he really believe she was so cruel as to do such a thing in the face of his agony? Had she truly been that type of person?

She lowered her gaze against the tears that filled her eyes. "What will you do with her?"

"I will turn her over to the authorities—today, in fact. I have already sent word to the Admiralty."

"Blast, Chase! This is incorrigible!" Mr. Atherton shouted, jabbing his hands through his hair and storming across the room like a madman. "They will hang her, and you know it. You throw her to the dogs without so much as an explanation or a by-your-leave. You owe her that much."

Chase clenched his jaw and slowly raised his gaze to Percy. "I owe her nothing," he hissed. "And I will hear no more about it!" He gave Mr. Atherton such a spiteful look as to silence him immediately.

"And then what will you do, Chase?" Katharine interjected before the two men could come to blows.

"Admiral Troubridge is nearly recovered. I will return to sea."

A sharp pain gripped her from within, sending a lump to her throat. "But what of William? You have made such strides with the boy. It will break his heart to see you leave again."

"He will survive," Chase said bluntly. "I will hire another governess."

Shame and sorrow rose like bile in Katharine's throat as she stood and walked to the window. A barrage of dark clouds advanced across the sky and engulfed the bright morning sun, just as she had blighted Chase's happiness. The more she had tried to control her brother's life, the worse it had become. She had transformed her own pain and fears into a sword of revenge and had planted it in the heart of an innocent woman, and in the process, she had stabbed her own brother, as well. *What have I done, Lord?*

"It is what you prayed for."

"No." She raised the back of her hand to her nose, stifling a sob.

"No, what?" she heard Chase ask behind her.

She spun on her heels and gave her brother a pleading look. "This is not right, Chase. I am quite sure there is a valid reason for her actions."

"For once, I concur with Katharine," Percy added. "Let us bring Miss Dawson down here. Talk with her."

Chase stood and rose to his full height, clenching his fists at his sides. He stared at them with a look that would send even the bravest of officers aboard his ship scurrying off to do his bidding. "I never wish to see her again. It is done. Now be off, the both of you, and leave me alone." He swung away, shouldered past Percy, and marched from the room, the usual lift in his walk gone along with everything else.

Rumors among the servants had reached Dominique's ears—rumors that she would be sent to prison that very night. Truth be told, the thought brought her some relief, for she would be glad to leave this room, this house, and all its memories. She had just endured five of the longest, most miserable days of her life. Even the time she and Marcel had spent starving and dodging villains on the streets of Paris could not compare with the agony of these past days—the torture of hearing William's sweet voice in the hall asking for her. . .and then his retreating sobs as the housekeeper ushered him away; the ache that nearly tore her heart in two when she heard the admiral halt at her door during the night and hesitate as if contemplating whether to speak to her.

On one such occasion, she had rushed to the door and leaned her head against it, if only to hear his breathing. Quietly she had pleaded with him to open the door, hoping he would allow her to at least tell him how sorry she was—for everything. But no sooner did she call his name than she heard his footsteps retreating down the hall.

Reaching up, she brushed her fingertips over her throat and swallowed, wondering what it would feel like to be hung. Would her neck break right away? Or would she dangle there in agony, suffocating until God finally took her home?

Sinking to the floor, Dominique crumpled into a heap and sobbed. *Oh God, why did You bother to send me here? What good have I done? Naught but hurt all the people I love, including Marcel.* She had been unable to save him, after all, even though he had saved her so many times. Squeezing her eyes shut, she allowed a flood of tears to pour down her face and land on the wooden floor below. She watched them bead into tiny pools before soaking into the wood. Then, leaning her cheek against the sodden boards, she hugged herself and gave into the sobs that now wracked her body.

Minutes later, she sat and took a deep breath, trying to quiet the uncontrollable whimpers that continued to rise to her lips. Crying would solve nothing. She knew that. Maybe her real purpose here had been only to help Larena find her way back to God.

Dominique glanced over the room she had come to know so well. During the past days, voices had slithered out to her from the dark corners, telling her God had abandoned her, but she knew she only had herself to blame—for her weakness, her fear. In just one week, when she did not make it to the rendezvous spot, Marcel would die. She only prayed his death would be quick and painless.

Moving to the bed, she knelt beside it and folded her hands over the coverlet. She prayed for the admiral, for the healing of his heart. She prayed that someday he would be able to love again—although her own jealous heart shriveled at the thought. "And, Lord, send William a mother who will truly love him and care for him as if he were her own."

When the lock clicked and the door creaked open, Dominique assumed it was Larena with her supper, so she did not rise, did not make an attempt to wipe the tears streaming down her face.

Light footsteps echoed through the room. The door thudded shut, but no other sounds reached Dominique's ears. Slowly she raised her gaze to the doorway.

"I beg your pardon, Mrs. Barton." Dominique shot to her feet and swiped at her moist face. "I did not know it was you."

"You were praying?"

"Yes."

"For William and my brother?" Her tone was incredulous.

Dominique nodded.

Mrs. Barton drew a deep breath, shifted her gaze away, and wrung her hands together, staring out the window. She swallowed as if fighting back some deep emotion. When her eyes met Dominique's again, a moist sheen covered them.

Dominique approached her. "Something troubles you, Mrs. Barton? Has something happened to the admiral or to William?" She could find no other reason for Mrs. Barton's distress, or for her presence here, and the thought that some harm had come to either of them sent Dominique's heart pounding.

"No, my dear. They are well." She reached out for Dominique's hands.

Dominique shrank back at first, unsure of the woman's intentions, but the gentle look in Mrs. Barton's eyes bade her to comply. Squeezing her hands, Mrs. Barton gave a soft chuckle and shook her head. "You think only of others—even in the face of death." The seeming kindness pouring from a woman who had done nothing but spit vile lies and insults toward Dominique caused the hairs on her skin to bristle. What was she up to? Surely she knew what Dominique was, what she had done.

"I must know," Mrs. Barton began in a sharp tone. "Why did you steal those documents?"

Dominique withdrew her hands and sighed. Yes, here was the woman she knew so well. "Did the admiral send you?"

"No. It is I who wish to know." Her brown eyes seemed to pierce through Dominique. "Please, you must tell me."

"It is as you have been told. I intended to give them to the French." Dominique moved to the bed and gripped the post, unable to look at the displeasure she was sure burned in Mrs. Barton's eyes.

"But why?"

"They have my brother. They threatened to kill him if I did not do what they said."

"Who has your brother?"

"Lucien Bonaparte."

Mrs. Barton gasped. "Napoleon's brother?"

"Yes." Dominique gave a reluctant nod. "By some strange twist of fate, I find we are related—cousins third removed."

Mrs. Barton walked toward the coal grate and stood staring at it for several seconds.

The silence grated over Dominique. "You have what you came for. You were right about me all along. Now if you would be so kind as to leave." She nodded toward the door, turned her face away from Mrs. Barton, and then wrapped her arms about her chest. The last thing she needed was to suffer the vainglorious gloating of a woman who despised her.

The silk of Mrs. Barton's gown shuffled, but the sound grew louder, not softer. "I have come to offer you my apology."

Dominique snapped her gaze around, wondering whether she had finally lost her mind or perhaps fallen asleep on the floor, her dreams fabricating a lie born of desperation. "I do not understand."

"I have come to see that I have been wrong about you." Mrs. Barton patted her cinnamon hair that always reminded Dominique of dark, polished wood. "You made my brother happy, and you loved William as if he were your own son."

She made the statement matter-of-factly, as if it were the only logical conclusion to a long experiment. Except her experiment had given no quarter for an opinion other than her own—an opinion that had thrashed Dominique with distrust and cruelty.

"Besides," she added, "you have shown me that character and morality are far more important than title and nationality. In addition"—her tone softened, and there was a slight wobble in her voice—"you have shown me forgiveness, the type of forgiveness that can only come from God."

"But I am a spy." Dominique wrinkled her brow, still unable to grasp the change in Mrs. Barton's attitude.

"With good cause, my dear. It proves you are loyal to your family. This is all I ever wanted for Chase. Someone who will love him, make him happy, and remain loyal to him." She chuckled, and a faint smile broke onto her lips. "There you were, right under my nose all the time, and I could not see you because of my prejudice."

Dominique regarded Mrs. Barton, unable to utter a word, unable to make sense of the drastic change in her.

Mrs. Barton withdrew a wad of papers from a pocket in her gown and shoved them toward Dominique. "Here."

"What are these?" But as soon as Dominique grabbed them, she knew. They were the documents. She shook her head. "What?"

"Go save your brother, mademoiselle." Mrs. Barton grinned and folded her hands over Dominique's.

Dominique's eyes widened. "I do not understand."

" 'Tis my fault you are in this mess. I do not want to see you hanged, nor your brother die because of me."

"But I am trapped here. And the admiral will throw me in prison tonight."

"I know. That is why I have come. We haven't a moment to lose."

"You will help me escape?" Hope began to rise above the despair shrouding Dominique's heart.

Mrs. Barton nodded, her eyes alight with excitement.

"How will I. . .I have only a week, and I must find a ship to Lihou. And I have no money."

"I anticipated that." Mrs. Barton reached into her pocket and pulled out a velvet satchel clanking with coins. "Take this."

"I cannot." Dominique shook her head and backed away.

"Please. I insist." Mrs. Barton thrust it toward her.

Dominique grabbed the satchel, nearly dropping it for the weight of the coins within. "Does this not make you a spy, as well? How can you betray your country, your brother?"

"Chase will forgive me." Mrs. Barton shrugged. "You know these skirmishes. Napoleon will never dare attack Britain. 'Twould be naught but a fool's errand, and he knows it. And your brother's life is far more important."

Dominique was not as sure about Napoleon's intentions as her new friend seemed to be. She gazed into Mrs. Barton's eyes. "I cannot come back. You understand?"

"Yes, I do." Mrs. Barton swallowed and lowered her gaze. "And it grieves me greatly. I wish with all my heart that you could stay and make my brother happy. But it is not to be."

Dominique's heart shrank at the thought she would never see Chase again. "Please take care of him."

Mrs. Barton squeezed her hand and smiled. "You know I will. But. . .I believe God is in control."

Dominique blinked. That made two. Two members of this household, both of whom had previously denied a need for God, now encouraging Dominique in her faith. A tiny burst of joy erupted within her but was quickly smothered by shame at her own weak faith. Hadn't Rev. Newton encouraged her to believe—to truly believe in the power and presence of God?

"I will return shortly." Mrs. Barton headed toward the door. "Pack your things."

"Where are you going?"

"Never you mind that." Hand on the doorknob, Mrs. Barton turned, a mischievous twinkle in her eye. "If what I am about to do does not succeed, then when I return, I intend to break you out of this house."

CHAPTER 24

Chase sifted through the papers at his desk, their contents—a mass of numbers and charts—blurring before him. It was not the effects of liquor that dazed his focus tonight, but the unsettling events of the day. Ever since the confrontation that morning with his sister and Percy, Chase had been unable to find peace. Then an hour ago, his sister had stormed into his study, offering him a tongue-lashing reminiscent of their childhood days.

Chase shook his head, still bewildered at her change in attitude toward Miss Dawson. When Dominique had been an innocent governess, his sister had hated her. Now that she was deemed a spy, she loved her.

But at the moment, it was neither of these encounters that caused Chase's empty stomach to convulse. The most harrowing event of the day was yet to come.

The marines were due any moment to take Miss Dawson away. He had no choice. If he waited much longer, he would be arrested for treason himself.

He glanced toward the window. What had begun as a bright, sun-glazed day had soon been shrouded in clouds as dark as coal, a deathly covering that seemed to grow darker as the day progressed. Now as early evening snatched what remained of the daylight, rain began to splatter over the panes of his window. At first the streaks were straight and narrow, but soon, as the rain pounded harder, they twisted around one another in chaotic detours of eerie colors cast by the streetlamp.

Tossing his quill pen to the desk, Chase shoved back his chair and stomped across the room. Lifting the lid of a small box atop the mantel, he grabbed a cheroot, then knelt and lit it in the coals of the fire. He knew what he was doing was right. She was a traitor, and traitors must be punished. It was the code by which he lived, the code he'd sworn upon when he had committed his very life to His Majesty's Royal Navy.

Then why did the grinding feeling in his gut tell him he was making a terrible mistake? He tried to shake it off as his own foolish emotions, no doubt caused by his shameful infatuation with the blasted woman, but the words his sister had hammered into his ears not an hour ago rang forth like warning bells.

She had come crashing into his study without so much as an announcement of her presence, swishing her skirts in an air of puerile determination.

"I have discovered the reason for Miss Dawson's betrayal."

"I care not. Go away," he had retorted.

"I will leave as soon as I have had my say." She'd drawn her lips into a thin line and planted her hands upon her hips in a way that said she would not entertain any objections.

No amount of demanding or beseeching would persuade her to leave him be, save perhaps physically hauling her from the room—he could have easily done so if he had the heart to care one way or another, but at that time, he did not—so he had crossed his arms over his chest and heard her out. When she informed him that Miss Dawson's brother was being held captive and would be killed by Napoleon's men, the news had struck him like a cannonball in the belly, though outwardly he had remained unmoved.

She had continued her tirade, but he heard not another word as the knowledge sped through his mind, adding sense to the myriad of unexplained moments he had spent with Miss Dawson.

Marcel. The few times she had spoken of him had brought her to tears. Of course. Chase chided himself. Why had he not seen it?

Rising from the fireplace, he took a puff of his cheroot, hoping the tobacco would calm his nerves and clear his head.

In the face of his stubborn stance, his sister had finally marched from the room in a huff, leaving him to suffer in a wake of tormenting emotions. Never had he doubted a decision, even one that had cost him dearly.

But now he felt unsure of everything.

Especially Miss Dawson. . .*Dominique*. Had her forced deception been the reason for her inability to return his affections? Could she have cared for him, after all? The scar on his cheek began to itch, and Chase rubbed it until it burned. He had thought his first lieutenant—his best friend—had cared for him as well. Until he had stabbed Chase in the back.

Thunder grumbled in the distance, and a gust of wind slid between the loose panes of his window, sending the candle's flame quivering. He swallowed and glanced upward.

She was upstairs. So close. It would take him only a minute to reach her, to see her, to speak to her and find out for himself. But his pride and the pain grinding through his heart kept him rooted in place. Regardless of her motives, she admitted her treachery. And he had already informed the Admiralty that the spy had been caught. The marines would be here any minute.

The decision was made.

Bang, bang, bang. His thick oak door thundered, and Chase's heart ceased beating. They had arrived. He tossed the cheroot into the fireplace. Every ounce of his soul seemed to scream in agony as he opened the door, expecting the bright red uniforms of the marines and knowing that when he saw them, Miss Dawson would be lost to him forever.

His heart sparked to life again upon seeing, instead, a white-faced Sebastian in the fierce grip of Midshipman Franklin. He could not find his tongue until Franklin said, "Admiral, may we come in?"

"Of course." Stepping aside, he allowed them entrance then closed the door. "What is this about, Franklin?"

"Sir." The man released Sebastian and saluted. "I found your butler down at the Chaucer again."

The normally rigid Sebastian seemed to shrivel into the wood floor as he took a step back, his eyes darting about the room.

"He had these, Admiral." Franklin shoved a stack of papers toward Chase, and after a quick perusal, he recognized them as more of the same documents he had planted for the spy—for Dominique.

Franklin eyed Sebastian with disdain. "He was giving them to a group of men."

Chase rubbed his eyes, his mind reeling. Could he have two spies in his house? Surely not Sebastian, his loyal butler all these years. He turned toward the man who had attended him so faithfully and narrowed his eyes as the pain of yet another betrayal pierced him. "What have you to say about this?"

Sebastian's lip trembled slightly. He kept his eyes on the ground. Then as if some unseen force surged through him, he lengthened his stance, straightened his coat, and set his gaze firmly upon Chase.

"Do not presume to believe that I have enjoyed polishing your boots, dressing you, managing your home, and attending your every whim all these years," he began in a loud voice, although Chase detected a quaver in the stern tone. "And for what? A mere forty pounds a year?" He snorted with such rage that there might as well have been fire shooting from his nostrils.

A fire that now burned within Chase. "You said you were content." He could barely spit out the words between his gritted teeth.

"Content?" Sebastian tossed his chin in the air. "To be ignored? Treated as if I were born only to wait on you? As if I were not human, not even a man?"

"So you resort to this?" Chase thrust the documents in the air. "Betraying not only me, but your country?"

"I have no country. England has done naught for me."

Chase took a step toward the man, his fist itching to strike him in the jaw. Sebastian flinched but held his ground. How could Chase have been so unaware of the butler's dissatisfaction and defiance? He clenched his jaw as he scanned through the memories of the past seven years—the times he had been home. Truth be told, he hardly remembered his dealings with Sebastian. Perhaps that alone proved he had valued him as no more than an object of service.

With a grunt, Chase faced Franklin. "What happened to the men he intended to pass these to?"

"We lost them, sir."

"Who were these men?" Chase shoved his face toward the butler.

"Men who were to pay me a great deal of money."

Clutching Sebastian's collar, Chase lifted him off his feet as a loud thump on his door halted him.

"Enter." Chase commanded as he dropped Sebastian with a snort. The butler tumbled backward, arms flailing, but managed to remain upright.

In walked two marines, their scarlet coats bright against their white facing and breeches. The man on the left stepped toward Chase and saluted. Two leather straps crossed his chest, joined in the center by the marines' badge, one of the straps housing a service bayonet. "Lieutenant Wilkins to pick up the prisoner, sir."

Chase returned his salute. *The prisoner.* He glanced at Sebastian, whose courageous facade had suddenly melted into a pool of quivering flesh in the presence of the marines. Only one prisoner was to be escorted to Newgate, but suddenly he found himself with two.

Chase stood at the bow of a frigate, crossing his arms over his chest. A numinous wind played with his loose hair. Before him, the sea churned in white, frothy swells as the ship sliced through the dark waters. Strangely, he could not remember how he had gotten here. He didn't care. He was back at sea. And the nightmare of the past few months loomed behind him. Bracing his boots against the sodden planks, he gripped the railing as the ship rose and plunged over another mighty wave. Water sprayed his face, and he took a deep breath of the salty air, an elixir that sparked every fiber within him back to life. He lifted his face, offering thanks to God for somehow bringing him back to sea—where he belonged.

It was then that he noticed the unusual color of the sky. Massive ribbons of violet and red wine swirled in a chaotic dance above the tumultuous indigo waters, making it seem as if the sky were a moving, breathing, living thing. Burgundy clouds hovered over the horizon, shielding the bright orange of a setting sun and blanketing the scene with an eerie mauve. Was it an incoming storm, perchance? Not like any he had ever seen.

Something else was amiss. He closed his eyes. Where was the creak of wood, the flap of sails, the snap of the rigging? No sounds of the ship reached his ears, only the crashing of waves against her hull.

He spun on his heels, intending to inquire from his officers their exact location, but not a soul was in sight, not a sailor in the yards above, nor on the deck, nor even manning the wheel.

Instantly the ship slowed. The winds lessened until not a whisper of a breeze stirred past his ears. He gazed across the ocean. The sea became a mirror of dark glass.

"Chase."

The sound of the familiar voice melted over him. He turned. Melody stood before him. Though the wind had ceased, her white silk nightdress billowed behind her like a creamy wake. The final rays of the sun, piercing the dark clouds, set her golden hair aglow.

His heart swelled to near bursting. Had he died and gone to heaven? Dismissing that thought as highly improbable, he simply smiled. "My love."

She returned his smile, her blue eyes sparkling.

"How. . ." He reached out to embrace her, but she shook her head and took his hand instead. Her fingers gripped his with a firmness and warmth that took him by surprise.

Disappointment stifled his elation as the realization hit him. "I am dreaming again, aren't I?"

She nodded and tilted her head slightly, giving him that "It will be all right" grin that always eased his agitated soul.

"Let us stay in this dream forever." He swallowed and brushed his fingers through her hair. "Please don't leave me again. I cannot bear it."

She turned and pointed off the starboard side of the ship. A light appeared in the distance, reflecting like a golden spiral off the dark water. He squinted toward the vision as a tiny boat formed out of the violet haze, a lantern hanging at its stern.

"Who is it?"

"You shall see." She squeezed his hand.

As the boat drifted closer, Chase's breath caught in his throat. Dominique sat within it, gripping the railing, her eyes flickering about, fear tightening the delicate lines on her face.

Chase started to yell to her but stopped. Melody's presence, his love for her, his loyalty to her, kept him silent. "I do not understand," was all he said.

Melody turned to him. "Go to her, Chase. She needs you."

He shook his head and slid a finger over her skin, as soft as he remembered it. "There can never be anyone but you."

"But don't you see?" A shadow of a grin passed over her pink lips. "There must be. You and William need her."

Chase shifted his gaze from Dominique, still drifting aimlessly over the inky water, back to Melody. A dark void of understanding swallowed his momentary joy. "I will never see you again, will I?"

"Not in this life." She gave him a knowing look, but not one devoid of hope, nor devoid of the love they had once shared. "Now go to her." She placed a gentle kiss upon his cheek. Closing his eyes, Chase relished her touch, her presence, fighting back the burning behind his eyes.

He turned his face to meet her lips, but she was gone.

"No!" He bolted up in bed. Sweat poured from him, saturating the shirt he had fallen asleep in. Cursing, he jumped from the bed, stripped the sodden garment from his back, and paced the cold room. He raked his fingers through his tousled hair and gripped the strands until they hurt. *Why must you torment me so?* He wasn't sure if he was talking to God, Melody, or his own demented mind.

"Go to her," Melody's voice echoed in his head—in his heart.

"No. I will not. I cannot!" he shouted. "She will never replace you." He glanced around the room, hoping Melody would appear to him again, speak to him. But he knew she would not—ever

279

again. He smashed his fist atop his desk, toppling a bottle of ink. A pool of liquid black seeped over the wood, oozing beneath his quill pen, his pocket watch, and covering everything in its path in darkness, including his heart. A heart he had finally opened, allowing light to enter. But then the blasted Frenchwoman had lied to him, deceived him. How could he ever trust her again?

Chase took up a frantic pace across his rug in step to the beating of his heart. He rubbed his knuckles, still sore from his attack on the wall earlier in the week. "God, if You are there and You are still listening to me, please tell me what to do. Please help me."

His thoughts sped over the past two months. Dominique's sweet smile and bright amber eyes glittered before him. Her presence had consumed the house from the moment she had entered, sweeping away the cobwebs of bitterness, hatred, and sorrow. *My word*. He could not deny the change in Katharine, Larena, Percy, William— himself. Dominique had shown nothing but strong faith, tenderness, forgiveness, and she had filled this home with love and joy again. Was her intense love for her brother her only real crime?

Would you not have done the same for your own sister? For Melody?

The thought sliced him like a sword in the gut. Would he? Would he have betrayed his country to save Melody from death? If he could bring her back now, was there anything he would not be willing to do, to sacrifice?

Chase searched his conscience, peering around every dark corner—places where secrets and truth resided—until his head ached from the strain. Even as an admiral of the fleet, he found he could not answer that question with a definite no. How much less could he expect from a lady torn between two countries?

He glanced at his door. He had not turned Dominique over to the marines. Faced with making an immediate decision, Chase had handed over Sebastian instead.

The man had been caught in the act, and Chase had no choice. Still baffled by the butler's betrayal as well as hatred simmering in Sebastian's normally placid eyes, Chase had to accept some of the blame for Sebastian's actions. Since Melody's death, he had been naught but a harsh taskmaster and had not taken the time to understand his butler's past—his French mother's untimely death, the scurvy that had stolen his father's life while at sea. Why hadn't Chase paid more attention to the traitor brewing beneath his very eyes? Huffing, he rubbed the back of his neck. Since no documents were actually turned over, Chase intended to speak on the man's behalf and perhaps lighten his sentence.

As for Dominique, Chase had no idea what to do. He knew he should turn her in. He knew she was a spy for France.

But something in his gut had told him to wait, a voice that had been silent for many years, or maybe a voice he had turned a deaf ear to for far too long. Now a sudden urgency filled him. He must speak with her and hear the truth behind her betrayal from her own lips.

Dashing into his dressing closet, he snatched a shirt and threw it over his head; then, grabbing keys and a candle from his desk, he blasted from his room, made the few short steps across the hall, and halted before Miss Dawson's door. No light shone from beneath it. She was asleep, no doubt. He threw back his shoulders, drew in a deep breath, and unlocked the door before he could change his mind.

"Miss Dawson," he whispered as he approached the bed, not wanting to alarm her.

No soft form lay curled on the bed. He held the candle high and surveyed the room.

Chase felt as though every ounce of his blood rushed back to his heart and weighed it down like an anchor.

Dominique was gone.

CHAPTER 25

Today Dominique would rendezvous with the Frenchman.

She gripped the railing of the tiny sloop as it descended upon another wave. Feeling the familiar flip of her stomach, she leaned over the side—just in case. The bubbling foam atop the azure water slapped the hull of the ship and seemed to laugh at her. Why did the sea relish torturing her so?

Coarse snickers of the crew pricked her ears, only adding to her torment. She dared not turn around. She had seen enough of these loathsome men the past few days to put an imprint of horror on her brain forever.

Smugglers.

She had heard they were not as bad as pirates, but the close association forced upon her by her present journey had all but discredited that commonly held opinion. Thanks be to God, they had left her alone thus far. Perhaps her constant heaving over the side of the ship had dissuaded them from any romantic notions. The thought sent a coil of shivers up her spine.

Pressing a hand over her belly, she straightened her stance and shielded her eyes against the sun, now a handbreadth above the horizon in its descent, casting an array of sparkling diamonds over the royal blue water. Despite her queasy stomach, she could understand the admiral's love of the sea, untamed in its beauty and power—in many ways just like him. She missed him. Her heart longed for him, and she knew the pain of losing him would never truly go away.

After an arduous journey by coach to Plymouth, which had lasted the better part of a week and during which Dominique had not slept but for an hour here and there, she arrived filthy, smelly, and exhausted, only to discover that the only passage she could procure to Lihou was on a ship run by smugglers.

How she managed to barter with these salt-encrusted miscreants for her passage and not pass out from fear, she could only attribute to God's presence, His strength urging her onward. If anyone had told her just six months ago that she would be alone on board a smuggler's ship heading toward the isle of Lihou to plead for her brother's life from egotistical French maniacs, she would have laughed in his face. Now, for some reason, an unusual strength kept her from giving in to the quivers that periodically struck her, threatening to dissolve what little courage she had into a puddle at her feet.

She had seen the man in black—her angel. A few brief glimpses on shore and one on this ship, but his appearances grew less frequent the farther she traveled from London. Did that mean God was not with her? Yet she knew that was not true, for she felt His presence more each day.

"Land, land," a man standing on a yard above her bellowed. "Lihou. Three points off the port bow."

The ship erupted into a flurry of activity as further orders were given, and men clambered up the ratlines to adjust the sails. The creak and groan of yards and halyards and the flap of sails—now familiar sounds to Dominique—drifted over her, telling her they were making a turn, or a tack as they called it. Clinging to the railing, she shielded her eyes from the sun and squinted toward the brown ribbon of land that grew larger on the horizon. So that was Lihou. Excitement rose within her. She had made it.

Perhaps Marcel was already there.

The captain came alongside her and tipped his floppy hat. His eyes were narrow slits of black that sat too far apart on his head and, combined with his long triangular nose, made him look like a vulture—a fitting look for a smuggler, she supposed.

"We'll row ye ashore, miss, but my men will not be waitin'

more'n an hour afore they return t' the ship."

Dominique turned her face away as the man's foul breath, tainted with the evening's meal of fish and hard biscuits, assailed her. She nodded and took a step back from him, trying to avoid his arm brushing against hers. An hour. That was all she had been able to negotiate with these miscreants.

One hour to save her brother.

He cocked his head. "What be yer business on Lihou, miss, if I may be askin'? Meetin' a lover, perhaps?" He leered at her through yellowed teeth.

"Of course not." Dominique took another step back, disgusted by his vulgar perusal. " 'Tis none of your business, Captain. And I'll thank you to honor our bargain." She clutched her valise to her chest, as she had done through the entire voyage, never allowing it to leave her sight. Which also meant she hadn't slept very much and now found herself in a constant battle with the ache that weighed heavy upon her eyelids.

Moments later as the sun sank below the horizon, the ship eased in beside the island, and the anchor was tossed into the water with a resounding splash. The captain ordered one of the boats to be lowered, and two of the men assisted Dominique over the side and down a wobbly rope ladder. Traversing the teetering boat nearly ended with her headfirst betwixt the thwarts, but she finally settled into a spot at the stern. After several minutes of rowing, during which her stomach still protested vehemently, the keel of the boat struck shore. Two of the men jumped out and hauled the bow of the boat onto the sand.

"I'll carry ye ashore, miss." One of the smugglers plunged into the shallow water and held out his hands. He smacked his lips, a fiendish twinkle in his eyes.

She gave him an icy glare. "I would rather swim with sharks."

Chuckles erupted from the man's companions, and he narrowed his eyes upon her and took a step back.

Gathering her skirts, Dominique swept both legs over the side. Freezing water bit her skin as she sloshed ashore and trudged onto the sand, her boots squishing. When she turned to remind the men to wait for her, they were already piling back into the boat. The man who had asked to carry her to shore pushed the craft from the beach and jumped in. Turning, he doffed his floppy hat and gave her a mock bow. "Then swim with the sharks you will, miss."

"You cannot leave me!" Dominique screamed, blood rushing to her clenched fists. "Our bargain."

Heinous laughter was her only reply, and within moments, the tiny vessel was only a bobbing mirage upon the water.

Fear and loneliness gripped Dominique, replacing her anger. How naive she had been to expect to find honor among thieves. How was she to get Marcel and herself off this island?

Oh Lord, please give me the strength. Her stomach twisted into a knot as she gazed out over the sea, the final arc of the setting sun flinging orange, yellow, and violet across the span of the sky and over the darkening waters. Wavelets crashed at her feet, leaving behind crescents of foam glittering in a rainbow of colors. The vastness and beauty of the ocean before her made her feel tiny and insignificant.

Gripping the valise, Dominique squeezed it until she heard the crackle of the documents. She had everything these Frenchmen wanted. Surely they would release Marcel into her hands and allow her and her brother to go free. Where that was or how they would get there did not matter right now. All that mattered was saving Marcel.

Dominique couldn't help but smile as she thought of her new friend, Mrs. Barton—Katharine—and how she had helped Dominique escape. *Lord, You do choose the most unlikely people to do Your work.*

"As I have chosen you."

Dominique chuckled. *Indeed, Lord. Indeed.*

Her smile quickly faded, however, as her thoughts drifted to the admiral. No doubt he would be as angry at his sister for her betrayal as he was with Dominique. She prayed he would come to understand Katharine's reasons, and someday Dominique's, as well. *Please help him to forgive me, Lord.*

Swerving around, Dominique faced the island—where she

would either save Marcel or lose her own life. The white sand of the beach splayed out from the water like a smooth fan ending in a bed of pebbles that eventually led to larger rocks, finally leading to a cliff that loomed above her. Dark green ivy hung over the top of the precipice where Dominique could make out trees above. A light breeze brought the smell of salt and moist foliage to her nose. Peering through the deepening shadows, she took a step. The white sand crunched beneath her shoes as she searched for the easiest route up the embankment, knowing it would be best to make her climb before darkness overtook her. Why hadn't she thought to bring a lantern? Tiny crabs skittered over the sand with each step she took. She wished more than anything she could run and hide under a rock right alongside them. But no. She was tired of being afraid. God was on her side.

As she carefully traversed the pebbles and rocks, she glanced up to see the man in black standing at the foot of the cliff. He leaned against the craggy rocks and watched her from beneath the shadows of his hat. She was no longer surprised to see him, and his silent presence reminded her of something Rev. Newton had said. She might always feel afraid, but God's promise of His strength and presence remained. A recent verse she had read in Joshua came to her mind: *"Be strong and of a good courage; be not afraid, neither be thou dismayed: for the Lord thy God is with thee whithersoever thou goest."*

Yes, God was with her. He would protect her and help her. Had He not done just that all along? Dominique allowed her mind to traverse the past few years: enduring her parents' untimely deaths, begging for food on the streets of Paris with Marcel, stealing the Admiralty documents, holding harrowing meetings with the Frenchman. Though she had never ceased to be afraid, God had given her the ability to do all these frightening things—things that she never would have thought possible before. She swallowed and glanced up at the darkening sky where the first stars peeked through the curtain of night and began to twinkle down upon her. He would be with her now.

She knew it.

The man in black nodded, and she thought she saw the briefest shadow of a smile alight upon his lips before he turned, stepped toward the rock wall. . .

And disappeared.

Somehow, deep inside, she knew she would never see him again. It was as if God had allowed her to see the angel for a short while to reassure her of His presence.

Following him, Dominique stubbed her toe upon a jagged rock and stifled the scream that rose to her lips. Burning pain seared up her foot and leg, but she pressed onward until she came to the place where the man in black had disappeared. A narrow pathway etched out of the massive rocks led upward. At the base of it, right where the angel had stood, a flower grew, thrusting its bright yellow petals out from a tiny crack. Dominique halted and eyed it curiously. How could such a delicate flower thrive surrounded by nothing but cold, hard rock? Then she realized with a smile that the Lord was showing her a vision of herself, and if He could take care of this flower and make it flourish despite its frightening surroundings, then He would do the same for her.

Clambering upward, she braced herself against the boulders on each side, more than once scratching her fingers and arms against the craggy, damp rocks. The crash of the waves echoed between the walls like peals of thunder, drowning out all other sounds, especially the pounding of her heart that seemed to increase with each step upward. The fear would not subside. It was increasing, but she knew now that it was of little importance how she felt on this harrowing journey. God was with her.

Finally, as she reached the cliff top, a blast of wind swept over her, loosening her hair from its chignon and carrying with it the scent of salt and flowers. Lights flickered through the trees ahead, and, taking in a deep breath, she headed toward them.

She had not gone three steps when she heard a rustling behind her, and a rough hand grabbed her by the throat. "*Nous vous attendions*, Mademoiselle Dawson," a man growled.

Unable to speak, all Dominique could do was allow the man to drag her forward into the trees and down a pathway and then shove her into a clearing filled with men. Flickering light from lanterns perched upon boulders scattered at the edge of the forest cast an evil glow over the faces of the mob. All eyes shot to her. Gasping, she scanned the crowd, looking for Marcel. Two men dressed in the ostentatious, jewel-studded silks of the old regime stood in the center of the pack. One she recognized as her French contact. At least ten more men wearing the blue and white tailcoats and tall blue hats of the French Infantry stood at attention, bayonets by their sides.

Panic gripped Dominique. Where was Marcel? What were these beasts up to?

"Ah, Mademoiselle Dawson. So good to see you again." The Frenchman took a step forward, exposing his crooked teeth in a grin, and doffed his colorful bicorn. "Me, I had wagered you would not come."

"Then I hope you did not lose too much money, monsieur," she replied with a confidence she in no way felt.

"Dominique." A voice that ignited a spark of hope within her shot through the crowd, and Marcel appeared beside the French-man, a beaming smile on his face. Dressed in a black waistcoat and tan breeches, his hair tied neatly behind him, he did not appear harmed in any way.

Quite the opposite. Unease churned in her empty stomach.

"Marcel," Dominique sobbed, resisting the urge to run to him.

He started toward her, but the Frenchman held out his arm, blocking his way.

"First, have you brought *tous les documents?*" He flung his purple cape over his shoulder and held out his hand.

"Oui. They are in here." Dominique clutched her bag tighter to her chest and willed her legs to stop shaking before these men noticed.

"No ruse—how do you say?—trick, this time." He grinned, and venom seemed to drip from his lips.

Dominique shook her head, her gaze darting over the men, landing upon a taller man hiding in the shadows of a tree behind the crowd.

The Frenchman gestured for her to approach. "Let me see them."

"First, allow Marcel to come to me."

He blinked. *"Absolument non."*

"Come now, monsieur." Dominique pursed her lips. "Do you think we would run away with your precious documents? Where would we go?"

The Frenchman cocked a brow toward Marcel and snorted. "You said she was meek." He shot his beady gaze back to her and shrugged. *"Très bien. Allez. . .*go." He flicked his fingers out in front of him.

Marcel walked cautiously toward her, glancing back at his captors, then hastened to her side. He opened his arms, and Dominique flew into them, laying her head upon his shoulder. He seemed to have grown during their separation, taller, more muscular. Drawing a whiff of his musky scent, she listened to his strong heartbeat and silently thanked the Lord. She took a step back and wiped the tears from her face. "You look well, my brother."

"They have been good to me, Dominique." He nodded then furrowed his brow. "But you have been so very brave."

"I could not lose you." Emotion burned in her throat as she gazed into his ocean blue eyes and ran her fingers through his dark curls, the strong features of his face reminding her so much of their father. "I will not lose you," she said with more determination.

"Assez, assez," the Frenchman barked as he approached them. *"Maintenant, les documents."*

Opening her valise, Dominique grabbed the bundle and shoved them toward him. Taking Marcel's hand in hers, she pulled him beside her and took a step back while the man perused them. He fingered his oily mustache, sifting through the pages, his eyes alight with cruel excitement.

"Excellent."

Dominique squeezed Marcel's hand, relishing the feel of him beside her. She had saved him, after all. She cast a quick glance his way just to ensure he was not a dream, a vision. He did not look her way but kept his gaze forward.

Dominique's palms grew sweaty, and her hand almost slipped from Marcel's. "Now you have what you asked for. Let us go," she demanded with all the authority she could muster.

Marcel stiffened beside her.

The Frenchman handed the documents to the man behind him then folded his arms over his silk coat and studied her.

Dominique shifted her boots in the dirt, still moist inside from the seawater, and tried to meet his imperious gaze. Wind howled through the trees surrounding them, sending the branches fluttering and initiating the eerie hoot of night owls. Yet he said not a word. One of the soldiers shifted.

Something was amiss. Every nerve within Dominique pricked to attention. All she wanted to do was grab Marcel and run.

"But no. I fear we cannot do that," the Frenchman finally said with a sneer.

The infantrymen raised their bayonets.

Dominique's heart crashed into her ribs then crumbled into a heap in her sodden boots.

"What of your bargain, monsieur?"

"We do not bargain with Englishwomen."

Marcel turned Dominique to face him. "It will be all right, Dominique. Their cause is a good one."

Every fiber in Dominique went suddenly numb. "I do not understand, Marcel. What are you saying?"

He swallowed, his Adam's apple bobbing in his throat as it always did when he got caught at something. He shot a glance at the Frenchman before facing her again. Still he said nothing as his eyes searched hers.

Her gaze wandered to the Frenchman. An evil grin twisted his lips.

She faced Marcel. "You were with them. . . ." Dominique uttered the words that her mind still refused to admit. "All this time."

"It is not what you think, Domi. You were never in any danger from them." He gripped her shoulders.

"Danger?" Anger raged through her. She snapped from his grasp and pounded his chest. "Do you know what I have been through? I could have been hung for treason!"

Marcel grabbed her wrists. "They never would have let that happen."

"You stupid boy." Dominique dropped her hands to her sides and felt her heart sink further into a deep mire.

"Uncle Lucien has taught me much." Marcel gave her a pleading look. "He cares for me, and I am sure he will care for you, too. He has been like a father to me, Domi."

"You have a father, Marcel. Or have you forgotten him already?"

Marcel lowered his gaze. "That is not fair." He kicked his boot in the sand. "I told you I would take care of you. Uncle Lucien can provide for us, give us a name. He has great plans to ensure our futures." Marcel's eyes glittered with excitement. "I have met Napoleon. He intends to make me one of his elite Guarde des Consuls. His Imperial Guard. Can you believe it?"

No, she could not believe it. Dominique shook her head, wanting to cover her ears with her hands and stop this nonsense. How could her brother betray her?

"I did it for us, Dominique," he continued in a pleading tone. "This is our chance, chérie. I told you I would take care of us. Now we will have position, title, and wealth."

"No, Marcel. They are using you. Don't you see?"

Marcel swiveled his gaze to the Frenchman. "Tell her, Vicomte."

The Frenchman smiled—one of those smiles that reminded Dominique of a snake about to devour its prey. "Cheer up, mademoiselle. It works out for everyone, does it not? You and your brother will be cared for. Napoleon will win the victory at sea." He waved a jeweled hand through the air. "Everyone will be happy."

Everyone but her. For she would not serve Napoleon, nor his cause. And she would not allow her innocent brother to be a part of his wicked schemes to rule the world.

"Shall we go, then?" The vicomte gestured behind him.

Dominique clutched Marcel's hand. "This is madness. Come with me, Marcel."

"Are you daft? I cannot, Dominique. This is my home. We are related to Napoleon. He will soon be emperor. Think of what that will mean for us."

"You see how he treats his relatives. Do not make a pact with the devil, Marcel. 'What shall it profit a man, if he shall gain the whole world, and lose his own soul?' "

"*Assez.* We go now," the Frenchman roared.

Dominique released her brother's hand. She could not force him to leave with her. "Go with them, Marcel. But I cannot."

The vicomte pivoted on his heels. "I am afraid you have no choice, mademoiselle. My orders are to bring you back, as well."

Alarm cinched her heart, but she threw back her shoulders. "I will not go with you."

"Then you will die." With a snap of his fingers, the infantry cocked and pointed their muskets upon her.

"Die! This was not part of our bargain," Marcel shouted. "Take her with us. I assure you, she will change her mind later on."

"No. She has been nothing but a bother to me, an annoying little gnat, as she will be to His Excellency. I have neither the patience nor the time to deal with her." He straightened the lace at his cuffs and spun around.

"Shoot her."

Marcel flung himself in front of Dominique, stretching his arms wide. "Then you will have to shoot me, as well."

Fear spiked through her. She pushed against Marcel, trying to shove him out of the way, but he was too heavy to move and stood his ground, keeping her behind him with one arm.

The Frenchman slowly turned around. "Very well. Shoot them both," he said with the same tone with which he would order a drink.

Oh Lord, save us. Dominique wrapped her arms around her brother and squeezed her eyes shut.

CHAPTER 26

T hat will not be necessary."

Chase marched into the clearing, the pistol in his hand pointed directly at the Frenchman's chest. Behind him, he heard his seven marines emerge from the shadows of the trees, then the cock of their muskets as they aimed them at their enemies.

The Frenchman's eyes narrowed and snapped to Dominique. "You tricked us."

Ignoring him, Dominique slowly turned, her amber eyes locking upon Chase's and widening with both surprise and something else. . .joy?

"Chase."

The sweet sound of his Christian name upon her lips seeped through him like soothing balm over an open wound. Egad, but it was good to see her again. He glanced over her shoulder. But not with ten bayonets aimed at her heart. Terror like he had known only once before froze the blood in his veins. He could not lose another woman he loved. He could not.

Trust Me.

The voice that he had heard over and over again these past days eased through him—the voice that had answered him when he had cried out in agony, in despair, seeking guidance, seeking answers.

The initial shock lifting the Frenchman's features soon faded, replaced once again by a bellicose impudence. "You are outnumbered, Admiral."

"It will not matter. My pistol is aimed at you."

The Frenchman spat to the side.

Marcel, the brother whom Chase had heard betray Dominique, glanced at Chase over his shoulder. No maliciousness stormed in his gaze. Young. So very young. So easily fooled by these men with their vain promises of glory.

"I have a better plan." Chase glared at the Frenchman. "Give me the documents and allow myself, Miss Dawson, and her brother to go free. Then you may scurry back to the hole where Napoleon hides himself and tell him he will never defeat His Majesty's Royal Navy."

The Frenchman's face became a bloating mass of scarlet. He glanced over his shoulder as if searching for someone then snapped his gaze forward again. With a snort, he puffed out his chest. "On the contrary, monsieur. We will keep these documents and promptly kill all of you and your men." Keeping his gaze fixed upon Chase, he slowly retreated.

In all his years in command, Chase had learned the scent of fear on a man, and the stench coming from the Frenchman overwhelmed him. "I am afraid I find your terms most disagreeable." Chase gave the man a sardonic grin. "Surely you cannot expect me to abide by them."

"Non," the Frenchman retorted. "I expect you to die." He snapped his fingers.

A musket fired.

Chase ducked and fired his weapon as a shot zipped past his right ear. Its ominous buzz echoed through his head. Far too close.

"Fire!" he yelled to his marines. Drawing his other pistol, he shoved Dominique behind him, pushing her to the ground.

Gunfire cracked like feral whips all around him.

Waving aside the smoke, Chase aimed his pistol toward the Frenchman.

But the viper had already disappeared into the forest.

Dominique. Dropping behind a boulder, Chase peered through the acrid haze, coughing. Finally, he saw her. She and her brother had sped into the trees for cover.

Confident they were safe for now, Chase fired at one of the French soldiers. The man clutched his shoulder and dropped to the ground.

More shots thundered through the clearing. Then the firing ceased. Nothing but the coughs of the living and moans of the wounded filled the air. Chase knew he must not give his enemy time to reload.

"Swords!" he shouted, and the swish of blades against scabbards bounced through the dissipating smoke.

Plucking out his own blade, Chase sliced through the thick vapor and forged toward the infantry, taking on the first man he came upon. Blade against blade they parried, the clang of their swords echoing through the night air. Sidestepping the Frenchman's lunge, Chase brought his sword about and ploughed it into the man's arm. With a shriek, his opponent clutched the wound before flinging the tip of his blade toward Chase in a whirlwind of steel. Chase countered the attack with an ease born of practicing his swordplay until exhaustion relieved the tension of his unrequited affections for Miss Dawson.

A look of dread cast the poor Frenchman's face in gray as no doubt the realization hit him that he was outmatched. As Chase drew up his sword for another charge, the man simply dropped his blade, turned, and fled into the night.

With a shrug, Chase scanned the area for another enemy but found that either his men had dispatched them or the rest had run away.

He stormed across the clearing. "Grab the lanterns. Gather the wounded and ready the boat," he ordered the men, kneeling to check on one of the marines who had been shot. Still alive, thank God.

Dominique. Oh Lord, let her be safe. A wave of terror struck him.

Grabbing a lantern, he dove into the forest, frantically brushing aside branches. Then he saw her, crouched behind a bush with Marcel.

"Chase." She raced into his arms, and he swallowed her up in his embrace, taking in a deep breath of her and finding it the best scent he had ever smelled.

"You came for me. After what I did," she sobbed, looking up at him, her eyes glassy pools of wonder.

He brushed a curl from her face and eased it behind her ear, but he could not find the words to tell her how he felt.

Over her shoulder he saw Marcel rise to his feet.

Dominique's gaze shot down to Chase's arm. "You are hurt," she gasped, peeling back the fabric of his shirt.

Following her gaze, he saw a red stain marring the white linen. He had not even felt it. "It is nothing. We must go. I am sure there are more Frenchmen about."

Marcel laid a hand on Dominique's shoulder. "I am so sorry, Dominique." He dropped his gaze to the ground. "What have I done?"

"Never mind that now." She brushed her fingers over his cheek.

Chase took Dominique's hand and led the way, holding the lantern before them. They had only to get to the cliffs then climb down to the shore, where not twenty yards to the north, his longboat awaited.

As they emerged from the trees onto the top of the embankment, a blast of salty air struck him. He took a deep breath, hurrying Dominique and her brother along as fast as he could over the rocks and thorns.

Almost there.

He squeezed her hand and said a prayer of thanks to God for saving her.

The cock of a pistol, ever so quiet, clicked behind them.

Before Chase could turn around, Marcel uttered a loud "No!" and flung himself in front of Dominique. The crack of the weapon reverberated through the night air.

Marcel crumpled to the ground.

Dominique screamed and dropped beside him.

When Chase looked up, he saw the Frenchman's wicked grin leering at them from the trees to their right. "I was aiming for the girl, but killing the traitorous whelp will suffice."

Chase set down the lantern and drew his sword. "You have proven you can shoot an unarmed boy. Now let us see how you fare blade to blade against a man."

The momentary twinge of fear that crossed the Frenchman's distorted features soon tightened into resolve as he swept his sword from its scabbard and held it out before him. "I warn you, monsieur, I have won many honors with my sword and beaten men far more skilled than you."

" 'Twill be a shame, then, for you to die at the hand of an Englishman." Chase advanced over the rocky ground, a grim smile stretching his mouth.

Dominique's stomach convulsed then tightened into a knot. She removed Marcel's coat and pressed it upon the burgeoning circle of blood on his chest. "Marcel," she cried. "Oh Lord, please do not take my brother."

Marcel's lids fluttered open, and he moaned. "Domi. . ." His breath grew ragged. The sharp scent of blood stung her nose.

"Rest now. We will get a doctor. You will be all right." She kissed his forehead even as the ringing of swords behind her tore away the hope of her words.

She glanced over her shoulder. Chase swooped down upon the Frenchman, slashing a path before him as his foe jumped back in quick frenzied leaps. Darting to the side, the Frenchman swung around and sliced the tip of his blade across Chase's chest.

Dominique shrieked. A line of dark maroon formed on his blue waistcoat.

Chase stood erect and confidently poised. "Is that your best, monsieur?" he asked, twirling his sword out before him, taunting his enemy.

The vicomte charged forward, his face the color of a sweaty beet, and once again the two swords clanked hilt to hilt. The men gritted their teeth and ground their swords together. The muscles beneath Chase's torn shirt bulged under the strain. Fresh blood glistened from his wound.

Then, as if only waiting for the right moment, he shoved the Frenchman. The man stumbled backward over a boulder. Before he could regain his composure, Chase pummeled him with blow after blow, the man barely fending them off, so quickly they came.

Dominique had witnessed her father's swordplay from time to time, but she had never seen anything like this. Chase fought with the skill and confidence of an admiral of the fleet and the ferocity of a savage. Terror sent her heart into a wild, uncontrollable beat. The Frenchman was not without skill himself. What would become of her, of Marcel, if Chase were to die? Glancing down at Marcel, she pressed down upon his wound. He uttered a guttural moan. A tear slid from her face and landed on his chest. *Oh Lord, do not let me lose both of them.*

The ringing of swords drew her attention back to the fight, an eerie, ghoulish battle in the flickering light of the lantern. Chase sidestepped an overzealous thrust of his enemy then turned and met his blade from behind. She still could not fathom why he had come to her rescue. To hate her, to despise her, yes, but never to risk his life for her. Not after what she had done.

With a growl that made Dominique's skin crawl, the Frenchman charged Chase, knocking him off his feet and tossing him to the ground. Chase's head hovered over the side of the precipice.

With a maniacal cackle, the Frenchman raised his sword to plunge it into Chase's heart.

Dominique screamed and sprang to her feet, intending to throw herself against the villain.

Suddenly Chase raised his feet, tangled them around the Frenchman's legs, and toppled him to the dirt with a thud. Flipping upright, he grabbed his sword, kicked the Frenchman's aside, then thrust his boot upon the man's neck. Choking, the man stared at Chase with horror. Chase lifted his sword and pivoted its tip over the man's chest.

"No, Chase." Dominique touched his arm. No matter what the Frenchman had done, killing a defenseless man would not be right.

As Chase looked at her, the fury melted from his eyes. Removing his boot from the Frenchman's neck, he sheathed his sword then brushed his thumb over her cheek.

Groaning, the vicomte rolled on his side.

Chase rushed to Marcel. Dominique knelt beside him as he lifted the blood-soaked coat and checked the wound. He said nothing. He didn't have to. Dominique could tell from the stiff lines on his face that it was serious.

He hoisted the moaning boy over his shoulder without effort. "We need to get him to my ship immediately. I have a surgeon on board."

"Will he live?" She clung to his sleeve. "Tell me he will live."

"You must pray, Dominique." He gave her an earnest look, his eyes filled with uncertainty.

Nodding, she grabbed the lantern and followed him down the same narrow pathway she had climbed when she had first arrived. Only this time, she did not concern herself with tripping or scratching her palms. She was not worried about the French. This time, Marcel's curly dark hair swayed before her as his head fell limp over Chase's shoulder. This time, she was consumed with the terrifying thought that her brother would die. *Lord, You could not have brought me this far only to watch him die. Please, Lord.*

Her prayers fell silent, drowned out by the crash of the waves and the fear that choked the breath in her throat and jumbled the thoughts in her head. Instead, she concentrated simply on following Chase.

They scrambled over the jumbled labyrinth of boulders and reached the white fan of the beach. Before them, a sea of ebony stretched to the horizon, interrupted only by the moon's reflection off the pearly froth atop the waves. Chase turned right, and Dominique followed him along the shoreline, their boots sloshing through the waves that clawed at their feet.

A bright flash lit up sea, followed by a thunderous boom. Dominique shot her gaze upon the dark waters where another flash of white revealed the dark silhouette of a ship before it faded into darkness.

Boom!

The roar pounded in her ears and sent a quiver through the water.

Chase halted, and she came up beside him.

"What is it?"

"Apparently my ship has encountered the French," he said matter-of-factly. "We cannot return yet." He glanced over the dark, jagged bluffs bordering the shore. "We must hide. This way."

Chase strode toward the cliffs with a confidence that helped ease Dominique's fear. In the face of so much danger and uncertainty, he never complained, never showed any fear, and never faltered in making a quick decision. She supposed that was why he was an admiral. Yet she had rarely seen this side of him at his home. There on land, amidst the shrill tongue of his sister and the comical badgering of Mr. Atherton, he had seemed naught but a fish out of water.

Still holding Marcel over his shoulder with one hand, he grabbed hers with the other and assisted her as they wove through the massive boulders littering the beach, dove around an uneven rock wall, and came upon a shadowy opening in the base of the cliff. Taking the lantern from her, he held it before him then ducked and entered a small cave.

He gently placed Marcel on the soft sand toward the back and put the lantern beside him.

"Stay here. I will alert my men and make sure the light cannot be seen from shore."

A massive red blotch stained the shoulder of his blue waistcoat and seeped onto his shirt. Dominique knew it was not his blood.

He must have seen the terror in her eyes, for he stopped and lifted her hand, placing a kiss upon it. "Be brave for just a little while longer. It will be all right."

When he left, Dominique felt anything but brave. Marcel groaned. "Dominique." Dropping by his side, she squeezed his hand.

"Marcel." She brushed the dark curls from his face, noting how white he had become. "I need you. Be strong, Marcel."

Lifting the coat, she winced at the oozing pool of blood. Quickly she pressed the coat back upon the wound, willing the flow to stop, praying with all her might that it would. Marcel did not even moan. *Oh God.* Her breath came in rapid spurts. The eerie, craggy walls of the cave began to spin around her.

"Dominique." Marcel's voice was weak, as if he spoke to her from the end of a long tunnel.

"Do not try to talk, Marcel. We will soon be on the ship." She glanced at the dark entrance to the cave. "The surgeon will save you." The surgeon must save him. *Oh Lord.* Her throat suddenly went dry. She began to tremble.

"Dominique." He opened his eyes, so blue, but the clarity had dissipated, leaving only a hazy sheen.

She pressed a finger to his lips, unable to speak for the lump in her throat.

He brushed it aside. "Let me speak, ma chérie." He coughed and winced. A trickle of blood spilled from his lips. "I was a fool. Taken in by Lucien, by Napoleon. I thought they cared for me."

Dominique wiped the tear that slipped from his eye. His face had gone ghostly white. Beads of sweat crested his hairline. The realization of what was happening sailed through Dominique's mind, but she refused to allow it a place to anchor.

"I only wanted to be a part of something important," he continued, his voice cracking. "To be somebody important. To make you and Mother and Father proud."

The blast of cannons thundered in the distance.

"But we are so proud of you. We always have been."

"It was all so exciting, you know." He squeezed his eyes and moaned.

"I know. Let us not speak of it now," Dominique said. "When you are well, I will give you a good spanking, rest assured." She forced a chuckle that faltered on her lips.

A brief smile flitted across his lips, which had now turned purple.

Dominique heard footsteps behind her.

Marcel gave her hand a weak squeeze. "I have caused you so much pain."

"Pain? You saved me, Marcel." Tears flowed down her cheeks as her heart shrank into a black hole. "You saved my life. I would be dead if not for you."

He opened his mouth, but only a gurgling sound emerged.

"You cannot leave me," Dominique wailed and clutched his shoulders. "I will not allow it, do you hear? I need you!"

"You do not need me any longer, *chère soeur*." His voice was a mere whisper now. "Look how strong you have become." He tried to smile. "I am proud of you."

Dominique shook her head. "No, I do need you."

He reached up and touched her cheek. "It grows dark, I am afraid."

Dominique grabbed both of his hands. "Cling to Jesus, Marcel. Trust in Him now more than ever."

He nodded, his breath ragged, his chest heaving.

His blue gaze darted to her. Then the look of love that filled his eyes went completely blank.

Dominique fell into a heap upon him. "No! Marcel. . . No," she sobbed. "Oh Lord! No, no, no! Why have You done this? Why?"

Strong arms grabbed her shoulders and lifted her from her brother's body then turned her around. She fell against Chase's chest. He held her until the sobs that raked over her quieted to tiny ripples.

She clung to his waistcoat. "He is gone."

"I know."

"I cannot believe it. I do not understand why God allowed this. I did everything He wanted."

Chase sifted his fingers through her hair then kissed the top of her head. "This is not your fault."

The crunch of sand sounded behind them. Chase spun around, hand on the hilt of his sword. Dominique rose and stared aghast at the man who stood at the entrance to the cave. He fingered a jewel embedded in his richly embroidered black waistcoat, out of which bounded a flurry of lace from his shirt beneath. A gust of wind blew in behind him, swinging the ends of a white sash that hung around his waist and fluttering his purple velvet cape fastened around his chest by a gold-tasseled braid. A high, stiff collar that reminded Dominique of the cliffs along the beach guarded the back of his neck. Short dark hair sat in waves on his head while thick, bushy sideburns forested half his narrow cheeks. Standing with the regal authority of a prince, he placed one hand on his hip and smiled at her.

What remained of Dominique's hope melted into the sand beneath her feet.

"Are you not going to introduce me?"

Dominique wiped the tears from her face and took a deep breath. "Chase. . .Admiral Randal, my cousin. Lucien Bonaparte."

CHAPTER 27

Dominique grabbed Chase's hand, knowing these might be her last moments with him. He squeezed hers in return but quickly released it as he took a step toward Lucien.

With a snap of his jeweled fingers, Lucien summoned three French infantrymen, who stormed in behind him and leveled their bayonets upon Chase.

The admiral snorted and crossed his arms over his chest. He slid in front of Dominique.

"Ah, so *vaillant*, Admiral." Lucien eased a hand into a side pocket. His eyes sparkled with cruel intelligence. "But what would I expect from so fine a British officer?"

Lucien's dark gaze shot over the tiny enclosure. "Where is Marcel?" He peered toward the back of the cave. A frown wrinkled his brow. Suddenly he charged past them, nearly toppling Dominique before he knelt beside the lifeless boy. For a moment, Lucien simply stared at him. Uttering a deep sigh, he dropped his head into his hands.

"*Qu'est-ce qui se passé?* What happened?" His voice that only a moment ago brimmed with pompous authority now clogged with emotion. He shot a fiery glare at Dominique as if she were the cause of the travesty before him, then returned his gaze to Marcel, taking the boy's hand in his.

"He is dead, monsieur." Dominique fired the words at him like a cannonball, hoping to wound him, but in the end, saying them aloud only sliced a larger hole in her own heart.

"Your man, the vicomte, shot him."

Lucien shook his head and kept his gaze upon Marcel, rubbing his hand as if the gentle action would somehow bring the boy back.

Dominique watched him curiously. Gentle sobs rippled down his back. Were they real? Or rather was his display of affection some sort of ruse? Had he really cared for Marcel?

"*Non, mais non!* I did not mean for this to happen," he finally said, his voice cracked and hollow. "Oh, my sweet boy. Marcel."

Dominique knelt on the other side of her brother, peering at Lucien, but his face was lost to her in the shadows. "What do you expect when you use a boy as a pawn in your heinous game of power?" she hissed, anger and agony seething in her voice.

She knew Lucien Bonaparte was unaccustomed to being spoken to in such a manner. But she no longer cared. Marcel was dead. They were trapped. It was all over.

Oh Lord, bring us home quickly—she brushed a finger over her brother's pasty white cheek—*to join Marcel.*

Swiping the back of his hand against his nose, Lucien slowly rose. He turned his back to them and faced the wall of the cave. Dominique cast a quick glance at Chase and saw the same astonishment in his eyes that she experienced in light of the brutal Frenchman's emotional display.

Flinging his cape over his shoulder, Lucien spun around, his face set in stone. Only the moisture glistening in his eyes betrayed his inner turmoil.

"I will kill Vicomte D'Aubigne for this."

"More deaths will solve nothing," Chase said.

"Death comes to us all, Admiral." Lucien sneered then stole a glance at Marcel. He swallowed. "And to some, far too soon." He seemed to choke on the words.

Dominique rose and joined Chase, still overcome by the sudden change in her cousin. Perhaps Marcel had been right and Lucien *had* become like a father to him.

"You have your documents. What do you want with us?" Chase demanded.

Lucien fingered the jewel-encrusted broach fastened to his cape and shifted his gaze between Chase and Dominique. The sorrow of Marcel's death seemed to have shrunk him in stature while deflating his bloated superiority. He opened his thin lips to speak but snapped them shut and looked away.

"Let the girl go," Chase ordered him as if Lucien were one of the sailors on his ship. "She did what you requested. She is of no further use to you."

Dominique gripped his arm. "No, Chase."

Her heart swelled with both pride and fear for the man who stood so bravely in her defense. Cakes of mud smeared his white breeches; torn and bloodstained, his shirt hung in shreds around his thick chest; and the gold buttons that once adorned his blue waistcoat were either missing or dangling by threads. A moist blotch of dark purple marred his shoulder where locks of dark brown hair had escaped his queue and hung about him wildly. Despite the threat of death hanging over her, despite the agony in her heart, Dominique thought him the handsomest man she had ever seen.

"Never fear, Miss Dawson is of little consequence to me." Lucien waved at her as if she were naught but an annoying bug. "But I had thought to keep you, Admiral." His sunken eyes barely grazed over Chase before they fixated on the void of the cave. "An admiral in His Majesty's fleet would be *très* important for us, your knowledge, your skill." The tone of his voice sank lower with each word, draining all the threat from his statement.

Chase cast a calm glance at Dominique. "Then take me and let her be."

Fear once again drained the strength from Dominique's legs, causing them to wobble. "No. I will not lose you. Not because of me."

Lucien pursed his lips and gazed toward the mouth of the cave where three of his men still aimed their weapons upon Chase and Dominique.

Outside, the blast of cannons had ceased, and only the rhythmic crash of waves echoed through the narrow cave. A cold breeze swirled the cape at Lucien's feet and sent a chill over Dominique.

"*Baissez vos armes.*" Lucien gestured toward his men, who quickly lowered their weapons and stood at attention.

A twinge of hope flickered within Dominique, a spark she dared not allow to grow, for she knew the guile of these Bonapartes. Beside her, a slight motion caught her eye, and she glanced down to see Chase fingering the hilt of a knife housed on the side of his belt. Her heart restricted. It would be suicide to attack Lucien Bonaparte.

Lucien rubbed the back of his neck and stared down at Marcel. "I have seen enough death for one night."

Without so much as a glance at them, he sauntered past Chase and Dominique. The admiral began to lift his knife, but Dominique pressed upon his arm and shook her head. She knew Lucien well enough to know something was amiss—something that might end up in their favor.

Lucien ordered his men to leave the cave; then he faced Dominique and Chase with a somber look. "I have come to oppose many of my brother's imperial ideas." The lines at the corners of his mouth tightened. "I currently find myself in his disfavor." He threw back his shoulders as if he had just made a grand decision. "I am thinking of moving to Rome."

Dominique gaped at him in disbelief.

"I fear my brother has gone—how do you say?—*fou*. . .mad," he continued with a sigh. "He will declare himself emperor soon. And you should also know that he intends to bring most of Europe under his domination."

Chase shifted his stance, his brow wrinkling. "Why are you telling us this?"

"Because I am setting you free."

The words drifted through the air, bouncing off the cold walls of the cave but never seeming to form into any sensible pattern.

"You release us?" Dominique asked.

"Unless you prefer imprisonment? That can certainly be arranged." Lucien grinned—a wide, spurious grin that quickly snapped back into a frown. "Non, you may go." He waved them forward.

Chase remained frozen in place. "Do you take us for fools? We will not fall for your trickery again."

Lucien frowned. "I assure you, I am quite sane and quite serious." He raised his brows then poked his head around the front of the cave and blasted a string of French commands to his men—words Dominique recognized as orders not to shoot them and to allow them to leave.

Lucien faced them again. "*Allez, allez.* Your boat awaits. My men have not harmed your marines."

Dominique glanced at Chase. Mistrust glittered from his gaze.

"Why do you wait?" Lucien barked.

"You Frenchmen have a habit of shooting people in the back," Chase responded.

"Do not test my patience, monsieur," Lucien stormed, his eyes simmering. "Leave now, or I may change my mind."

Dominique glanced back at Marcel. "I will not leave my brother." She shook her head and swallowed a lump of pain. "Not to rot alone in this cave."

"I will give him a proper burial." Lucien's expression sank as he glanced at Marcel.

"Non. He will not be buried in France, not by you—not by those who caused his death."

Chase's gaze took in Marcel then landed on Dominique. A glimmer of concern pierced the imperious glare she knew he must maintain in the face of so many enemies. He lightly touched her arm. "We will take him with us."

Dominique glanced at the still form of her brother and wiped another tear sliding down her face. He looked so peaceful. "We will bury him at sea. Father would have liked that."

Dominique stood at the bow of the brigantine and wrapped her arms about her chest as she stared upon a sea as dark and thick as ink. A half moon flung sparkling dust upon the tips of choice waves as it made its way across the sky. The smell of the sea—salt, fish, and freedom—wafted about her, tousling her loose hair and ruffling her skirts. Taking in a deep breath of it, she praised her Father in heaven and found it surprising that she could still do so.

Only an hour ago, she had buried her brother. Sewn into a burlap sack, he had slid into the sea from a plank around which stood the admiral and his crew. The mighty Word of God had been read, and then, just like that, Marcel had slipped away from her, out of her sight, out of her life, and into eternity. Now he rested at the bottom of the deep, alongside countless heroes before him. Despite his betrayal, he was and always would be a hero to her.

The strong one.

The boy who had become a man on the streets of Paris.

"*And the sea gave up the dead which were in it; and death and hell delivered up the dead which were in them: and they were judged every man according to their works. And death and hell were cast into the lake of fire. This is the second death.*"

Dominique remembered the words from the book of Revelation and knew in her heart she would see Marcel again. Truth be told, the eternal world had become much more real to her than the wooden planks beneath her feet or the salty air she breathed. These past months, she had witnessed not only the Lord's protection, but also His mighty hand. God sat on the throne and was as active now in the affairs of men as He was in days of old.

She gripped the railing as the ship heaved over a swell. The salty spray showered her. The creak of wood and snap of sails reached her ears. Why was she not sick? She had never been able to sail before without losing the contents of her stomach. She laughed in amazement as a sudden strip of light streaked the horizon, blazing upward into the sky.

A new day dawned.

A new life seemed to burst forth within her heart.

For God had become her strength, just as His Word declared. She had only to keep her eyes on Jesus, regardless of the fear she felt inside. And as He promised, He had seen her through to accomplish His will. For it was always His will that would be done in the end—even Marcel's death. She swallowed a lump of sorrow. She would miss her brother, but he was in a far better place. A smile lifted her lips as she envisioned him in heaven, riding horses with Father or sitting with Mother, excitedly telling her of his

M. L. TYNDALL

adventures. Someday she would join them.

But not yet.

She had not seen much of the admiral since they had boarded the merchantman-privateer he had procured in London, busy as he was with the running of the ship, especially with the possibility of French gunboats still lurking about. Though the vessel was not one of His Majesty's ships, Chase had assured her it was both well armed and well manned. Many of the crew aboard had sailed under his command before and were extremely loyal.

"What do you have in store for me now, Father?" She gazed upward as the stars began to fade under the fiery sunrise.

Chase had come to her rescue, yes, but she had no idea what his true feelings were. How could he not be angry with her for her deception? Would he take her back as governess? Or would she have to fend for herself on the streets of London? If so, she knew now that the Lord would take care of her. But the loss of the admiral and his son would surely damage her heart beyond repair.

Yet love had beamed in Chase's eyes when she had first seen him on Lihou, had it not? Or had that just been wishful thinking?

Dared she hope that he could forgive her? Dared she hope that he could love her?

She bit her lip, pondering these things, when from behind, strong arms wrapped around her. Chase's spicy scent set every nerve on fire.

"I love you, Dominique." His warm breath sent a tingle over her neck as his soft words melted her heart.

She turned toward him, hope flickering to life. "After what I did? After I stole your documents? Gave them to the French?" Then it suddenly dawned on her. She took a step back from him. "Sacre bleu, the French have the Admiralty papers." She flung her hand to her mouth.

Chase grinned.

"How can you be so cavalier?"

"Ma chérie, they were fake. Planted in my study by the Admiralty. In the hands of our enemy, they will help our cause rather than harm it."

He knew about me all this time? Dominique blinked. "But how. . . how did you know I—"

"I didn't." He raised one brow. "All I knew was that I possibly had a spy in my household. Truth be told, and much to my deep humiliation, I never suspected you."

"I am so sorry, Chase." Dominique lowered her gaze to the sodden planks below. "I never meant to hurt you." Her thoughts drifted to Marcel. "Now I know how it feels to be betrayed by someone you l—"

"Love?" He placed a finger beneath her chin and lifted her gaze to his.

Dominique searched his eyes, warm and inviting, no longer shielded by a cold veneer. "But how can you. . .after what I have done?"

"With the help of God—and my sister, of all people." He chuckled. "I have come to understand your reasons—not agree with them, mind you, but understand them." He moved his fingers from her chin to her cheek and began to caress her skin.

This could not be happening. Was she dreaming? *Oh Lord, could the man really love me?*

His eyes grew sad. "I am so sorry for your loss, Dominique."

She gazed at the purple stain on his blue waistcoat and cringed.

The last remnant of Marcel.

No, not true. Her brother would always live in her heart. "Now I, too, understand the pain of losing someone you love more than your own life," she added, her eyes shifting to the wound on Chase's chest, realizing how close she had come to losing him, as well.

"But you have not turned from God in anger as I did."

"I wanted to at first. I could not understand why, after all I suffered to save Marcel, the Lord would end up taking him." Dominique gazed out across the sea. Ribbons of yellow and orange stroked the horizon and cast glittering jewels upon the water. "But I have come to believe that was His plan all along. Though my heart feels as though it has been blasted to bits, I know the Lord will see me through, and it will all work out for good."

A breeze danced through Chase's hair, lifting it from his

shoulders. "Perhaps it was God's plan to take Melody, as well. Maybe I believed that all along, and that is why I was so furious at Him." Chase snorted. "As for turning out for good. . .well, I pray someday I shall have just a fraction of your faith, Dominique. You inspire me."

"Do my ears deceive me, or did I hear you say that nasty little word *pray*, Admiral?" she teased him.

"Aye, I will admit to it. I have begun to speak to the Almighty again." He shifted uncomfortably and drew his lips into a thin line.

"And has He spoken back?"

Chase nodded and smiled. "In more ways than one." Then his smile faded. He eased a lock of hair from her face. "When I thought I might lose you, my world collapsed. All the fears of Melody's death surrounded me like a fleet of enemy ships, but I called out to God. I cannot explain the peace that came over me, not a peace that ensured you would not be taken from me, but a peace that said God loved me and I could put my trust in that love." His stubbled jaw tightened. He rubbed his eyes and looked away.

The arc of the sun crested the horizon, instantly setting aflame the rippling azure waters and flinging sparkling nets of gold and crimson into the sky.

Slowly his warm brown eyes met hers again.

"I never want to be without you, Dominique."

Before she could respond, he covered her lips with his, caressing them as if she were the most precious thing in the world. Gentle, loving kisses that began to grow in intensity. Crushing her against him, he claimed her mouth as his own. Dominique grew dizzy with the feel of him, the taste of him. A warm flutter radiated out from her belly and sped through her until nothing else mattered to her but being in Chase's arms.

Chuckles erupted from behind them. Chase withdrew, a mischievous grin on his face. "Forgive me. I am so overcome by you that I fear I forgot we were not alone," he whispered.

She knew exactly how he felt. Dominique's skin flamed, but she dared not glance across the deck at the sailors, who no doubt were enjoying the spectacle. Instead, she faced forward and clutched the railing, raising her face to the beauty of God's creation, allowing the morning breeze to cool her passions. "So does this mean you will not dismiss me as governess?" She cast Chase a coy look.

"Nay, I intend to dismiss you." He sternly fisted his hands at his waist. "You cannot expect an admiral of the fleet to harbor a known spy within his home."

Dominique's insides crumbled. Truth be told, she could not. "I understand," she said, wondering where she would find lodging.

"But a wife, now that is a different matter altogether." He winked. "That is, if you will do me the honor?"

Dominique flung herself into his arms and showered him with kisses.

Stepping from the carriage, Chase removed his hat and gazed up at the Randal house—his house. Whenever he had returned home before—especially after Melody's death—he had felt only despondency coupled with an urgency to leave as soon as he could, even before he had put a foot inside the door. This time as his gaze took in the three massive white columns guarding the front of the home and the ornate ironwork on the porches above encasing sparkling french windows, joy and excitement bubbled within him at the prospect of finally coming home.

"Darling."

"Ah, yes, forgive me." He turned, held out his hand for Dominique, and assisted her from the landau. Her chestnut hair fluttered from beneath her bonnet and glimmered as a ray of sun alighted upon her. She gazed at him with those amber eyes now brimming with love and admiration—for him. He still could not believe it.

He paid the driver then turned to her and held out his elbow. "Shall we?"

Placing her hand on his arm, she smiled, and he believed at that moment that all his happiness in this whole world rested within that smile alone.

Feeling a lightness in his step that he had not known in years, he swaggered to the front door, Dominique on his arm. Before they could reach it, the door slammed open and his son blasted from within the house like a cannonball.

William dashed toward them, his blond head bobbing, his blue eyes glowing. "Father, Father—Miss Dawson."

Katharine stepped out behind him and leaned against the front wall, her hands clasped before her and a smug grin plastered on her lips.

Chase scooped the leaping boy into his embrace and gave him a tight squeeze, savoring the feel of his son and the warm touch of William's arms encircling his neck.

Chase kissed him on the forehead. "Good to see you, Son. I have missed you so much."

"You have?" The boy giggled with delight.

Chase nodded and tousled his hair, vowing to God to be a better father. With God's help, he would keep that promise. Not that he wouldn't return to sea—for that was his duty, his job. But he would never let his love of the sea come before his love for God or for his family.

Never again.

"Miss Dawson, you came back, too?" William exclaimed with a wide grin.

"Your father came to get me, William." She leaned in and kissed him on the cheek.

"I am so glad you found her, Father."

"So am I, Son." Chase flung a sultry glance at Dominique. "So am I."

Holding William in one arm, he grabbed Dominique's hand, and they entered the front door as a family.

Katharine looked at them both, joy skipping across her eyes—a joy Chase had not seen in years. "I see you have found what you were looking for."

"Aye, that I did, dear sister."

Releasing his hand, Dominique plucked off one of her gloves and waved her left hand in the air before Katharine. A golden ring sparkled on Dominique's finger, drawing Katharine's gaze.

She flung her hands to her mouth. "Oh my word. How? When?"

"Just yesterday," Chase answered. "We obtained a special license."

"And my good friend Rev. Newton performed the ceremony," Dominique added.

William's confused gaze wandered from Chase to Dominique.

"What does this mean, Father?" He scrunched his tiny nose. "Does this mean Miss Dawson can be my new mother now?"

Chase gave his son another squeeze and kissed him on the nose.

"No, William. It means she already is."

ABOUT THE AUTHOR

M. L. TYNDALL

MaryLu Tyndall dreamed of pirates and sea-faring adventures during her childhood days on Florida's coast. She holds a degree in math and worked as a software engineer for fifteen years before testing the waters as a writer. Her love of history and passion for story drew her to create the Legacy of the King's Pirates series. MaryLu now writes full-time and makes her home with her husband, six children, and four cats on California's coast, where her imagination still surges with the sea. Her passion is to write page-turning, romantic adventures that not only entertain but expose Christians to their full potential in Christ. For more information on MaryLu and her upcoming releases, please visit her Web site at www.mltyndall.com or her blog at crossandcutlass.blogspot.com.

OTHER BOOKS BY

M. L. TYNDALL

Legacy of the King's Pirates Series

The Redemption

The Reliance

The Restitution